DALTON'S BLUFF

by

Ed Law

Dales Large Print Books
Long Preston, North Yorkshire,
BD23 4ND, England.

British Library Cataloguing in Publication Data.

Law, Ed
    Dalton's bluff.

    A catalogue record of this book is
    available from the British Library

    ISBN   978-1-84262-562-0 pbk

First published in Great Britain in 2006 by Robert Hale Limited

Published in Large Print 2007 by arrangement with
Robert Hale Ltd.

Dales Large Print is an imprint of Library Magna Books Ltd.

Printed and bound in Great Britain by
T.J. (International) Ltd., Cornwall, PL28 8RW

CHAPTER 1

'Keep moving,' Deputy Vaughn demanded. 'That noose is waiting for you in Applegate.'

Dalton bit back an oath and kept his fevered gaze on the river, now just a quarter-mile away. With his handcuffed hands held before him and the rope around his waist tugging him on, he staggered another pace. He'd been walking since first light and now his gait was more the process of him throwing out his legs and stopping himself from falling rather than walking.

For the tenth time in the last few minutes Dalton scraped his rough tongue over his blood-encrusted lips and dreamed of thrusting his head beneath the water and drinking until either he drowned or the river ran dry.

But the river might as well not be there.

Even when he reached it, Deputy Vaughn might not let him drink. The lawman could continue his relentless journey through the water, but keep Dalton's rope under such a tight rein he wouldn't be able to lower his head to drink.

So, with more hope than confidence, Dalton imagined tasting the sweetness of the cool water and, as he closed his eyes and dreamed of the relief that'd bring, he stumbled. His ankle turned and he fell to his knees.

As Dalton was already at the furthest extent of Vaughn's rope, the loop around his waist yanked him forward and ploughed his chin into the dirt then dragged him on. Vaughn grunted, Dalton's weight pulling him back and halting him. Then he hurried his horse on.

On his chest, Dalton scraped across the ground, squirming as he fought to regain his footing. But with his hands cuffed together, he couldn't get leverage on the ground and he bumped and scraped over rocks.

If Vaughn had stopped for just a few seconds, he could have stood, but it was a full minute before he managed to roll on to his side and gain enough traction against the ground to climb to his feet.

When he was walking again, Vaughn used his bulging canteen to swill out his mouth and spit to the side. Then he provided a sly smile, perhaps suggesting that Dalton's stumble had encouraged him to start devising a new punishment, but then he snapped round to face the front.

Dalton resumed his steady stagger forward and fixed his gaze on the river, willing Vaughn to stop there. But then Dalton noticed why Vaughn had turned. They wouldn't be the only people by the water.

A sole rider stood sideways to them. He was watching their approach on the edge of the river with the water lapping at his horse's hoofs.

Dalton's heart lurched. This man was the first person he'd seen since his capture and his presence surely meant that Vaughn would have to let him drink.

Vaughn leaned forward in the saddle to consider the man. Dalton could by now read the varying degrees of Vaughn's bad moods from the set of his back and he judged him to be on guard for potential trouble from this man. But Vaughn needn't have worried. The man hailed them.

Vaughn hailed him in return, offering his name and learning that the man they were approaching was John Stanton. He continued at a steady pace towards him. Twenty yards before him, he halted.

Dalton carried on walking, heading past Vaughn to ensure he got as close to the water as possible, hoping that while John was watching them, he might reach an outlying puddle. But Vaughn drew in the rope, halting him at his side.

Dalton swayed to a halt and tore his gaze from the inviting water to consider John. He was thickset, his buffalo-hide jacket and the furs slung over his horse suggesting his line of business. And the firm-set jaw and steely eyes that glared at Dalton suggested he enjoyed solitude and would take no nonsense from any man.

'What's he done to deserve this?' he asked, his upper lip curled back in a sneer.

Vaughn snorted a laugh. 'Don't know where to start answering that. He's a violent critter and that's a fact. But when I get him to Applegate, he'll pay for the trouble he's caused.'

John narrowed his eyes as he looked Dalton's form up and down.

Dalton chose that moment to plant his feet wide, hunch his shoulders some more, and let his parched mouth drop open, trying to appear as pathetic as he could.

'He don't look like trouble,' John said. 'He looks half-dead. You giving him food and water?'

Vaughn bent at the waist to spit on the ground.

'No point wasting that on a man who'll swing in a few days.'

John provided a sharp intake of breath. 'Ain't telling you your job, but he should still get water or he won't live long enough to pay for whatever crimes you reckon he's done.'

'What's that got to do with you?'

John raised his eyes to consider Vaughn.

'Nothing. I just don't like to see anyone suffer.'

'Tell that to the family and friends of the man he killed.'

John looked away to point across the river, the determined swing of his head appearing to dismiss the issue of Dalton's brutal treatment from his mind.

'Anyhow, as you're heading to Applegate, if you see a wagon train heading this way I'd be obliged if you'd tell them I'm still waiting for them.'

Vaughn's shoulders relaxed with John's less confrontational attitude.

'Been waiting long?'

'Two whole days.' John nodded towards the distant mountains, their jagged outlines blue and faint in the afternoon heat haze. 'They're heading to the other side to start a new life, but I'm getting to think they might

9

have started it without me.'

Vaughn looked at the mountains. 'There's good land over there, then?'

'Yeah, land aplenty and valleys galore for anyone to start a new life.'

'I'll remember that.' Vaughn stretched. 'But I reckon I'll rest up first. Been travelling a while.'

Vaughn swung out of the saddle, still clutching Dalton's rope, then placed the rope on the ground. He rooted around and found a forked twig, which he pushed into the ground over the looped end of the rope.

'That twig is to secure you,' he said, turning to Dalton. 'If you dislodge it, you know what you'll get.'

And with that taunting promise made, Vaughn chuckled to himself then led his horse down to the river.

Dalton shuffled after him, but Vaughn had ensured that the maximum extent of the rope would stop him ten yards from the river. He halted and watched Vaughn water his horse while keeping his back deliberately turned, goading Dalton into disobeying him and giving him a chance to administer yet another beating.

The hot sun beat down on Dalton's bowed back as he glanced at John, but he'd already turned away to stare across the river, looking out for the wagon train. Dalton dismissed his last lingering hope that this man might help him and stared at the water. He rasped his tongue over his lips as he weighed up the pleasure of gulping several mouthfuls of cool water against the pain of the beating that would follow. The water won.

He rolled his shoulders and settled his stance, practising the actions that'd let him gulp down the most water in the shortest possible time. Then he ran with all his strength, pounding the ten yards in a few long strides, and hurled himself to the ground, sliding on his belly until his head dunked into the edge of the river. He buried his face in the coolness and gulped.

Vaughn had denied him sustenance for so long that after his first gulp, nausea clutched his throat and he dry-retched. But then he gulped again and dragged water into his empty stomach.

He heard Vaughn shouting at him, his tone both annoyed and delighted with Dalton's defiance, but Dalton was counting the gulps. He'd hoped to get three swallows down before Vaughn stopped him, but he'd managed five before a hand slammed on his back and bodily lifted him from the ground before setting him down on his feet.

With his eyes closed, Dalton threw back his head and let the water in his mouth seep down into his grateful guts, then looked at Vaughn. But it was to see a pile-driving blow crunch into his cheek. Dalton was so weak he collapsed, but he got lucky.

He was still standing beside the river and the blow rolled him into the water. He came to rest on his belly and thrust his head below water then slurped in another gulp before Vaughn pulled him up. This time, he dragged Dalton away from the river before throwing him to the ground.

And then he started to punish him, whipping him with the knotted end of the rope. Stinging blow after stinging blow rained down on Dalton's wet back as he tried to escape from them, but no matter in which direction he crawled, they continued to hammer down on him.

But then the blows stopped. The beatings had never stopped that quickly before and Dalton steeled himself for the next round of brutalizing, but instead, he heard John speak.

'Stop beating him,' he ordered.

'I'll do anything I want to my prisoner,'

12

Vaughn snapped, then paused letting Dalton hear John grunt his disapproval. Vaughn lowered his voice. 'Do you want to know what he did?'

'Nope. That man may be the most evil critter who ever lived, but you got no right beating him for drinking water.'

Vaughn snorted as Dalton rolled on to his side and looked up. Vaughn and John were facing each other ten paces apart with their feet set wide and their shoulders hunched.

'Obliged,' Dalton croaked. 'And I ain't no evil man. I didn't do–'

'Be quiet,' Vaughn roared, swirling round. He advanced on Dalton with his fists raised, but then stomped to a halt and straightened. 'I got fine hearing, John, and that had better not be a gun you've just drawn on me.'

Dalton crawled to the side to see past Vaughn and saw that his captor was right. John *had* drawn a gun and had aimed it squarely at Vaughn's back.

'Seeing as how you can't deliver a man to justice without treating him like an animal, I reckon as I'll take custody of him.'

'You won't. You'll lower that gun, and then me and my prisoner are leaving.'

'That ain't happening. I could do with

visiting Applegate to see what happened to the wagons. And while I do that, I'll see he gets to a decent lawman like Sheriff Melrose.'

Vaughn flexed his shoulders, his face darkening, his fists opening and closing.

'I'll give you no trouble,' Dalton shouted, 'if you treat me fairly. I reckon I can answer the charges against me.'

Vaughn flared his eyes, as Dalton knew he would – any mention of the fact that Dalton wasn't a cold-hearted killer always sent him into an uncontrollable rage.

Then Vaughn threw his hand to his gun and turned at the hip, his gun clearing leather as he swirled round to aim at John using the same lightning speed that had captured Dalton earlier.

But John was aware of the possibility of Vaughn turning on him and he fired.

Two simultaneous crisp shots destroyed the quiet of the hot afternoon. Then Vaughn and John stood still, staring at each other, smoke rising from the barrels of both their guns. John stood square on, facing Vaughn, who stood twisted.

The motion of both men had been so quick that Dalton was unsure whether either man had hit the other, but then he saw John

14

straighten up, his hand shooting up to clutch his chest beneath the heart. Then he keeled over, his face burying itself in the dirt.

Dalton closed his eyes a moment, then darted his gaze to Vaughn, who was still half-turned away from him, his stance frozen as he watched John's twitching form.

But then Vaughn stumbled a pace. His legs buckled and he came tumbling down to collapse on his side. Dalton couldn't help but deliver a whoop then hurried to Vaughn's side and threw him on his back.

He knew the precise location of the keys to his handcuffs. He thrust one hand into Vaughn's jacket and tore the gun from Vaughn's limp grasp with the other. The key emerged coated in blood.

Dalton danced back, his gaze fixed on Vaughn, still unsure as to whether his captor was dead but ensuring he gained as much as he could from the situation.

He jabbed the key into the lock, heard the handcuffs spring open, then shrugged them away. Then, with his hands free, he struggled his way out of the rope to stand free for the first time in two weeks.

'Vaughn,' he grunted, turning the gun on the lawman, 'things have just changed around here.'

He glared down at the deputy sheriff, but the man was oblivious to Dalton's demand as he twitched then stilled. Dalton continued to watch him, seeing that Vaughn still lay supine, then paced to his side and kicked him in the chest, but received no complaint. He watched Vaughn's head loll so that he pressed a cheek into the dirt. And his open mouth didn't move the dirt before him.

With only the slightest of cheer in his heart, Dalton accepted that his cruel tormentor was dead, but he still kept one eye on him as he hurried over to join John. He hunkered down beside him and rolled him on his back. Although John's eyes were open, they were glazed and his breathing was shallow.

Dalton had little knowledge of doctoring but he guessed that water might help. He turned to go to the river, but John threw out a hand and grabbed the trailing end of his jacket.

'Stay,' John grunted. 'He got me with a good shot. Must have slowed up.'

'I'm obliged.'

John winced, his body racking backwards, then he fixed Dalton with his steely gaze.

'Tell me one thing,' he breathed. 'Were you...? Was you...?'

16

'You didn't take a bullet defending no outlaw if that's what you're asking.'

A faint smile played on John's lips.

'What did you do?'

'I killed a man, but I did it to save other innocent people, a bit like you just did.'

John nodded. He opened his mouth to say something else, but the words were low and unintelligible.

For several more minutes Dalton sat with him, keeping a silent vigil as his breathing slowed until it finally stopped. And then Dalton was alone with two dead men and before him was the freedom he never thought he'd enjoy again.

He stood, pondering how best to use that freedom, but then saw movement nearby. He flinched round until his gaze alighted on the other side of the river.

Edging out into the water was the first wagon in a sprawling line of wagons – the very people John Stanton had been waiting to meet.

And they would reach him in a matter of minutes.

CHAPTER 2

Dalton shrugged inside his new and slightly baggy clothes, then stood back from the two mounds of earth and stones he'd hastily scraped over the bodies of John Stanton and Deputy Vaughn. He had been practical and swapped his torn and battered clothing for John's clothes, then claimed his belongings, but he had dignified his saviour's memory by burying him.

He also reckoned that the people in the wagons would have noticed him, even if they hadn't seen what he had been doing. So, if he ran with the bodies unburied, they would reach the obvious conclusion that he'd murdered them. Now, he just had to acknowledge the wagon train, wait until it had passed, then head off to enjoy his freedom.

He mounted John's horse and nudged it forward to stand on the edge of the water.

The driver of the lead wagon, a grey-haired and wiry man, had almost waded through the river. He was carefully picking a route,

19

checking that there weren't any channels or dangerous currents. Five other wagons had lined up on the edge of the water, the people noting his route. Eight other wagons had stopped further back and were corralling their livestock.

The lead man hailed Dalton, then headed his wagon out on to dry land and pulled up beside him.

'You waiting for us?' he asked, leaning forward in his seat.

Dalton shrugged, unwilling to say too much as anything he said could require him to lie and so perhaps cast suspicion on his actions.

'Just enjoying the view.'

'I'm Virgil Wade.' Virgil's roving gaze passed over Vaughn's horse, which was now mooching by the side of the river, then moved on to consider the two graves. 'What happened here?'

As Dalton had had only limited time before the wagons reached him, the location behind a small mound was the most private place he could find for the graves and, in his haste, he'd forgotten about Vaughn's horse. Clearly, Virgil was the kind of man who missed nothing and Dalton saw no choice but to set off towards the mound, beckoning

Virgil to follow him.

Virgil called over his shoulder for Jacob to take the reins. A younger man, who Dalton assumed was his son, climbed out of the wagon and into the seat to take the reins from him. Then Virgil jumped down to join Dalton, who led him from the trail.

They waded through the long grass until they reached the graves.

'Two men died in a gunfight,' Dalton said, bowing his head. 'I buried them.'

'Any idea who they were?'

Dalton was about to confirm that John Stanton was one of the men, but an idea came to him.

'Some papers they had on them showed that a deputy sheriff from Harmony called Vaughn was escorting a wanted man, Dalton, to Applegate. I reckon the prisoner fought back and got the lawman's gun off him.'

'You could be wrong.' Virgil tipped back his hat and glanced around. 'Somebody could have bushwhacked them – like the Spitzer gang.'

'Perhaps you're right,' Dalton said, shrugging. 'There's plenty of danger out here for unwary travellers.'

Virgil gave a short nod, but he continued

21

to glance around. Dalton watched him and from the nervous darting of his eyes, he decided that he was concerned because of his own fear of the dangers of the trail and not because he didn't believe Dalton's story.

Dalton relaxed as he joined Virgil in heading back to the wagon.

'It may sound selfish,' Virgil said, 'but at least John Stanton wasn't one of the dead men. We can't give you a description, but have you seen a man who looks likes he's waiting for us?'

Having planted the idea in Virgil's mind that a man called Dalton was dead, Dalton was already thinking about how he'd assume a new identity, but Virgil's comment about not knowing what John Stanton looked like set his mind racing. Instantly, he decided to try a bluff.

'Perhaps I didn't explain myself. I am John … John Stanton.'

'I read your letter,' Virgil said, narrowing his eyes. 'It made me think you'd be older.'

A letter had been amongst John's belongings and Dalton made a mental note to read it when he got the chance.

'Apologies for that.'

Virgil smiled and pointed at the line of wagons that were now fording the river.

'Then I'd be obliged if you'd help me get them across the water.'

Even before Dalton could nod, Virgil shouted orders to the next wagon that would reach the riverside. And as that wagon emerged on to dry land, Dalton quickly thought through the implications of his bluff.

If he couldn't convince these settlers he was John Stanton, they were sure to reach the obvious conclusion that he'd murdered the two men. But if they did accept him, he could accompany them to their final destination, then begin a new life with a new identity.

Pleased with his sudden decision, Dalton made himself useful by lining the wagons up on dry land, then introduced himself to each group and repeated that everyone should avoid the long grass where he'd buried the bodies.

But it was only when the tenth wagon rolled onto dry land that Dalton learned that taking on a new identity would not be as simple as he'd hoped.

A young, red-haired man was sitting beside a woman. This man passed the reins to the woman then jumped down from his wagon and stood beside Dalton, peering at the distant mountains and shaking his head.

'Hard to believe there is a way over them,' he said.

'It sure is,' Dalton said, turning to join him in looking at the mountains.

The man patted Dalton's back. 'Then I sure am glad we hired the best damn guide around.'

Dalton nodded then directed the next wagon to head on by, but the wagon had stopped before the comment filtered through to his thoughts.

And then he couldn't help but wince.

These people reckoned *he* was their guide and they expected him to lead them to their final destination. And with mounting shock, he realized that to do that he would have to find a route over the mountains when he didn't know what was on the other side of those mountains, or on this side, or even what the name of the mountains was.

Dalton sat beside the camp-fire, enjoying his broth, but eating slowly to avoid anyone learning just how desperately hungry he was.

The first few hours spent under his new identity had gone smoothly.

By late afternoon the wagons had safely crossed the river after which the group had

24

said prayers over the graves of Deputy Vaughn and John Stanton and erected simple crosses labelled Vaughn and Dalton.

Then Virgil had insisted that they cover a few more miles that day, but everyone else reckoned that spending time fishing to replenish their provisions would be more useful. Virgil had still urged them to carry on but a round of grumbling from everyone persuaded him that they should settle down for the night.

While they settled, Dalton had distanced himself from the group, avoiding anyone drawing him into conversation in which he might have to tell more lies. He used the moments when nobody was looking his way to rummage through John's belongings and search for a map. But he didn't find one and, aside from the letter, neither did he uncover any more details about the man whose identity he had assumed.

And the letter provided little help. It had an illegible signature and was a short message agreeing to his terms for the mission and offering a payment of one hundred dollars.

Luckily, nobody looked at him in an odd way as he went about his business and Dalton slowly relaxed as he accepted that the settlers had never met John Stanton before.

And so as he spooned the meal into his mouth, he planned his future actions.

He hadn't lied to John as his saviour lay dying. His crime had not deserved Deputy Vaughn's relentless pursuit, capture and brutal treatment. Nine months ago in the town of Harmony, Dalton had killed a worthless and corrupt man to save innocent lives, but as that worthless man was a lawman, he had faced the noose.

Now, the Dalton who had faced those charges was dead and buried and a new Dalton had a chance for something he had only dreamed of before – a fresh start amongst people who wouldn't prejudge him as being an outlaw.

But he could only enjoy that fresh start if he became the man this group wanted him to be.

When Dalton had eaten his broth, he took his bowl down to the river to wash it, then sat on a boulder on the edge of the water, contemplating. From here he could see the dark and jagged outline of the mountains against the night sky and he reckoned that at the undoubtedly slow speed this wagon train would travel, they were several days away, perhaps weeks.

And that would give him time to search for a route he could lead them on. That route would prove to be a difficult one with rivers and ravines to ford and forests to hack through, and dangers of a more human kind might confront them. But as the settlers expected to face hardship, they wouldn't know that better and safer routes were probably available. Provided Dalton found them a place where they could settle down, they should accept that he was who he claimed he was.

Feeling confident now with his situation, Dalton watched everyone mill around, seeing in the group's quiet efficiency that they had been travelling together for some time.

But he noticed a man and woman standing apart from the group beside their wagon. They were watching him and talking, their closeness and low tones suggesting they were concerned.

And when Dalton searched his memory for a previous encounter with them, he recalled that the man was the one who had told him he would be their guide. He was Newell Boone and she was Eliza. He had assumed they were married. Although on noticing they both had red hair, he revised his assumption to their being siblings.

There was still a chance someone might have information about John Stanton and so might suspect he wasn't that man. So, rather than delay an inevitable problem, he beckoned them over with a short wave and a wide smile.

Newell and Eliza glanced at each other and she said something to Newell, which Dalton thought might have been her saying that there was nothing to worry about. Then they set off towards him.

Dalton stood. He kept his stance casual and his expression relaxed as Newell swung to a halt before him and raised a foot to place it flat against the boulder beside the river. Eliza stood beside him with her arms folded.

'I believe in plain speaking,' Newell said, leaning on his knee. 'So, why don't you see fit to talk to us?'

'I'm sorry,' Dalton said. 'I'm not ignoring you. I just haven't got round to spending time with everyone.'

'I understand that, but after the letters Father wrote to you, I thought you'd at least want to speak to Father.'

'I thought Virgil Wade wrote to me,' Dalton said, then regretted offering such a lame comment.

Newell narrowed his eyes. 'Henry Boone wrote to you. What makes you think it was Virgil?'

Dalton shrugged. 'He's your leader.'

Newell snorted and glanced at Eliza, who echoed his snort.

'He likes to think he's leading us,' she said.

'Yeah,' Newell said, 'but this wagon train is Father's. It's just that he ain't well enough to lead us right now.'

'Newell,' Eliza said, placing a hand on his arm, 'he won't ever lead us again. Accept that, please.'

Newell glanced at her and although his back remained rigid and his expression firm-jawed, when he spoke his tone was soft.

'I won't accept that and neither will Father, and until he says otherwise, he is still our leader.' Newell swung round to face Dalton. 'But I want to know why John thinks Virgil wrote to him.'

Dalton glanced away, desperately sifting through various excuses. His cheeks warmed as he failed to think of a lie that would resolve the even bigger lie he'd told. But Eliza resolved his problem for him.

'You've embarrassed him,' she said. 'Just because you know lettering, it doesn't mean everyone does.'

Newell winced, colour rising in his cheeks, and Dalton provided a bashful smile.

'Sorry. I got me some learning. I was reading the letter earlier – you might have seen me. I can make out some words, but not all of them.' Dalton shrugged and rocked from foot to foot. 'To be honest, I got someone to read to me and then write back, but perhaps I didn't hear or remember all the details.'

Newell closed his eyes, breathing deeply, then opened them.

'I'm the one who should apologize. I didn't think. I guess from your viewpoint, Virgil looks as if he's our leader.'

Dalton nodded then leaned forward and lowered his voice.

'And he sure didn't volunteer the information that he didn't write to me or that he wasn't in charge.'

'*He* wouldn't.' Newell stepped aside, letting Eliza take Dalton's arm and lead him to the wagon.

'You can see Father now,' she said, 'but keep the visit short. He's dying–'

'He's ill,' Newell snapped, hurrying past them to stand before the wagon.

'He is *dying*,' Eliza said as she stopped. She released Dalton's arm to place both hands on her hips. 'He's got a week, perhaps more, perhaps less, but he's dying.'

Newell opened his mouth, his jaw rippling with the words he wanted to snap back, but then he slapped a fist against his thigh and swirled round.

'Just wait here and I'll check he's still able to see you.'

Newell climbed into the wagon, leaving Dalton facing Eliza.

'Don't be hard on him,' Dalton said. 'It's hard for some people to accept things like that.'

She flashed a smile. 'You're a kind and perceptive man. My brother is, too, but perhaps too kind sometimes.'

Dalton could think of nothing else to say or ask that wouldn't risk adding to the lies he'd already told these decent people. And for the first time he felt a twinge of shame for what he'd done. Unable to face Eliza's pleasant smile and trusting eyes, he looked away towards the distant mountains.

Presently, Newell emerged and signified that he could see Henry, so Dalton jumped on to the wagon.

Inside, Henry Boone lay beneath a blanket in a clear area amongst the family's stored furniture, his wizened form providing the slightest of bumps. His face was gaunt and

sallow, but the deep-set eyes held the determination and intelligence of a man who
should be leading this wagon train.

Unfortunately, the stench in the wagon
confirmed that Eliza was right. It reeked of
death. Sweet, cloying, permeating every
scrap of cloth and piece of stored furniture,
the reek was impossible to ignore, a smell
that said this man was close to the end.

A bony and liver-spotted hand slipped out
from beneath the blanket and beckoned
Dalton to come closer.

Hunched over and breathing through his
mouth, Dalton approached him and sat
cross-legged beside his bed.

'Listen,' Henry said. His voice was deeper
and more assured than Dalton had expected, but he still expelled a wave of rank
air that curdled Dalton's stomach. 'Newell
can't accept I don't have much longer, but I
will die soon and before I die, I want to see
where my people will settle down.'

Henry displayed an arc of blackened
teeth, the fragile smile appearing to acknowledge that he was unlikely to get his wish,
then he waved towards a chest at his side.

Dalton moved to open it, but when Henry
grunted and gestured again, he collected the
folded blanket that rested on the top. He

brought it to Henry, who opened it, his tense jaw, intense gaze and shaking hands confirming that this simple action required all his failing strength and concentration to complete. When the blanket fell away, a simple wooden sign lay on his hands, and Henry swung it round to face Dalton.

'Sweet Valley,' Dalton read aloud. 'The name of the new settlement?'

'A fine name for a fine town.' Henry busied himself with folding the blanket over the sign, but his hands shook so badly the sign slipped. Dalton rescued it, receiving a murmured thanks. 'And how long will it take you to lead my people to a place worthy of this sign?'

Dalton placed the sign and blanket back on the chest, heaving a sigh of relief, as Sweet Valley wasn't a specific location, but a dying man's dream of an ideal place to live.

'Five days, maybe a week.'

A snorting cackle emerged from Henry's lips.

'Honest men make bad liars. Don't tell me what I want to hear. Tell me the truth.'

Faced with Henry's unquestioning acceptance of his role, Dalton found that no matter how much trouble it might make for him, he couldn't lie to a dying man.

He laid a hand on his bony shoulder. 'No matter what I have to do, you'll see Sweet Valley. I promise.'

Henry stared into Dalton's eyes, then nodded.

'I know what that promise means and I accept it. I reckon that from on high, I will be able to see Sweet Valley, and even if I die on the way down, I'll have seen it.' Henry stared hard at Dalton, his gaze boring into him, but Dalton could find nothing to say in reply. 'So, when you see the valley for the first time, take me out of this wagon and show it to me. That's all I ask.'

Henry closed his eyes, the gesture effectively ending their meeting.

But Dalton still sat beside him for another few minutes, listening to his rasping breathing. Only when Henry delivered a low snore did he leave the wagon.

'How is he?' Eliza asked, drawing him away from the wagon.

Dalton glanced around, seeing that Newell had gone.

'Asleep.'

'Good. He does that a lot these days. Did you tell him the truth about how long it'll take to get over the mountains? Virgil reckons it'll take at least two weeks, and he can't last that long, never mind the time it'll take to get to somewhere where we can settle down.'

'I didn't lie, but I promised I'll do everything I can to get him there.' Dalton ventured a smile. 'Why did he even make this journey in that condition?'

'He never told us he was ill. I guess he must have been fighting to avoid showing it for a long time, but when we neared Applegate, he collapsed. Virgil bought him a potion from a snake-oil seller, but that made him worse. And since then, he's just become weaker with every passing day.'

Dalton tried to think of something comforting to say, but found that he couldn't face talking any more now that his bluff could hurt such decent people. He bade Eliza goodbye, then headed to the river, leaving her to slip into the wagon.

But when he'd settled down on the boulder by the river he looked towards the mound of earth that covered the body of the real John Stanton.

'I promise you, John,' he whispered under his breath, 'I won't let you down. I really won't. Whatever it takes and no matter if my bluff fails, I will get these settlers to Sweet Valley.'

CHAPTER 3

Dalton's first few days with the wagon train passed without any major problems.

Virgil didn't even consult him before they set off each day. Instead, he steered the wagons on a straight course across the plains towards the mountains, driving them on with a determination to cover as many miles as possible before the light dimmed.

Each day they closed on the mountains, but their forms grew so slowly that Dalton reckoned he still had several days before he had to trust his luck and choose a route.

But for now, nobody asked him for details of the terrain ahead, and neither did Dalton encourage that debate by letting himself get drawn into conversations where he'd be forced to lie or change the subject.

And his bluff weighed heavily on him. These people had every year of past hardship etched into their lined faces and work-calloused bodies. He didn't enquire into anyone's past, but assumed everybody had a reason for seeking out a new life in a new land. And the potential cost to them of trusting a man, who might not be able to find that new land, shamed Dalton into avoiding contact with them.

At night, the group did relax from the rigours of their journey. They placed the wagons in a circle with a heaped fire in the centre. The children milled and chased each other within the circle while the adults entertained themselves with simple pleasures such as swapping stories, singing, or playing games. In particular they enjoyed a game in which two competitors threw horseshoes at a spike in the ground. Jacob, Virgil Wade's son, was proficient at this game and usually emerged as champion.

Like Dalton, Eliza and Newell distanced themselves from the entertainment. If this was because their father was dying or because they were annoyed that Virgil had assumed control of the group, Dalton couldn't tell. But he didn't speak to them to find out, as he found it hard to talk to people who would suffer the most from his possible inability to direct them.

He did watch them, looking for signs of distress that might herald Henry's impending demise. He saw none and although Eliza assumed all the caring duties, many people passed by their wagon to offer help and to ask about Henry. From the snippets of conversation that Dalton overheard, he learned that his condition had even improved slightly.

On the fourth night, when he'd collected his meal, Eliza sat beside him. She said nothing other than to smile at him and they ate in silence, but afterwards, she took his plate and pointed to Henry's wagon.

'Father would like to talk to you again,' she said.

'What about?'

'He said it was a personal matter.' She leaned forward, a flash of intrigue in her lively eyes. 'I'll feed him later. You can see him first.'

Dalton still wavered, knowing that he would be unable to lie to Henry.

'He's a sick man. Are you sure I should bother him?'

'He knows his own mind, as he always has.' She placed a hand on his arm and squeezed. 'I know you're a quiet man who doesn't like to waste time on idle chatter, but Father likes that in a man. And I do, too.'

She ushered him away and, with her bemusing comment still on his thoughts, he headed into the wagon.

Henry was sitting up, with more colour in his cheeks than the last time he'd seen him.

'You look well,' Dalton said with all honesty.

'I *do* feel better. Odd that, but I like the nights now that it's getting colder.' Henry gestured to the flapping cloth at the back of the wagon. 'And that must mean we're making good progress.'

'We are. But this is the easy part. We'll travel more slowly later.' Dalton settled down beside Henry. 'But you had a personal matter you wanted to talk to me about.'

Henry chuckled, the sound rasping. 'I do have a personal concern that only a dying man with a comely daughter would raise. I reckon you're a man who likes plain speaking. So, you said in your letter that you'd thought of settling down one day. Are you still considering that?'

Dalton gulped as he instantly saw the direction this conversation was taking.

'I am,' he said, his tone cautious.

'And now that you've met Eliza, do you think you and she might...?' Henry raised his eyebrows.

Dalton sighed. Until Eliza had uttered her cryptic comment before he'd come into the

40

wagon, he hadn't thought about her at all. Now, he found to his surprise that the insinuation didn't disconcert him.

'It's hard to say.'

'I know I'm putting you in a difficult position. You don't want to lie to a dying man, but at least tell me you'll consider her. Jacob Wade is the only man here who could be suitable, and he ain't.'

Dalton shrugged. 'Aside from watching him play that game with the horseshoes, I haven't talked to him, but he seems a fine young man.'

Henry shivered. 'Ain't got the energy for the details, but the Wade family are no good, no good at all. And where we're going, Eliza won't meet many men. I'd hate to die without knowing one of my kin will give me grandchildren.'

Dalton considered Henry's wicked smile and he returned it.

'You're a fiendish old man and that's a fact.'

Henry cackled, the sound ending in a burst of coughing, but the merriment still played in his deep-set eyes.

'I like you, John. You won't lie and you won't give up. Do what you will and I'm sure Eliza will get her claws into you. Now, I'm

41

hungry. Send her in.' Henry winked. 'But I won't keep her long if you want to talk to her later.'

Dalton patted Henry's shoulder then left the wagon.

Eliza was loitering nearby and she hurried over to join him.

'What did he want?' she asked, rising on her toes to peer over his shoulder at the wagon.

'Like you said, it was a personal matter.'

'And did you promise him he'd get to see Sweet Valley? He's been better these last few days and there has to be a chance.'

Dalton considered her hopeful expression and although supporting her suggestion would provide him with a ready explanation, he shook his head.

'That wasn't what he wanted to ask me.'

'Father tells me everything,' she said, her voice low and hurt as she hunched her shoulders and folded her arms.

Dalton placed a hand on her shoulder. 'It was nothing to worry about, and now he's hungry. That has to be another good sign.'

'It is.' She patted his hand, then rocked her head up to look at him and gave a wicked smile that proved she was her father's daughter. 'But if you won't tell me what he

42

said, I'll have to see what I can get out of him.'

'Don't pester him,' Dalton said. He smiled. 'Perhaps we can ... we can talk later after you've fed him.'

She nodded. 'I'd like that.'

He gestured through a gap in the circle of wagons.

'And maybe we could walk down to the creek. It looks like it'll be a fine night.'

Her eyes flashed before she looked away, breathing deeply, and Dalton thought he might have been too forward, that she'd refuse, but she smiled.

'That would be nice. So long as Newell approves.'

'Later, then.'

She turned to the wagon and Dalton was sure she gave a short skip, but then she halted. Her shoulders shook. Then she swirled round, her eyes blazing.

'That was the personal matter he talked to you about, wasn't it?'

'I ... I...' Dalton stammered as she advanced on him.

She stabbed a finger against his chest, punctuating her points with repeated stabs.

'He told you I'm growing into a spinster woman, didn't he? He told you that where we're going there just aren't any men, didn't he? He told you that you should … should woo me, didn't he? Go on. Deny that.'

'I can't. But it wasn't like that. He just said that—'

She delivered a stinging slap to his cheek that resounded around the circle of wagons and, from the corner of his eye, Dalton saw several heads snap round to watch them with interest and amusement.

'You can forget whatever plans you and Father have dreamed up because I will not go walking down by the creek with the likes of you.'

She swirled round, her long skirt swinging, and flounced to the wagon.

While rubbing his cheek, Dalton watched her climb into the wagon, then immediately climb back out again to collect her father's meal, then disappear inside.

Dalton was aware that several people were still watching him and murmuring to each other with curiosity in their tones, but he ignored them and continued to watch the wagon.

Presently she emerged, but she saw that Dalton was watching the wagon and turned on her heel. She slipped away through the gap between Henry's wagon and the next one, muttering under her breath, then walked off into the night, heading down to the creek.

But just as she disappeared from view, she glanced back over her shoulder.

And then she was gone.

Dalton watched the darkness between the wagons for another minute, then shook himself.

'Dalton,' he said to himself as he headed after her, 'you're in serious trouble.'

When he was beyond the circle of wagons, he stopped and waited for his eyes to adjust to the dark.

The half-moon was low and providing some light, but deep shadows pooled on the ground. Dalton squinted and slowly Eliza's form resolved standing by the creek and looking into the water.

The creek was around ten feet wide and the water's gurgling as it brushed over rocks came to Dalton on a light and sweet breeze. He watched her bend and cup a handful of water, which she drew up to her face, but she didn't drink.

Slowly, she let the water drip down to the creek, the droplets small balls of fire in the moonlight, then she cupped another handful. She appeared so serene, her gestures almost suggestive of ritual. Dalton rocked from foot to foot, uncertain as to what he should do.

When he'd followed her he had been sure that she had wanted him to do just that, but now he was less sure. Had her last glance back been her way of requesting his company? Or had it meant something entirely different?

One thing was certain – a bad guess would have repercussions.

He watched her through another cycle of cupping water and letting it drip to the creek, then made his decision and set off. Whether she wanted to see him or not, he detected in himself an urge to see her and at the very least explain himself.

But he still paced carefully, placing his feet to the ground in the pools of inky blackness and avoiding startling her until he was closer and could call out to her.

When he'd walked to within twenty paces of the creek, she straightened and threw the last handful of water over her shoulder. Her shoulders and arms shook, although as she had her back to him, he couldn't tell what she was doing.

But then she swirled round to look down the creek.

46

'Jacob,' she murmured, backing a pace, her tone startled, 'is that you again?'

Dalton opened his mouth, meaning to apologize, but the words died on his lips. He had not been the one to startle her. A man was standing, emerging from the shadows between two rocks.

'It ain't,' the man said, 'Eliza Boone.'

'Who ... who are you? What do you want?'

'You know what we want.'

'We?' she bleated, then flinched. The first note of a scream tore from her lips but then died as another man emerged from behind her and slapped a hand over her mouth.

Both men must have been hiding in the shadows down by the creek, possibly waiting for her, and neither of the men was from the wagon train.

'You two,' Dalton shouted at the top of his voice, ensuring that they and anyone else who was nearby heard him, 'step away from Eliza.'

Dalton heard an instant commotion erupt from behind him and confident now that he'd alerted everyone to the danger, he broke into a run. He didn't have the gun he'd taken from John on him and could see that both men were packing guns, but he didn't slow as he closed on them.

The man holding Eliza from behind turned her round to face Dalton, and barked out a command that he stay back, but heartened by Dalton's presence, Eliza fought back. She stamped on the man's foot, elbowed him in the stomach, and squirmed and struggled in his grip.

The other man hurried along the creek to help him, his body turned towards Dalton, his gun drawn.

Dalton slid to a halt and raised his hands slightly.

'You won't get away with this. Help is a-coming. Put down that gun, release Eliza, and run while you still got the chance.'

The man darted his gaze up past Dalton, where Dalton could hear pounding footfalls as several men hurried out through the wagons and others shouted that Eliza was in danger.

He moved to join his associate in holding Eliza, but she bent at the waist and threw herself forward, the movement making her assailant slip on the wet ground beside the creek and they both came tumbling down.

Dalton broke into a run, hurtling across the ground towards them.

The standing man glanced up at him, then ran, splashing through the shallow water and away. Then Dalton reached the struggling twosome.

He slapped a hand on the man's back and dragged him away from Eliza to stand him straight, then delivered a round-armed slug to his jaw with all the pent-up anger of the last few minutes behind it.

The man reeled to the ground as Dalton grabbed Eliza's shoulders, lifted her from the ground and threw her in the general direction of the approaching help from the wagon train. Then he stood between her and the man, waiting for him to rise.

When the man came up, his hand reaching for his gun, Dalton kicked his hand away. Then he thundered a blow into his cheek, wheeling him away into the creek where he landed on his back with his arms and legs splayed, a huge splash spraying water around him.

Dalton stomped down into the shallows, ready to capture him, but the man rolled backwards and this time, when he came up, he stood crouched in the water with his gun drawn.

Dalton immediately danced back, the man too far away for him to reach, then dived to the ground.

A gunshot ripped out. Dalton heard the

whine as it scythed into the dirt, a few feet to his side. Dalton pressed himself flat to the earth, trusting that Eliza had had the sense to keep running, and that in the poor light the man wouldn't be able to see either of them from the creek.

A second shot peeled out. Dalton winced, but then realized the report had come from behind him, a fact confirmed when he saw the man roll out of the creek on the other side and run off in the direction the other man had fled.

Dalton still stayed down, ensuring that the man wouldn't hit him with a wild shot, but the man didn't fire again and by the time a surge of people joined Dalton, both men had disappeared into the gloom.

Several men were keen to chase after them, but Virgil called for order. Everyone still continued to murmur, but sufficient quiet returned for Dalton to hear the clop of hoofs as the men secured the horses they must have left nearby.

After a short discussion everyone agreed that there was little chance of chasing after and securing the raiders in the night. Several people reckoned these men were with the Spitzer gang, a group of bandits they had been warned about in Applegate and who terrorized the area and specifically preyed on travellers.

'Is Eliza all right?' Dalton asked, when everyone turned to head back to the wagons.

'She is,' Virgil said, 'and that's entirely down to you.'

The group raised a clamour of support for Dalton's actions and, embarrassed by the congratulations, he wended his way through a crowd of backslapping men until he reached Newell, who was standing outside Henry's wagon.

'What did they want?' Newell asked, his eyes wide and staring, his demeanour more shocked than pleased.

'Eliza, apparently. They knew her by name.'

Newell winced. 'Why did they know that? Why did they know that?'

Dalton reckoned he wasn't expecting an answer, and he patted his back and headed past him. But standing on the other side of the wagon was Eliza and, like Newell, she didn't look pleased, her eyes were blazing and her actions jerky as she brushed dust from her skirt.

'That must have been a terrible shock,' Dalton said.

'It was,' she said through clenched teeth.

'Did you recognize them?'

'No.'

Dalton accepted that she didn't want to talk about her ordeal and he moved to pass by her, but she raised a hand, halting him.

'But I *did* recognize you.'

Dalton smiled. 'I'm just glad I was there and could help.'

'I didn't mean that. I mean why were you there in the first place? I went down to the creek to bathe and you followed me. You… You… You disgust me. I thought you were different from the likes of Jacob Wade, but you're just as pathetic as he is. Never ever do that to me again.'

Dalton flinched back, shrugging. 'I'm sorry. I thought…'

He turned and headed away, sighing and shaking his head.

'And John,' she called after him. 'Thank you. I'm glad you did follow me.'

Dalton stopped to nod, then headed away.

While the wagon train prepared to move out on Dalton's fifth day with the group, Dalton avoided Eliza. Although Newell did look at him and give a rueful smile, as if acknowledging that he was embarrassed at not being more grateful the previous night.

All the settlers were tense; the encounter with the Spitzer gang had subdued everyone. For the first time since Dalton had joined the wagon train they had maintained a permanent watch through the night. The gang hadn't returned and when the wagons moved on outlying riders scouted around, ensuring they got advance warning of any more raids by these notorious bandits.

Despite this, the wagons made good speed, everyone appearing eager to get to their new life where they hoped they wouldn't have to deal with such problems.

And last night's incident soon left Dalton's immediate thoughts as his first big decision crept up on him.

So far, he hadn't needed to advise Virgil as to the direction they should take. The wagon train had just headed across the plains towards the mountains, but now the land was rising.

Ahead, the deep indentations of gorges and ridges were slowly revealing themselves and their foreboding presence confirmed that if he chose the wrong route, he could lead them into an impassable dead end.

He continually peered ahead, running his gaze over the various potential routes and hoping he would see which one would give him them the best chance of success. But all routes appeared equally treacherous and Dalton slowly accepted the truth of his dilemma. Henry Boone wouldn't have hired a guide in advance if the route ahead was an obvious one and for him to lead them to Sweet Valley would require a huge slice of luck.

As the day wore on, the moment when he needed to discover just how lucky he would be arrived. A river, perhaps the same one as the one where he'd met the wagons, was lazily swinging in to block their path and he had to choose between fording it or heading upriver.

Dalton darted his gaze around as he searched for which alternative would be the better.

And it was then that he had the stroke of luck he'd hoped for.

A rider was arcing in towards the wagon train from the river and had a hand held high as he hailed them. Since Dalton had joined the group, this was the first traveller they'd encountered during the day.

Virgil shouted orders down the line of wagons for everyone to be on their guard, but Dalton judged that this man wouldn't give the same sort of trouble as the Spitzer gang had. He hurried his horse on to speak to him privately and perhaps glean information about what was ahead.

'Howdy,' he called. 'You heading in any particular direction?'

The man introduced himself as Loren Steele, then pointed to the mountains.

'Going that-a-way.'

Dalton kept his face impassive, avoiding reacting to this good news.

'That's where we're heading. You been over them before?'

'Nope.' Loren leaned forward in the saddle, smiling. 'But it sure is good news that we're heading to the same place. Be obliged if you'd let me join you.'

Dalton bit back his disappointment, then glanced back to see that Virgil Wade was speeding his wagon to join them, with riders flanking him and glaring at Loren.

'Ain't really my place to say.'

Loren rocked his gaze from Dalton to the advancing Virgil, then nodded and stayed quiet until Virgil joined them. Then he made his pitch.

'I ain't no trouble,' he said. 'I ain't no burden. I can help with anything and ask for nothing in return, and I got no needs other than to enjoy good company.'

Virgil didn't reply immediately, sizing Loren up with his steady gaze, then he looked around, perhaps to see if this man had any associates. He glanced at Dalton.

Dalton had caught only fleeting glimpses of the Spitzer gang in the dark, but he was sure he would recognize them if he met them in daylight. And he saw nothing in Loren's placid gaze and honest expression to alarm him. He nodded to Virgil, who returned the nod then pointed towards the wagons, signifying that Loren could ride along with them. Then he turned to Dalton.

'Do we cross the river?' he asked.

Dalton took a deep breath and entrusted his first guess to luck. Loren had been riding away from the river and, as his horse's flanks were wet, he must have forded it. So, that suggested there wasn't an obvious route on the other side of the river.

He pointed upriver. Without further word, Virgil headed his wagon off along the side of the river.

Dalton watched the wagon pass by, then turned to follow, but Loren hadn't moved and was still watching him.

'So,' he said, 'you're guiding these people, are you?'

'Sure am,' Dalton said. 'I'm John Stanton.'

Loren's gaze remained expressionless as he gave a slow nod.

'Well met, John ... Stanton.'

Dalton caught an odd intonation in the way Loren uttered the name and the slow way he'd used the full name was also odd.

He dismissed that from his mind and turned to follow Virgil, but as he rode off, he had the distinct impression that Loren was watching his back.

The steadily rising trail that Dalton had chosen presented no problems that day and neither did anyone catch sight of the Spitzer gang. So, when they made camp that night, Dalton was in good spirits, and those good spirits had infused the rest of the group.

He studiously avoided Eliza and the only time their paths crossed was when Dalton slipped out of the circle of wagons to collect water from the river. She happened to be standing in his way, but she turned and started talking with the guard assigned to keep an eye on anyone leaving the circle.

After that, Dalton did what he normally did in the evenings and sat apart from the group, watching everyone and enjoying the sight of their relaxed camaraderie.

As darkness fell, Virgil posted another two

men outside the circle to watch out for the bandits and issued orders that nobody should leave the circle unaccompanied. But within the circle, the group built up the fire, raised their voices and laughed loudly at any comment.

Dalton quickly saw that this wasn't because everybody had forgotten the near tragic events of last night, but was in direct defiance of those events. If the Spitzer gang were close, everybody was letting them know that they weren't frightened and that they would prevail.

In spite of his earlier apparent suspicion, Loren didn't look at him again, although Dalton had the impression that he was avoiding looking at him. But Dalton accepted that if he were paranoid about every encounter he would never survive this journey. He dismissed his worries from his mind so that he could enjoy watching everyone have fun.

The game of throwing horseshoes at a spike started up and tonight Jacob Wade was even more impressive than normal, winning every match and eventually taking on all comers and defeating them. The game was over seven shoes and Jacob lost only one or at most two rounds before winning each game.

As the night wore on Jacob was indefatigable, his face beaming and the air frequently receiving a firm punch as he won yet again. The only time he moved away from the spike was to receive the congratulations of the watching people. Dalton couldn't help but notice that he always talked to someone close to wherever Eliza happened to be sitting and often glanced in her direction.

But he didn't speak to her and neither did she look at him while he was close.

Dalton had never played a game of this kind before and so had no desire to participate. But after Jacob had won his twentieth straight game by defeating Loren Steele with four perfect throws, Jacob boasted that nobody would ever beat him again.

His boast received catcalls aplenty, but nobody stepped forward to challenge that claim and Dalton surprised himself as much as anyone when he found himself rising to his feet and pacing into the circle of watchers to stand before him.

'You can't say you can defeat anyone,' he said, 'because you haven't played me yet.'

Dalton glanced around the watching circle, seeing both Eliza and Loren lean forward with interest, and hearing everyone else welcome him with a huge cheer. He acknowledged the encouragement with a short wave, then returned his gaze to the beaming Jacob.

'Then,' Jacob said, rolling his shoulders, 'it's time to find out if you're a good loser.'

CHAPTER 4

Dalton reckoned he'd set himself up for a quick defeat, but he got plenty of encouragement from a group eager to see the boastful Jacob defeated by a man who had already proved his worth. And he milked the situation, pacing around behind the mark, sizing up the spike from various angles, crouching down then standing as he chose the best angle from which to throw.

He'd watched the others throw and noted that many threw the shoe high in the air, aiming to land it on the spike, but Jacob threw hard and low, trusting his accurate aim to catch the spike and hang on. He decided to use Jacob's tactic.

His first throw worked perfectly, slamming into the spike then spinning around it and coming to rest with the spike in the centre of the shoe.

A huge cheer rippled around the circle of watchers as Jacob grumbled about the throw being a lucky one, then took his place behind the mark. And perhaps Dalton's unexpected success had rattled him because his shoe flew a foot or so over the spike, giving Dalton the lead.

Spurred on by the success of his first throw, Dalton tried the same tactic for his next two throws, but he missed the spike both times and, with Jacob catching his shoe around the spike, he lost both rounds.

After that, he threw his fourth shoe with more care and less strength and it landed in the dirt in front of the spike, then slid across the earth to nudge up to the spike. In response, Jacob delivered an accurate throw, but it hit the spike and ricocheted, landing further away than Dalton's throw.

The loser always took the first throw of the next round and, with the game tied and with only three throws remaining, Dalton appraised his opponent.

Jacob strode back and forth considering the spike from a variety of angles and repeatedly rocking his arm up and down as he tested the weight before throwing.

Eventually he threw, but even after all his preparation, the shoe emerged from his hand with too low a trajectory and ploughed into the dirt four feet short of the spike, then stopped dead.

Jacob muttered an oath under his breath,

kicked at the dirt, then swung round and stomped past Dalton.

'Bad luck,' Dalton said.

'I'll get you next time,' Jacob grunted.

Dalton smiled as he considered Jacob's hunched shoulders and downcast eyes.

'There's nothing at stake here,' he said, still smiling. 'Don't take it so seriously.'

Jacob snapped his head up to glower at Dalton, his glaring eyes confirming that he took all competitive situations seriously. Dalton shook his head as he turned away, but he did wave to the watchers, encouraging everyone to support him.

Somehow, he'd rattled his opponent more than anyone else had tonight and the watchers did their best to strengthen Dalton's position, clapping and shouting encouragement. And as he took up his position, he noticed Jacob look around. His gaze centred on Eliza, who was talking animatedly with Newell.

Dalton nodded to himself, reckoning that he had understood the situation and the reason why he had been the one who had rattled Jacob. Confident now of his ability to beat him, he cleared his mind of all distracting thoughts and concentrated on beating Jacob's poor throw.

He centred his gaze on the spike as he weighed the shoe in his hand then threw it, but as it left his hand, a light flashed in his eyes, dazzling him and making him flinch. The shoe flew wildly away, landing ten feet to the side and five feet beyond the spike.

A collective sigh went up from the watchers as Dalton straightened then looked around for what had dazzled him. And Jacob was thrusting his hand beneath his jacket while sporting a smug grin.

Dalton stared at him as Jacob held his hand out, inviting him to take the next throw.

Dalton collected both shoes then paced to the side to keep his back to Jacob and threw the shoe using his previous tactic of aiming strongly at the spike. The shoe clanged into the spike and although it didn't catch, it dropped to the dirt a few inches from the spike, leaving Jacob in the position of needing an accurate throw to win the game.

Jacob took up his position behind the mark, walking slowly by Dalton.

'Reckon as I'll beat you this time,' he said, swinging his arms and grinning.

'If you have to cheat to win, you're welcome to it.'

'No such thing as cheating in this game.' Jacob crouched, then rocked his hand back and forth. 'All that matters is to win.'

'And does that apply to everything?' Dalton glanced over Jacob's shoulder to look in Eliza's general direction.

Jacob straightened then turned to look at Eliza. He turned back, his smug grin re-emerging.

'Yeah. I'll beat you at everything, old man.'

Dalton nodded. 'I reckon I understand. But what I don't understand is why you reckon that beating me at this childish game will impress a woman like Eliza.'

Jacob resumed his crouched stance and rocked back his hand, ready to throw.

'This is just a part of it.'

'For you, it's the *only* part.' Dalton waited for Jacob to swing his hand forward before delivering his final comment. 'You can have this game, I'll have Eliza.'

Jacob flinched as he threw, Dalton's taunt causing his aim to veer, and the shoe flew over the top of the spike to land five feet on, then roll onwards for several more feet. Jacob swirled round to glare at him.

'I thought you didn't believe in cheating.'

'I never said that. I can beat you any way I choose, kid.' Dalton held out his hand. 'And now it's your throw again – one each for the game.'

Jacob grumbled as he collected both shoes. He threw one to Dalton's feet then rolled his shoulders and took up his position.

'You forget, old man,' he muttered while staring at the spike. 'I'm Eliza's age, I know her better than you do, and I'm staying. I'll beat you to her just like I'll beat you at this game.'

Jacob glanced at Dalton, his eye flared, then he turned to look at the spike and threw the shoe.

If it hadn't been for Jacob's arrogance, Dalton would have been impressed as the shoe flew at the spike, hit it, then slid into place around the spike to sit nudging up to it – a perfect throw and unbeatable.

Jacob slapped his hands together then straightened and walked past Dalton without further comment, letting his good throw say everything he needed to say.

Dalton hefted his shoe and considered how he could match Jacob's throw, finding in himself a surprising yearning to succeed. A few minutes ago he had had no interest in even playing this game, and he didn't share Jacob's desire to show off in front of Eliza.

But now the competitive urge had taken him over and he had to find a way to beat Jacob.

66

He pulled his hat low in case Jacob tried to dazzle him again then stared at the spike as he rocked his arm back and forth. He couldn't beat Jacob's throw, but as the bluff he'd been carrying out since he'd joined the settlers required him to ride his luck, he decided to trust that luck again and use the same tactic as for his first throw.

He thrust his arm back, then hurled the shoe at the spike with all his strength. The shoe blurred through the air, then cracked into the tip of the spike. It caught, then swirled round and round. Applause and cheering broke out, but Dalton still stared at the spinning shoe, the strength he'd used letting it spin for many seconds.

But the shoe didn't come loose and nestled down on top of Jacob's shoe.

'A tie,' Virgil Wade declared, coming into circle with his arms held wide. 'A fair result after the best game of the night.'

'We got to throw again,' Jacob shouted, slapping his hands on his hips and pouting, 'and prove who's the best. And that's me.'

Virgil looked at Dalton, but Dalton reckoned he'd pushed his luck far enough with his last throw and shook his head.

'A tie is a fair result for me.'

Jacob grumbled and even stamped a foot.

Then the three men stood in a silent group, each man glancing at the others. Dalton could see from Virgil's gleaming eyes and proud smile that he approved of his son's competitive spirit, but that only helped to convince Dalton he didn't want to continue with the game.

He started to confirm that as far as he was concerned the game had ended with honours even, when Newell Boone emerged from the circle to stand over the spike. He stared down at it, rocking his head from side to side, then beckoned them to join him.

'We don't need another game to see who's won,' he said. 'We already know. John's shoe is the nearest to the spike.'

'What?' Virgil and Jacob snapped together as they hurried over to join Newell.

Dalton followed and saw that Newell was right. Jacob's shoe had been touching the spike, but Dalton's throw had been so powerful it had pushed the shoe away to leave his being the only one touching the spike. The gap was only an inch, but it was still there.

'See,' Newell said. 'John won the game.'

'Jacob's shoe was touching the spike,' Virgil said. 'The best John could do was to tie. He couldn't win.'

'He could,' Newell declared, miming the

action of Dalton's shoe hitting the spike and pushing Jacob's away with his hands, 'but only if he knocked Jacob's shoe away, and that's just what he's done.'

'*That* is not the rules of the game.'

'It is. The nearest shoe wins.'

'Not when the first thrower touches the spike.'

Newell sneered. 'You just made that rule up.'

Dalton watched the two men knock this argument back and forth, waiting for an opportunity to butt in and state that he didn't mind settling for a tie, but he saw that Virgil and Newell weren't arguing about this game. A simpler power-struggle was coming out into the open – perhaps for the first time – and one in which neither man was prepared to back down.

But one of them had to relent and, as the circle of watchers broke up in disgust at their pointless argument, Virgil's position of arguing that the nearest shoe shouldn't win started to sound desperate.

And to Dalton's surprise, Virgil suddenly backed away.

'All right,' he said, waving a hand in a dismissive manner as he turned his back on Newell, 'if this means that much to you, I'll declare that John has won.'

'That's only because he did,' Newell said, folding his arms.

'He didn't,' Jacob muttered, advancing on Newell. 'You cheating Boones can't deny me.'

Newell glanced at Jacob, shook his head then turned away, but Jacob broke into a run, thrust his head down, and slammed into Newell's side. The sudden nature of his action caught Newell unawares and he wheeled his arms and legs as he fought to keep his balance, but Jacob carried him on. The two men tumbled to the ground.

Within seconds, both men were rolling over each other, throwing dust up as they tried to land flailing blows on the other man. Wild scything punches connected on arms and shoulders, but from so close neither man could inflict much damage on the other.

The watchers stood bemused and rigid, Dalton getting the impression that even if they were on guard to repel the Spitzer gang, violence amongst their own numbers was rare. And it was only when Eliza fought her way through the circle of watchers and tried to get a restraining hand on Newell's back that everyone broke out of their spell.

Dalton and Virgil hurried towards the fighters. Newell had now pinned Jacob on his back and was shaking his shoulders, knocking his head back into the dirt.

Virgil reached them first. He nudged Eliza aside, then looped his hands under Newell's armpits and lifted him off Jacob, who used his freedom to throw a wild punch at Newell. His fist whistled through the air a foot short of Newell's chin. Then he rolled to his feet and hurled back his fist ready to aim another punch at him, but Dalton grabbed Jacob around the chest from behind.

Newell and Jacob squirmed and struggled, trying to wrestle themselves clear and land a punch or a kick on the other man, but when Virgil and Dalton dragged them apart, they slowly desisted.

Dalton heard Virgil murmur placating words to Newell, and Eliza joined them, shaking her head.

'Let me go,' Jacob whined.

'I will,' Dalton said, keeping his voice low as he spoke into Jacob's ear, 'but only when you're not so loco.'

'You don't know what this is about.'

'I got an idea and I'll give you a good piece of advice – beating on Eliza's brother sure ain't the right way to impress her.'

Jacob snorted. 'That ain't got nothing to do with why I hate the Boone family. They don't lead this group. We do.'

'We both know you don't hate *all* the Boone family.' Dalton relaxed his hold of Jacob's chest to give him more leeway. 'I know this is hard for you, but you got to be sensible.'

'Leave me alone. I don't need your pity.'

Dalton detected a change in Jacob's tone, with hurt feelings replacing his anger, and he released his grip to let him stand free.

'Then take a different piece of advice. No matter whose fault this is, you all have to live together. Shake Newell's hand.'

Jacob rolled his shoulders. 'I'll never do that.'

'Then do it for Eliza.' Dalton moved from behind Jacob to stand before him. 'Or you'll stand no chance against me.'

Jacob sneered. 'I already have everything I need to impress her. You'll see.'

Jacob brushed by him and paced towards Newell, who glared at him, but then swung away and left the circle of wagons. A few moments later another man returned, confirming that Jacob had taken over his guard duties.

With the cause of the fight having left,

Virgil released Newell and headed off after his son.

Everyone else dispersed, disappearing into their wagons with barely a word or glance at each other, and neither Eliza nor Newell looked at Dalton as they headed to Henry's wagon.

With the area clearing in a matter of minutes, Dalton turned on the spot to find that only one person remained – Loren Steele.

'Now,' Loren said, smiling as he glanced in the direction Jacob and Virgil had gone, 'you dealt with that situation well, John Stanton.'

Then Loren tipped his hat and turned away.

In the morning nobody mentioned last night's incident, although from the significant glances he detected being exchanged, Dalton judged that most people were embarrassed but not surprised by the confrontation.

He also noticed that more people than usual called in on Henry Boone's wagon to check that he had had a restful night.

When they were ready to move out, in accordance with the normal routine, Virgil took up the lead position and, with a few terse questions, requested instructions on their route today. As Dalton hoped that the river would have flowed from the higher ground down a route they could follow, he directed him to continue following the winding path of the river, keeping to its side.

For most of the morning they travelled at a steady rate. When the sun had burnt off the early mist Dalton saw that the river was now flowing down a valley, its sides becoming increasingly steep. And they were closing on a range of jagged peaks and rocky ridges. But Dalton continued to hope that when they reached them the terrain would resolve itself into something less formidable than it appeared to be from further away.

For the whole morning this possibility remained. The steep-sided valley, and occasionally the thick forest, closed in so that there was room for only one wagon to pass easily beside the river.

But later the flat and gently rising land on either side of the river provided easy travelling, with the steep valley-sides and thick forest staying several hundred yards back. And on several occasions the sides of the valley became shallow enough to provide a passable way out of the valley if the route ahead were to became blocked.

As the day wore on those occasions

became less frequent and the times when the land narrowed became more frequent.

Dalton began to feel that disaster would be around the next bend in the river. So, as they rounded each bend, he ensured he was at the front so that he'd be the first to see what was ahead. Each time, he hoped his luck would hold and that a path which this group could follow would be ahead.

But the valley continued to narrow and, just as the valley sides loomed on either side and he was fighting down his mounting panic, he rounded another bend.

Ahead, the valley straightened and a long and steep ascent caused the river to roar and spray over the rocky bed, and that ascent led to a solid ridge, with the land beyond disappearing from view.

Dalton couldn't help but let his gaze linger on the summit of that ascent, noting that beyond nothing was visible other than the clear blue sky. Even the jagged peaks were invisible behind this significant ridge.

He hoped that his luck would hold and that once they'd crested the ridge, there would be a negotiable continuation of their route. But he gave no sign of his concern as he shouted encouragement to everyone to follow and the wagons headed up the incline in single file.

Dalton centred his gaze on the blue sky, hoping he would soon see an indication that the terrain would be passable beyond the ridge.

But he got the first inkling that his luck was about to run out when he was half-way up the slope. He caught the first glimpse of the peak of a bluff that poked out from beyond the ridge, pines sprouting up from its top like unruly hair.

And as he closed on the crest of the ridge that bluff spread out to cover the whole of the route ahead.

Dalton fought back the growing feeling of despondency that threatened to overwhelm him. He speeded up to ensure he was well ahead of the group and so give himself time to decide where they would go next.

But when he crested the top, he could see no possible forward route.

He drew his horse to a halt and peered up the winding extent of the river, but it disappeared into a precipitous gorge. Both sides of the gorge were too steep for a rider to climb and perhaps even a man.

Dalton locked his gaze to the bluff that blocked their way on this side of the river, but the sides were vertical and even overhanging in places. And the slope on the other side of the river was rocky and ended in an overhang at the top.

There just wasn't any way forward from this position.

'Which route do we take now?' Virgil shouted from behind him as his wagon crested the ridge.

Dalton drew his horse back, still glancing around in the forlorn hope that he might find a path, but seeing no way out. Virgil drew his wagon to a halt and Dalton glanced at him, seeing his features reddening by the moment.

But it was Jacob who poked his head out from the wagon and delivered the simplest assessment of their situation.

'You've led us in the wrong direction,' he said, a certain smugness in his tone. 'What kind of guide are you?'

CHAPTER 5

Dalton forced himself to ignore Virgil's and Jacob's agitated complaints and peered around, searching for a possible way out of the dead end he'd led them into.

But he could see no route ahead and could think of nothing to say that would avoid him losing the settlers' confidence. The only possibility was for them to double back and for him to search for another route upwards.

'Well?' Virgil asked, his tone determined and demanding an answer. 'What are we going to do?'

Dalton turned and watched the next wagon crest the ridge, then raised his eyes to look down the snaking line of wagons trailing further clown the slope.

Beyond the last wagon, movement caught his eye. He took a deep breath and turned in the saddle to look at Virgil.

'Keep your voice down,' he said, 'and look as if we're unconcerned, but move everyone over the ridge and seek the higher ground beside the gorge.'

Dalton pointed to the highest point the wagons would be able to reach below the most precipitous part of the gorge.

'Why?' Virgil asked, his eyes narrowing with suspicion.

'Because we're being followed and we need to prepare for the worst.'

Virgil gulped. 'You... You sure? Is it the Spitzer gang?'

Dalton couldn't help but notice the stammer in Virgil's voice.

'Don't know who they are, but they're staying back and for me, that means trouble. But don't worry. I've taken us to the best place to defend ourselves and we will prevail.'

Virgil hunched forward in his seat, then gave a quick nod and turned to pass an order down the line of wagons for everyone to move up over the ridge and make camp at the highest point they could reach. The driver of the next wagon looked at the impassable terrain ahead, but as Virgil had used a stern voice that left no room for debate, he followed his instructions.

As the wagons rattled past Virgil muttered further orders. From several of the wagons men jumped down then hurried along the line of wagons with rifles in hand and keeping out of the view of anyone who was further down the slope. They moved so swiftly that Dalton noted that this group must have a prearranged routine for dealing with trouble when on the move.

Loren crested the ridge between the sixth and seventh wagons, but when he saw the commotion beyond the ridge he needed no encouragement to join them with gun in hand, ready to repel a possible attack.

But Dalton, despite his assurance when he'd spoken to Virgil, wasn't sure that an attack would come. If the men were the Spitzer gang, it would suggest they had been followed intentionally into a trap. But he hadn't seen the Spitzer gang since they'd run them off, and if it hadn't been for his predicament, he'd have taken their presence as a hopeful indicator of his having chosen a passable route.

But whether the following men were trouble or not, he was relieved that they'd headed into the straight stretch of valley at just the right time to give him an excuse that would cover up his bad directions.

When the last wagon had passed him, Dalton and five other men remained and they hurried on foot along the ridge and hunkered down on the edge of the tree-line.

From there, Dalton could see the river flowing down the steep ascent for several miles, but could see no sign of the riders.

Nobody worried about this, and Virgil murmured the opinion that this provided further evidence that these men *were* following them and were keeping themselves hidden. Dalton viewed Virgil's ready suspicion with some surprise, judging that he almost expected an attack.

Virgil ordered them to spread out. He and Jacob stayed on the edge of the trees, two men headed into the trees, and Loren and Dalton took up positions on clear land near the river.

They lay down on a wide and flat rock that would cover them from anyone looking their way from below provided they didn't make any sudden movements that would let anyone see them against the sky.

For ten minutes they remained quiet, until Loren spoke up.

'So, John Stanton,' he said, still keeping his gaze downriver, 'you led us into this dead end to escape these men, did you?'

Dalton again caught Loren's emphasis on his full name. He hadn't heard him use anyone else's full name, but he responded as if the question had no sinister intent.

'Like I told Virgil, I ain't taking no chances.'

'That's good to hear, John Stanton.'

Dalton took a deep breath. 'We're all friends here, Loren Steele. You can call me John.'

'Obliged, John...'

Dalton waited for Loren to complete his adopted name, but even when it didn't come, the implied accusation still hung in the air. That intent could be real and Loren could have reason to suspect his identity was false, or it could just be his own guilt worrying him.

Either way, Dalton tried to keep his concern quiet, but as the long minutes passed, he found he had to give voice to that concern.

'You got a problem with me?' he asked, keeping his tone calm.

'Why you ask?'

'The way you say my name. It strikes me that you don't like me.'

'You really want me to answer that?'

'Yeah, and quit answering everything I ask with another question.'

Loren laughed with a single low snort, then shuffled back from the edge of the rock to lie looking up at Dalton.

'Then I'll say it, but I don't know how to speak without asking a question.'

Dalton shuffled back to lie beside Virgil.

'Then just say it.'

Loren took a full minute to answer, during which time Dalton noted where his horse was. If Loren was about to reveal that he knew he wasn't John Stanton, he reckoned he could slug Loren's jaw, disarm him, reach his horse, and gallop away before anyone could stop him.

'Are you...?' Loren rubbed his jaw, rocking his head from side to side as Dalton flexed his fist behind his back. 'Are you pursuing Eliza Boone?'

The question was so unexpected that Dalton flinched back.

'Eliza!' he spluttered, then glanced down the ridge towards Virgil, who put a finger to his lips. Dalton lowered his voice. 'What you mean?'

'I mean that as I might get me the hankering to stay with these settlers when they get to where you're leading them, I've been looking at who's here. But there ain't much in the way of unaccompanied women here.'

'Except Eliza.'

'Yeah. And you've been looking at her a lot.' Loren smiled. 'And no matter what

84

other people say about me, I ain't a man to take another man's woman.'

Dalton hadn't realized he had been watching Eliza a lot, but he searched Loren's clear eyes, seeing no hint in them that this question was anything but honest.

'Then I'll tell you the truth. I don't know. Sometimes we're friendly, but most of time we ain't. So, I guess she's free and I won't stand in your way just as you won't stand in my way.' Dalton glanced over his shoulder towards the trees, then leaned towards Loren. 'Jacob Wade might think otherwise, but he ain't got much to offer beyond an ability to throw horseshoes. You can deal with him.'

Loren laughed. 'Obliged for your understanding, John Stanton.'

Dalton shuffled to the edge of the rock to peer down the valley.

'John, please.'

Loren joined him. 'Then John it is, John.'

With that, they settled themselves to look down the side of the ridge.

An hour passed with still no sign of anyone approaching. Loren remained resolute in his surveying of the valley below, but Dalton noticed that the men to his side were glancing amongst each other and muttering.

Eventually Virgil called those men into a huddle and murmured instructions, then hurried over the ridge, doubled over, to join Dalton and Loren.

'You sure we were being followed?' he asked, drawing Dalton back from the edge. 'Nobody else has seen these men.'

'I'm sure that at least two riders were behind us and making no attempt to get closer.'

Virgil nodded. 'And once we've found out what they want and seen them off, how far do we have to backtrack to get back on the right trail?'

'Several miles.'

'I'm guessing it's a few more than that. We've probably lost a whole day with this detour.'

'Better to lose a day than risk an attack from the Spitzer gang.'

Virgil didn't reply immediately, and when he did, his voice was low.

'You may be right, but that wasn't your decision. I guess you're used to making decisions for yourself, and when you're on your own like you were down by the creek, you make damn fine ones. But you wasn't on your own here and you got to accept that if you got a problem, you come to me.' Virgil slapped his own chest. 'I'm in charge here and I'll decide what to do.'

Dalton considered mentioning that Virgil wasn't strictly in charge, but as his own position was precarious, he shrugged.

'You'll get no argument there, but what would you have done?'

'I'd have stayed on the right route and not lost us a whole day.' Virgil raised himself to look down the river, then sighed. 'But now that we have lost that time, I choose to stay here and wait them out. But that was my decision, not yours. Understand?'

Dalton raised his hands, smiling. 'You won't get any more misunderstandings from me. The moment I have a problem, I'll come to you.'

Virgil patted Dalton's back, then ran, doubled over, back to the tree-line.

Dalton watched him leave, then settled down, but he saw that Loren continued to look at Virgil.

'I got me a pebble in my boot,' he said, 'you reckon I should ask him what to do about it?'

'Might be wise,' Dalton said, enjoying hearing Loren support him for the first time. 'You don't want him to think you're threatening his authority.'

Loren snorted. 'Authority is earned and he ain't earning mine.'

'You not approve of his tactics?'

'Of course I don't. You don't sit around waiting for an attack. You make sure that an attack doesn't happen in the first place.'

Dalton was considering how he could ask what Loren's tactics would be without showing that he didn't have any better plans of his own, when he saw movement down the valley. He pointed.

Loren rose slightly to look down the valley. A half-mile down the slope two men were riding through the trees. They were taking a route that kept them hidden from casual sight, but which would still let them cover distance at a reasonable rate.

Dalton slipped back from the edge of the slope and with a few hand-gestures conveyed what was happening to the others.

Virgil nodded, then beckoned for all the men to join him.

When everyone had grouped together, he whispered quick instructions to two of his men to take up positions fifty yards down the slope. There, they would hide and wait until the riders had passed them.

Then, he ordered, they would surround these men and subdue them with warning gunfire. They would use deadly fire only if forced to.

His men hurried off to carry out their instructions as Virgil and Jacob spread out along the ridge, leaving Loren and Dalton in the middle and directly ahead of the route the riders would take.

Dalton noted Loren's firm jaw and the set of his thin lips.

'Orders ain't getting much better, are they?'

'Nope. And I ain't getting myself killed for that man.' Loren shuffled closer. 'What you expect these men to do?'

'It depends on whether they know the area. If they don't, they're just following us. If they do, they won't take kindly to us surrounding them.'

Loren nodded, his quick smile signifying that Dalton had summed up his own misgivings; then, along with Dalton, he lowered his head and kept quiet.

Down the slope the two riders closed. Dalton slowly discerned their faces. He had caught only fleeting glimpses of the bandits before, but these men had broadly the same build and, on balance, he reckoned it was highly likely that they were the same men.

He glanced at Loren, the slight narrowing

of his eyes conveying his concern. In response Loren shuffled down, his gun aimed firmly down the slope.

At a steady pace the two riders passed the point where Virgil's men had slipped into hiding, then headed for the brow of the ridge.

Dalton looked past them and saw the two defenders raise themselves from hiding, but even before they'd stood up one of the riders swirled round in the saddle. The defenders had been right behind him and Dalton could see no way that he should have seen or heard them, but as the bandit threw a hand towards his rifle, Virgil jumped up.

'Fire!' he shouted.

The men down the slope and at the top of the ridge fired a barrage of warning shots, the lead tearing into tree-trunks a few feet above the bandits' heads.

'What you–' one bandit shouted, but Virgil cut him off with a stentorian command.

'Put those hands were I can see them or die where you stand!'

The riders glanced at each other and an unspoken message passed between them. Then they yanked their reins to the side and hurried through the trees, disappearing from view in a matter of seconds.

Several wild shots hurtled back through the trees from them and Virgil's men loosed off several rounds in return, but with nothing to aim at but trees, Virgil quickly shouted out an order to desist. Then he directed Jacob to head back to the wagons and find out what had happened to everyone.

As Loren slapped the earth before him in irritation at their getting away, Dalton leaned to him.

'At least Virgil proved they ain't friendly,' he said.

Loren snorted a hollow laugh. 'At least that.'

When the men from further down the slope arrived, Virgil directed everyone to take up defensive positions in an arc which would stand between the wagon train and the forest. Already, Jacob had reached the wagons and men were peeling out to take up positions before the wagons.

Virgil and the other two men hurried off to join them, and Dalton moved to follow, but Loren slapped a hand on his arm, halting him.

'I've had enough of following Virgil's orders,' he said, 'and I guess you have too. I ain't sitting out in the open for the rest of the day waiting for those bandits to attack.

Are you with me, John Stanton?'

'Sure am, Loren Steele.'

'Then come on. Let's find out what they want the proper way.'

Loren winked and without further discussion they hurried down the slope, then swung round to follow the men. Even with the undergrowth being dense and the trees being tightly packed, on foot they made good speed and, at first, the trail the men had made as they brushed through the undergrowth was easy to follow.

After following for around 200 yards they found the bandits' abandoned steeds. But Loren declared that they'd then head off on a route that would run parallel to the river and which would bring them out somewhere near and above the wagons – the ideal place to launch an attack.

Fuelled on by a need to head them off, they sped off, running with large strides and vaulting fallen trees. They made too much noise for a stealthy approach but they didn't dare risk not reaching the bandits before they attacked the wagons.

Their wild chase soon caused them to lose all signs of the trail they'd been following. Dalton slowed to look around for further signs of the men's passage, but that let

Loren take the lead.

Dalton could see no hints in the dense forest of the right direction to take and the tightly packed trees limited his vision to a dozen yards or so. If he had been on his own, he had no doubt he'd have become lost within minutes.

But Loren knew exactly where to go and he weaved around trees and ducked under branches with Dalton trailing in his wake. Then he took a rapid turn and set off in a different direction, the move so sudden that Dalton kept running for several strides, then had to slide to a halt and resume chasing after him.

Their general route was always uphill and whether Loren could see or hear something Dalton couldn't, or was just guessing, Dalton didn't know. But one thing was certain, Loren knew where he was going and Dalton could only hurtle after him as if he were chasing Loren and not the two bandits.

A few paces behind Loren, Dalton continually peered ahead, looking out for their quarry and he noticed a lightening ahead first, but when he found the source of the lightness, it was with a shock. One moment, they were brushing through undergrowth. The next, they emerged on to bare land.

Loren slid to a halt, Dalton ploughing into his back and pushing him forward a pace, but then they both danced back, wheeling their arms in sudden panic.

They were high, the ground was stony, and they were just a few feet away from the edge of a sheer drop of around a hundred feet. Around them, fallen trees awaited wind or gravity to drag them to the bottom. Below were the wagons, a line of men kneeling and looking away from them and towards the direction from which they expected an attack. And none of them was expecting that attack to come from higher up the sheer rock face.

Dalton bent at the waist and opened his mouth to shout a warning to them, but then a gunshot sounded, the lead winging a few inches past his hat. Dalton just had enough time to see the people below swing round to look up, but then he leapt to the ground to lie behind a fallen trunk, searching for the direction of the shooter.

The few feet of rock snaked around the top of the ridge on either side of him with the trees a solid curtain on one side and the drop on the other, but Dalton couldn't see the men. He glanced at Loren lying beside him and he returned a shake of the head.

On their bellies, they shuffled back into the trees, only one more shot scything past them. Then he and Loren crouched down between two fallen trees.

'At least everyone knows where they are,' Loren said.

'Yeah, but we could do with knowing exactly where they are or we won't be able to do nothing.'

Loren considered. 'They won't sit around waiting for us to find them. They'll come for us, and we have to be somewhere unexpected.'

'And where...?'

Dalton didn't complete his question as Loren backed up his theory with a staggering level of confidence. He stood and backed out of the trees to stand in full view on the stony stretch of land. Then he hurried along the edge of the drop.

Dalton wavered, fearing Loren would pay for his theory with lead, but no gunfire came and Dalton accepted that somehow Loren had read the bandits' tactics with surprising accuracy. He followed him, slipping along the edge of the sheer drop and jumping over fallen trees until he reached Loren.

His colleague had stopped in the gap between three fallen trees. Loren knelt down nearer the tree-line and Dalton lay down by the edge.

He glanced over the side, noticing that below, the defenders were looking up and had trained guns on this ledge. And the slope here was less steep than elsewhere. It was still almost precipitous, but most of the slope was climbable, and several men were venturing upwards in a quest to help them.

Dalton gestured down with a calming hand signal, signifying that they had some control over the situation, but Loren slapped a hand on his arm, beckoning him to lie flat.

Dalton did as ordered and looked out through the gap between two of the trees.

Further along the ledge a man was venturing out at the precise place where they had been hiding a few moments ago and was looking around.

Loren and Dalton exchanged a glance and swung their guns on to the log before them, waiting until he presented a clear target. The man loitered on the edge of the trees, standing with his back to a tree and glancing around. But then he slipped around that tree to look in their direction and Loren and Dalton ensured he paid for his mistake.

Together, they loosed off a volley of shots. Several peeled bark away, but at least two slammed into the man's chest rocking him back on his heels and knocking him into the tree. He took a stumbling pace, keeled over to his knees, then fell, clutching his chest, over the side of the ledge and disappeared from view.

Dalton heard several cries of alarm from below as the people at the bottom saw the man fall. He heard a thud as the man hit the ground, but then a gunshot pealed out. Both Loren and Dalton swirled round, their guns swinging to the side as they searched for the man who had fired.

And that man emerged from the trees, just ten feet in front of them, and fired down at them. The shot scythed into rock and hurtled away as Dalton and Loren scrambled for better cover behind the logs.

Flat on their bellies and with their senses alert for any movement, they edged out to look for the man, but he had returned to cover. Long seconds passed with Dalton darting his glance back and forth, but no further gunfire came.

Loren and Dalton exchanged silent glances, signifying and confirming with their eyes where they reckoned the man was. And that was standing behind one of the trees in front of them. The trees were just far enough apart for a man to slip through as long as he kept his elbows in, and that meant he could move to new cover in a fraction of a second.

Except they didn't know which tree he was hiding behind and he knew exactly where they were. Dalton aimed his gun at chest-height at the nearest tree while Loren aimed at the one to the side and they waited for the man to show himself.

Dalton, with his heightened senses, trusted himself to fire on pure instinct the moment the man ventured out, but with no hint as to which tree he was hiding behind, the waiting preyed on his nerves. He started to wonder whether the man could have sought different cover while they had been diving for their lives.

He glanced at Loren, who darted a glance back, his raised eyebrows confirming that he also thought this man wouldn't have the patience to wait this long.

And that did it for Dalton. Loren's hunches had been right so far and he decided to back this one. He stood slowly. Loren saw his intent and nodded with a short gesture, then paced over the logs to stand outside them. Then he took a long pace to the side, walking sideways, aiming to get a different angle on the trees and bring the man into view.

He took another pace, his view of the trees shifting and letting him see behind the trunks, but the man was still not visible. He took another pace. Still he didn't appear and, from this angle, Dalton reckoned he ought to be able to see him.

Dalton winced. The man couldn't be where he expected him to be. He glanced at Loren, but he was swinging his gun round to aim at Dalton's head.

For one shocked moment, Dalton thought his worst fears were justified, that Loren had really known his true identity and was about to kill him. But Loren fired, the slug hurtling over Dalton's shoulder, a cry emerging from behind him.

Dalton turned on his heel, seeing the blur of a man leaping at him before he piled into his side. Dalton just had time to note that he must have been lying behind one of the fallen logs. Then they wheeled backwards.

On the very edge of the slope Dalton dug his heels in and slid to a halt. He and the man stared into each other's eyes, the man's eyes glazing from Loren's possibly terminal gunshot.

Then Dalton saw a flash of metal as the man swung his gun up to aim at his chest. But his injury had slowed him, giving Dalton time to react more quickly. He swung his gun round and tore a shot low into his assailant's stomach at point-blank range.

The man folded and swayed backwards, but then a shot from behind hammered into him and he rocked forward to fall against Dalton, pushing him back.

Dalton scrambled for purchase, but he was on the edge of the slope. Pebbles and stones slipped away from his questing feet. Loren shouted something to him as the man, with his last dying action, hurled his arms around Dalton's chest and collapsed.

Dalton's trailing heel landed on air and he tumbled backwards, the man's dead weight dragging him down. Dalton hurled his arms wide, reaching for something to grab, but he was already too far from the edge and, as he rolled round to face downwards, below was the terrible long drop to the wagons.

CHAPTER 6

Dalton blinked groggily as his surroundings swayed and swirled around him, then focused.

He was lying under cover in a wagon, and by the look of the stored furniture, it was Henry's. A cold towel lay on his bare chest. He moved to rise but a wave of nausea hit him and forced him to flop back onto his back.

'Don't move,' a voice said beside him. 'You got hurt.'

Dalton needed a moment before he worked out that Henry Boone had spoken. He let his head roll to the side to look at him.

'What happened?'

'Didn't see it myself but from the way everyone tells it, you and Loren sneaked up on the Spitzer gang. But one of them took you down with him and you both came hurtling down to us, going head over heels. You sure had plenty of luck to avoid breaking every bone in your body.'

'Yeah, I sure had plenty of luck.'

'And you had plenty more in ending up in here. Eliza is a fine carer.' Henry winked. 'But you could have found an easier way to win her heart.'

'What you mean?'

'I mean getting yourself all beat up just so she can look after you. It's sneaky, but it's sure to work.'

Dalton joined Henry in chuckling then raised the towel to look at the purple bruises beneath. He winced and dropped it back on his chest, but the towel slid off his chest and to the floor.

Dalton muttered to himself then rooted round for it, but only succeeded in knocking over Henry's chest and tumbling the town sign in the folded blanket to the floor. Dalton flopped back on his bedding and prepared himself for rescuing the mess, but Eliza poked her head into the wagon, then climbed inside.

She stood hunched with her hands on her hips, surveying the damage.

'I thought you'd be one of those fools who wouldn't lie down and rest.' She picked up the sign and righted the chest. 'But I didn't think you'd wreck the wagon while you were busy being stupid.'

She continued to complain but Dalton lay back, enjoying her chiding of him. When she'd fussed around him, he pointed out of the back of the wagon.

'Have we moved on?'

'No. We're staying here for the night. So you can rest and concentrate on getting well. I do not want to waste any more time than I have to looking after the likes of you.'

'You don't have to do this at all.'

She pointed a firm finger at him. 'Do not tempt me.'

Dalton glanced at Henry, who narrowed his eyes, suggesting he should change the subject. So, he nodded down at his chest.

'How bad is it?'

'You'll be fine. You didn't break any bones.' She considered his chest. 'But you got some bad bruising, and not all of it from the fall.'

Dalton glanced down, seeing that the faded yellow bruises from Vaughn's beatings still marred his exposed skin.

'I guess I've seen some trouble before.'

'How did you hurt your wrists?'

Dalton fingered the band of bruises around his left wrist, the remnants of two weeks spent in cuffs, then looked up, but saw only openness in her gaze and nothing other than a desire to make conversation.

'Can't remember,' Dalton said, avoiding creating a complex lie that might cause him problems later.

'Then don't think too much. You had a nasty bang on the head.'

'Yeah, but I need to show everyone where to go.'

Dalton rubbed his brow as he searched for the best way to word an excuse that the bang on his head had affected his memory, but Eliza shook her head.

'You don't need to worry about directing us for a while. Sheriff Melrose from Applegate arrived. He was after the Spitzer gang, but he's staying with us to show us where to go.' She turned to leave the wagon. 'And when you're fit enough to talk, he wants to speak to you.'

Dalton listened to the early morning birdsong. Last night he had slept fitfully, partly because he couldn't find a way to lie comfortably, and partly because of his concern about an impending encounter with Sheriff Melrose.

He couldn't believe that the lawman wouldn't know the real John Stanton, so his new identity was sure to come to an inglorious end within seconds of meeting him.

He had helped this group and saved lives. So, they would speak up for him, but he couldn't think of a story that would explain his actions before joining the wagons that wouldn't draw attention to the dead bodies back beside the river. Melrose had probably never heard of Deputy Vaughn and Dalton, but no matter what story he accepted, it would look bad for him.

Henry was still sleeping beside him as Dalton decided he had to get away from the wagon train. When he'd been Vaughn's prisoner he'd vowed that he'd sooner die than be anyone's prisoner again and even if he had little chance of evading the lawman in his injured state, he had to try.

He rolled from his bedding and knelt, flexing his back. Muscles complained, confirming that riding would be uncomfortable, but he gritted his teeth and slipped into his shirt, then jacket. The weight on his skin chafed his bruises and scrapes, but he reckoned he'd have to get used to it.

After nodding a farewell to the sleeping Henry, he slipped out of the wagon and glanced around. Nobody had risen from their slumbers yet; all the wagons were closed and quiet. Loren slept outside but was out of view.

Over at the edge of the ridge two men sat huddled, staring down the river, the only approach to this location. He watched them, reckoning that keeping watch at this time was a thankless task and, from the men's unmoving postures, they were probably dozing in a semi-conscious state.

He'd alert them when he headed down-river, but he could excuse his actions by explaining that he was scouting around. When he failed to return, they would raise the alarm, but that would give him several hours in which to find a place to hole up.

He didn't want to risk spending time searching for food, reckoning that a gun and a horse was pretty much all he needed. So he headed for his horse, shuffling past the line of wagons with short paces, but when he passed the last wagon, he flinched. A man was sitting back against the sheer rock face and watching him, a blanket drawn up to his chin.

The man stood, the blanket fell away, and Dalton couldn't help but notice the star on his chest.

'You shouldn't push yourself too much,' Sheriff Melrose said. 'You took a bad fall.'

'I got a job to do,' Dalton said, deciding that making a run for his horse was impossible, but detecting no suspicion in Melrose's tone.

'I can see that. I'd heard about you, John, but I always took you to be an older man.'

Dalton limited himself to a smile, fighting to avoid revealing the wave of relief that overcame him.

'And I'd heard about you. I always took you for a younger man.'

Melrose provided a relaxed laugh and went to the back of the last wagon. He took a ladle from beside the water barrel, filled it and held it out to Dalton, who took advantage of Melrose's assumption that he had been looking for sustenance and drained the ladle.

'I won't keep you outside for long,' Melrose said. 'But I just need to hear what happened from your viewpoint.'

'No problem.'

While dunking the ladle, he covered the details in a matter-of-fact manner. Melrose nodded frequently. When Dalton had finished he wandered around in a small circle, rubbing his chin and considering.

'But why bring the wagons here? I'd figure you'd head through Green Pass. That's a far easier route than any other.'

'And we will go that way now. When I saw

we were being followed, I came here to make a stand. If I had been on my own, I'd have doubled back and taken care of the problem, but...' Dalton shrugged, then took another gulp of water and returned the ladle to the barrel. 'Perhaps I did wrong, but it's hard to know what's right when you're protecting the lives of this many people.'

'I understand the problem. And I guess it's what I might have done in the same situation.' Melrose turned to his blanket, but then glanced back at him. 'You need to rest, but can I ask you one more thing?'

'Go on,' Dalton said. He steeled himself for what might prove to be a tricky question as Meirose drew him away from the last wagon.

'I've never heard of Loren Steele, so I didn't ask him this – what impression have you formed of these people?'

'They're decent, hard-working families looking to start a new life.'

Melrose nodded, his downcast eyes suggesting he was debating whether to ask another question.

'Any of them strike you as being less decent than the others?'

'What you getting at?'

Melrose sighed. 'I intend to stay with you

a while longer, but I'd prefer it if you kept this to yourself. The men who attacked you *were* the Spitzer gang, four men led by two gunslinger brothers, Fritz and Herman.'

'Only two men attacked us.'

'And that means the other two are still out there – and they're the brothers, the worst of the bunch.'

Dalton rubbed his ribs. 'Don't worry. As soon as I'm fit enough, I'll help you defend everyone against them.'

'I know you will, but I didn't join you because I was after them. Someone beat Marcus Wilcox, a snake-oil seller from Applegate, to death in a frenzied attack. Certain facts suggest that someone on this wagon train killed him.'

Dalton looked away as he considered, then shook his head.

'These people are decent men and women. Are you sure the Spitzer gang didn't kill him?'

'I thought it was them at first. Marcus had a thousand dollars on him and whoever killed him stole it. Everything pointed to the Spitzer gang, except they had a real alibi, for once. But this wagon train left town on the day of the murder, and I reckon the Spitzer gang followed you because they'd worked out someone here stole that thousand dollars.'

'I ain't questioning your actions, but that don't sound like much of a reason to follow us for a week.'

'Like I said – certain other facts point to the culprit being with this wagon train.'

'And you won't tell me what those facts are.' Dalton considered Melrose's impassive face, then shrugged. 'You could search the wagons for the money, I guess.'

'And I might find it, but that won't prove nothing. When people like me ask difficult questions, groups like this have a habit of providing excuses for each other. And in my experience, it's the newcomers like you and Loren who often take the blame.'

Dalton provided a rueful smile. 'Yeah, I know that.'

Dalton looked away towards the gorge as he considered his dealings with these people. He'd been more worried about anyone discovering his real identity than looking out for anyone else acting suspiciously. But nobody had given him cause for concern – except one – although his dispute with Jacob had been on a personal level. Then Dalton remembered something Jacob had said.

'You've just thought of somebody,' Melrose said, interrupting Dalton's thoughts. 'Don't keep your suspicions to yourself. I'll do the thinking while you get these people over the mountains.'

'Then I'd suggest Jacob Wade. He said something to me...' Dalton sighed, his sudden suspicion not sounding quite so damning now that he was voicing it. 'It was probably nothing, but he told me that soon he'd impress someone. Perhaps that means he's stolen a thousand dollars.'

'It could. Anything more?'

'No, I don't...' Dalton glanced away, another thought coming to him now that he was considering the Wade family's actions in a suspicious light. 'His father has acted oddly, too. I'm guessing it took some effort to catch up with us.'

'It did.'

'That's because Virgil has pushed us to cover as many miles as we can each day.'

Melrose nodded. 'And that means he's either eager to get to where he's going, or eager to get away from where he's been.'

'Yeah.' Dalton shrugged. 'But when you think like that, everybody's actions could be suspicious, even mine.'

Melrose laughed. 'And with your reputation, you're the only person here I do trust. Obliged for the information.'

Dalton smiled and moved to turn away, then turned back.

'One other thing, if you wouldn't mind.' Dalton rubbed his chest and winced. 'But I could do with some rest. Could you direct them for a while?'

'No problem. I assume you were heading up Green Pass, around the bluff, keeping below the ridge and then over Blind Man's Canyon.'

'It's the best way to go,' Dalton said, keeping his expression blank.

'Then I'll take them as far as the canyon.' Melrose smiled. 'And you'll be pleased to hear I'm planning to see your old friends Eddy and Tucker Malone there.'

Dalton raised his eyebrows and put on a smile.

'That's good news. What you seeing them about?'

'They left a message that they knew something about Marcus Wilcox's murder, but when I got back to Applegate, they'd headed off to disappear down another glory-hole in the canyon. You know what they're like.' Melrose leaned forward and lowered his voice. 'We'll have to hope that your friends will be able to tell me something I can use when we get there.'

As the wagons headed up the pass that John Stanton would have known about, Dalton devoted his resting time to thinking. Based on Melrose's estimate of their likely speed, he had four days to get well enough to leave the wagon train, or find a way to avoid meeting Tucker and Eddy Malone.

However much he tried, Dalton couldn't think of a plausible excuse to be away during that meeting, but as regards returning to health, he improved faster than he expected.

Eliza was a bountiful source of energy. She maintained a matter-of-fact demeanour, neither engaging in casual conversation nor spending a moment longer with him than she needed to. But Dalton got the impression from her terse comments and gentle chiding that she enjoyed seeing one of her patients improve and that their enforced intimacy of a sort was helping to patch over their previous misunderstanding.

With her devoting as much time to caring for him as she did to her father, after just two days Dalton felt that he was fit enough to leave the wagon and pace around.

So when they settled down that night he rolled from his bedding and flexed his back before he stood. His back was still sore and complained with every movement, but at least he could move around freely and he reckoned he'd be able to ride in the next day or so.

Outside, he heard voices, which he assumed were Eliza and Newell, but when he emerged from the wagon he found it was Eliza and Jacob. Their tones implied a casual conversation and Jacob's posture suggested he had been passing and had just stopped, but they both silenced and turned to him. Eliza smiled. Jacob did not.

'Good to see you're mending,' Jacob said with nothing in his blank tone suggesting he was being honest.

'Thanks to Eliza,' Dalton said. He nodded to her, then looked around. Loren was leaning back against the next wagon, looking straight ahead. He raised his voice. 'And I'd have probably died without Loren's help.'

Jacob snorted, his sneer confirming that he wasn't exactly pleased with the result of Loren's bravery. But Dalton had no interest in his petulance and continued to look at Loren, noting that although most of the people had looked in on him while he'd been resting, Jacob and Loren were the only people who hadn't. Jacob's failure to see

114

him he could understand, but after facing danger together, he thought Loren and he should have reached an understanding.

While Loren continued to avoid looking at him, Eliza fussed around him, checking his bandages and admonishing him for leaving the wagon without her permission.

Jacob watched Eliza's attention leave him with his upper lip curled back in a sneer. In response, Dalton wriggled and murmured a few comments to prolong the time she'd spend with him.

When she'd finished, Eliza declared that he was well enough to go on a short walk. She also stated that she needed water for Henry. She looked at a bucket standing beside Dalton. Then she looked at each man in turn, but neither man moved. With a snort she moved to grab the bucket to fetch the water herself. But that encouraged Jacob to hurry past her and lunge for the bucket.

Dalton had caught Eliza's hint, but he didn't want to risk carrying anything heavy yet. Then, seeing Jacob moving, he also lunged. The sudden movement sent a bolt of pain ripping through his back but he still clamped a hand on the bucket first. He stood, stooped, wondering whether he could straighten his back. Taking advantage of the delay, Jacob also grabbed the handle and the two men tugged.

'Stop it, you two,' Eliza said. 'I'll get the water myself.'

Dalton raised his eyes to look at Jacob and the two men locked gazes. Dalton was the first to raise his hand.

Jacob grinned, but then his eyes glazed, perhaps as he realized that going on an errand would find favour with Eliza but give Dalton time to be alone with her. He snapped his hand up and straightened.

With plenty of low muttering about all men being idiots, Eliza slipped between them and took the bucket herself, then headed away.

'So,' Jacob said, 'it seems neither of us is fetching the water.'

Dalton straightened slowly. 'Maybe next time we'll get to decide once and for all who'll fetch things for her.'

'Maybe we will, but I know who that person will be. And I reckon you do too.'

'Yeah.' Dalton turned to climb back into the wagon, finding that the thought of going for a short walk had now turned sour. 'I do.'

Jacob slammed a hand on Dalton's shoulder and swung him round. In his weakened state, the action bent Dalton double.

'And we both know we got a fight coming

to us, John.' Jacob flexed his fist. 'Now might be the right time for it.'

Dalton stayed bent double while he confirmed that Jacob's sudden action hadn't hurt him, then looked up. Jacob had raised his fists and his blazing eyes said he wasn't in the mood for placating words. Before he'd sustained his injuries, Dalton would have retaliated but in his present state, he wouldn't be able to provide a good account of himself, and Jacob knew it.

'Soon, Jacob, soon, but not today.'

'I knew you were a yellow-belly.' Jacob hurled back his fist ready to pummel Dalton, who flinched away, a hand rising to ward off a blow, but it never came.

Loren had sneaked up on Jacob. He grabbed his hand as he swung it back. He held the fist in his firm grip behind Jacob's back.

Jacob struggled, but Loren held him close to his chest, thrust his arm up in a half-Nelson, and whispered something in his ear that made Jacob gulp. Then he patted him on the head as if he was granting favour to a child, and pushed him away.

Jacob stumbled, then swirled round to glare at Loren and Dalton in turn.

'You'll pay for that now, both of you.' Then

he stormed round and made off before either man could reply, leaving Dalton and Loren alone.

'Seems I'm obliged to you for saving me again,' Dalton said.

'No problem, John Stanton, no problem at all.'

Dalton continued towards the wagon, but a twinge rippled across his back and eroded his fragile good mood. He turned back.

'I thought you'd agreed to call me John,' he snapped. 'Being as we've fought side by side, I'd be obliged if you'd do that.'

Loren gave a slow nod. 'I'll do that, John....'

Loren turned and headed away, but he passed the wagon that he'd previously been standing beside and continued walking. He acknowledged everyone he passed with a nod until he slipped out between two wagons. There, Sheriff Melrose was sitting and he passed by him, then continued for twenty paces before stopping to look up at the route ahead.

Dalton raised his gaze to look in the same direction. They had now achieved some height; behind them the plains stretched away. They were heading towards a flat ridge of land between two peaks, beyond which

Dalton presumed they would start the downward trek. The ridge was close and Dalton was sure the estimates of their progress were right and that he had not much more than a day to find a good excuse to leave the wagon train.

He was about to climb into the wagon, but the odd nature of his confrontations since he'd come outside tapped at his thoughts. He could understand why Jacob didn't like him, but Loren hadn't appeared friendly either. Loren had claimed that he was interested in Eliza, but he had *done* nothing to suggest that that was the case and unless Loren was being devious in his courting, Dalton didn't believe that excuse.

As he had more worrying matters to deal with, he could leave the issue unresolved but, for a reason he couldn't fathom, he didn't like the idea that a man who was as resourceful as Loren didn't like him. So, instead of climbing into the wagon he followed him, acknowledging the people he passed with nods and the occasional short chat about his improving condition.

Sheriff Melrose smiled at him as he passed and he continued until he joined Loren, who despite the fifteen minutes it'd taken Dalton to reach him, was still staring up at the route ahead.

They stood silently for a minute. Loren was the first to speak.

'Would you have chosen this route, John?' he asked, looking at the low ridge between the peaks.

'I would.'

'And how many times have you headed over Blind Man's Canyon and the ridge beyond, John?'

Dalton looked over Loren's shoulder, seeing that Sheriff Melrose was out of hearing-range, but near enough to detect any friction between them. He guessed that Loren had chosen this spot for precisely that reason.

'Time for some straight talking, Loren,' he said. 'We fought together against the Spitzer gang, but you never came to see me afterwards.'

'Didn't want to bother a man who was getting himself all fixed up.'

'Then I'm obliged for your consideration.' Dalton took a deep breath. 'But you claimed you had an interest in Eliza, yet you don't even talk to her.'

'Not all of us care to make fools of ourselves squabbling with kids over buckets of water.'

Dalton glanced away, wondering whether

to push this matter, but he was sure Loren was hiding something and this was an ideal time to find out what it was.

'Loren, just tell it to me straight. Why don't you like me?'

Loren turned from his consideration of the landscape to look at Dalton.

'Why think that? I saved your life, didn't I?'

'You did, but I don't reckon that means what it ought to mean.'

Loren rubbed his jaw, then swung away to look around.

'So, you really want to hear it, do you, with Sheriff Melrose just a few paces away?'

'He's far enough away. He can't hear us, as you intended when you stood here. So, no more questions, no more insinuations, no more snide comments, no more avoiding my questions. If you got something to say, just say it.'

'All right.' Loren looked deep into Dalton's eyes, his craggy features hardening to solid iron. 'Who are you and what have you done with John Stanton?'

CHAPTER 7

Ever since Loren had joined the wagon train, Dalton had half-expected that he would unmask him, but he still couldn't stop himself gulping. But Loren hadn't mentioned his suspicion to anyone else and there had to be a reason for that, so he decided to answer honestly.

He placed a hand on Loren's shoulder and led him away from the wagons, smiling. Loren returned the smile in case anyone was looking at them. A hundred yards from the wagons, Dalton stopped and stood square on to Loren.

'My name is of no importance,' he said, 'and I've done nothing to John Stanton.'

'Then where is he?'

'I won't lie. I'm sorry, but he's buried back beside the river.'

Loren's right eye flickered with a momentary twinge, this being his only reaction.

'You kill him?'

'Nope. He saved my life.'

'And you're repaying his memory by

pretending to be him.' Loren snorted. 'If you knew the man he was, you'd know how pathetic that is.'

'I only knew him for a few minutes, but I know you're right.'

'And that's the first thing you've said I do believe, Dalton.'

Dalton sighed. 'So, you already knew who I was.'

'Yeah. I asked around. It didn't take long before I heard the story of the dead outlaw and the lawman.'

'Then why avoid confronting me with your suspicions?'

'I just wanted to know how long it'd take you to tell the truth.'

'And with a lawman so close, you must know how hard it was for me to tell you that. And that must prove things ain't what they seem.'

With this admission, Loren looked aloft and his shoulders relaxed.

'There's always a chance of that.' He sighed, his glazed eyes suggesting he was recalling old and fond memories. 'I knew John some years back. When I heard he was leading these people, I reckoned I'd ride along with him awhile and swap some old tales. Except he's dead and you're pretending to be him. You must see why I got suspicious.'

'I do, but why didn't you tell Melrose?'

'John would have known. Out here, you're on your own and you make your own justice. So, I'll tell you this – I ain't interested in hearing no lies, but I will work out what happened to John and, if necessary, I'll deliver my own justice in my own way.' Loren slapped his holster and narrowed his eyes. 'Don't bother watching your back, Dalton, because I'm watching it for you.'

Loren turned away, but Dalton clamped a hand on his shoulder and halted him.

'And I ain't interested in hearing no lies either. You didn't tell Melrose about your suspicions, not because you want to deal with me, but because you don't want Melrose to learn of my suspicions about you.'

Loren sneered. 'You got nothing.'

'The Spitzer gang were following us and you knew what they'd do, where they'd go, and how to stop them. And that means you've met them before, except you didn't mention that.'

'And why does that matter?'

'It matters because it means you didn't join us to meet an old friend, but for some other reason, and I reckon it had something to do with why Sheriff Melrose is here. So,

125

Loren, don't watch your back because I'm watching it for you.'

Dalton raised his hand and let Loren pace away, shaking his head. He watched him leave, then turned to look at the ridge.

For the day after Dalton's encounter with Loren, the wagon train snaked up several passes at a steady pace. Dalton felt stronger than he had the previous day, but not strong enough to ride and he sat up in the wagon, pondering his complicated situation.

Sheriff Melrose did call in on him to confirm that he was taking the best route and Dalton could only nod while silently noting that if he had still been directing everyone, he would have never found this route.

That night they negotiated the topmost pass. The ridge for which they had been heading was now just a few miles ahead, its bare and rocky length a short saddle between two snow-flecked peaks. After several days of travelling with high and steep sides protecting them from the prevailing winds, a harsh and grit-filled wind whipped around them. In a matter of minutes the temperature dropped, forcing everyone to search for extra clothing.

Tomorrow they would reach Blind Man's

Canyon, and if Dalton couldn't find a reason to be elsewhere for a while, he didn't relish the thought of leaving and making his own way over such inhospitable terrain.

In the wagon, Henry Boone huddled beneath several blankets, his previous appreciation of the falling temperature having now departed.

'Tell me about Sweet Valley,' Henry said, his teeth chattering, 'and warm me up.'

Dalton winced as he lay on his back in the wagon. For most of the last few days Henry had been silent, but Dalton had been dreading that their close proximity would lead to inevitable questions he couldn't answer.

'I could,' Dalton said, 'but you have the sign. You must have a vision of what you want.'

'It has to be a valley.' Henry chuckled. 'And it has to be mighty fine.'

'And you can put your mind at rest. It will be.' Dalton remembered something the real John Stanton had said. 'Beyond the mountains, there's land aplenty and valleys galore for anyone to start a new life.'

Henry smiled and raised himself. 'And when will we get there?'

'Not long now.' Dalton flashed a smile, but Henry's brow furrowed with the hint of another impending question and Dalton asked one of his own to deflect him. 'Why do your family and the Wades hate each other?'

Henry sighed and flopped back on his bedding.

'That is a long and painful story.'

'Then just tell me the basics.'

Henry didn't reply immediately. His breath wheezed, then he rolled his head to the side to look at Dalton.

'We moved on after the flood, but I first thought about a fresh start when both our wives died. They got a fever, throats all swelled up...' Henry raised a bony hand to swipe away a tear. 'Damn fever came from somewhere and at the time nobody cared about nothing but stopping it, but once it'd moved on to torture some other poor souls, we both got to thinking.'

Henry offered no more details, and Dalton spoke up.

'Virgil blamed your wife for giving the fever to his wife....'

'And I blamed his. But who's to know who's to blame? And as we never will, there's no way we'll ever talk again.'

'Have you tried to make peace with him?'

'He came to see me after we'd left Applegate. He'd bought a potion to make me feel better, but it didn't and I won't suffer his company again.'

'If he was prepared to try once, perhaps you should try again while you still can, for both your families' sakes.'

'Perhaps, but how can I forgive him for what his wife did to mine?'

Dalton could think of nothing to say in response. He slipped out of the wagon. He discovered that Loren was scouting around, then asked if there was anything he could do to help. Eliza allocated him the task of collecting wood from the sparse trees, and completing this simple activity increased his confidence in his returning strength.

At Melrose's insistence the group found extra logs to take with them, Melrose providing the explanation that 'Stanton' would have advised them to do the same.

As working in the thinner air had already tired him, Dalton returned to the wagon before anyone could ask him why that might be so, and spent the night huddled up with Henry.

The next day Dalton rose early. He felt fitter than he had done for a while and, despite his predicament, a curious optimism threatened to burst out, as if he was emerging from a cocoon or a prolonged hibernation.

Melrose insisted that they set off as early as possible and Dalton decided he needed to start riding again. As Loren was at the back of the wagons, he rode beside the lawman. His bruised chest complained at first, but the rolling motion also eased the remaining soreness in his muscles.

'Learnt anything to suggest that either Virgil or Jacob Wade is guilty of killing Wilcox?' he asked by way of starting a conversation.

'Nope,' Melrose said. 'I'm putting all my hopes into Eddy and Tucker knowing something. But I'll tell you one thing for sure, I'll watch their reactions when I do ask them.'

Dalton nodded. He had been planning to steer the conversation round to the possibility that he might scout around to look for the Spitzer brothers and so not visit Blind Man's Canyon, but an alternative idea came to him.

'Perhaps you can do that before you get there.'

Melrose turned in the saddle. 'What you suggesting?'

'You've told everyone you're accompanying us but you didn't reveal the real reason. If you were to announce you're investigating the murder of Marcus Wilcox and that Eddy and Tucker know something about it, the guilty person might panic himself into doing something rash.'

Melrose rocked his head from side to side, frowning.

'If I did that, he could go after the Malone brothers. But then again, I don't think the killer will kill again. I reckon Marcus's murder was an act of rage, not malice.' Melrose nodded, beaming. 'I'd heard good things about you, and I can see they're justified.'

'Shall I think of an excuse for us to stop so you can tell everyone?'

'You're right that the sooner I say something, the sooner the killer can start worrying, but I won't do it just yet.' Melrose pointed ahead, then winked. 'And we both know where the best place to do it is, don't we?'

Dalton kept his expression blank, but when Melrose continued to smile and gave no hint as to where that place would be, Dalton slowly matched his smile, as if he'd just seen his intent.

'Yeah,' he said. 'That sure is the best place.'

Dalton then rode in silence to avoid Melrose detecting his discomfort, but he didn't have to wait long before he discovered where Melrose would try to expose the killer.

Before noon they reached the end of the flat terrain before the ridge. Throughout the morning, Dalton had assumed that this flat stretch of land would continue until they reached the ridge between the two peaks. Then they would crest the ridge to see the land beyond. He had assumed that Blind Man's Canyon would emerge beside them at some stage, but he was wrong.

When they stopped, the last ridge was just a mile or so ahead and almost level with them.

But on first glance it might as well be 1,000 miles. Between that ridge and their current position there was nothing; the ground dropped away into a deep canyon, its base lost in the mists below, the deep gash stretching away on both sides seemingly for ever.

'Blind Man's Canyon,' Melrose announced to Virgil as he drew his wagon up at the edge of the sharp drop.

'What you bring us this way for?' Virgil murmured, blinking rapidly as he considered the huge drop into the canyon below.

'It's the best way.'

Virgil turned to Dalton for support, but Dalton just pointed across the canyon to the ridge opposite and smiled.

'Like he said, it's the best way. I never promised it'd be easy.'

Virgil jumped down from his wagon and shuffled to the edge, then stared ahead with his hands on his hips and his hat tipped back. But Melrose joined him and pointed to a rocky outcrop which burst out of the opposite side of the canyon.

'Don't worry. Many is the prospector who's visited that outcrop, searching for the gold they're all convinced is there.'

'So,' Virgil mused, looking down again, 'there *is* a way down.'

'For man and horses, there is. But for these wagons, we'll have to be more inventive.'

Virgil sighed. 'Then it's a good job we got plenty of rope.'

'And the logs,' Melrose said, patting his back.

By mid-afternoon, Virgil had organized the group into making a frame over which they'd lower the wagons down the side of the canyon. He looped rope over two crossed logs, with a third log anchoring the structure on the edge of the drop.

Further back from the edge, a four-horse team were tethered to a rope that wound around a series of stays hammered deep into the ground and around which the rope would slowly pass and control the wagons' descent.

Dalton had expected that Melrose would now mention the fact that when they reached the bottom he would discover who had killed Marcus Wilcox, but he said nothing.

As Dalton was apparently familiar with the terrain, Melrose suggested that he go down on foot first to secure the area below. Dalton didn't think that he could refuse but to Dalton's surprise, Loren, the only other person aside from Melrose who didn't have a wagon to protect, volunteered to go down with him.

Dalton led him to the edge of the canyon but then, without fuss, Loren took the lead. As soon as they'd disappeared over the side, he put them on a trail down the canyon side that was obvious as soon as Dalton was on it, but which wasn't visible from the top.

Dalton quickly saw that Melrose had chosen the ideal place to descend. The canyon side where they'd lower the wagons was sheer, but elsewhere a man on horseback could ride down. But he also saw that the distance they'd have to lower the wagons was considerable and was further than he thought they could cover safely.

He kept these thoughts to himself and rode behind Loren, concentrating on keeping his footing on the slippery ground. But later, he discovered that his initial fears weren't justified and that Melrose's plan was a wise one.

Approximately half-way down there was a wide ledge on to which he planned to lower the wagons. Then the settlers would have to stay there, perhaps for the night, and lower the wagons on the second stage of their journey tomorrow. That was safer than lowering them the whole distance in one go.

Loren and Dalton arrived on this ledge just as the first wagon appeared over the side of the canyon. Neither man had spoken so far and, as the wagon came down towards them, Dalton noted Loren's refusal to meet his eye. He presumed he wasn't interested in rekindling their previous argument.

From this lower position, Dalton had a clearer view of the terrain on the other side of the canyon. The route upwards was not as sheer, there being terraces that a wagon train in single file could snake up. As he waited for the first wagon to arrive, he considered various potential routes, and Loren, with no trace of sarcasm, drew his attention to one in particular.

Then they stood to the side of the ledge and guided in the approaching wagon, which landed safely. In short order they unhooked the wagon, signalled for the rope to return, and manoeuvred the wagon away.

Dalton couldn't help but notice that the first wagon had been Virgil's. Clearly, the group's assumed leader wouldn't let anyone do something he hadn't first proved to be safe and viable.

The first wagon had come down unaccompanied but, after it had proved that the technique was safe, several people joined the next wagon. Later, livestock came down until the ledge became crowded.

But the sun also set behind the peak to their side and it became clear that no matter how cramped they became, they would have to stay on this ledge for the night.

Henry's wagon came down last, with Eliza and Henry inside, but Newell stayed back to help Sheriff Melrose and Virgil dismantle, then bring down the frame they'd built.

As soon as they arrived everyone joined them in setting up the frame for the second half of the journey. Everyone worked late into the evening to ensure that they could start on the second leg as early as possible tomorrow.

By the time they'd completed the task night had fallen. Everyone all but collapsed into exhausted huddles. A frugal cold meal was passed around and, from the frequent glances that Melrose shot Dalton's way, Dalton reckoned he was now waiting for an opportunity to use Dalton's idea in the one place from where nobody could leave.

But Melrose bided his time until the conversation around the campfire drifted towards a suitable point.

'So,' Virgil asked at last, turning to Melrose, 'how much longer are you staying with us?'

'I'm afraid this is as far as I can go,' Melrose said, 'but I reckon Dalton is fit enough now to direct you the rest of the way.'

'And we're most obliged that you stepped in and helped.'

'No problem. But I still wanted to come here to see these two prospectors, Eddy and Tucker Malone.' Melrose leaned back, pausing as he awaited the inevitable question.

'What was so vital you had to come all this way just to see two men?'

Melrose rubbed his brow as if he was debating whether to answer, then shrugged.

'Someone killed a snake-oil seller, Marcus

Wilcox, then stole one thousand dollars off him.'

Several people drew in their breath during the quiet that descended on the group. Dalton lowered his hat and glanced around, searching for anyone who appeared more shocked than they ought to be.

He saw Newell flinch and look up, his gaze seeking out Eliza, who also reacted in the same way. And Virgil's wide eyes and hunched posture suggested either surprise or perhaps concern as he looked at the campfire in the centre of the ledge.

'That's a shock,' he said.

Melrose shrugged. 'It is, and apparently, the Malone brothers in the canyon know who killed him. Tomorrow, I'll know who I have to track down.'

'And why have you only seen fit to tell us this now?'

'There wasn't no need for me to say anything.'

'There was. I need to know everything that affects this wagon train.'

'This doesn't.' Melrose leaned forward as if he was about to say something more, and perhaps that he had reason to suspect that the murder of Marcus Wilcox *did* affect this wagon train. But he said nothing more, and neither did Virgil.

The group sat in silence awhile. When someone did break the silence it was to start an unnecessary debate about the arrangements for the second leg of their journey down the side of the canyon the following day.

Melrose didn't join in this conversation and wandered off to stand on the edge of the canyon, but as he left he glanced at Dalton, who waited for a few minutes then followed.

The two men stood on the edge of the canyon, looking out into the blackness beyond.

Melrose kept his voice low. 'The route up the side of the canyon is treacherous in the dark. The route down is treacherous in the dark. We're in the one place where nobody can come in or out and we have a killer amongst us who knows he'll be uncovered when we reach the bottom tomorrow. He'll have to do something and he'll have to do it soon.'

'Then I hope it's soon and not when we're lowering the wagons tomorrow. Desperate men can do desperate things.'

'They can, but I wouldn't have gone along with your plan if I thought he'd be that desperate. But still keep on the look-out for anyone acting oddly tonight and anyone eager to be the first to head down tomorrow.'

'Or the last.'

Melrose nodded. 'Either way, someone will leave this wagon train before we reach the bottom, and whoever that is, I'll follow him.'

Dalton sighed as he watched Melrose move to the position he'd marked out to sleep tonight.

'Yeah,' he said to himself, 'and I hope that person ain't me.'

To avoid raising concern, they'd agreed earlier that although they'd keep watch tonight, they wouldn't let anyone know what they were doing.

Dalton had chosen to stay awake first.

When everyone had settled down, he sat back against his saddle, flexing his back whenever he sat in one position for too long, and watched the moon sink towards the horizon. With their horses and livestock corralled at the back of the ledge and the wagons pressed together tightly, the ledge was still, most people choosing to sleep under cover.

Dalton noted that Loren slept apart from the group on the edge of the ledge and that Melrose slept on the other side of the wagons, close to the only route away from the ledge.

Melrose had said he slept light but had asked Dalton to relieve him when the moon set.

Dalton doubted that anyone who decided to run in the night would be able to leave quietly and he frequently let his eyes close as he dozed in fitful spells. But he came awake after one such spell to find that the moon was dipping close to the peak to his side.

He stood, stretched, then paced on a steady tour of the ledge, ensuring he didn't look as if he was deliberately visiting Melrose to check on him. He walked to the edge, looked out into the dark well of the canyon, then paced around the endmost wagon to the clear space beyond. Melrose was sleeping hunched under his blanket, either sleeping or looking as if he was sleeping.

Dalton had agreed with him not to make any unnecessary noises and he paced slowly around the perimeter, eventually passing by him, but he scraped his feet along the ground, raising enough noise to wake a light sleeper.

The lawman offered no sign that he'd heard Dalton and Dalton stopped in front of him. He looked down at him and smiled at his lack of attentiveness.

'Melrose,' he whispered, 'you awake?'

He waited, but received no answer – not even a low snore – and he dropped to his knees and shook his shoulder.

Melrose just rolled over, his stiff body thudding to the ground and, as the blanket rolled with him, Dalton saw the revealed earth.

Wetness, inky and thick in the moonlight had pooled where Melrose's body had lain: blood.

CHAPTER 8

Dalton confirmed that Sheriff Melrose was dead. His neck's gaping second mouth had given the lawman no chance of surviving, and although he couldn't find the knife, he looked for prints leading away from the body.

He saw nothing to confirm that the killer had either left the ledge or returned to the wagons to sleep.

'Is he dead?' Loren said from behind him.

Dalton swirled round, his hand reaching for his gun, but Loren was standing casually and peering at the lawman.

'I didn't hear you sneak up on me.'

Loren slipped past Dalton and knelt beside Meirose. He raised the blanket, winced, then draped it over his head.

'And from the looks of this, that was Melrose's downfall. This is the work of someone without a conscience and no desire to face a man head on.' Loren rose. 'You want to tell me who you suspect?'

'Melrose didn't bring you into his confidence for a reason.'

'Then don't make the same mistake.' Loren spread his hands. 'I don't trust you and you don't trust me, but if you reckon I know more than I'm prepared to reveal, telling me what you know won't add to my knowledge.'

Dalton couldn't find a flaw in that logic and he swung round so that he had a clear view of Loren's face when he spoke.

'Melrose suspected that someone from this wagon train killed Marcus Wilcox. The Spitzer brothers are probably after us to get hold of the thousand dollars the killer stole off him. And the killer has now killed Melrose to stop him seeing Eddy and Tucker Malone.'

Loren's expression remained impassive throughout these revelations.

'I guess everyone will figure most of that out for themselves. But now that your plan to force the killer into the open has gone wrong, you got to come up with a different plan or more people could die.'

'I know.' Dalton shrugged. 'Perhaps we should turn back.'

'That's one option.' Loren considered Dalton. 'But I know that Eddy and Tucker knew John Stanton. Meeting them wouldn't be good for you and–'

'And that would be sufficient motivation for me to kill Melrose. But I didn't do it. I can't prove that, but I didn't.' Dalton set his hands on his hips and returned Loren's steady gaze. 'So, can you convince me you didn't have a reason to kill him?'

'I got the same problem. I didn't do it, but I can't prove it.' Loren raised his eyebrows. 'The only difference is, I didn't have a motive to stop him seeing the Malone brothers.'

'That I know of.'

Loren's gaze flickered with a sudden emotion, but Dalton couldn't tell what it was and he blinked it away. Then the two men stared at each other, but as neither offered anything more, they headed to the wagons.

Loren located a tin plate and beat it on the ground until he roused a group of bleary-eyed and complaining people, who looked at the dark sky, shivered, then complained some more. But they soon quietened when Dalton relayed the bad news.

'Sheriff Melrose is dead,' he reported, 'murdered, and somebody from this wagon train killed him.'

The hubbub this revelation raised continued for some time but when Melrose's body had been confirmed dead, Virgil called for a meeting.

Everyone sat in the centre of the ledge and voiced their concern about what had happened, but nobody was as worried about who had killed Melrose as they were about what they should do next. Newell summed up the general mood for resolving this practical matter.

'This mean we have to turn back?' he asked.

'It sure doesn't,' Virgil said. 'We'll bury him. Then we'll keep going.'

Newell looked away as Virgil glared at him, but Virgil continued to glare, confirming he wouldn't voice an objection, then looked at each person in turn, receiving several nods but no headshakes. His gaze ended at Dalton.

'But I still assume,' Dalton said, 'that one of us will head back to Applegate.'

Dalton heard Loren snort as Virgil raised his eyebrows.

'There's no need.'

'A lawman's died and we can't just let those prospectors know what happened. It might be months before they meet anyone else.'

'We ain't even telling them.'

Murmurs grew around the group as

everyone looked at each other, but Dalton voiced their concern.

'You can't *not* tell anyone.'

'I can. We've come here to make our own rules and live our lives the way we want to live them. We take care of our own and don't need no interference from anyone.'

'A death of an innocent man is where we have to accept interference.'

'You don't have a say in this. You're only with us until we reach our destination.' Virgil gestured around the group, his hand studiously avoiding picking out Dalton and Loren. 'We accept what we want to accept.'

'You can, but Melrose died from a knife slash across the throat while he slept.' Dalton stood and set his hands on his hips. 'So, I sure ain't risking going to sleep if that's what you're prepared to accept.'

'I trust my people. His killer doesn't have to be anyone I'm leading.'

Dalton looked up the short distance of visible canyon-side above them, then edged to the side to peer into the dark at the remaining drop down.

'If Melrose had died anywhere but here I'd have agreed, but we're in the one place where nobody can sneak up on us. Whoever killed Sheriff Melrose is amongst us and we got to face up to that.'

'And we will. But you didn't get my meaning. I said the killer doesn't have to be one of us.' Virgil flashed a smile without warmth. 'I trust every person here, but two people joined us and–'

'Hey!' Loren shouted stepping forward and joining the debate for the first time. 'You can't accuse me of that.'

'Like Loren said,' Dalton said, 'hey!'

As several people voiced support for Dalton and Loren, that support gathering momentum, Virgil raised his hands, calling for calm, then looked at each man in turn.

'I didn't accuse either of you. I was just stating a possibility.'

'You were. Don't state it again.'

Virgil glared at Dalton, then shrugged.

'I will when the time is right. In our new life, we'll make our own justice and we'll work out amongst ourselves who killed Melrose. Then we will deal with the problem ourselves, but we don't need outside help.'

As this was close to the philosophy Loren had championed earlier, Dalton glanced at Loren, who stepped forward.

'Fine sentiments,' he said. 'But for that to work, you must have a clear idea as to how you'll unearth the truth. So, do you?'

Virgil's eyes flickered with momentary doubt before his usual impassive expression returned.

'That is my concern, not yours.'

'As John Stanton said, if we're to trust each other sufficiently to get a good night's sleep, knowing what you plan to do is very much everyone's concern. I ask again, how will you work out who killed Melrose without outside help?'

Murmured support drifted round the group, as Virgil remained quiet. Dalton glanced at Newell, wondering if he'd step forward with a reasonable argument as to how they should proceed. He had been the first to voice Dalton's suggested policy of turning back and seeking help. But he just stared at a spot before his feet, his furrowed brow suggesting that many thoughts were racing through his mind, but not ones he wished to voice.

At last, when the people who had dared to express their concern had silenced, Virgil spoke up.

'Don't worry. Remember this – guilty people always slip up. This evil person will not keep his crime hidden from the honest gazes of our good people for long.' Virgil bored his gaze into Loren, then moved on to look at each person in turn. Many people looked away and Dalton almost expected someone to blurt out a confession under his resolute gaze, but when he'd traversed the group, he pointed down the canyon side. 'But for now, we must put this tragedy aside, as we have put others, and face our next challenge of getting to the bottom of the canyon.'

'I say we don't do that,' Dalton said, his being the only voice raised in objection.

Virgil turned to glare at Dalton.

'Why?'

'Last time, most people went down in groups on the wagons. Can any of us trust the others enough to be alone with a potential killer suspended hundreds of feet above the ground?'

'I can,' Virgil snapped, giving Dalton's question no chance of gathering support. He lowered his voice, his tone a mixture of sarcasm and accusation. 'I'll even accompany you if you're that worried.'

Virgil's comment could have many meanings and to Dalton it almost sounded like a confession. Dalton narrowed his eyes.

'I'd prefer to sort this out before we risk our lives.'

'We can't do that, and I won't let you tear

150

this group apart with suspicion and fear. We will carry on as normal and wait for whoever did this to expose himself.'

And with that statement of intent, Virgil slapped his legs and stood up, effectively ending the debate and drawing everyone's attention to the fact that first light was brushing the horizon.

The meeting broke up as the group prepared to head down to the bottom of the canyon. Only Loren remained to stand with Dalton.

He looked at him, his eyes hooded and his jaw firm, suggesting he'd heard something that had helped him form a suspicion, then he joined the others.

Despite Virgil's proclamation that the group shouldn't be suspicious of each other, Dalton noted that everybody eyed everyone else during their preparations to move down. And, once they'd buried Melrose, just about everyone inspected the rope and frame as if they might find a fatal flaw in the arrangement.

As had happened the last time, Virgil volunteered his own wagon to go down first. Even more than the first time, this act helped to stem the tide of growing concern, and afterwards everyone appeared shame-faced at doubting the others. A new sense of getting the job done took over and they started acting as a group again.

As they wanted to observe everyone, Dalton and Loren didn't volunteer to go down on foot to await the wagons and, as the route to the bottom was easier to negotiate than yesterday's, two other men went down.

But now that the wagon lowering was under way, Dalton didn't see anybody acting oddly. And even that curious dismissal of past misfortune that he'd noticed after Eliza's attempted kidnapping, and which had been admirable then, was repeated with Melrose's murder not being referred to again.

One by one the wagons disappeared over the side and reached the bottom safely until they'd reduced the remaining task to just three wagons. Newell insisted that Eliza go down with Henry on the next wagon, but that he should stay back.

And then, aside from the horses, Virgil, Jacob and Newell were the only ones left for Dalton and Loren to observe. As Jacob and Virgil drew up the rope after Henry's wagon had been unhitched below, Newell joined Dalton and Loren.

'The Wades?' he said, without preamble,

his expression and posture relaxed, as if he'd come over to discuss a minor matter.

'That's my assumption,' Dalton said.

'I'm keeping an open mind,' Loren said.

Newell swung round to watch Jacob and Virgil. Jacob happened to glance their way, then snapped his head around as if he'd realized he'd been seen looking at them.

'What makes you think that,' Dalton said, 'aside from the fact you don't like them?'

Newell snorted. 'Nothing.'

Loren patted Newell's back. 'I admire your honesty, but we need more if we're to voice a suspicion openly.'

Newell's jaw twitched, perhaps as he suppressed an urge to mention a real reason why he suspected the Wades, then he gave a curt nod.

'You're right. I'll go down with Jacob on the next wagon. I have some questions I'd like to ask him alone.' He glanced at Loren, then at Dalton. 'Perhaps you might have something you'd like to ask Virgil while you're up here alone.'

Loren didn't reply. He walked away to help hitch up the next wagon, but Dalton stayed back to give Newell a grim smile and a nod. Then they all moved back to the edge, but when the next wagon was secure and Newell suggested his plan, Jacob flared his eyes.

'I will not go down with you,' he said, then folded his arms.

'Do not accuse me,' Newell snapped, pointing at him.

'Newell,' Virgil urged, 'you will avoid talk like that.'

As Newell grunted his irritation, Jacob shook his head.

'This ain't got nothing to do with Melrose's murder,' Jacob said. 'I just don't want to go down with a Boone.'

'That ain't right,' Newell muttered, his eyes flaring. 'Because we all know there's one of us you—'

'Newell,' Virgil shouted, cutting him off, 'this is not the time to air disputes. Right now, we have to get the wagons to the bottom safely.'

'Then stand up to your son for once and maybe there won't be so many disputes.'

Virgil snorted his breath, but then glanced at Jacob and, with a short nudge of the head, ordered him to get in the wagon, then he shook his head at Newell.

Jacob smirked as if he'd won an important point of principle. He sat in the wagon with his legs dangling over the backboard. He glanced around, his grin showing that he wasn't afraid of the height and that he was even enjoying the thrill of being lowered down the canyon.

He was still smirking when he disappeared from view, and Newell didn't mention the matter again as they lowered the wagon.

When that wagon had reached the bottom and they'd dragged up the rope, Loren considered the sullen Newell, then faced Virgil.

'And who should go down in the last wagon?' he asked.

Dalton caught the sarcasm in his tone, as there was no need for any of them to accompany the wagon. Earlier, several other people who were confident of their ability to negotiate the slippery canyon side, hadn't risked sitting in the wagons and had gone down on foot. And all the men here had stayed to the end because they could do just that, but Virgil replied as if the question had no agenda.

'Perhaps you and John should go down next and enjoy the view. Jacob sure wasn't scared about putting his life in other people's hands.'

'Then we'll do just that,' Loren said, his dry tone suggesting to Dalton that only Virgil's taunt had encouraged him to make that gesture.

Dalton didn't feel a need to make such a gesture, but Newell looked at him, his significant glance encouraging him to let him talk privately with one member of the Wade family.

So he joined Loren in sitting inside the last wagon to make the journey to the canyon bottom.

Inside, the weight of the belongings and furniture had been spread evenly across the wagon and, to maintain that balance, Dalton and Loren sat at opposite ends facing each other. But neither man felt the need to display bravado by looking outwards.

They waited quietly while Newell and Virgil checked the ropes. Then, with much creaking followed by a sudden lurch, they rose from the ground and swung out over the drop.

Dalton had no particular fear of heights, but after his recent fight with the Spitzer gang, he was pleased that the wagon was covered and he didn't have to look down as they dangled high above the ground.

The two men sat silently until the wagon began to descend in short drops. Then Loren smiled.

'We've watched everyone for the whole

morning,' he said. 'So, who do you suspect now?'

'Still Jacob Wade,' Dalton said, 'maybe Virgil.'

'Getting all friendly with the family the Wades don't like ain't a reason to suspect them.'

'It might just be that, but you got to admit it was mighty odd that Virgil forced us to carry on and not fetch help.'

'It was, at that,' Loren conceded with a sigh, 'but I reckon he believes what he says. He wants to start a new life, free from out-side pressures. He wouldn't kill to start that life.'

'Perhaps he wouldn't, but maybe Jacob would and, as Virgil would never accept that his son is capable of doing wrong, he'd act to cover up his crimes.' Dalton considered Loren. 'And your suspicion?'

'Newell Boone,' Loren said with a surpris-ing amount of confidence. 'Marcus Wilcox was a snake-oil seller and Henry Boone is an ill man. Perhaps Newell wasn't impressed when Marcus's potion didn't work. He sure reacted when Melrose revealed who the dead man was.'

'Yeah, with surprise, as if he didn't know Marcus was dead.'

'Perhaps.'

Dalton shrugged, accepting that when people voiced suspicions, every action could appear significant. He shuffled across the wagon, then leaned out to look down. He judged that they were less than half-way down, swaying at least 200 feet above ground. Then he looked around until he located the outcrop of rock where they would meet Eddy and Tucker Malone. It was several miles away, so he still had time before he would have to find a way to avoid them. He drew his head back in.

'So,' he said, 'let me see if I understand our suspicions correctly. Virgil and Newell, the two people we suspect, somehow worked together to persuade us to get in this wagon when we didn't need to. And they're both above us and are in sole charge of the rope that's stopping us from plummeting to our deaths.'

'That's the situation.' Loren winked. 'But don't look so concerned. If one of them cuts the rope, at least while we're on the way down we'll know our suspicions were right.'

Dalton chuckled at Loren's grim humour, but try as he might to avoid it, he couldn't help but peer outside again to confirm that the descent was progressing safely.

Two doubled and crossed ropes were beneath the wagon and they looped up into a giant knot which connected those ropes to the main rope fifteen feet above the wagon, forming a tight canopy. All the ropes were solid and intact and Dalton ran his gaze up the taut main rope to the top where Newell and Virgil were out of his view as they controlled the horses that were lowering them.

He was about to slip back into the wagon, but then movement caught his eye and his gaze darted back to the rope above the giant knot.

There, two feet above the knot, twine had frayed apart and a length of that twine dangled free. Even as he watched, another strand spiralled away and, in a moment of shocked horror, Dalton realized what had happened.

Someone had already sliced through the rope and the weight of the wagon was slowly splitting that rope.

Within seconds, the rope would break and they would both plunge to their deaths.

CHAPTER 9

Dalton darted his head back into the wagon.

'The rope,' he said, 'it's breaking.'

Loren stared at Dalton, his wide-eyed gaze drinking in Dalton's shock, then he joined him at the back of the wagon, their combined weight dipping them lower.

As they looked up, Dalton was sure the wagon jerked downwards and that the rope had frayed even more in the few seconds in which he'd been inside. The thickness of the rope was now less than half its original width.

He looked down, but it took over twenty minutes to lower each wagon and he reckoned they were fifteen minutes or so from reaching the ground.

The wagon lurched as the rope frayed again, convincing Dalton that they didn't have those fifteen minutes.

'We have to lighten the load,' Loren said, 'and reduce the strain on the rope.'

Dalton nodded, no other plan coming to

him, and turned. Inside were the total belongings of a family and he balked at destroying them, but if this wagon plummeted that would happen anyhow.

As Loren grabbed the first armful, he shouted down that everyone should watch out. Then he hurled the nearest sack out.

First, they hurled clothes down, ensuring they didn't hurt anyone with their unexpected actions, and Dalton heard people shouting below, demanding to know what they were doing.

Dalton stopped hurling sacks down for long enough to shout back that the rope was breaking. Then he looked up.

On the ledge, the shouting had attracted Virgil's and Newell's attention and they were peering over the side. From so far away, Dalton couldn't discern whether or not their expressions were shocked, but when the wagon lurched again, that concern fled from his mind.

Since he'd first seen the frayed rope they'd lowered by only a few feet, and more and more cords were breaking away on the straining rope.

'We got to start throwing the heavy stuff over the side,' he shouted.

'Agreed,' Loren said. He pointed at a cupboard strapped to a dismantled table, then lay on his back to kick away the side-boards so that they could topple it over the side quickly.

Dalton moved to join him, but then saw another length of rope fray and part, even hearing the snap and feeling the wagon lurch down another foot.

'Don't bother,' he said. 'We'll never lighten the load fast enough. The rope's going to break any second now.'

Loren lay on his back with his feet raised for a moment, then he hurried over to join Dalton and look up. He winced, then grunted his agreement and they both stared around, looking for a safe berth to leap for on the near-vertical side of the canyon.

There were numerous protruding rocks, scrubby trees, and ledges where a desperate man could perch for a while, but the face was twenty feet away and too far for them to jump to. Dalton did notice that the falling clothes had persuaded everyone to move out of the way, but in looking down, his gaze alighted on a ledge, around five feet wide and ten feet long. It protruded further than any others and could both be reached from a wagon dangling beside it and be rested upon, but it was fifty feet below them.

He drew Loren's attention to it.

'The rope will never last that long,' Loren murmured. 'We got to jump for it now and trust our luck to grab hold of something.'

'I reckon I've pushed that luck too far already.' Dalton stood and swayed, then righted himself. 'We got to get to the rope above the frayed length.'

Loren looked up and although Dalton saw him shake his head at the likelihood of their having enough time to succeed, he stood and gestured to Dalton to take the lead.

Dalton grabbed hold of the nearest rope, then pulled himself up. But the combined effects of his healing injuries and the lack of purchase for his feet on the side of the wagon meant that though he put lots of effort into climbing he managed only to drag himself up a few feet.

He stopped using just his arms to pull himself up, and braced his feet against the rope. Then he began to make progress, dragging himself up the rope towards the knot and possible safety.

Below him, Loren watched his slow progress, then tried a different method. He tore through the cloth, then climbed onto the cupboard, gaining height faster than Dalton had. He swayed with his arms outstretched then leapt for the rope above his head and hung on, his feet dangling beneath him. Then he climbed, hand over hand, up the rope before his strength gave out.

He covered several feet in four swaying lunges. That brought him to a point where he could dangle beneath the knot. He swung from side to side until he looped a foot around the nearest rope, then, with his weight spread over two ropes, he climbed on to the knot that connected all the ropes.

He glanced at the fraying length of rope, shivered, then darted a glance downward.

'Hurry! You ain't got time to admire the view.'

'I am,' Dalton grunted as he dragged himself up another few inches. 'I just wish I'd used your method.'

'I had to see the wrong way to do it to find the right way. Now hurry!'

Loren leaned down as far as he could and thrust down a hand. But his fingers were still feet away from Dalton's hands.

'Get above the fraying rope. I'll be fine.'

'Stop talking and climb.'

Loren thrust his hand down another foot and Dalton dragged himself up another clawed handhold. One glance at the fraying rope convinced him he'd never reach the top in time and he decided to use Loren's climbing method. He let his feet fall away from the rope to dangle free, then swung himself from side to side, kicking up higher each time.

Loren shouted encouragement at him and, on the third swing, he looped a foot around the nearest rope and hung on, trapped sideways and unsure as to how he could use his new position.

From above, Loren directed him to get both his feet up, then to brace himself between the two ropes. Dalton did as ordered and that released some of the tension from his arms, giving him the freedom to walk his hands up the rope and gain height quickly.

He flexed himself, ready to walk his feet higher, but then a hand slapped down on his arm and tugged. Dalton suffered a terrible moment where he reckoned his weight would drag them both down, but Loren braced himself against the knot and lifted him.

Dalton lunged and locked his hands on Loren's shoulders. When Loren stood the two men scrambled over each other before separating and standing on either side of the knot.

Then the rope split, its end coming in a rush of bursting cords, deep snaps and sudden drops.

Both men leapt upwards to grab hold of the rope above their heads.

Dalton had a giddy sensation of the ground falling away as the wagon plummeted from him, receding into the distance, and he tore his gaze away to check that Loren was hanging on. But then he saw that the canyon side appeared to be falling away, too.

He heard the wagon crash to the ground, then closed his eyes, unable to work out what was happening. When he opened them he was rushing in towards the canyon side. In shocked horror, he realized that releasing the tension of the wagon's weight had sprung the rope back up. With only his and Loren's weight now on it, the broken rope was flailing wildly, snapping back and forth and hurtling them in towards the canyon wall.

Dalton had just a moment to prepare himself and then they slammed into the side.

They were lucky in that they both hit sideways, but the jarring was so great that it shook Dalton's grip free of the rope. He saw Loren also come free, but then he was falling, pressed flat to the side of the canyon and sliding down an almost sheer slope.

When the Spitzer gang had put him in this

position, he'd fallen head first and had lost consciousness the first time he'd hit anything, but this time he headed down feet first and that let him slow his progress.

He thrust out his arms and legs, scrambling for purchase in the loose rock of the canyon-side. His foot caught and slowed him and then he was sliding again. A trailing hand grabbed hold of scrubby vegetation, which came loose, but slowed him again. Then he slid down over loose grit, throwing up huge plumes of dust around him as he scythed down, but again he slowed.

For the first time since he'd seen the fraying rope, he started to believe he'd survive the journey to the bottom. With renewed hope he remembered the ledge that had been fifty feet below him. He darted his head around, searching for it. At that precise moment he slammed into the ledge.

His legs buckled and his momentum lunged him forward and almost carried him on, but he diverted his motion by throwing himself to the side and, on his belly, he slid to a halt, half-on, half-off the ledge. He took a deep breath, enjoying his good fortune and the relatively safe position he was in, then he saw a blur of movement ahead.

The shouting he'd been hearing, and which

he'd thought he'd made himself, registered and he realized that Loren had been tumbling on broadly the same path. And he would reach the ledge in a matter of moments.

Dalton rose to his knees then jumped to his feet, his outer foot barely catching on flat ground. Then he sprinted forward and threw himself to the ledge with his arms outstretched.

Loren might have been tumbling but he'd seen the ledge earlier than Dalton had. As he reached it he threw out his hands and the two men locked grasps. And then they both pushed backwards, their actions uncoordinated but both trying to find purchase on the ledge and avoid Loren's momentum dragging them down.

With an ungainly scrambling and much kicking, they came to rest. Loren lay half-hanging over the edge with his chest on the ledge and his feet dangling. Dalton lay on his side with his feet braced against the rock face and his head dangling so that he looked down the side at the people below.

'No sudden movements,' Loren whispered beside him, 'and we can both get back on this ledge.'

'Wasn't thinking of doing any of those,'

Dalton said, still trying to focus on his upside-down view of the world, 'but how are we going to get down from here?'

Loren rocked his head to the side to join him in looking down.

Other ledges and handholds were below them, but they were still over one hundred feet above ground level.

'I don't know,' he said. 'But whatever we do, we'll have to do it on our own.'

It took Dalton and Loren nearly an hour to pick a route down the side of the canyon.

At first they had to trust their own ability to find ledges below them that they could reach. Several times they reached safe berths to rest up, then found that there was no route down from there and they had to climb back up and try again.

But once they'd covered the first thirty feet of their journey the people at the bottom were able to shout up about what was ahead and so help them pick the best route down.

Then they made quick progress. Dalton even began to enjoy the challenge of climbing down. But he didn't relish the encounter they'd have to face when they reached the bottom.

And as they took so long to climb down,

Virgil and Newell had reached ground level by the time they scampered down the last ten feet to join everyone. They received many pats on the back, but both Loren and Dalton stepped clear of the support to stand alone facing the two men, one of whom had tried to kill them.

'Are you all right?' Virgil asked, his tone and staring eyes registering concern which Dalton, in his annoyed state, chose not to believe.

'Yeah,' Dalton said, 'your attempt to kill us failed and now we can—'

'I didn't do that. Believe me.' Virgil turned to Newell, imploring him with his wide hands to support him, but Newell lowered his head. 'Newell was with me the whole time.'

Dalton and Loren glanced at each other and, in Loren's burning eyes, Dalton saw that, like him, he was determined to get to the truth this time.

'It was one of you two,' Loren said. 'So, tell us your stories and I reckon we can figure out which one of you is lying.'

'Neither of us is lying. We were together all the time and neither of us cut the rope.' Virgil again looked to Newell for support and again Newell didn't meet his eye.

'Then perhaps it was both of you.'

'That,' Virgil said, pointing a firm finger at Loren, 'is your anger speaking. It's more likely that somebody cut the rope earlier–'

'You're damn right I'm angry. Now, tell me what happened!'

'Perhaps,' Dalton said, as Virgil shook his head, 'that *is* what happened.' He glanced at the wrecked wagon, then at the other wagons standing further away. 'Somebody could have cut the rope while it was down here with the previous wagon and Newell and Virgil were too busy finding reasons to argue that they didn't notice the cut.'

Newell looked up for the first time, his narrowed eyes and pained wince suggesting that Dalton's guess at what they'd been doing was correct.

'But who?' Loren said, shrugging.

'Jacob was the last person down before us. He could have done it before the rope went back up.'

Virgil snorted and waved his hands high above his head.

'If you're now saying it happened on the ground, anyone could have done it.'

'They could,' Dalton said, 'but at the very least you got to question your son.'

'And,' Loren said, 'search for the money

Marcus Wilcox's killer stole. Wherever you find it, it's sure to prove something.'

Virgil's eyes blazed, perhaps suggesting he would never accept comments about his son being guilty, but then he swirled round to present his back to everyone. Dalton expected him to refuse to take any further part in this questioning. He looked at Newell, hoping he'd assert his authority, but Newell didn't look at him and it was Virgil who eventually poke up. His voice was low and trembling with barely suppressed hurt and rage.

'I deplore the accusations you've levelled at my people. This is the sort of behaviour we are trying to distance ourselves from. When this is over, both of you will leave us and we will find Pleasant Valley on our own.'

'Sweet Valley,' Dalton said, 'you're looking for Sweet Valley.'

Virgil turned. 'We have never officially assigned a name to our new settlement and I say it'll be Pleasant Valley and I will lead my people there without influence from anyone. Is that clear?'

'It will be clear, but only after you've called for Jacob and we've heard his story.'

Virgil snorted his breath through his nostrils, then roared at the top of his voice, the sound echoing in the canyon.

'Jacob, come here and show these worth-less people how the Wades stand up to groundless accusations!'

As the echoes faded away, Dalton couldn't help but notice that Virgil locked his gaze on Newell and that Newell still didn't meet his eye.

But Jacob didn't emerge. Virgil's demand was so strident he must have heard it and everyone looked around, murmuring and raising their eyebrows at his defiance. Virgil didn't call for him again. He stood with his arms folded and his glazed eyes refusing to acknowledge that his son was actually defying him by keeping him waiting.

As Virgil's jaw muscles tensed and his cheeks reddened, Dalton felt a twinge of sympathy for him. He now saw Virgil for what he was. He had many faults, but he wasn't a killer.

Virgil was the father of a wayward and now murderous child, who couldn't accept that his own blood could do wrong, but as the seconds passed and Jacob still didn't emerge, Dalton watched Virgil's authority seep away.

If Jacob were hiding in fear of the reper-cussions, nobody would trust him again.

And every passing second only put further pressure on Virgil to admit something he could probably never voice voluntarily.

People fidgeted. The muttering grew. One person, then another, slipped away to search the wagons, and when they didn't find Jacob, others joined them to look further away, but still they didn't find him.

Soon, only the four men at the centre of this crisis were left standing by the wrecked wagon. Virgil stood with his arms folded and his chin high, no sign of panic in his resolute gaze. Newell's eyes were downcast as he failed to acknowledge the problem. And Loren and Dalton stood together exchanging significant glances that confirmed that they both now knew who the guilty person was and that their problems would soon be over.

People drifted further and further away in their search. A check of the horses found that one was missing, but it was only when someone shouted out that they'd discovered a second horse was missing that Newell snapped out of his torpor and joined in the search.

Dalton and Loren hurried after him, but when he headed into Henry's wagon they stopped and debated how they could best help. But they never got the chance to start searching, as Newell emerged from his wagon and reported his terrible discovery.

Newell had checked on his father, but his eyes were wide and shocked as he hurried over to clear ground and attracted everyone's attention.

'What's wrong?' Dalton shouted as people milled in.

'It's Eliza,' Newell said. 'She's missing, too.'

CHAPTER 10

The ten minutes after the discovery that two people were missing from the wagon train were fraught and frantic. Virgil emerged from his state of denial but replaced it with another form of denial and organized everyone into carrying out a systematic search of the surrounding area.

Dalton and Loren stood back and let him complete this sensible check, but Dalton did encourage Newell to tell them what he knew. Newell shook his head and led them into Henry's wagon instead.

Henry was shaking, a hatred of his position burning in his sunken eyes. He was a man who would once never have let this situation occur and he hated himself for his current impotence. In terse sentences punctuated with harsh bursts of coughing, he told them what had happened.

Soon after Jacob had reached the ground, he had slipped into the wagon where Eliza had been comforting Henry after the journey down. He'd slapped a hand over her mouth then tried to place a pillow over Henry's face, but Eliza had struggled so much that he'd relented and taken her from the wagon. He knew nothing else about what had happened and, despite his pleas, nobody had come to the wagon to check on him until now, that fact causing him as much pain as everything else had.

Presumably before kidnapping Eliza, Jacob had sliced through the rope, but Henry had no information to confirm whether this was true. With the distressed Henry then beginning to repeat himself, Newell beckoned for them to leave, but Dalton lingered.

'Don't worry,' he said, placing a calming hand on his shoulder. 'Everything will be fine.'

'It won't,' Henry bleated. 'I'm dying. I ain't got long. I can't do nothing. I need her. I won't see her again.'

Henry continued to ramble, his words becoming unintelligible. This time Newell urged them to leave with more determination.

The three men emerged from the wagon and, without consulting the people scurrying around, headed for their horses. Quickly, they mounted up and debated the quickest way to pick up Jacob's trail.

But in those few moments they received an addition to their numbers.

'You ain't welcome here,' Newell said.

Virgil shrugged and continued pacing to his horse.

'So, you've decided to speak your mind. But I don't care. I'm coming with you to ensure justice for my son.'

'He killed Marcus Wilcox and Sheriff Melrose. He tried to kill John and Loren and my father, and I don't like to think why he's taken my sister.'

Virgil stopped to point a firm finger at Newell.

'Do not accuse him without proof. I have had enough of the unfounded accusations against my family from–'

'Both of you,' Dalton roared, 'be quiet!'

To his surprise, both men did fall silent, but having gained some control, Dalton found that he had nothing he wanted to say to men who put arguing over a family dispute above action when a killer had abducted a woman. So, he just glanced at Loren and the two men hurried their horses on without looking at the other two.

Dalton heard Newell trot after them and then Virgil chase after him, but, as both men stayed quiet, he concentrated on helping

Loren find Jacob's trail. It didn't take long. Few people came to the canyon and two riders travelling together presented an obvious trail to follow. Dalton asked if the trail could be Tucker's and Eddy Malone's, but Loren pointed to the outcrop, some miles away in the opposite direction, then confirmed the trail was fresh.

The trail headed off down the canyon towards lower land and, in a brief and quiet conversation, Loren let him know that the canyon carried on for many miles. It would take many days before they came out on to the plains.

Again without consulting Newell and Virgil, Dalton and Loren followed the trail at a gallop. The other two men followed them, but kept their distance both from each other and the leading men.

Dalton glanced back to confirm that these were the only people who had joined the chase. He noticed that further back the settlers were getting into their wagons and were looking as if they were moving on. Then the land dipped and they disappeared from view, leaving them with just the two trailing and distrusting men following them.

'Well,' he said, turning back to look at Loren, 'at least one thing's come out of this

– we two can start to trust each other.'

'Nope,' Loren said, turning to Dalton. 'I still don't trust you.

For an hour the four riders headed down the canyon. The trail they were following remained clear with two riders heading down the centre of the canyon. The tracks were recent, but whether they were closing on Jacob or not, Dalton couldn't tell.

The group was silent, but from his companions' reddened faces and stern jaws Dalton guessed that passing time was not cooling anyone's temper and that the previous confrontation could easily flare up again.

Loren was the first to risk speaking. They had rounded a jutting outcrop of rock and ahead the canyon presented a long and straight section for several miles. The men placed their hands to their brows and peered ahead, but there were no untoward movements. As clear water flowed from a nearby spring and crossed their path, Loren called for a rest.

Nobody disagreed. When they'd dismounted Loren stood before Virgil.

'Now we've all had time to calm down, can we at least agree to work together to find Jacob and Eliza?'

'I have no trouble being fair with any man,' Virgil said.

Loren nodded and turned away despite Virgil's less than obvious acceptance, but Newell snorted.

'And what do you know of being fair?'

'More than Henry ever knew.'

'Virgil, Newell,' Dalton urged, but both men faced up to each other and were oblivious to anything but finding another reason to argue.

'My father led this wagon train with a lot more respect for others than you ever have.'

'Respect is just another word for weakness and being weak won't get us somewhere where nobody can come along with their nasty plagues and–'

Newell stabbed a firm finger at Virgil's chest.

'One more insinuation is all I need and I'll–'

Virgil batted the finger away. 'And you'll do what?'

Newell stood toe to toe with Virgil; a long-delayed confrontation between these men was just seconds away.

'This is the worst possible time for this,' Loren shouted at them.

Both men continued to glare at each

other. Then they shoved each other's shoulders as they worked themselves up to trading blows.

Before that happened, Dalton turned away in disgust and took the reins to walk his horse along the length of spring water. Loren joined him and the two men left the shouting and sounds of scuffling behind them.

'This is ridiculous,' Dalton said. 'We'll never track down Jacob and Eliza if we can't stop arguing amongst ourselves.'

'And what do you expect?' Loren said. 'None of us trust the others.'

'We don't, but I expect us two to be sensible enough to put aside our differences until we find them.'

'And that's what the new John Stanton reckons, is it?'

'I reckon.' Dalton stopped and faced up to Loren. 'And I never knew the real John Stanton like you did, but I reckon that's what he would have done.'

Loren snorted his breath through his nostrils and advanced on Dalton.

'Don't ever tell me what John Stanton would have done. You ain't worthy of his name and you never will be.'

'And you're right. I'm trying to act like

him, but what I don't understand is why a man whom John Stanton called a friend won't look for the good in me and give me a chance. I've saved your life and you've saved mine and surely that's good enough for the two of us to at least not be enemies.'

Loren looked away, his eyes flashing, perhaps with hurt.

'Never say that again. Every moment you continue to call yourself John Stanton just helps remind me you ain't him. I'll give you a chance when you start acting like the man whose name you've taken.'

Dalton rubbed his chin, then nodded.

'In that case, I'll start now. You don't trust me, and I don't trust you, and neither of us trusts them two.' Dalton pointed at the squabbling Newell and Virgil. 'One of us has to start trusting someone, and that person will be me. So, I trust you.'

'Why?'

'You knew what the Spitzer gang would do, but I reckon you were just following your instincts and not using any inside knowledge.'

'That's right, and it's something John Stanton would have known without insulting me with accusations.'

'Yeah, he did have instincts.' Dalton glanced at the canyon-side, then at the ridge above. 'And now, I'll use mine.'

Dalton mounted his horse, swung the reins to the side and headed straight for the canyon-side.

'What you doing?' Loren shouted after him, but Dalton had had enough of dealing with and explaining himself to everyone. He kept going.

Dalton rode on to the side of the canyon, then headed for a terrace between two rock strata that cut upwards and which he reckoned would get him most of the way to the top of the canyon.

From here, he could see Newell and Virgil down by the spring-water. Dalton's sudden departure had encouraged them to end their flaring argument and both men were mounting their horses to hurry after him. Loren had already mounted up and was trotting after him. Half-way up the terrace, he caught up with him and repeated his question.

'I'm doing what you said I should do,' Dalton said. 'I'm thinking like John Stanton. He wouldn't blindly follow Jacob's trail, always being one step behind his quarry. He'd figure out where he was going and get there first.'

'You got some idea as to what he'd do, but

you're going about it all wrong. You won't prove nothing here.'

'Then leave me and find him your way.'

'We got to stick together. Even Newell and Virgil realize that.'

'Then I tell you this: if my hunch is right, you'll stop facing me down and accept me for what I am – a decent man doing my best in a difficult situation. And you'll accept that I didn't kill your friend and that you got no reason to look for reasons to hate me.'

Loren didn't reply. They reached the top of the terrace in silence, then switched back to head towards a second terrace. Below, Virgil and Newell were hurrying up the first terrace to catch up with them.

'I can accept that,' Loren said at last. 'But only because there ain't no way your hunch is right. You ain't John Stanton.'

Dalton stopped for long enough to acknowledge Loren's acceptance and that gave Newell and Virgil time to catch up. Virgil wasted no time in reiterating Loren's concern.

'I'm just trying to bring this to an end quickly,' Dalton said, turning to continue on up the slope. 'I reckon I understand Jacob. He'll head up the canyon-side the first chance he gets.'

'I understand my own son better than you ever will,' Virgil said.

'Do you?' Dalton shook the reins and carried on, forcing Virgil to hurry on to ride alongside him. 'Perhaps you're more concerned with countering the accusation that he's a killer than to hear the truth.'

'Which is?'

Dalton glanced back at Loren, who narrowed his eyes, encouraging him to be subtle.

'Perhaps this is all a misunderstanding. Perhaps circumstance has forced Jacob into actions he wouldn't otherwise do.'

'Go on,' Virgil grunted.

'He loves Eliza and he wants to get to Sweet Valley to start a new life with her. And if he has to do that without us, he will. So, he'll head over the ridge and try to find a place for them to settle down. We need to get to him first before that love forces him into doing anything else he'll regret.'

None of the men argued with this viewpoint and for the first time the group set off with a shared purpose. Even so, Dalton glanced at Loren, who returned a slow shake of the head and mouthed that Dalton wasn't John Stanton and his hunch would fail.

The four men stood on the ridge, looking out at the land beyond. The journey up the side of the canyon had been easy. They hoped that the wagons had found an equally easy passage and so would already be looking out at this vista.

But after hearing Henry's vision of Sweet Valley, Dalton had formed a picture of the land beyond the mountains as being a green and lush landscape, filled with numerous places for his people to set down.

Instead, under the harsh afternoon sun, the ground was brown, hard-baked and unable to sustain life. Clearly, even if they resolved this crisis, this group's odyssey wasn't over.

Then they headed along the top of the ridge. The south peak that Dalton reckoned Jacob would need to slip by to readily reach the other side of the ridge was still several miles away. And they rode towards the peak while constantly looking out for anyone cutting across ahead.

But as they approached a sudden sharp rise Dalton began to feel that Loren was right and that his hunch would prove to be wrong. In an odd way he had been trying to live up to the name of John Stanton, a man he didn't know and could only understand from the reactions of others. And his impending failure provided the final proof that he'd never be worthy of that name.

Virgil was the first to voice that concern, slipping his horse nearer to the canyon's edge and pointing out various downward routes. And Newell even supported him, looking down and reporting that they could see for miles and Jacob wasn't visible. Loren said nothing, letting his silence and the apparent failure of Dalton's hunch say everything he needed to say about Dalton.

At last Dalton called a halt at a point where the land ahead became treacherous. He directed everyone to take cover behind an overhanging group of rocks, where they could look back over the previous few miles of the ridge and wait for Jacob to show himself.

'He'll just get further away,' Virgil grumbled, 'if we wait here. I'll go after him on my own.'

'He has my sister,' Newell said. 'I'm going with you.'

'You won't. I will never travel again with–'

'That *is* enough,' Loren said with quiet authority. 'We'll all find out whom we can trust soon enough. If Jacob is coming, it won't be long before he's here.'

Virgil and Newell snorted, their flashing eyes and bunched fists showing they were prepared to carry this argument on until they traded blows, but then they slumped down to slip into cover. And with that being the limit of the agreement they could reach, they waited.

A half-hour passed, then an hour, and Dalton felt the last lingering hope that his hunch would be right slip away. He could think of numerous things Jacob could be doing with Eliza while they waited here, none of them pleasant.

But then he heard something.

At first he thought he might have been mistaken, but then it came again – the steady clop of hoofs – and they were closing fast.

The men glanced at each other, conflicting emotions of irritation, hope and anger registering on everyone's faces, but then common sense took over and they shuffled down to await the approaching people.

And, from the loudness of the hoofbeats, they would pass close by, perhaps fifty yards away. Dalton risked a glance out and saw that there were two riders – Jacob and Eliza.

Jacob rode at the back, a gun drawn and resting on his lap. Eliza rode up front, her head held high and her back straight with defiance and perhaps some fear.

With his eyes, Dalton signified to the others that it was Jacob and Eliza who were approaching and that they should wait until they'd passed. Then he shuffled down. But Virgil ignored him.

Loren had seen the signs of his defiance more quickly than Dalton had and moved to slap a hand over his mouth and hold him down, but Virgil was already on the move. He squirmed away from Loren's questing hand and vaulted out from behind the rocks to stand clear.

'Jacob!' he yelled. 'It's going to be all right.'

Jacob swirled round in the saddle to face him, then shook the reins and hurtled his horse towards him, hoofs skating on the hard surface.

'Eliza,' Newell shouted. 'Get away!'

Eliza turned her horse but still glanced around, uncertain as to which direction to go. By the time Dalton had shouted at her to head away, Jacob had halved the distance to them and Virgil was running towards his son.

Newell rose and chased after him. Dalton shouted at him to stay down but he ignored him.

191

Virgil skidded to a halt and stood before his son's speeding mount, but Jacob swung it past him. Virgil still lunged for him, but missed and fell to his knees. Then he hurried after him as Jacob galloped towards Newell.

Only the presence of the rocks behind Newell stopped him from running him down. But Jacob drew his horse to a halt, then leapt from his mount. He caught Newell around the neck and knocked him over. Then the two men rolled across the stony ground, entangled.

They came to a halt with Jacob on top. He wrapped both hands around Newell's neck and bore down on him. Both Loren and Dalton trained their guns on them, but with the fighting men being so entangled, neither man dared to fire.

Dalton hurried out from his cover, leaving Loren behind him. By now Virgil had regained his footing and he reached the two men first, then swung round to stand guard over his son with his gun drawn.

'Stay away, John,' he ordered. 'It was always coming to this and now these two will sort it out.'

Behind him, Jacob lunged down with all his weight on Newell's neck, his face darkening and his eyes bulging as he threw every ounce of energy into squeezing the life out of Newell.

'Don't kill him,' Dalton shouted.

Dalton didn't expect Jacob to respond. He'd merely spoken to stop Virgil shooting him as he steadily moved closer, but Jacob snapped his hands up to leave Newell lying gasping and clawing at his throat.

'I'm doing nothing,' he shouted. 'This man did everything and blamed it all on me.'

Dalton spread his hands, keeping them away from his gun.

'Then let's talk about it, but in the proper way and not with guns drawn and you with your hands at his throat.'

'This is the only way. We're aiming to live our lives our own way and we'll deliver justice our own way.'

'This ain't justice.'

'It is.' Jacob rolled his shoulders and set his hands together, ready to bear down on Newell again. 'This man killed Marcus Wilcox because he made his father ill. Then he killed the sheriff to cover it up and tried to kill you to make it look like I was the guilty man.'

This version of events was so different from what Dalton believed that he was stunned into momentary silence. The only thought that came to him was to keep Jacob talking and keep him from attempting to strangle Newell again.

But then Newell spoke. His words came broken and gasping.

'Don't believe him, John.'

'It's true,' Jacob roared, then bore down on Newell's neck again. 'You tried to poison Eliza against me.'

Dalton broke into a run as Virgil swung his gun round to aim at him. A single gunshot rang out. Dalton just had time to register that Loren had fired and winged Virgil's gun away, then he brushed past Virgil and launched himself at Jacob. With his arms outstretched he piled into Jacob's chest, knocking him away from Newell and the two men rolled away.

Dalton used his momentum to keep the roll going, ensuring that he dragged Jacob as far away from Newell as he could. When they came to a halt the two men lay on their sides facing each other.

'I beat you,' Jacob said, grinning. 'She came with me.'

'Only because you kidnapped her.'

Jacob twisted and forced Dalton to roll with him until Dalton landed on his back with Jacob sitting astride his chest.

'I took her away from you.' Jacob clamped a hand on his throat. 'And you backed the wrong man.'

Dalton doubted Jacob could exert enough pressure to strangle him with just one hand and he glanced to the side to see that Loren was running towards them. But Virgil stood in his way and grabbed his arm. Then the two men struggled. Eliza had come to a halt and was now edging closer to them, but she was out of danger.

Newell lay on his side, gasping and fingering his throat.

Dalton accepted he'd get no help from anyone else and swung round to look up at Jacob. He grasped both hands around the hand holding his neck and strained, then levered it away, but Jacob didn't put up much resistance and instead lunged to his side. When his hand reappeared, he was clutching a rock, jagged and glistening.

He thrust his hand up then brought it down like a dagger aiming for Dalton's head. Dalton wrenched his head to one side and the rock parted his hair before it sparked into the rocky ground where his head had just lain.

Jacob grunted his irritation then raised the

rock ready to dash it down again. He held it in both hands and took his time, aiming to bring it down in the centre of Dalton's chest in a pulverizing blow.

Dalton flailed his arms, seeking to gain purchase and buck Jacob, but Jacob settled his weight down and raised the rock high above his head.

Dalton still strained but his questing right hand landed on a stone. It was only as wide as two fingers but it was all he could reach and he hurled the stone overhand at Jacob's face. The stone brushed past Jacob's raised arms and smashed into his bared teeth. Blood sprayed, accompanying a wince-inducing crack of teeth, and Jacob flinched back.

Fuelled on by his brush with death, Dalton surged forward, rolling Jacob on to his back and crashing his head into the solid rock surface behind him. Then he wrested the rock from Jacob's hands and raised it high above his head ready to dash it down on his chest in the same way as Jacob had aimed to kill him.

'Don't,' several voices screeched from behind him.

Dalton almost ignored them, every stored-up ounce of anger at Jacob's actions since he'd joined the wagon train threatening to burst out and make him smash Jacob to oblivion.

But he lowered the rock and let it fall to the ground. He turned. Virgil and Loren stood behind him, each having hands on the other, each restraining the other man.

'I'm not like him,' Dalton said. 'I'd never kill out of anything but desperate need.'

'And you've misunderstood him,' Virgil said. He tore himself away from Loren, hurried to Jacob's side, and knelt beside him. With shaking hands, he raised his head. A deep spasm contorted his face.

He withdrew a hand. Thick blood, dark and sticky in the afternoon sun coated the hand, as Jacob lay with his head rocked back, still and sprawled, oblivious to the debate as to his guilt.

Jacob died a few minutes after his fight with Dalton. The fall on to rock had caved in his skull. He didn't regain consciousness.

Now he lay in the shadow of the rocks with his father standing over him in silent guard.

Nobody questioned Dalton's role in his death. He had been saving his own life when Jacob had accidentally hit his head and died. But despite the lack of comment, Dalton reckoned Virgil would think through the incident and it wouldn't be long before a different version of events formed in his mind.

As regarded proving who had killed Marcus Wilcox, Dalton reckoned the truth of that had died with Jacob. The dead man didn't have the stolen money on him, Newell wouldn't dignify his accusations by defending himself, and Eliza confirmed that Jacob had said nothing other than to claim that he was only taking her away out of love.

Newell quickly recovered from his ordeal. With Jacob dead the group decided to return to the wagon train. In a line, they trooped along the top of the ridge.

They rode at a sombre pace. They let Virgil ride up front, leading Jacob's horse with his body draped over its back. Eliza and Newell rode behind him, neither person speaking after Jacob's doomed love for Eliza had ended in the worst possible way. Loren and Dalton brought up the rear, but again, neither man felt inclined to talk.

They hoped to intercept the wagons further along the ridge. Although Dalton accepted that travelling quickly was inappropriate, he still hoped they would be lucky and find them before sundown. A night spent alone with this unhappy group would do nobody any good.

The sun was setting over the peak ahead when he caught the first sight of other people, but there were only two of them and neither person came from the train. They were riding towards them from the canyon, heading from the opposite direction to the way he expected the wagon train to travel.

The group halted and waited for them.

'From the look of that body,' one of the men shouted, 'you got to them first.'

Dalton and Loren exchanged a glance, both men shrugging.

'You seem to know what happened here,' Loren said.

The man nodded, then pointed at Jacob's body.

'We met the wagon train. I'm guessing that's the man who took off with the woman and that's–'

'It was not like that,' Virgil said, swinging his horse around and advancing on the two men.

Both men raised their hands and smiled.

'No offence meant. We didn't come to start no arguments. We heard there was trouble and we came to help. Just sorry we got here too late.'

Virgil turned his harsh glare on Dalton. 'Yeah, we're all sorry somebody else didn't get to Jacob first.'

Virgil continued to glare at Dalton, but Dalton was oblivious to Virgil's taunt. He'd realized who these men were and knew the question that was coming. And even after several days of considering his response to it, he could think of no words that would explain himself to Tucker and Eddy Malone, two people who knew the real John Stanton.

Tucker and Eddy looked at each person in turn, then glanced at each other, and Dalton could almost hear the question coming closer to both men's lips.

'We were hoping to spend some time with our old friend, John Stanton,' Eddy said, at last. 'They told us he was with you. Where's he gone?'

Virgil flinched, then pointed at Dalton. 'He's here.'

Both men snorted, then shook their heads.

'He ain't John Stanton,' they said in unison.

CHAPTER 11

Dalton could say nothing in response to the confirmation of his false identity, so his only option was to run, but he never got the chance.

Unseen by him, Virgil drew his gun and turned it on his back, and Tucker and Eddy joined Virgil in covering him from the front.

In short order, Dalton found himself disarmed and kneeling with his hands on his head and with Tucker Malone standing guard over him.

Newell and Eliza remained quiet and Loren didn't even look at him, but Virgil had no such reticence. He paraded back and forth, extolling ever wilder theories about Dalton's activities and working himself up into believing that a man who had assumed another's identity must have committed all the crimes Dalton had blamed on his son.

Tucker and Eddy broke into Virgil's ranting to ask Dalton the only question that interested them – what had happened to John Stanton?

And when Dalton gave them the answer that he was dead, Virgil pieced together the full circumstances of the incident back at the river that had put Dalton in this position, putting that situation in the worst possible light.

'He's this outlaw, Dalton,' he said to Tucker. 'He feigned his own death. He used your friend to escape from a lawman, then repaid him by killing both men and insinuating himself into my wagon train.'

'It wasn't like that,' Dalton said.

'And how can we believe you when you've lied to us for a week?'

Dalton carefully considered his answer, but didn't get the chance to use it. Tucker Malone loomed over him.

'All I want to hear about is what you did to John Stanton,' he said, aiming his gun at Dalton's head. 'And when you've told me, I'll kill you.'

Dalton ignored the gun and met Tucker's fiery gaze.

'And if you were John Stanton's friend, you'd know he wouldn't have wanted you to act like that.'

Tucker stamped a foot. 'Don't tell me what John would have wanted.'

He threw back his hand ready to slap

202

Dalton's cheek. Dalton flinched away, but the blow never came and he looked up to see that Tucker was now looking over Dalton's shoulder.

Dalton turned to see that Loren had dismounted and stood with an imperious hand raised.

'I knew John Stanton, too,' he said, 'and I'll tell you what he was like.' He paced towards the group to stand beside Dalton. 'He was just like Dalton, loyal, trustworthy, brave beyond reason, and always willing to look for the best in people.'

Tucker and Eddy glanced at each other then lowered their heads, but Virgil sneered.

'You knew John?' he said, intoning each word with heavy accusation.

Loren swung round to face Virgil. 'I did.'

'And yet you've never mentioned that.'

'I didn't, and for the same reason that's on Tucker's mind. I wanted to know what happened to John. If Dalton had killed him, I'd have killed Dalton, but I've spent time with him, seen the kind of man he is, and I know he didn't kill John. I doubted him, but now I'll speak up for him.'

Virgil swung round to look at Eddy and Tucker, but the two men were looking at each other. With brief grimaces and darting eyes, they debated what they should do in the way only people who have spent lots of time together can. They ended their silent discourse with a nod and turned to face Loren.

'You're right,' Eddy said. 'John wouldn't have wanted us taking no revenge on an innocent man.'

Tucker looked at Dalton. 'We'd be obliged if you'd tell us what happened and then we'll be on our way to mourn our friend.'

Loren held his hand out to Dalton, letting him speak first.

Dalton nodded and stood up. He lowered his hands to his side and took a deep breath.

'Like Loren here says, I was—'

'Loren?' Tucker spluttered, swirling round to face Loren. 'You're Loren, Loren Steele?'

'Yeah,' Loren said, his tone resigned and defensive.

'Loren Steele, John Stanton's oldest friend and partner?'

'That's me.'

'The Loren Steele who stole John's wife and destroyed his life?'

Loren firmed his jaw. 'I never aimed for that to happen, but I guess I might have done that.'

Tucker and Eddy rolled their shoulders,

their original belligerent stances replacing their resigned attitude.

'So, you're the man John talked about when we sat up in Blind Man's Canyon, drinking to past miseries.' Tucker snorted. 'And whenever he got down, he'd describe all the things he'd do to you if he ever found you.'

Loren sighed. 'I can't blame him for that.'

'And he ain't here no longer.' Tucker chuckled. 'But we sure as hell can do 'em to you.'

The group rode at a quicker pace than before across the ridge. Dalton and Loren rode together in the centre of the group with Tucker and Eddy's guns trained on their backs.

Despite his son's body on the back of his horse, Virgil was now in the mood to hurry. Eliza and Newell remained quiet, but Virgil made up for their silence by building up his case against Dalton and Loren. He twisted everything that had happened since Dalton had arrived, putting both men at the centre of the settlers' misfortunes.

With Tucker and Eddy adding their own low opinions of Loren, Dalton had no doubt that by the time they reached the wagon train the evidence against them would have reached damning proportions.

'So, you got secrets, too,' Dalton said to Loren when they reached a point where the ridge narrowed and forced the group to ride in twos.

'Yeah,' Loren said. 'But as you've said to me, don't believe everything others say.'

'I don't.' Dalton looked ahead. They only had another minute to talk before the group would bunch up again. 'Why did you really seek him out?'

'In short, she died three years ago, and I got to thinking he should know that and perhaps get a chance to forgive me, or beat me to a pulp.'

'From what you've said about him, I reckon he'd have forgiven you.'

'He would, and the fact he never got the chance meant I had to protect his memory.'

'And you did that when you spoke up for me. Implying I was worthy of John's name meant a lot to me.'

'Yeah, but you've been trying so hard to live up to that name that you've missed one thing.' Loren frowned. 'You weren't the only one trying to be like John.'

After that admission, they returned to silence and the sun was close to disappearing behind the approaching peak when they caught the first sight of the wagon train.

The line of wagons had reached the ridge, then headed down the other side for several hundred yards to rest up in a visible but protected spot.

The sight of the wagons subdued Virgil into silence as he led them down the slope. As usual when sundown approached, everyone was sitting outside in a rough circle within the wagons, a fire in the centre, but nobody so much as acknowledged their arrival.

As Eddy and Tucker so obviously had their guns drawn and a body lay over one horse, this wasn't surprising. Virgil stopped just outside the circle of wagons and dismounted, then signified that the others should follow and spread out around their prisoners. Then they trooped closer.

The circle of upturned faces and eyes bored into the group, but several people darted their gazes around. At first, Dalton thought they were trying to understand what they were seeing, but then he noticed that several people repeatedly looked towards two of the central wagons.

Dalton stopped and swung round to face one of those wagons as a man stepped into view from behind that wagon, a second man emerging from behind the other wagon.

Two crisp shots peeled out. Dalton saw out of the corners of his eyes that Tucker and Eddy hurtled backwards, their chests holed. Even before they'd hit the ground two more shots ensured they wouldn't get up again.

And then the two men paced into the centre of the circle. Although Dalton had never seen either man before, he was sure who they were – the Spitzer brothers, Fritz and Herman.

'You took your time,' Fritz, the elder brother, said. 'We've been waiting for you.'

'Yeah,' Herman, a squat and surly man, said. 'Now give us the money.'

'We don't have it,' Virgil said. 'Jacob didn't steal it.'

'Then that's bad news for you,' Fritz said. 'We've been tracking you up passes and over that canyon for a week and we ain't in the mood to wait. The only reason your people are still alive is because you were bringing the money back. Now, give it to us!'

Fritz glanced at his brother, who turned on his heel, then aimed his gun along the line of sitting people. His grin and frequent licks of his lips as he nudged his aim on to the next person showed that he'd have no compunction about firing and that he was just picking his first target.

Away from the circle, Dalton glanced at Loren, who spread his hands, rueing his unarmed status, then glanced at the bodies of Eddy and Tucker. The loaded guns of both men were lying beside their bodies, but to use them, they'd need a distraction, and soon.

'Which one shall I take out?' Herman asked, glancing at his brother.

'Pick one of the older ones first. Then we'll–'

'Stop this,' Newell shouted, stepping forward. 'Jacob may not have had the money on him, but he did steal it.'

Fritz darted round to aim his gun squarely at Newell.

'Then tell me where it is and you'll get to live.'

Newell stopped ten paces from Fritz, then pointed, his gaze resolute as he looked at Virgil's wagon.

'Search that wagon and you'll find the money.'

Herman and Fritz glanced at each other, then sized up Newell, their suspicious gazes hinting that they reckoned this was a distraction. In response, Dalton and Loren edged short paces towards the guns on the ground. But then Virgil roared with frustration.

'Do not believe that man's lies about my son,' he said. 'Jacob did not steal anything.'

Fritz licked his lips. 'Be quiet. We just want the money.'

Fritz grunted an order to Herman, who hurried into Virgil's wagon.

Again, Dalton shuffled a pace closer to Tucker's body, the gun just five paces away, while keeping his gaze on the other outlaw, waiting for a moment when he was distracted. But as clothes tipped out of the back of the wagon and Herman's annoyed tones rent the air, Fritz's gaze didn't waver from his steady consideration of the circle of people.

Presently, Herman emerged, tearing a jacket in two in his rage, and hurled the pieces to the ground.

'And now,' he roared, stamping his feet and drawing his gun, 'somebody will pay for that.'

'You sure it ain't in there?' Fritz asked, peering at the wagon.

'Sure am.' Herman's annoyed gaze centred on Newell. 'And you've just wasted my time.'

He raised his gun to aim at Newell, who stood tall, even puffing his chest and refusing to cower. Behind him, Dalton used the distraction to slip closer to the gun on the ground, judging that he might be able to reach it before Herman reacted, but Virgil surprised him by raising a hand.

'Before you kill him,' he said, 'you should take the money he was keeping from you.'

'We were trying to do that,' Fritz muttered.

'Then search Henry Boone's wagon. You'll find the money in there.'

'We are not spending the whole night following you people's orders. If we go in there, we'd better find it.'

'You will,' Virgil said, his voice calm. 'I'd stake everything on it.'

'You have,' Fritz muttered with grim assurance, then directed Herman to check out the wagon.

Herman kept his gun on Newell a moment longer then, with an irritated slap of a hand against his thigh, walked to the wagon. He climbed inside, muttering to himself about just what he'd do if this proved to be another piece of misdirection.

From inside Dalton heard Henry utter a strangulated cry, but then a louder screech of delight emerged.

Then Herman leapt down with Henry's

chest held aloft, which he threw to the ground. He kicked away the town sign, pulled out a bag, which he ripped open, thrust a hand inside, then withdrew a bundle of bills.

'That had nothing to do with me,' Newell said, his tone bewildered.

'Don't care,' Fritz said. 'We got what we wanted.'

Newell looked back at Virgil, who stood with his arms folded and a smug grin appearing such as Dalton had seen before on Jacob's face.

'But I care,' Newell said. He fell to his knees, his hands coming up to hold his head. 'I've lost everything. Everyone will reckon I stole it.'

Twenty paces behind Newell, Dalton glanced at the gun to his side, but he was in Fritz's line of sight and judged that he couldn't reach it. To his side, Loren was nearer to the other gun, but, in looking around, he again saw Virgil's grin, an expression no man who had just lost a son should have even if he'd defeated the family he hated.

And that grin gave Dalton an inkling of who had killed Marcus Wilcox and why. He shot a glance at Loren, then set off walking towards the Spitzer brothers. Herman dropped the bag at his feet and swung round to join his brother in turning their guns on him.

'Stop where you are,' Fritz said, 'or die.'

Dalton paced by Newell then halted. 'I just want the bag.'

Herman snorted. 'We're not giving this up.'

'You can keep the money. I just want the bag.'

'What you mean?'

Dalton raised his hands then walked slowly to the pile of discarded belongings from Virgil's wagon. He kept his movements steady as he emptied a sack, then threw it to Herman's feet.

'Use that. It'll be easier to carry the money.'

Herman shrugged, his gaze incredulous, but with his tone guarded, Fritz directed Herman to do as Dalton had suggested.

'Why say that?' he asked, his eyes narrowing.

'And why are you interested? You don't care what happens to us now.'

'I don't, but tell me anyhow.' Fritz smirked. 'Or I take the bag.'

'There's something in the bag,' Dalton

said, pointing.

'Oh?'

'Nothing valuable,' Dalton blurted as Fritz's eyes widened, 'but something that'll prove who stole the money, and we need that information to sort out our problems. After all, you don't want the man who really stole the money to come after you, do you?'

Herman straightened after loading the money into the sack. Fritz grabbed the empty bag, then tore it open to look inside.

'There's something in here that'll prove who killed Marcus Wilcox and stole this money, is there?'

'Sure is,' Dalton said using his most honest voice.

Fritz looked inside, then thrust a hand in and rooted around. His eyes flashed and he chuckled.

'Now, that sure is going to be a surprise to whoever–'

'No!' Virgil shouted, his face reddening as he broke into a run and pounded across the ground towards Fritz.

'Stay back,' Fritz ordered, turning at the hip to face him, but Virgil kept running.

The two outlaws didn't even glance at each other as they both fired, hitting the running man low. Virgil folded over the shots but staggered on, his momentum carrying him forward until he dived to the ground at Fritz's feet, a trailing hand thrusting out for the bag, but catching Fritz's ankle.

And then he rolled to the side, dragging Fritz to his knees.

Dalton broke into a run. He saw Herman swing his gun round to aim at him, but Loren had now reached Eddy's gun. A shot pealed out and tore lead high into his chest, wheeling him to the ground. And then Dalton was on Herman and rolling over his body as he lunged for his gun.

Fritz turned to him on one knee. As Dalton used Herman as a shield, he tore a shot into his own brother's body. Then Dalton slapped the gun on Herman's chest, sighted Fritz and fired. His single shot tore into his left shoulder and knocked him on to his back.

Dalton trained his gun on Herman but the outlaw was still. Then he swung the gun back up to aim at Fritz, who twisted round and stood up, then hunched over, ready to return fire. But the other settlers had reached their own discarded guns and the circle echoed to the sound of repeated gunfire as everyone worked off their frustration by holing the outlaw.

As Fritz's body twitched and writhed to a deadly crescendo of gunfire, Dalton hurried to Virgil's side. He was still breathing, but the outlaws' gunfire had ripped into his belly and Virgil was barely breathing.

Dalton turned away to see Eliza hurry into Henry's wagon, while Newell loitered nearby, perhaps torn between joining his sister and trying to resolve the family feud before Virgil died.

Dalton moved to follow Eliza and check on Henry, but Loren hailed him. He turned to see that Loren had collected the bag and was wandering over to him, peering inside it. Then he tipped it up, but nothing emerged.

'It's empty,' he said, not sounding particularly surprised.

'Sure was,' Dalton said, 'but Virgil thought there might be something in it.'

Loren nodded. 'And he couldn't risk that that something would prove Jacob's guilt.'

'Maybe that is...' Dalton winced. Eliza was emerging from the wagon and she looked at Newell, her mouth framing the other words that Dalton had dreaded hearing since he'd joined these people. 'But we'll have to work that out another time. Henry is dying.'

216

CHAPTER 12

Dalton slipped his hands beneath Henry's limp body and lifted him from his bedding, the old man's weight no greater than that of a child's. His breathing was shallow and his mutterings were unintelligible, but Dalton paced out of the wagon, through the circle of people and away towards Sweet Valley.

Only Eliza and Newell hurried on to join him and they headed to a small outcrop where they could see the landscape ahead. Under the weak rays of the setting sun, the terrain beyond the ridge glowed with a deep redness, the panorama of ridges and canyons stark and uninviting.

'Show me Sweet Valley,' Henry croaked.

Dalton turned Henry round to face the barren terrain, but the old man's eyes remained closed.

'It's beautiful,' he wheezed. 'Make sure my people are happy there.'

'I will.'

'Tell me... Tell me....'

Dalton guessed what he wanted and he

started to describe an idyllic place where they would settle down, but Henry uttered a low sigh, then flopped. Dalton glanced at Eliza, who buried her head against Henry's chest, and Newell rested a hand on his father's shoulder.

They stood there for a while, seeing the redness that had consumed the landscape fade to dull brown. Then they headed back to the wagons.

Loren was waiting a respectful distance from them. As he walked back with them he reported that Virgil had died.

With no family left to state the Wade family's needs, Newell and Eliza agreed that they would find a spot near by to bury Virgil and Jacob so they could watch over them for the rest of their journey. But both agreed that Henry wouldn't rest too close to them.

Fifty yards from the wagons, Dalton passed Henry's body to Newell. Then he and Loren slowed so that Newell and Eliza could lead the way. But when they were out of earshot, Loren confirmed that the family feud would continue after the deaths.

'Your bluff worked,' he said, holding up a letter. 'But it was no bluff. There really was proof in the bag. This had slipped down into the lining.'

'What does it say?'

'Virgil wrote to Marcus Wilcox. He paid him a thousand dollars to poison Henry Boone real slow.'

Dalton winced. 'That doesn't prove he killed Marcus.'

'Perhaps not, but I reckon Marcus wanted more money, or maybe Virgil had to silence him. Either way, he stole back his own money and hid it in Henry's chest when he visited him.' Loren sighed. 'It seems he hated Henry so much, he was prepared to lose his own son.'

'Sounds possible.' Dalton looked back towards Sweet Valley, then at the ridge. 'But that just leaves the question of what we should do now.'

Ahead, Eliza and Newell had reached the wagons and had placed Henry's body in his wagon. While everyone gathered around, Newell collected the town sign and they headed back to them, their heads bowed and their pace slow.

Loren shrugged. 'They're the only ones who know the truth about you, and me for that matter. I guess it's up to them.'

Dalton nodded and waited to face the people, who were now, by virtue of Virgil's death, in charge of this wagon train.

'Father made you promise something,' Eliza said, not meeting Dalton's eye. 'I hated it at the time, but it doesn't seem quite so bad any more...'

Eliza looked at Dalton with an unspoken question in her watering eyes and, just like the first time Henry had mentioned it, the thought didn't sound too worrying.

'Maybe we can talk about it one day,' Dalton said, 'if I stay.'

'I hope you will.' She gulped. 'We need you to lead us.'

'We do,' Newell said, fingering the town sign. 'The last week has proved to me that Father was the man to lead this wagon train and not Virgil. But I'm not the right man either. Every time I had a chance to take control, I let it pass. There's only one man for this job, and that's you.'

Dalton pointed at the terrain beyond the ridge.

'But I have no idea about what's ahead. I can't lead you.'

'Yeah. You got no idea what's ahead, but none of us has.' Newell offered the sign to him. 'But that doesn't matter. A leader doesn't lead because he knows where to go.'

Dalton didn't want to take the sign, but Eliza and Newell nodded in encouragement,

220

and Loren held his hand out, directing him to lead these people on the remainder of their journey.

'You didn't let John Stanton down,' he said. 'He couldn't have done any better than you have.'

Dalton sighed. Ahead lay a place where he could settle down and perhaps find the peaceful life he'd craved. He had promised Henry he would find that place no matter what the cost and no matter if his bluff failed.

And it had cost plenty and his bluff had failed, but he had no doubt that with these people beside him and with good friends like Loren to help him, he would fulfil the promise he'd made to Henry. And, seeing Eliza smile at him for the first time in a while, perhaps he could fulfil the other promise he'd made, too.

'All right,' he said. He took the town sign from Newell and held it aloft. 'Tonight, we bury our dead. Tomorrow, we find Sweet Valley.'

This Large Print Book, for people
who cannot read normal print,
is published under the auspices of

THE ULVERSCROFT FOUNDATION

Nurses' Aids Series

PRACTICAL NURSING

NURSES' AIDS SERIES

Nurses' Aids Series

Practical nursing

ELEVENTH EDITION

REVISED BY
Margaret Clarke
B.Sc., S.R.N., R.N.T., Orthopaedic Nursing Certificate,
Neurosurgical & Neurological Nursing Certificate
*Lecturer in Nursing, Department of Biological Sciences,
University of Surrey; formerly Ward Sister and
Nurse Tutor, St George's Hospital, London*

FOREWORD BY
Dame Muriel Powell
Chief Nursing Officer, Scottish Home and Health
Department, St Andrews House, Edinburgh

BAILLIÈRE TINDALL · LONDON

© 1971 *BAILLIÈRE TINDALL*
7 & 8 Henrietta Street, London WC2 8QE
A division of Crowell Collier and Macmillan Publishers Ltd

First Edition, June 1938
Tenth Edition, January 1965
  Reprinted, April 1968,
  English Language Book Society Edition,
  November 1969
Eleventh Edition, September 1971

Publisher's note
Miss Marjorie Houghton wrote the first nine editions of this book,
and the tenth in collaboration with Miss Mary Whittow.

I SBN 0 7020 0385–9 Limp edition
I SBN 0 7020 0395–6 Case edition

Published in the United States of America by
The Williams & Wilkins Co., Baltimore

Made and printed in Great Britain by
William Clowes & Sons, Limited, London, Beccles and Colchester

Foreword

EACH new edition of *Aids to Practical Nursing* has taken account of current advances in medical practice and the consequential changes in the practice of nursing. This edition goes even further. Miss Clarke, who has undertaken to revise the text, has certainly brought it up-to-date in a technical sense. She has also introduced much new material which will considerably broaden the perspective of students and pupils in their approach to nursing practice.

No one could be better qualified than Miss Clarke to demonstrate the application of scientific principles in the practice of nursing. In clear and simple language she applies the principles involved in such a way as to stimulate the reader to think more deeply about the reasons for doing things. The section on the decision-making aspects of observation will be of interest to teachers of nursing as well as to their enquiring students.

Miss Clarke also writes as a nurse with considerable experience of dealing with every day practical nursing problems. In particular, the chapter on the patient and his reaction to illness reveals both her wide knowledge of nursing and her sensitivity to the needs of patients and their families.

For many members of the nursing profession, including myself, *Aids to Practical Nursing* will always be associated with the name of Marjorie Houghton, a most distinguished nurse whose influence will long be felt in this country and overseas. This latest edition is a worthy successor to previous issues in this remarkable series and one with which, I believe, Miss Houghton herself would have been happy to be associated.

MURIEL POWELL

June 1971

Preface

Aids to Practical Nursing was the textbook I found most useful as a student nurse. Information was easy to locate, and concise, yet important details were there. For this reason, I considered it a great honour when I was asked to carry out a revision of this very popular book.

Whilst retaining those qualities of the book which are so useful to students, both in their day-to-day practical work and in revision for examinations, I have emphasized principles in nursing, in the hope that this will help nurses to be adaptable and thoughtful. I believe it is with individuals who can criticize existing methods and devise new ones, that the future of the nursing profession lies.

Today, the patients of this country are beginning to participate more in determining the kind and quality of care they are given, due to greater knowledge of biology, medicine and nursing, acquired in schools and universities and through the mass media. The concept of the welfare state has caused patients to become clients of the health services; and nurses should be open to the opinions and ideas of their clients. An understanding of the difficulties which our clients face when they are ill, expecially if they are placed in the strange environment of a hospital, should enable nurses to encourage patients to express opinions of the service they receive. I have devoted one whole chapter (Chapter 3) and part of another (Chapter 15) to an outline of some of the reactions of both patients and their relatives, to illness and hospitals.

Since the last edition of this book, developments in medical care have been reflected in the more widespread involvement of nurses in cardiac monitoring and with care of patients on artificial respirators. Some guidance in these techniques has been included in this edition (Chapters 10 and 13).

There is also a new grouping of procedures, together with a

separation of basic nursing from more technical procedures. For example washout procedures are grouped together in Chapter 23, whilst techniques involving slow 'drips' of fluid are discussed in Chapter 21.

New chapters have been introduced, dealing with the care of patients with pyrexia (Chapter 14), the unconscious patient (Chapter 12) and barrier nursing (Chapter 16).

A great deal of previous material on bandaging has been omitted, since the introduction of new ways of fastening dressings has reduced the number of bandages used in hospitals. As aspects of fluid and electrolyte balance are covered in various chapters throughout the book (Chapters 6, 11 and 21), there is no separate chapter on this topic in this edition.

Throughout this book I have referred to the nurse as 'she' and to the patient as 'he' except where the patient is quite obviously a woman, may I explain that this has been done to aid clarity of expression and no discrimination was intended, either against male nurses or female patients.

It is my hope that this book will help nurses in their task of comforting the sick, both mentally and physically, and enable them to nurse and encourage their patients back to physical independence and into full family life.

Thanks and Acknowledgements

To my own students who teach me so much. To Dame Muriel Powell for writing the foreword.

To Dr Geoffrey M. Stephenson, Department of Psychology, University of Nottingham, for reading Chapter 3 in draft form.

To Miss P. McCann and Mrs S. Harrison, Clinical Instructors, St George's Hospital, London, for bringing me up to date with the nursing preparation and care of patients undergoing diagnostic procedures.

To Miss M. Boss, B.SC., Department of Physics, St George's Hospital, London, for discussing with me the use of radio-isotopes in medicine.

To Mrs Mary Summers for her help and kindness during the 6 months she worked with me.

To the publishers who helped and encouraged me. To the audiovisual aids department, University of Surrey, for photographing some disposables and instruments.

To Peter Southgate, Department of Biological Sciences, University of Surrey, for some photographs from which line drawings were prepared.

I gratefully acknowledge permission to reproduce illustrations as follows: Fig. 1 from Camera Talks Ltd; Fig. 3 from *Radiography*, the journal of the Society of Radiographers; Fig. 4 from Baillière, Tindall & Cassell Ltd, *Nursery Nursing: A Handbook of Child Care* by G. E. M. Meering and A. B. Stacey; Fig. 7 from British Cellophane Ltd; Figs 18–25 redrawn from figures supplied by the Chartered Society of Physiotherapy and the Royal Free Hospital; Fig. 26 from Talley Surgical Instruments Ltd; Fig. 28 from Portex Limited; Figs 29, 35, 70 and 71 from Dr N. A. J. Heymer, St Bartholomew's Hospital, London; Figs 49–51 from Vickers Ltd, Medical Group; Fig. 57 from the North East Metropolitan Hospital Board; Fig. 58 adapted from *Emergencies in Medical Practice* by courtesy of E. & S. Livingstone Ltd; Fig. 59 from Avon Medicals Ltd; and Fig. 63 from the *Nursing Times*.

May 1971   MARGARET CLARKE

Contents

1

The historical background of nursing

A STUDY of the historical background of nursing is not only of great interest; it also enables us to understand and appreciate the influence of the past on professional nursing as we know it today. A few of the salient points are briefly outlined in this introductory chapter.

Nursing in Past Ages

Records of the early civilizations show that many of the diseases with which we are familiar are at least as old as history. Ancient India, Egypt, Assyria and Greece gave the physician a place of honour in civil life. Much of the practice of medicine was, however, inextricably mingled with religious practices. In the fourth century B.C. the Greek physician Hippocrates laid the foundation of rational medicine when he stated that disease was due to disordered function of the body, often the result of disobeying the laws of health, and not to the work of evil spirits or the wrath of the gods as was formerly believed. His treatment was based on close clinical observation of symptoms and signs, and his medical notes, clearly but simply written, are still regarded as models.

However, even in Hippocrates' time we find no mention of skilled nursing by specially trained attendants. Treatment was carried out by the physician or his pupil assistants, and the general nursing care of the patient was in the hands of the women of the household or of slaves. Midwives are frequently mentioned in early days, and midwifery was usually a hereditary family profession. The 'man midwife' and the obstetric physician were innovations of the seventeenth century.

The Christian Era

The teachings of Christ that service to the very humblest living creature was service to God, and that it was the duty and privilege of the strong to bear the burdens of the weak, inspired the early Christians to seek out those needing help, and to go beyond the narrow limits of their own homes ministering to the bodily and spiritual needs of the sick and poor. The Order of Deaconesses was formed and, working with the Deacons under the Bishops, became the first organized visiting service. A group of wealthy and influential Roman matrons, friends and followers of St Jerome in the fourth century A.D., also included nursing among their Christian duties, although they did not form an order.

In the mediaeval period, when the Church was the great intellectual and social force in all the countries of Christendom, the religious orders were responsible for the care of all who needed help, whether from sickness, poverty or old age. It is interesting to note that many of the large monasteries (some housed 3000 inmates) had houses both for monks and for nuns, and that the supreme control of the dual establishment was often in the hands of a woman, the Abbess. These women were undoubtedly great figures in their day and age. Their knowledge was wide and their administrative abilities of a very high order.

At the time of the Crusades, in the twelfth century, the military orders were founded. The most powerful and the most famous was the Order of the Knights Hospitallers of St John of Jerusalem. This order had a 'langue' or branch in every country of Christendom. They founded and maintained hospitals first in Jerusalem and later in Rhodes and Malta. The nursing was performed by 'serving brothers', but there was a subsidiary women's order whose members nursed in the hospital at Jerusalem, though not in any other hospital of the Order. In the sixteenth century the Order was suppressed in this country, but was re-established in a different form in the nineteenth century. Now everyone is familiar with at least some of its activities, the St John Ambulance Association and the Voluntary Nursing Corps being the best known.

The Sisters of Charity

In France in the seventeenth century the most important nursing order was that of the Augustinian Sisters. They staffed the largest Paris hospital, the Hôtel-Dieu. These sisters must have been very over-worked. The practice, common at that time, of putting as many as six patients in one bed, made their wards very over-crowded, and in addition to nursing they had to do domestic work, including the washing, which they did in the Seine. Their nursing work was also necessarily limited by the required attention to religious duties, their working day being directed by the priests and not by the physicians. It was not considered suitable that celibate nuns should know much about their patients' bodies or their diseases, so that efficient nursing was hardly possible. The sisters led a life of total self-abnegation and gave loyal and kindly service to the sick, but in those circumstances it was quite impossible that the sick could receive adequate nursing care.

A French priest, Vincent de Paul (afterwards canonized), took an extremely practical interest in the administration of charity both in hospitals and in the homes of the poor, and when visiting the Hôtel-Dieu he was greatly impressed by the need for a more efficient service. With the aid of several influential ladies who had worked with him under the name of 'Dames de Charité' in a voluntary visiting service, he took a house in Paris, and there gathered a group of country girls of good character who were to be trained to work in the Hôtel-Dieu with the Augustinian Sisters. His great helper was a Mlle Le Gras, who became the first Superior of the Sisters of Charity, the nursing community which grew from this small beginning.

St Vincent instructed the sisters that they were to give implicit obedience to the physicians—this was very revolutionary teaching —and also that they must take no vows nor be tied to a cloistered life, but go wherever they were needed. Indeed, it was not long before the sisters were to be found all over the country, nursing in the homes of the people, in hospitals and in homes for the aged and insane, and from 1654 they rendered service on the battlefield in many campaigns. It is noteworthy that St Vincent considered that their general as well as their professional education was important, and wished the sisters to have instruction in reading, writing and arithmetic.

The Dark Ages of English Nursing

From the disestablishment of the monastic orders by Henry VIII until the reforms of the nineteenth century, England had no nursing orders comparable with the Augustinian Sisters or the Sisters of Charity. The existing charitable foundations had to staff their institutions with such women as they were able to hire, and the status of nurses was hardly as good as that of a domestic servant in a good-class house. In the private house the patient was nursed by the women of the household or by such 'professional nurses' as were available, and there is no doubt that the Dickens' characters Sairey Gamp and Betsey Prig, although caricatures, are representative specimens of that type. The public conscience awakened slowly, stirred by the pioneers and progressive leaders in all branches of science and the professions. The more advanced physicians advocated the training of educated women for real nursing service; the religious bodies, especially the Society of Friends, felt that the appalling social conditions so largely due to ignorance and neglect must be remedied. The latter half of the nineteenth century also saw great advances in medicine, surgery and all scientific knowledge.

Nursing Reforms of the Pre-Nightingale Period

The examples of the communities of the Sisters of Charity in France and the Deaconess Institute at Kaiserswerth near Düsseldorf in Germany inspired the foundation of the many communities in this country in the middle of the nineteenth century. The Kaiserswerth Institute was a new venture that was fast proving itself eminently successful. A German pastor and his wife, Theodore and Frederica Fliedner, had started a small home for discharged women prisoners, and had shortly afterwards added a hospital to their activities. Here they trained a succession of young women of good character and upbringing to be deaconesses. Their duties included nursing in hospital and in the home, home management and the care of young children, and religious visiting. They received practical instruction from the pastor's wife, theoretical instruction in their professional duties from the physicians, and ethical lectures from the pastor. It was an attempt to give an organized training; and though Florence Nightingale, who received practical hospital training at the Institute, clearly saw that the nursing and hygiene could be improved, she was greatly impressed by the moral tone.

Mrs Elizabeth Fry, of the Society of Friends, knew the Fliedners and their work, and one of her many activities was to found the

Protestant Nursing Sisters in 1840. The Park Village Community in north-west London was the first order under the Church of England, but their work was that of visiting rather than nursing. Miss Sellon in Devonport was the head of a band of Sisters of Mercy who gained most of their nursing experience in all too frequent epidemics. Some of these sisters accompanied Miss Nightingale to the Crimea and were often referred to by her as the 'Sellonites'.

In 1845 St John's House was started as a training school for nurses under religious direction. The head of the community was a priest of the Anglican Church. The nurses went to King's College Hospital for practical experience and also received instruction from the doctors at the hospital. Later this order took over the entire nursing in that hospital until a lay training school was established in 1885. The St John Sisters also nursed in the Metropolitan and Charing Cross Hospitals.

The sisters of another Church community, that of All Saints, nursed in the wards of University College Hospital for more than twenty years.

The Nightingale Era

When Miss Nightingale was asked by the Secretary at War, Sidney Herbert, to take a band of nurses out to the Crimea to give the same care to our soldiers that the Sisters of Charity were already giving to the French, the great opportunities of a life of preparation for such a task had come.

This woman of wide education and high social position had from her youth been imbued with the idea that the care and comfort of the sick, and the promotion of health in the family, was work for women of character and education. In spite of home opposition she managed to see all that there was to see of training on the Continent; she was, however, to set standards of practical nursing and hospital administration far in advance of any that she found. At the time of the Crimean War Miss Nightingale was in charge of a small hospital for gentlewomen in Chandos Street.

Her first difficulty when she accepted the task of organizing a nursing service for the army in the Crimea was to find a sufficient number of experienced nurses of reliable character, and to refuse the numerous offers from the totally untrained and unfitted.

Florence Nightingale saw that in many quarters this innovation of women in the army hospitals would not meet with favour, and she was most anxious not to take the type of woman who would make the work yet more difficult.

When she arrived in Scutari she found a lack of all provision for the care and comfort of the sick and wounded, and an indifference to this dreadful state of affairs that aroused her to a fury of organization and unsparing work. Conditions were as difficult as they could possibly be, red tape obstructed her on all sides, the army doctors resented the presence of women and, sad to record, her nurses did not all prove suitable, some drank, some were unable to stand the dreadful conditions, others found her a hard supervisor and were continually bickering. Certainly Miss Nightingale spared none, herself least of any.

The soldiers looked upon her as an angel, officialdom regarded her in quite another light, but the public made her their national heroine, and when she returned, broken in health, a grateful country presented her with a large sum of money (£9000 of which had been subscribed by private soldiers). With this money she founded the Nightingale Training School at St Thomas's Hospital. The pupils in this school were 'trained to train', so that they could in their turn fill important nursing posts throughout the country; and this was only one of the activities of a woman who was almost a continual invalid for the rest of her life, but it was one to which she gave much personal attention.

In addition to laying the firm foundations of the modern system of nursing training, this one woman was responsible for the complete reorganization of civil and military hospitals, and for many reforms improving the sanitation and hygiene of the army, particularly in India.

Professional Organization

The increasing demand for the 'Nightingale Nurses' and the opening up of this new profession to educated women meant, of course, that the profession increased rapidly in numbers, and the question of organization and registration on the lines already instituted for the medical profession soon arose. Miss Nightingale herself was opposed to state registration. She always regarded nursing as a vocation, not as a profession, but it is strange that this far-sighted woman could not see the necessity for protecting both the public and the nurses from exploitation by those who were untrained or partly trained.

There is no doubt that the opposition of the most influential person in the nursing world must have been a great factor in delaying state registration for so many years.

The first organized body of trained nurses was that formed by Mrs Bedford Fenwick in 1887 and known as the British Nurses' Association. Mrs Bedford Fenwick, before she married Dr Bedford Fenwick, was Miss Gordan Manson, Matron of St Bartholomew's Hospital. The British Nurses' Association was incorporated by Royal Charter and became the Royal British Nurses' Association. With much opposition from within the profession and from without, efforts were made to get a Nurses' Registration Bill through Parliament, but without success. The first Registration Act was passed in 1901, not in England, but in New Zealand.

In 1894 the Matrons' Council of Great Britain and Ireland was formed. In 1898 the council wholeheartedly accepted Mrs Bedford Fenwick's proposals for an International Council of Nurses. The object was to admit to membership all national nursing groups which had developed, or were trying to develop, professional self-government and a settled professional status. The International Council is mainly concerned with organizing international interchange of nurses, promoting the advance of nursing service and nursing education and the economic and social welfare of nurses throughout the world. It has links with a number of international organizations; including the World Health Organization.

During the long period from 1887 until after the First World War the struggle for registration in England dragged on. In 1916 the College of Nursing was founded by leaders of the nursing profession and by other influential persons impressed with the need for greater professional organization. A draft scheme for the State Registration Act was drawn up. With amendments to this and to the original Bill presented by the Royal British Nurses' Association, a New Bill was sponsored by the Minister of Health, and became in 1919 the Nurses' Registration Act.

The College of Nursing was granted a Royal Charter in 1929; it is now the Royal College of Nursing with headquarters in Cavendish Square, London, and branches throughout England and Wales. A Scottish Board in Edinburgh and a Northern Ireland

Committee in Belfast are local headquarters for the Scottish and Northern Ireland Branches. It is the largest organization of Registered Nurses in this country and its activities are many. The professional association department of the College is chiefly concerned with forming and implementing professional policies and giving help where required to the individual nurse. The educational side of the activities of the College covers a wide field in preparing nurses for posts in hospitals and in the fields of public health and occupational health, including preparation for teaching and administration in all these areas.

Until recently the United Kingdom organization in membership with the International Council of Nurses has been the National Council of Nurses of Great Britain and Northern Ireland, which was a federation of professional associations, nurses' leagues and fellowships. In 1962 agreement was reached between the National Council and the Royal College of Nursing that the two bodies should amalgamate to form one united organization which would in future represent British nursing internationally under the name of the 'Royal College of Nursing and National Council of Nurses of the United Kingdom'. Membership of the new organization is on an individual basis and this national body is therefore no longer a federation of associations and leagues and it should be noted that all registered nurses, whether on the General or a Special Part of the Registers maintained by the Nursing Councils of the United Kingdom, are eligible to apply for membership of the Royal College of Nursing and National Council of Nurses.

The State and Nursing

As has already been stated the first Nurses' Registration Act was placed on the Statute Book in 1919. This Act established the General Nursing Council for England and Wales as the statutory body responsible for forming and maintaining the Register of Nurses. Similar Acts established Nursing Councils with the same functions in Scotland and Ireland. The Council also has the duty of laying down conditions for the approval of hospitals as training schools for nurses, inspection of conduct of hospitals so approved and examinations for admission to the Register. Separate parts of the Register were set up for general trained nurses and for nurses trained in the care of sick children, fever patients and patients suffering from mental illness and mental deficiency. Originally there was a separate part of the Register for general trained male nurses; but subsequently this part was amalgamated with the part of the Register for general trained female nurses.

No further nursing legislation was enacted until 1943, when, under the Nurses Act, 1943, the Council was charged with the duty of forming and maintaining a Roll of Assistant Nurses, inspecting and approving hospitals where such training could be undertaken, and conducting examinations for admission to the Roll. The type of examination which the Council considered appropriate for this type of training is mainly concerned with the candidates' practical nursing ability and is known as the 'assessment'. Under the 1943 Act the right to use the title of 'nurse' was, with a few exceptions approved by the Minister of Health, limited to registered nurses, enrolled assistant nurses and students or pupil nurses undergoing training for admission to the Register or Roll. This Act also gave the Council the responsibility of registering as registered nurse tutors those nurses who are qualified in teaching in schools of nursing.

In 1949 further nursing legislation was enacted, and this Act was designed primarily to 'improve the training of nurses for the sick'. The main provisions of the Act as it affects nursing training were to give further powers to the General Nursing Council; to enlarge the representation on the Council and to set up in each of the Regional Hospital Areas Area Nurse Training Committees which are concerned with regional matters relating to the training of nurses. One provision implemented, at least partially, a recommendation of both the Athlone and the Horder Committees, namely that finance required for the education and training of nurses should be separated from the expenditure required for the maintenance of the hospital services. In 1957 a further Act consolidated the previous three Nursing Acts of 1919, 1943 and 1949. A private member's Bill, introduced into Parliament by Dame Irene Ward in 1960, had as its main objective the removal of the word 'assistant' from the title of the enrolled nurse. This Bill was supported by both parties in the House of Commons and was entered on the Statute Book in March 1961. It is a measure of the value of the work of the enrolled nurse and the recognition of her place in the nursing profession that this measure had the whole-hearted support of the majority of registered nurses.

A recent development in nurse training has been the setting up of integrated and experimental courses of nurse education. One pattern of these new courses is the 'two plus one' training for state registration, in which the first two years of training consists of carefully supervised clinical nursing experience with a related lecture course. The state registration examination is taken at the end of these two years. The third year is spent practising as a senior nurse in the ward team, before the student is placed on the register of general nurses.

Another type of course is the integrated course in which general nurse training, district nurse training, and health visitor training are combined in a four-year course. A course of this kind at Manchester University has become the first course in this country, on the successful completion of which the student is awarded a degree in nursing. A degree course with nursing as the major subject has been offered at Edinburgh University for some years.

Several universities now offer courses in which an honours degree may be combined with nurse training, whilst several hospitals offer a two-year nurse training course leading to state registration for university graduates.

It should be noted that the duties and responsibilities of the General Nursing Council are clearly defined and limited by Act of Parliament and by Statutory Rules approved by the Minister of Health.

In 1937 an Inter-Departmental Committee on Nursing Services was set up by the Minister of Health and the President of the Board (now the Ministry) of Education. An interim report was published in 1939 and contained many valuable recommendations for the improvement of recruitment to the profession, and of conditions within the profession, such as the setting up of a Recruitment Centre and the establishment of national scales of salaries for nurses. The outbreak of the Second World War interrupted the work of this committee, but in 1941 the Minister of Health set up a committee under the chairmanship of Lord Rushcliffe to draw up agreed scales of salaries and emoluments for State Registered Nurses employed in England and Wales, and for student nurses in hospitals approved as training schools by the General Nursing Council for England and Wales. The terms of reference were later widened to include nurses in the Public Health field, nurses trained in, or training for, tuberculosis nursing, assistant nurses and nurses employed in mental hospitals. A similar committee was appointed in Scotland. The recommendations of these committees were accepted by the Government and the extra cost involved was borne by the Treasury. The principle of nationally negotiated salaries and conditions of service for nurses in the hospitals and health services is now carried on by the Functional Whitley Council for Nurses and Midwives composed jointly of a Management Side and a Staff Side.

The implementation of the National Health Service Act on 5 July 1948, brought all hospitals, with a few exceptions, under State ownership. Under this Act every man, woman and child in the country is entitled to medical attention and hospital treatment as and when required. The great majority of the population between the ages of 15 and 65 years are either self-employed or working for an employer and therefore pay weekly social insurance contributions. Although only a part of the total sum collected from this source is allocated to the Health Service, medical and nursing treatment is available without charge to the individual. The full cost of the National Health Service represents a very considerable proportion of the total national income, but no one would argue against its importance for the nation and the individual. We have accepted this financial burden as right and necessary both as a means of alleviating suffering and promoting a standard of health which is vital for the future well-being of the nation. It is, however, the duty of all who participate in this work not only to endeavour to foster and maintain high standards of service but also to accept responsibility for ensuring that the nation's money is expended to the best advantage.

It is possible that in the future the National Health Service will place a greater emphasis on a fully coordinated service with preventive medicine playing an increasingly important role.

Since the inauguration of the National Health Service hospitals, general practitioner services and local health services have been administered separately from one another.

In a recent report on the National Health Service (Green Paper: *The Future Structure of the National Health Service*, 1970) it is proposed that Area Health Authorities should administer hospital and specialist services, family practitioner, ambulance, community health and nursing service, family planning clinics and the school health service, thus unifying the three separate aspects of the National Health Service.

A change in the training requirements of the General Nursing Council for England and Wales in the 1969 syllabus for state registration reflects the increasing importance of community health services. In this syllabus of training, students may be seconded to local authorities for 3 months for experience in district nursing and health clinics.

Mental Health

The treatment and care of persons suffering from mental illness or mental deficiency was, even at the beginning of the century, largely limited to custodial care which had as its object preventing the patient from harming himself or other people. The admission of patients and the administration of mental institutions were largely dictated by Acts of Parliament, the Lunacy and Mental Treatment Acts of 1890 to 1930 and the Mental Deficiency Acts of 1913 to 1938. Towards the end of the last century the Royal Medico-Psychological Association, a professional association of doctors primarily concerned with, and interested in, the treatment of mental illness and mental deficiency, initiated a course of training and an examination for men and women working in mental hospitals and mental deficiency hospitals and at that time referred to as 'attendants'. This step marks the beginning of true professional nursing in these fields. Since then great advances have been made not only in the medical treatment but also in the nursing care of the mentally disordered. As interest in and knowledge of mental illness increased so the old conditions in the asylums, with their padded cells, strait-jackets and locked doors, have given way to the development of the modern conception of the mental hospital as a 'therapeutic community'. The psychological, physical and social methods used in the treatment of mental patients now makes this a field of service for the nurse where kindness, intelligent understanding, sympathy and an ability to form good personal relationships are of outstanding importance.

The Mental Health Act, 1959, which has been implemented in stages since October 1959, provides for the treatment of patients suffering from mental disorders on the same basis as that of patients suffering from any type of physical illness. Admission to hospital in the case of mental illness or mental subnormality is now 'informal', that is to say the legal requirement that the patient should first be certified as being 'of unsound mind' no longer operates, although there is provision for compulsory detention in certain circumstances where this is in the interests of the patient and the public. The Act also places responsibilities on local authorities to provide for the care of the mentally sick and subnormal in the community.

Many patients are now treated in day hospitals, returning to their families in the evening, thus retaining their links with home, whilst others continue their normal occupations during the day, but go to hostels at night where they can receive supportive therapy.

Although special parts of the Register for nurses trained in mental and mental deficiency (now called mental subnormality) nursing were set up when the Register of Nurses was established, the Royal Medico-Psychological Association continued to be a recognized body concerned with the training and examination of nurses in this field. However, in 1947 the Association agreed that they would cease to carry out this function and that the General Nursing Council should be the sole body concerned with the training and examinations for the certificates of mental and mental deficiency nursing. When this change took place it was also agreed that nurses who had trained under the auspices of the Association and held the Association's certificate would be entitled to apply to be registered with the General Nursing Council without undergoing further training or examinations.

2

The hospital community

The Hospital and the Community

In Chapter 1 we tried to indicate in outline how the nursing profession has grown through the ages, sometimes making great strides forward and at other times apparently lost in an age of general indifference to the welfare of the 'common man'. Just as the progress of nursing has reflected the social outlook of a particular age or century, so also have the hospitals and the health and welfare services.

Student nurses at the time of entry to the training school have to adjust themselves to new surroundings and may be somewhat bewildered by the many aspects of hospital life. The student may also have preconceived ideas about the hospital and about nursing, which bear little resemblance to reality. It may be worth while, therefore, to consider very briefly the function of the hospital in the community at the present time.

First we think of the day-to-day function of caring for the sick who lie in the beds in the wards or enter the casualty or out-patient departments. The hospital has to carry on its work day and night. There can be no moment in the twenty-four hours when the sick are not in need of medical attention and nursing care. This affects not only the medical and nursing staffs but also the ancillary staff and lay workers; porters, orderlies and domestic workers must be available for a 24-hr service, and other departments ancillary to medicine, such as dispensaries, laboratories, X-ray and physiotherapy departments, though not always providing a 24-hr service, have to cover a long span of hours and often to work at week-ends. These examples will serve to show that the organization of a hospital is, of necessity, complex and makes demands upon its personnel that are not equalled in many other spheres.

We must also consider the educational function of the hospital. In many of our larger hospitals, in addition to the training of nurses, the professional education of doctors, radiographers, physiotherapists, midwives and social workers is carried out. Many hospitals take part in the postgraduate training of medical specialists, although not forming part of an undergraduate medical school. Whatever the part played by the individual hospital in professional education we should not forget the role of the hospitals as health education centres. The aim of treatment is not only to cure or arrest disease but to restore the patient as far as possible to full activity. The motivation of the patient to get well is needed and he must be kept fully informed and instructed so that he can play his part in his own recovery and subsequent welfare.

A third function of the hospital is as an institution for clinical research. Research begins in the laboratory, but discoveries have to be put to the test if they are to have any practical use. In the last century Joseph Lister had theories about safe surgery which would abolish 'hospital gangrene' and septicaemia, from which so many patients died in hospital in spite of surgical skill. If, in the face of much opposition and scepticism, he had not had the courage to put his theories into practice 'antiseptic surgery' which opened the door to the great surgical advances of the twentieth century, would have been delayed for many years. From the days of Lister's triumphant vindication of his methods, research workers and clinical practitioners have striven to improve on this first great advance in the practice of safe surgery, until in this decade we have seen the discovery of chemical substances which can control sepsis to a degree undreamt of at the beginning of the century. Present-day methods of surgery are a great advance upon the cruder methods of antiseptic surgery, but Lister's work was the starting point. There are many examples which could be quoted to show that the close collaboration between the laboratory worker and the clinical worker in mitigating the sufferings of mankind is truly a part of the hospital service. The nurse is a part of the clinical research team, a team in which habits of accurate recording, observation and meticulous attention to detail are the first essentials.

A promising development is the recent growth of research into all aspects of nursing, including the quality of nursing care, being undertaken by nurses. A profession should both undertake research into its own practices, and educate its members about that research, so that current practice is based on the results of research. Nursing will then be based on accurate and controlled observation, not opinion.

The Hospital and the Individual Patient

Florence Nightingale once said that the hospital should 'do the sick no harm'. This somewhat sobering statement is well worth careful consideration. Constant vigilance is needed in all medical and nursing procedures in order that these may be carried out with the highest possible degree of competence. A hospital also needs to lay down and to demand strict observance of regulations designed to protect the patient, as for example in the storage, checking and administration of dangerous drugs, and in the measures necessary to prevent cross-infection in hospital wards. There are also less tangible dangers from which we have to guard the patient to the very utmost of our ability. The separation of a young child from his mother when admitted to a hospital ward, at a time when security and a link with familiar surroundings are most needed, is a source of harm to the child which may have lasting effects. Most hospitals allow the mother to be with her sick child as much as possible and in some instances to help with the care of the child.

Older patients too may have many difficulties in adjusting them-selves to the strange and even alarming hospital surroundings and the ward routine. It is most important that hospital staff should understand the difficulties involved, and help as much as possible. Each patient should be treated as a unique individual and helped to maintain his individuality and independence. Links with home should be encouraged, and relatives must be given the fullest information, so that they may feel they are partners in the process of helping the patient to recover.

The Hospital and the Community Services

Although the nurse training school is based on a hospital or group of hospitals, neither nursing nor medical treatment are, of course, confined within the hospital walls. The general medical practi-tioner, the Local Health Authorities and the hospital must understand each other's role and co-operate in the promotion of health and the treatment of ill-health. The student nurse will have opportunities throughout her training of learning about the care of patients in their own homes, the home nursing and midwifery services, their relationship with the general medical practitioners in the locality, the work of the public health nurse in family health care and her part in preventive medicine, which is largely the responsibility of the Medical Officer of Health and his staff. The student will also hear about the scope and value of medico-social work, probably from the hospital almoner, who can help the patient in many ways while he is in hospital and when he is discharged. It may be that the family is in need of financial help or that the patient will have to change his occupation on account of his illness, and so contact will be made with his employers or with the Resettlement Officer.

To meet fully the needs of the patient in hospital requires an understanding of his social, economic and family background; restoring the patient to an active life often necessitates the use of the resources of health, social and welfare agencies.

Nursing Ethics

Ethics means a code of moral behaviour, and under the term 'Ethics of Nursing' are included the values and rules of behaviour relating especially to nursing. The word 'nursing' means 'nourishing'; therefore it has come to mean tending and helping all who need it, especially the sick. The object in training nurses is to provide an adequate service to tend the sick, and to help in the preservation and promotion of the health of the community in general.

Those who enter this profession must have a real desire to do the work, and must be physically healthy.

Many qualities of personality must be developed during the period of training. Kindliness, sympathy and respect for each individual patient, regardless of age, sex, race or social class, are essential qualities for the successful care of the sick person and his anxious relatives, although the nurse must learn to be firm when necessary for the patient's good.

A nurse must have personal integrity, so that she can respect a patient's confidence about his private affairs. If she is told something that ought to be passed on to sister or the doctor, because it gives new light on the patient's illness or home situation, she should ask the patient's permission to pass it on. Better still, would be to persuade the patient to talk to sister or doctor himself, since information may be distorted in being passed through a second person. A nurse should be very careful to whom she reveals details about the patient's illness or condition. She should seek the patient's permission before giving information away to, say, employers or friends, however much kindly interest these people show.

Importance is rightly placed on complete reliability in carrying out instructions, and punctuality in giving drugs and recording observations. A nurse should be conscientious, so that nursing procedures are carried out properly, even though no one is watching and time is short. A short cut in a sterile procedure may result in cross-infection. Forgetting to remove a patient from a commode or bedpan may lead to the formation of a bed sore. Patients are unlikely to complain about being forgotten, since most feel a great deal of sympathy with overworked nurses.

The important thing is to maintain an ideal of service to the patient, so that what is best for the patient is foremost at all times. It is also important, however, to have sufficient humility to realize that a nurse does not automatically, and always, know what is best for the patient. Patients should be given a part to play in decisions about their welfare. This not only maintains their self-respect, but also encourages their independence, ready for a return to normal life.

Apart from the qualities already mentioned, a nurse needs to develop emotional maturity, and during the early days of her training she needs help and support from trained members of staff, so that she may gain this healthily.

Ethical Problems

There are many episodes which occur in a hospital ward which can upset a nurse emotionally, and a young student needs to be able to discuss these episodes with some mature persons whom she trusts. Then she can begin to understand her own emotional reactions and come to terms with them; neither suppressing them on the one hand, nor allowing them to upset her so much that she gives up her training on the other.

Episodes which may upset a student are, of course, very difficult to specify since each student is an individual, and will be affected by different circumstances from another individual.

The death of a patient invariably upsets the nurses in the ward concerned. A young student may be apprehensive before her very first contact with death and worry about how she will react. The topic should be discussed before the situation arises, so at least she will know what are the right things to do, reducing her anxiety in case she should do the wrong thing in a new situation. When a patient has died, she should be able to discuss her own reactions to the event. Most people are upset in this situation, and she should be made to realize that this is a normal reaction and not feel guilty that she is 'soft' or 'silly'.

Death of a young patient may be particularly upsetting, and may even bring uncertainties about her own religious faith. Being able to talk about the situation with a clergyman may help her.

News that a patient has an incurable condition can have a similar effect on the nursing staff. Here it is important to let the young student know that these things upset even mature members of staff. They learn, however, to forget their own upset, and put the well-being of the patient or relatives first, and by being helpful to others, tempered with an understanding of how they feel, can come to terms with their own emotions.

In addition, there are problems of conscience which arise, and which each nurse must resolve for herself, in her own way, in the light of her own philosophical beliefs, although talking them over with some trusted person may help.

Obvious problems of conscience are ones thrown up by recent developments in social reform and medicine.

Abortion. Should the nurse participate in the operation of abortion, if she herself strongly disapproves of abortion? If she does disapprove, should this be revealed in her attitude if she nurses a patient who has had an abortion? If she approves of abortion and sees a woman who is unfairly (as she judges) refused one, what should she do if she knows of another doctor who regards abortion more favourably?

Problems of resuscitation. Nowadays it is possible to maintain the heart beat and the exchange of respiratory gases by artificial measures. Sometimes a nurse may see a patient resuscitated whom she knows will only suffer a great deal if he survives. Although the decision is not hers, the situation may cause great stress to someone asked to nurse the patient.

The problems of abortion, resuscitation and transplant surgery have been well publicized in both the national and nursing press. They are not primarily nursing responsibilities, and most individuals are likely to have made up their minds on these issues in accordance with their own conscience.

However, the nurse may come up against other problems of conscience in her day to day work on the ward, and these are more likely to concern her.

For instance, what if she believes a patient should be given full information about his diagnosis and prognosis, and it is being withheld? She can ease her conflict, because the responsibility for this decision is a medical one. But what about this same situation when she is asked point blank by the patient if he is dying, and she knows he is, but the doctor's policy is not to reveal the information to the patient. Should she tell a direct lie? Possible solutions to this problem are suggested in Chapter 15 (p. 198). But although the nurse may cope admirably with the situation, it can still cause some conflict. Or what if she is asked the direct question by a patient, and by her flustered manner and evasiveness leads him to suspect the truth, which is being withheld? Again she will need to be reassured about the whole situation.

The nursing profession has traditionally emphasized that nurses should obey instantly the orders of medical staff and more senior nurses. What if these individuals tell her to do something which she believes is not in the best interests of the patient. Should she argue, or should she obey? This may be something seemingly rather trivial, like being told to go to coffee when a patient has just vomited and needs attention. Nonetheless it can cause conflict for a student, since the ideal of service to the patient, and that of respecting the judgement of her seniors, are now incompatible. What if senior nurses treat patients in a way of which she doesn't approve, and she sees all the other students in the ward following their example? For instance, if an elderly patient is being called by his Christian name, or 'Dad', without his consent or approval, should she follow the example set? Should she merely maintain her own standards, or should she attempt to change the attitude of other members of staff?

What if a patient is being positively mistreated or neglected? Do her loyalties lie with her colleagues, or should she complain and risk being victimized?

Away from the ward situations, the answers to these problems seem very clear, but issues become very much less clear in the ward situations, where a ward sister or staff nurse is much respected, and has a great deal of knowledge and experience. The individual may feel that there must be some explanation of their conduct which she just doesn't know. There should be someone to whom she can turn, to discuss these problems, so that she can see them objectively and then take action as dictated by her own conscience. All nurses, of course, do have a duty to complain if a patient is being mistreated, because a nurse's first duty is to her patient.

Subtle situations may be difficult to judge; when a patient is not being neglected but is just not being treated with the full respect due to a fellow human being, but here again, the first duty of any nurse is to 'nourish' the sick, and this surely includes the patient's mind and spirit, as well as his body.

3

The patient and his reaction to illness

PSYCHOLOGICAL EFFECTS OF ADMISSION TO HOSPITAL

What does it mean to an individual to be admitted to hospital? What emotions will he experience? How does he see the hospital?

People are admitted to hospital because this is the only place where the necessary treatment can be obtained. The patient, then, will be thankful and relieved that something is to be done to help him. At the same time, hospital is associated with pain and suffering, so that fear of the treatment and its outcome will be experienced. If this is the first time he has been admitted to the hospital, fear of the unknown will also be present. Thus, to the patient, the hospital presents both pleasant and unpleasant aspects which elicit behaviour of approach on the one hand, with the desire to get well, and avoidance on the other hand, with the desire to avoid pain, discomfort and uncertainty. This is a typical conflict situation, but one in which the approach or positive aspects invariably win out over the avoidance or negative aspects, and the patient duly presents himself at the hospital for admission.

The Hospital as the Patient Sees It

The Hospital	
Pleasant or positive aspects	*Unpleasant or negative aspects*
Treatment	Suffering
Getting well	Pain
	Unknown situation

Anxiety and Fear

However the knowledge that the hospital will help the patient to get well will not stop him from experiencing anxiety and fear. These emotions are responses to the unknown, or to situations which are anticipated as being unpleasant.

There are two reasons why a patient may experience these emotions on admission to hospital.

Fear based on imagination. One of these is because man is able to use his imagination to predict what may happen in the future. In so doing he may well imagine happenings much worse than the reality, and so suffer unnecessary worry. The best way to prevent this source of anxiety is to give the patient accurate and truthful information about what will happen to him, and his diagnosis. It is no good pretending that things will be better than they actually are in reality, as this will lead him to distrust what is said, and to rely more upon his own predictions than those of the staff.

Fear based on reality. Not all of a patient's worries are a result of imagination, however. There are plenty of factors actually present within the situation to provoke anxiety.

Fear that the treatment may not be successful may be uppermost in the patient's mind; he may fear death, permanent disability or a lengthy convalescence. He may be afraid that he will be unfit to perform his usual job and must look for another, perhaps at a lower salary. He may be anxious in case he is discharged from hospital without there being any improvement in his condition.

To many people, *pain* is an inevitable part of treatment and, indeed, it is doubtful if anyone can get through a stay in hospital without suffering some pain or discomfort, however slight. For instance, injections cause discomfort, although nurses invariably reassure patients that 'it won't hurt'. If a patient is admitted to hospital suffering pain from his illness, he may be apprehensive that he will not be able to get drugs when he needs them, as he no longer has control over their administration. Since there are few single bedded wards in our hospitals, pain must be suffered in public for the most part, and a patient may be afraid of making a fuss if he should be subjected to discomfort; this in turn, by increasing the tension in his muscles, may actually increase the discomfort he experiences. There are individual differences in the amount of pain which can be tolerated, some individuals' tolerance being very low, whilst others can withstand much higher levels. There will also be differences between patients in their readiness to complain of pain. Some will complain at what to them is a relatively minor pain, whilst others will bear quite severe pain without complaint. This may depend partly upon their prior expectations; to some, pain is an inevitable accompaniment of illness and therefore to be borne stoically. The patient's facial expression may show that he is suffering pain, even though he is reluctant to complain. Careful observation by the nurse, accompanied by enquiry, will ensure that any pain is promptly dealt with.

Worry about Relatives and Friends

Most people have responsibilities and duties to others, which they will be unable to fulfil whilst in hospital. A husband and father may be worried about his family and their financial support whilst he is away. This is more likely to be a problem to working class than professional men, since the conditions of employment of the latter are usually better. If he has a large family he may worry that his wife will be unable to cope while he is away, or she may have problems of discipline with the children. A wife will worry about the physical welfare of her family; who will cook, wash and clean the house for them? Bachelors or single women may have parents dependent upon them for financial or physical help. There may be anxieties associated with an individual's job. He may be worried that it will not be carried out properly in his absence, or he might fear that if he is away too long he may lose business if he is self-employed, or his job if he is not. If he is uncertain of the affection of his wife or girl friend, he may worry that she will desert him whilst he is incapacitated in hospital, and thus unable to give her the attention he would like to give.

Fear of the Hospital as a New Situation

Going into hospital for the first time will arouse many anxieties about the correct way to behave in an entirely new situation, whilst an 'old hand' though knowing the formal rules of behaviour will still be placed in the position of having to join and get to know a new group of people. The social structure of a hospital can be very confusing for one not used to it, with its many different hierarchies of staff: the doctors, nurses, administrative staff, laboratory and ancillary staff. Other patients in the ward can make a great deal of impact on a new arrival, particularly those whose beds are nearby.

The lack of privacy in a hospital ward can cause real distress to some people and, although bed curtains are the rule, these give no privacy as regards sound, and neither do they allow warning when someone is about to enter the bed space. Inhibited patients may be denied the emotional relief which weeping can bring, since this cannot be private. Lack of privacy when relatives and friends are visiting can also be a source of embarrassment and make for tensions in a relationship.

Possible Reactions to Anxiety, Fear and Conflict

People are interesting because each one is unique, and whilst most people have similar basic needs and emotions, the way in which these manifest themselves are infinitely varied. Patients are, first and foremost, people, and each is likely to react differently to the anxieties, fears, and conflicts occasioned by being ill. However, there are a number of fairly common ways of reacting to stress situations.

Denial. One effect of coming into hospital, although fearing it, may be *denial* of fear. It is a seemingly illogical action to bring one-self into a situation which causes fear. One way of justifying the action and making it seem logical is to forget or deny the fear provoking aspects and to concentrate upon the pleasant aspects of the hospital. This mechanism of denial may not be consciously recognized by the individual. The patient who reacts in this way requires information to allay fear as much as any other patient, since denial of fear involves its suppression, not its abolition, and this defence mechanism may not survive long in the face of the reality of hospital life.

Aggression. Aggression may be a way of covering up anxiety and uncertainty. The patient may feel defenceless and at the mercy of the doctors and nurses. He may react by attack. In adults, overt aggression is well under control, and it will only be manifest verbally. Thus a frightened individual when first admitted to hospital may appear rude and suspicious. He should be answered with sympathy, understanding and information, so that he will feel less uncertain and defenceless. To answer him with equal rudeness would increase his anxiety and justify him in his aggressive behaviour.

An *overtalkative* patient may also be covering up anxiety, and over-compensating in an effort to appear at ease.

Withdrawal. Other individuals may react by withdrawing into themselves, becoming very shy and timid, keeping their anxieties to themselves; perhaps hoping that if they don't express them, others won't realize that they are worried and anxious. Animal experiments which compare behaviour in a situation in which conflict or fear is present with behaviour in a situation in which there is no conflict or fear present, have shown that the variety of response the animal makes is much reduced, and he tends to produce old established responses rather than newly learnt ones in the presence of fear or conflict. The withdrawn patient, similarly, makes fewer and less varied verbal responses; sticking to well tried phrases, asking few questions.

Dependency

One quite common way in which patients react to illness is by dependency. That this reaction is quite common may be due to factors within the hospital situation which stimulate this reaction, as well as to internal factors of past experience and personality.

The social structure of the hospital is hierarchical, with the patient coming at the bottom of this hierarchy. Attitudes of doctors and nurses toward him are those of benevolent authority: their knowledge of his illness and its treatment are assumed to be greater than his, and they assume that they are better able to select the right treatment. It is both easier and less time consuming to present him with decisions made for his own good and to get his agreement rather than to consult him. The physical condition in which the patient finds himself is also a dependent one; he is dressed in pyjamas, he may be in bed; the nurse may wash him, feed him or change his position for him, just as if he were a child again.

As a child, when he was frightened or ill his parents must often have relieved his fright, made him feel less ill, by virtue of their greater knowledge and strength and their responsibility toward him. Depending on others, especially authority figures, was therefore rewarding in the past; it paid off, so the individual is likely to expect relief of his anxiety and fear if he depends on the doctors and nurses. Thus internal dispositions and external cues from the ward situation will be forces acting together to encourage dependence.

Individual's past experience Depending on others in past relieved fear and anxiety

Doctors' and nurses' role Dominant—behave with authority Have information Take decisions Give physical care

Present role of patient Dependent

Note: Note that doctors and nurses on the one hand and the dependent patient on the other play *complementary* roles.

The social class of the individual may be yet another factor affecting dependency. Working class people are much less used to questioning authority or demanding their rights and may be more submissive to authority than middle class people. To many working class patients, doctors and nurses are authority figures and the habit of submission to authority may be too strong to overcome whilst the individual is physically ill.

Social Cohesion

One very striking feature of the social group in some wards is its cohesiveness; the way in which the patients help one another and the ward staff. When a new patient is admitted to the ward, one of the 'up' patients comes and chats to him and tells him about the ward and its staff. The patients may help to make their own beds, they fetch urinals for other patients, they make tea and take it to patients confined to bed. If something troubles a patient, another will try to help by listening and reassuring, or he will tell the staff so that some action may be taken. A patient who has just been through the experience of being admitted to hospital and undergoing treatment is particularly well able to understand what others are suffering, and because he himself is in a similar position he is able to restore confidence and hope by example. Persons from very different backgrounds who would normally have little or nothing in common may become very close friends in hospital, and the friendship may persist when once they are both discharged.

How does this friendship and comradely feeling arise? Research has shown that individuals are more likely to seek the company of others when they are anxious and frightened or when they are faced with an impending threat. This is particularly so when they expect that others are experiencing the same emotions as themselves. Each individual is in a similar situation, and we tend to like people with whom we have something in common. In seeking the company of others, patients are bound to chat and interact with one another; the more two individuals interact with each other, the greater is the opportunity for them to get to know and to like one another. Thus a group of patients, anxious, and threatened by illness, may become very friendly towards one another and show what we call the 'better' qualities of human beings.

Physiological Effects

Anxiety and conflict, as well as producing possible psychological reactions of denial, aggression, withdrawal, dependency or social cohesion may manifest itself by its effect upon the body. A common effect of anxiety is an increase in muscle tone or muscle tension. When a doctor first examines a patient on admission, he may find the tendon reflexes to be very brisk; due to increased tone. The neck muscles, particularly, may be held continuously contracted in anxiety, leading to a 'tension' headache. Emotion can also have an effect upon the blood pressure; by causing constriction of the blood vessels, leading to a rise in pressure. This should be taken into consideration when recording a patient's blood pressure on admission. Other well-documented effects of emotion such as fear and anger include an increase in heart rate, modification of the respirations, dryness of the mouth and sweating of the palms. If these effects persist they can have an adverse effect upon the patient's recovery from illness.

NURSING MEASURES TO HELP THE PATIENT

If the nurse is to contribute as fully as possible to the patient's recovery, it is obvious that she must do all she can to keep his fear, anxiety and worry to a minimum, and help him to cope with that portion which is unavoidable. She can help to reduce his anxiety by ensuring that he is given information about what is to happen to him. This will prevent uncertainty and thus reduce the patient's apprehensiveness about the unknown. In other words, the nurse must communicate with the patient.

Communicating with the Patient

Communication is important on two levels:

(1) It provides the patient with information which is essential to him, and in exchange it provides the nurse with information about the patient. This is the formal, overt, information aspect of communication.

(2) Communication serves as a vehicle for the formation of an understanding relationship between nurse and patient. In talking and listening to her patient, the nurse is physically near to him, and this allows facial expressions and tone of voice to be assessed. It allows the two individuals to get to know one another; they pay attention to one another; they interact, and the more interaction there is between them the more opportunity there is for the verbal exchange to be pleasant or rewarding, and so they get to like one another.

Communication between nurse and patient can be non-verbal as well as verbal. Eye contact is important; the nurse looks to see if the patient is worried or in pain, as she passes; he sees her look; she smiles; he is reassured that someone is taking an interest in him. Communication by physical contact is also permitted between nurse and patient. Although massage of pressure areas is likely to do more physical harm than good, unless the lotion used is very carefully chosen, this does provide rhythmic, soothing contact for the patient. The nurse can help the patient by squeezing his hand whilst some painful procedure is carried out; allowing him to squeeze her hand will help to divert the patient's attention from the pain of the procedure.

In carrying out her day to day activities, in the presence of the patient, the nurse may be giving him information about herself and her attitudes. Any action (including speech) can be analysed at two levels, the overt purpose of the act, and the expressive, revealing component of the act. What we do, is guided by the intention of the individual and the job requirement; the manner in which the act is carried out is largely a function of personal differences between individuals; it is expressive; it tells us something about the person and his attitude to the job; it may even reveal something of his attitude to life. The way in which the nurse carries out a task for the patient may reveal her true attitude toward him. A nurse is bound to find that her immediate response to some patients is more favourable than to others, but if her attitudes toward all her patients are based on understanding and respect for the uniqueness of each individual, then she will do a great deal to help her patients to get well.

Information Aspects of Communication

The types of information a patient will require are:
1. What is wrong with him.
2. Information of what is expected of him; the role he is expected to play; the rules which apply to his behaviour. Included here should be information as to the right person to ask for further information of the different kinds he needs.
3. Information about other people in the ward, both staff and patients.
4. Information about his own future; what is to happen to him; what form his treatment will take; what the probable outcome will be.
5. Information that his family are in touch with the hospital and are being kept informed about his progress.

It is necessary to think about the patient and his capacity to receive information. There is a limit to the amount of information that a human brain can accurately accept and store in a given time. Any communication about something strange and unfamiliar will contain a great deal of information, and the patient may be unable to retain all of it. Anxiety on his part may reduce further the amount of detail he can recall. So it is important that not too much information is given at any one time. But one of the greatest needs the patient has is for information. What is the best way of resolving this problem? Ley and Spelman have shown that the initial part of a communication is remembered better than the later part. There-fore, the most important details should always be given first. If any information can be given in a permanent written form, this is obviously helpful. Name badges worn by all members of staff come into this category. If the patient knows that he can look to see the name and function of those who come to speak to him, he need not try to remember the significance of different uniforms, and the correct way of addressing the various grades of staff. This will help to prevent him worrying in case, for instance, he should offend sister by calling her 'nurse'. A booklet giving information about such things as visiting hours, shopping facilities, what to bring into hospital, who is the correct person to deal with what, can give the patient a measure of familiarity with the ward before he arrives. If he doesn't bring this booklet into hospital with him, it would be helpful to give him another, so that this information is at hand. The name of the consultant responsible for the treatment of the patient is often placed on the wall above the patient's bed. This could be placed so that the patient can see it. Ley and Spelman suggest that it would be helpful if the patient is encouraged to write down important information that he is given. This does not reduce the amount of information he can remember, whilst it does give a permanent record which can be referred to later.

A lot of the information a patient requires will come from the doctor rather than the nurse, but the nurse should be aware of what the doctor has told the patient so that she can make sure that the patient has understood. A great deal of skill is required on the part of the hospital staff to explain technical matters to the patient in terms he will understand, without appearing to talk down to him, or to underestimate his intelligence. It is not only insulting to the patient to give the impression of talking down, but it may give the unfortunate impression that the nurse knows no better. A long conversation with the patient in which he is encouraged to explain back to the nurse what he has been told is the best way of ensuring that he has understood; any misconceptions can then be cleared up right away.

Communication is a two way process if it is effective, so as well as giving information, the nurse will gain a lot by listening to the patient. Misunderstandings on the patient's part will come to light and can be corrected; further information about the illness of the patient or his social conditions may be obtained. Allowing the patient to talk can help him, because by verbalizing his feelings and his worries they become formulated. Real worries can then be dealt with, whilst imaginary ones can be seen for what they are.

The Patient's Need for Self-Respect

In ordinary life, any adult is responsible for ensuring that his own physiological, social and psychological needs are met, and most adults also take some responsibility for meeting similar needs in others. A man works to provide money which is used to supply the needs of himself and his family. A woman cooks, washes and cleans the home for her family. Even very young children carry out some 'caretaking' activities for themselves (e.g. feeding and dressing themselves). On admission to hospital, a patient may be unable to take complete responsibility for himself, and he certainly cannot take the amount of responsibility for others that he is used to. This decrease in the amount of responsibility taken may lead to a decrement in self-respect.

Self-respect comes partly from the way in which we live up to our own ideals and partly from the respect and love which others show towards us. The 'ideal self' towards which an individual strives is acquired from the society in which he lives. His ideals may not coincide with the ideals of society, but his own society is his reference point; it is the ideals of that society that he accepts, rejects or modifies; it is with those ideals that he compares his own. Independence and a sense of responsibility are valued in our society. An individual who undertakes responsibility for persons other than himself is treated with respect (morally if not financially). A husband and father is looked upon as a more worthy citizen than a bachelor. Thus the ideal self is likely to incorporate the acceptance of responsibility and a measure of self-respect will be lost if the individual is unable to fulfil his responsibilities.

If another person values us, then we feel there must be some intrinsic good in us which provokes that reaction from others. There is a tendency to accept the valuation of others, since we have learnt to rely on the judgement of others from childhood. The role taken by doctors and nurses towards the patient in hospital tends to reinforce any loss of self-respect, since they often take decisions about the patient without truly consulting him. Nurses treat the doctors with greater respect than they treat the patients. A patient is invariably dressed in pyjamas and dressing gown, whilst doctors and nurses are formally dressed; the patient is very often in bed, with the doctor or nurse looking down at him whilst holding a conversation. It is a very self-confident person who can maintain his self-respect under these circumstances.

The more a nurse can boost a patient's self-respect, the more she will aid his mental health, thus aiding his recovery and return to normal life. A nurse should never do for a patient anything he can do for himself, even though it is something she could do more quickly. She can help him by treating him with respect, not taking arbitrary decisions for him, but asking him about his preferences. She should not speak to the patient as if he were a child; neither should she underestimate his intelligence. She should never call a patient by his Christian name, nickname or such familiarities as 'Dad', 'Pop', 'Mum', 'Grandma', unless invited to do so by the patient. Strong disapproval is directed at both patient and nurse, if a nurse allows a patient to use her Christian name. Thus the use by the nurse of the patient's Christian name will be unreciprocated, and will give a flavour of adult–child relationship to any conversa-that they hold. In conversation with the patient, a nurse can help by asking the patient about his family and job. This maintains his links with the outside world and reminds him that he is useful and worthwhile. If she can ask his advice about something of which he has special knowledge, this will also boost his self-respect. At all times, the nurse should respect the individuality of the patient and show that she likes him for himself

Relief of Pain and Prevention of Sensory Deprivation

Everyone can appreciate that pain is a very unpleasant experience. Continued pain has adverse effects upon bodily functions; it can cause disturbances of gastric or colonic function, cardiac arrhythmia, a rise in blood pressure, alteration in the respiratory pattern, or curtailment of renal blood flow. Muscular spasm occurring over the area of pain may increase the discomfort of the patient. Pain will dominate the field of attention for the patient, diverting his attention from the more pleasant aspects of the environment. Everything possible should be done to relieve pain both for the sake of the patient's physical recovery and for his mental well-being. His facial expression may reveal the presence of pain, even in a patient who does not complain.

Pain occurs when there is excessive sensory input along different nerves of the body, but it has been realized recently that the absence of, or lack of variety in, sensory stimulation can also be extremely unpleasant. Experiments have shown that healthy young men find sensory deprivation difficult to tolerate, and in some it has produced hallucinations. In large adult wards there is usually plenty of activity, so that noise and movement are always present, but a patient who is placed in a single room or who has bedsides in position may have stimulation seriously curtailed. A confused, noisy patient is often moved from an open ward to a single bedded one, to allow other patients to rest. If the patient is then left alone because of shortage of staff, it could make his condition worse. Making a noise oneself is one way of increasing stimulation, since stimuli will come from both the ears and the throat and tongue. It is often at night when the amount of light is reduced that patients become particularly confused.

There is evidence that both intellectual and emotional development is dependent upon adequate stimulation from the social and physical environments. A child confined to bed, especially one isolated because of infection, could suffer from lack of stimulation. This is one reason why the maintenance of close contact between mother and child is so important whilst the child is in hospital.

The Importance of Sleep

Sleep is essential to mental health. Individuals deprived of sleep become fatigued and irritable; prolonged deprivation can lead to mental confusion and hallucinogenic states. Anxiety, fear, unusual surroundings, light and noise, can all act to prevent sleep. A certain amount of both light and noise will almost certainly be present in a hospital ward, but these should be reduced to a minimum.

Nursing measures that aid sleep include the provision of hot milk drinks; ensuring that the patient is physically comfortable; and letting him talk out his worries. If such measures fail, and the patient is allowed sleeping tablets, the nurse should ensure that these are given early enough to prevent their effect continuing when once the patient has been woken up the following morning. The ward should be as quiet and peaceful as possible during the hour before the patients are settled for the night. Excitement and stimulation will cause mental arousal and act to prevent sleep.

Care of the Patient's Relatives

The primary concern of the nurse is the well-being of the patient, but by including the relatives and friends of the patients within her sphere of responsibility she is indirectly helping the patient's recovery to normal health. It is important that the patient's links with home are maintained, and that visiting is encouraged. The patient needs to feel that his family still love him and are concerned for him. In effect, the relatives have entrusted the care of the patient to the nurse because of her specialized training; she is acting as their agent and should therefore try to include them in the patient's care whenever possible. The nurse should try to understand the relatives' point of view, their reactions, and their difficulties, so that she may be of the greatest help to the whole family.

Anyone who is fond of the patient will miss him whilst he is in hospital, since they cannot be with the patient the whole time. Thus, grief at separation will be experienced, as will anxiety for the patient's future. The presence of other patients and visitors at visiting time, if the patient is in a ward with others, has an inhibiting effect and may prevent the full expression of love and sympathy that will be felt. A wife or husband may be afraid for their own future and miss the support of their partner at home. It is most unpleasant to see the suffering of someone whom one loves and to be unable to share it, or to help, and there may be a recognized or unrecognized guilt at handing over the care of the loved one to strangers. There may be a feeling of failure that one cannot help the patient when he is in greatest need of help. If the nurse can bear in mind the possibility that these factors are operating, she can suggest ways in which the relative may help, so that he doesn't feel so useless.

A relative who is not used to hospitals and modern concepts of disease may misunderstand the treatment that is being given. This can cause great distress if, through misunderstanding, the relative feels that the patient is not getting the best treatment. So information, and access to the patient are the greatest needs of the relative. Although visiting is allowed daily in most hospitals, not everyone can get to the hospital during visiting hours if they are on shift work or at the mercy of the kindness of others to care for the children. Some flexibility on the part of the hospital authorities in allowing visiting 'out of hours' can do a great deal to help the whole family.

Fear of the hospital 'authorities', or a desire to cause them as little trouble as possible, may prevent a relative from actively seeking out a member of staff to ask for information. It is not sufficient for a member of the ward staff to sit in the office so that she is available to give information; she should seek out the relatives, giving them information about the patients' progress, treatment and prognosis, and affording them an opportunity to ask questions.

The way in which telephone enquiries are answered can also be a source of help or anxiety to the relatives. A relative may have walked some distance to a telephone box and have waited some time to obtain its use. He may be short of sixpences. Even today, there are people who are frightened of the telephone and get anxious and upset when they have to use it. A nurse answering a query should ascertain the name of the patient about whom the query is being made and the name of the enquirer. She should be prompt in gaining the necessary information from the person in charge of the ward. It is not sufficient to say that a patient's condition is 'satisfactory'. The word 'satisfactory' corresponds to a value judgement which depends upon the speaker's own standards. What is satisfactory to a nurse who has seen very ill patients may be far from satisfactory to a relative who knows the patient when he is well. Personal details about the patient's diet or activities will give more information to a relative than formal impersonal phrases. If possible, a message should be obtained from the patient himself.

A nurse who remembers that, no matter how busy she is, she is dealing with people and that people are individuals with problems of their own, will display that understanding and sympathy which are so necessary to the mental wellbeing of her patients, their physical recovery, and her own satisfaction in interpersonal relationships.

4

The physical environment of the patient

DURING his stay in hospital the ward is the patient's home, it is the place in which, as long as he is confined to bed, he must spend his day, eat and sleep, and where his personal toilet needs must be met. The planning of ward units has received a great deal of attention recently as new hospitals are built and older ones are modernized. Not so very many years ago the majority of patients spent most of their time in hospital in bed and were allowed to be up only for short periods at certain times of the day when convalescent. Now many patients are encouraged to get up to go to the bath and to the toilet and often spend a considerable part of the day out of bed. One feature of the newer ward units is the provision of more washing and toilet facilities and of a sitting-and-dining room where ambulant patients can have their meals, and where such recreations as playing card games and listening to radio and television can be allowed without disturbing ill patients.

The ward should be both comfortable and attractive. It should be light and airy, kept at a comfortable temperature, and in a good decorative state. Walls and cupboards should be decorated in washable paint or wall covering, so that they may be cleaned regularly.

The reduction of unnecessary noise should be the aim of every hospital and something which the nurse must always have in mind. This depends very much on the effort made by each individual member of the staff, but the provision of equipment which can be handled without noisy clatter (e.g. plastic rather than metal bins and pails) is a great help. Moreover in the planning of new buildings the type of construction has a bearing on noise and the provision of central departments for the cleaning and sterilization of equipment and for washing up dishes, make the ward a much quieter place than it can possibly be when these procedures are carried out in ward preparation rooms and ward kitchens.

The nurse should bear in mind the need of each patient for space and privacy. Little or no research has been done on the psychological effects on patients of the beds being close together, although it has long been accepted that overcrowding of wards makes cross-infection difficult to control. It is known that overcrowding does have adverse behavioural effects on experimental animals. It is not the nurse's fault, of course, if extra beds are put into a ward in emergencies, but additional care must be taken to ensure privacy for patients when space is cramped. Research has shown that patients do on the whole prefer to be with others in wards of around twelve to sixteen beds, but this might well be because few have the opportunity to try single rooms. The nurse must be meticulous in drawing curtains around the bed when intimate and personal procedures are carried out.

WARD CLEANING AND MAINTENANCE

The daily cleaning of the ward and its annexes is carried out by a separate domestic staff. Dust is liable to be heavily contaminated by pathogenic organisms, so cleaning must never be carried out by those responsible for patient care. Nonetheless, the nurse is concerned with the whole environment of her patient, and should ensure that it is clean, and that cross-infection does not occur. She will need to be capable of supervising and advising the domestic staff in their work.

Where nursing staff are able to influence the supplies department, they should ensure that items of furniture and equipment are bought which can be washed and dried, or can be disposed of after use. Articles should have a smooth surface, with no indentations in which dirt can accumulate. Floors should be sealed with polyurethane, or made of tiles, which can be washed. The vacuum cleaner used to take up dirt should have a collecting bag which is dust proof, and it should be possible to insert a paper bag lining into the dust bag which can be closed up with sticky tape and removed to be incinerated after each use. All members of the nursing staff should know the times at which routine cleaning is carried out, so that they may plan dressings and other sterile procedures accordingly.

Washing bowls and baths are particularly difficult to keep clean from the organizational point of view, since they must be cleaned between use, but there is rarely a domestic worker available for this job when baths and washes are being carried out. Ideally there should be enough washing bowls for each patient, but as far as baths are concerned there is, inevitably, a shortage of these in our hospital wards. If the nurse is helping the patient with his bath, she can get the bath cleaned, but quite often up patients go to have baths at what are convenient moments for them, but finding the bath dirty, do not know how to set about getting it cleaned, and do not like to worry busy people. There is no reason why cleaning materials cannot be left available so that patients can clean the bath after use, as they would at home. Otherwise, they must be told to ask the domestic worker to clean it for them.

Beds and lockers should be thoroughly washed over with an antiseptic solution and dried when a patient has been discharged. Clean bed linen, blankets and pillows will be used to make up the bed when it has been washed.

Clean linen is usually brought to the ward each day, to maintain a constant supply of each article in the linen cupboard. Dirty linen is put into bags and these are collected by the laundry porter. Nursing staff are responsible for keeping dirty linen from infectious patients separate from other linen. In special cases (e.g. enteric fever) the linen may be placed in disinfectant solution in the ward.

The Ward Kitchen

If the nurse is serving meals she should discard any cutlery or crockery which is not entirely clean, to be rewashed. Meal trays must be washed and dried after use, or they are a source of cross-infection. Any spilled food or milk must be cleaned up immediately.

Refrigerators should be defrosted and washed thoroughly by the domestic staff at regular intervals, at least once a week, and more frequently during hot weather. Surplus food supplied to the ward should be returned to the kitchen for disposal. Food scraps from the patients' plates are put into a polythene-lined bin from which they can be collected by a special porter. The lid of this bin must be kept closed.

Bed Pans and Urinals

These are the concern of the nursing staff. They should be flushed with cold water after use, then rinsed with disinfectant. Next automatic bed pan washers in which the bed pan can be enclosed to be flushed with cold and hot water should be used, and finally when it is clean, it should be sterilized in a tank of boiling water. (Minimum time for immersion in boiling water is 5 min.) It is essential that the bed pan is cleaned of all organic matter before being put in the sterilizer, since organic matter provides a protective covering for microorganisms, which thus escape destruction during the boiling process.

Treatment and Preparation Rooms

In modern hospital wards, provision is made for dressings and other sterile procedures to be carried out in a treatment room, away from the ward. Adjacent to the treatment room are two annexes, one a 'clean' preparation room where sterile equipment and lotions are stored and trollies can be laid. The other annexe is a 'dirty' utility room where instruments are washed and boiled, ready for return to the central sterile supply department. Dirty dressings will have been placed straight into a paper bag during the dressing. The bag should now be closed gently, taking care not to cause a great upward puff of air from the bag in the process, and sealed with tape before being put into the polythene-lined dirty dressing bin. Used disposables should be put into a separate polythene-lined bin. These bins are emptied by a special porter.

Ideally, the treatment room will be air-conditioned, but in many modernized wards rooms have been adapted as treatment rooms, rather than being purpose built, and an air-conditioning system is not possible. Every possible precaution should be taken to keep both the treatment and the 'clean' preparation room as dust free as possible. All surfaces must be washable, equipment should be placed in closed cupboards, windows should be closed, and no one should be allowed into the rooms unnecessarily.

PREVENTION OF CROSS-INFECTION

Whenever a group of human beings are together within a closed space, the number of microorganisms in the air increases. These microorganisms include ones from the respiratory tract, the skin and the clothes of the individuals. In a hospital ward there are not only many individuals within a defined area, but some of these individuals (the patients) may be more susceptible to microorganisms than usual. This is because they may have a wound which provides organisms with ready access to the body, or natural defence mechanisms may be less efficient than usual because of the illness itself. Another difference between, say a factory, and a hospital ward, is that in a hospital ward there may be patients, or indeed staff, carrying unusual strains of organisms against which other patients have no resistance.

It is especially important that the number of organisms in the air is kept to a minimum. Since, from the air, they can be breathed in, or get on to surfaces and bed clothes. Activities in the ward such as bed making should disturb the air as little as possible. Surfaces should be cleaned in a way that will prevent dust from rising in the air, thus vacuum cleaning and washing of floors, rather than sweeping, and washing surfaces with a damp cloth instead of dusting, is advocated; if a damp cloth is likely to damage a polished surface, it can be cleaned with a polish-impregnated cloth instead.

So that a nurse may maintain the best physical environment for her patients, in which there is no danger to them from cross-infection, she should understand the principles of microbiology, the conditions under which microorganisms survive and multiply, and the ways in which their growth may be inhibited. Given this understanding her nursing techniques will be safe, and she will be capable of advising and supervising the domestic staff in the cleaning of the ward.

Microorganisms

Microorganisms, for the most part, are either positively helpful to man (soil organisms, are an example), or at least do no harm. Some, however, are capable of causing diseases, and it is these with which the doctors and nurses are concerned. Harmful (pathogenic) organisms need fairly well defined environmental conditions for their growth.

The word 'growth' when used of microorganisms refers, not to the organisms getting physically bigger, as a human does, but to the multiplication of the unicellular organism, by cellular division, to form many identical microorganisms. Under ideal conditions a microorganism may divide at 20-min intervals. Thus, one cell divides to form two, then these in turn divide, forming four in all, and so on. It can be seen that it is most important to prevent this happening.

Their requirements for multiplication include a narrow range of temperature (around human body temperature), and of acidity–alkalinity. They also need both moisture and food substances in their environment. Thus the multiplication of many pathogenic organisms can be inhibited by depriving them of moisture; this is why surfaces should be dried and kept dry. Very high, or very low temperatures, will inhibit their growth, and a temperature of 100°C (212°F) for 5 min will actually kill most pathogenic organisms. Some chemicals, the disinfectants and antiseptics, cause damage to the cellular components of the organism, whilst antibiotics interfere with their metabolism. Gamma radiation destroys microorganisms and is an excellent method of sterilization for pre-packed dressings and equipment.

Some microorganisms have the capacity to protect themselves from adverse conditions, only to begin multiplying when conditions again suit their requirements. These organisms are termed 'spore-forming' organisms, and they are more difficult to kill than non-spore forming organisms. For instance, boiling for 5 min will not kill them, but higher temperatures as produced by steam under pressure will.

Human Defence Mechanisms

The interior of the living human body provides pathogenic organisms with conditions that meet their growth requirements, but human beings have evolved mechanisms which protect them against harmful microorganisms. An intact skin prevents organisms from gaining access to the body. Hydrochloric acid in the stomach and the lining of the alimentary tract, prevents organisms from entering the body by this route. Orifices of the body are lined with mucous membranes, and although a few organisms are capable of penetrating through genito-urinary membranes, these membranes do in general form a barrier to microorganisms. The respiratory tract is protected by cilia and mucus secretions, the cough reflex enabling particulate matter to be expelled. Inside the body protection from the harmful effects of organisms is by cells which engulf them. These cells are contained both in the blood (white blood cells) and in the tissues (macrophages and histiocytes).

In addition specific antibodies are formed which unite with specific organisms, rendering them harmless. These antibodies circulate in the blood stream. The reticulo-endothelial system is important in promoting the body's defence against microorganisms.

A wound interrupts the integrity of the skin surface, and allows the ready access of microorganisms. Absolute sterility is necessary for all objects coming into contact with a wound.

STERILIZATION

Sterilization in the microbiological sense means the process whereby a substance or body is rendered free from living organisms, and under this term are included various methods of killing bacteria and other microorganisms.

All instruments, utensils and dressings used in the conduct of surgical dressings and other procedures for which aseptic precautions are necessary must be sterile and must then be handled only by a person with sterilized gloved hands or with sterile forceps.

The word 'asepsis' implies the absence of microorganisms, while 'antisepsis' (against sepsis) usually implies the use of chemical disinfectants to kill microorganisms. Aseptic precautions in a ward or theatre imply that all dressings and appliances are sterile and that there is no risk of contaminating the wound and while similar precautions are taken with septic cases, additional antiseptic precautions may be taken to prevent spread of infection.

It cannot be too strongly emphasized that all dressing utensils and materials must be kept free from contamination with gross dirt even if they are to be sterilized before use. Any method of sterilization will be ineffective unless the equipment is thoroughly cleaned beforehand. Any organic matter, such as blood, pus or excreta, will form a barrier to full penetration by the sterilizing agent. A further point which is not always appreciated is that aseptic precautions are as necessary in dealing with an infected wound as with a clean one. The danger to the patient is increased if a fresh infection is introduced.

Sterilization of instruments and equipment used in surgical practice is usually effected by exposure to high temperatures for a sufficient length of time to kill all living organisms including spore-forming organisms. Other physical means such as exposure to gamma rays in an atomic pile or irradiation by radioactive cobalt are used and are particularly useful for sterilizing equipment which is readily damaged by heat, such as rubber articles and some endoscopes. Within the hospital, however, heat is the most generally used, and the most efficient agent, wherever its use is possible, in the form of high-pressure steam sterilizers (autoclaves) and hot-air ovens.

Disinfection by chemical agents is an ancillary method for materials and equipment which cannot stand exposure to heat, such as some endoscopes; chemical agents are also used for disinfection of the skin and the irrigation of body cavities.

Sterilization by Physical Means

Sufficient heat kills all forms of bacterial life, although those organisms which can take on a protective spore formation can withstand a higher temperature for a longer period than the less resistant, or vegetative, forms.

Autoclaving

Steam kills organisms by coagulation of the cell protein, provided that certain factors are present; the steam must be under pressure, dry and saturated. With these conditions fulfilled, the steam will condense when it meets the cooler surface of the articles in the autoclave and the latent heat released on condensation, will penetrate and kill the organisms. Autoclaving at a pressure of 20 lb. per in^2 (above atmospheric pressure) and a temperature of 126°C (260°F) for 20 min is an efficient method of sterilizing fabrics such as gowns, towels and dressings, and also instruments (Fig. 1). The latest types of high-speed, high-vacuum autoclave operating at higher temperatures reduce the time needed for sterilization. Rubber is readily damaged by exposure to high temperatures for long periods such as are necessitated during the process of creating a vacuum and subsequent drying process in all but modern autoclaves. Rubber gloves are usually autoclaved at a lower temperature, e.g. 121°C (250°F), for 10 min. The gloves should be very loosely packed in order to ensure full penetration of the steam.

It is important to remember that any sterilization by autoclaving is reliable only if the autoclave is correctly installed and efficiently operated, and the materials are packed loosely so that all parts are accessible to the steam. The operation of an autoclave is a serious responsibility and should be entrusted only to one who understands its working. Tests of efficiency, in addition to checking the accuracy of the pressure gauges and temperature readings, should be carried out at regular intervals; these include indicators, control tubes and bacteriological tests.

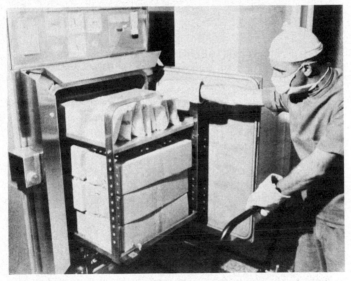

FIG. 1. Instruments and dressings may be sterilized in an autoclave where they are subjected to steam under pressure according to a pre-determined cycle.

Dry Heat

This kills microorganisms by oxidation, and provided that the articles to be sterilized are exposed to a temperature of 160°C

(320°F) for 1 hr all organisms and their spores will be destroyed. This method is suitable for all types of glass ware, including all glass syringes (but not glass and metal syringes where solder will melt in the high temperature in the oven) and some instruments such as knife blades and skin-grafting knives.

Other Physical Agents

Other physical agents in addition to heat will destroy bacteria, but, with the exception of gamma radiation, have not a very wide practical application in hospital practice.

Cold. Most organisms will survive exposure to very low temperatures but will not multiply. A practical application of this is the preservation of foodstuffs in cold storage.

Light. Direct sunlight kills many bacteria including the tubercle bacillus. The active agent is the ultraviolet radiation and these rays have been used to sterilize milk and water.

Drying. Moisture is as important to most bacterial cells as it is to tissue cells and removal of water will kill the cell. In certain circumstances, however, some bacteria can survive drying for considerable periods and are therefore likely to be present in dust. Examples are pyogenic organisms, diphtheria bacillus and the *Mycobacterium tuberculosis* in pus and sputum.

Gamma radiation. This agent is being increasingly used for materials which cannot be effectively sterilized by heat without damage. A number of packaged disposable items of surgical equipment, such as plastic catheters, knife holders and tubing; suture materials are also sterilized by this method.

Boiling. This method may be used in an emergency, but it is not recommended.

All pathogenic organisms in the vegetative forms are killed by 5 min immersion in boiling water, but the method is particularly open to human error.

(1) The water must be boiling for the full 5 min. The addition of cold articles takes the water off the boil and timing must begin from when the water begins to boil again.

(2) All articles must be completely immersed in the boiling water.

(3) Articles must be spotlessly clean before being immersed in the boiling water. Blood, pus, excreta, form a barrier, protecting the organism from the boiling water.

(4) For articles to remain sterile, they must be removed from the boiling water by means of sterile handling forceps, and must be placed onto a sterile surface and covered with a sterile lid, so that complete protection from contamination is obtained.

(5) A major source of danger of this method is that articles are wet when removed from the boiling water and moisture aids the growth of microorganisms. Thus the articles must not be contaminated with microorganisms.

(6) The articles to be sterilized must be constructed of materials not damaged by boiling water, and should be so constructed that all surfaces are in contact with the boiling water.

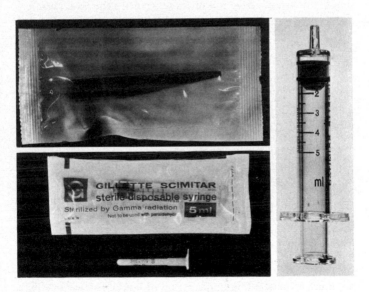

Fig. 2. Pre-packed syringe, needle and spigot.

Nowadays, all sterile equipment required for dressings and other procedures is sterilized centrally and delivered to the ward daily. Usually all the equipment required for a dressing or other technique is packed in a bag and then sterilized by steam under pressure. The nurse then needs to choose the appropriate pack and use an aseptic technique for the dressing. Syringes may be sterilized centrally in a hot oven or often disposable syringes are used (Fig. 2). These are sterilized by the manufacturers. Many other disposables are sterilized by gamma-radiation by the manufacturers and remain sterile until the packet is opened. Catheters, disposable instruments, airways, stomach tubes, are common examples.

Chemical Disinfectants

It is essential that the nurse should understand the necessary conditions for the effective use of these agents, otherwise chemical disinfection may be quite useless and may even be dangerous if it gives rise to a false sense of security. Therefore dilution instructions must be followed meticulously.

(1) To be efficient the disinfectant must be sufficiently strong and must be allowed to act for a sufficient length of time.

(2) With very few exceptions the disinfectant must be in solution; dry powders have very little effect.

(3) The disinfecting power of the agent varies with the number of organisms present; highly infected material is difficult to disinfect efficiently.

(4) The disinfecting power of the agent is to a certain extent dependent upon the nature of the medium containing the organisms, e.g. the germicidal power is lowered in the presence of pus since in this medium many of the organisms are inside the dead leucocytes and, therefore, it is difficult for the disinfectant to reach them.

(5) As a general rule it may be stated that disinfectant solutions are more effective hot than cold.

(6) Spore-forming bacteria and the acid-fast group (of which the *Mycobacterium tuberculosis* is the most important member) are much more resistant to the action of liquid disinfectants than they are to the action of heat.

Principal Groups of Chemical Disinfectants

A great many chemical substances are in use as disinfectants or antiseptics, many of them under proprietary names. The terms 'bactericide' and 'bacteriostatic', the former referring to substances which kill bacteria, and the latter to substances which inhibit bacterial growth, more accurately define the action of certain agents such as antibiotics than the words 'disinfectant' and 'antiseptic'. At the end of this chapter a list of disinfectants, antiseptics and lotions will be found, with some notes on their particular uses.

Oxidizing and reducing agents. Hydrogen peroxide in the presence of organic matter readily yields oxygen and in so doing acts as a mechanical cleansing agent removing pus and debris from a wound or cavity.

Potassium permanganate is an oxidizing agent with deodorant properties. Sulphur dioxide and formalin are reducing agents which alter the nature of the bacterial cell by removing oxygen.

Halogens. These substances are a group of non-metallic elements including chlorine, iodine and bromine, the first two, chlorine and iodine, having very wide uses as disinfectants.

The chief chlorine compounds used are eusol, Dakin's solution, chloramine and electrolytic sodium hypochlorite (Milton). These solutions liberate free chlorine which combines with proteins in the tissues and in bacterial cells. The solution has a cleansing as well as a disinfectant action since the protein of necrotic tissue and sloughs is dissolved and washed away. A chlorine derivative of xylenol, chloroxylenol, is known under a variety of proprietary names, e.g. Dettol and Osyl. More recent chlorine compounds are chlorhexidine (Hibitane), benzalconium chloride (Roccal) and hexachlorophane, which is used in antibacterial soaps, such as Cidal, and in a hand-washing cream, Phisohex.

Iodine, like chlorine, has the power of combining with proteins. It is relatively insoluble in water but will dissolve in a solution of potassium iodide. The commonly used preparation 'tincture of iodine' (Weak Solution of Iodine, B.P.) is a $2\frac{1}{2}$ per cent solution with potassium iodine in alcohol.

Salts of heavy metals. These substances are first adsorbed on to the surface of the bacteria and then penetrate the organisms and kill them. The bactericidal power of most of these chemicals is, however, reduced in the presence of serum and other organic matter. Water-soluble mercurial salts, in low concentrations, are effective disinfectants for many purposes but they are irritating to the skin, tarnish metals and become relatively inactive in the presence of blood, pus and other organic matter, such as excreta. Perchloride of mercury is one of the oldest of the mercurial disinfectants and is one in which the disadvantages just mentioned are most marked. Compounds containing very small amounts of mercury, phenylmercuric acetate and phenylmercuric nitrate, are suitable for chemical sterilization of some delicate instruments such as cystoscopes of the non-boilable type. Oxycyanide of mercury is another example of a mercurial disinfectant.

Cresol and phenol disinfectants. Carbolic acid is well known as the disinfectant introduced into surgical practice by Lord Lister. It is feebly acid in watery solution, but has a marked caustic action. A 5 per cent solution will kill all vegetative bacteria and most spore-forming ones in 1 hr; a 1 per cent solution will kill most non-sporing organisms in 10 min. Tar acid preparations (containing phenol, cresols, etc.) in the form of black disinfectant fluids, such as Cyllin, and white disinfectant fluids, such as Izal and Jeyes fluid, are specially suitable where large quantities of the solution are needed, as, for example, disinfecting excreta, bedpans and linen. Their disadvantages are that they are sticky and there may be some difficulty in rinsing and cleaning utensils afterwards, also the black fluids may stain linen. A proprietary disinfectant, Sudol, contains 50 per cent phenol and is a useful solution for general disinfection of such items as linen, baths, washing bowls and sanitary utensils. Lysol is a soapy solution of cresol containing 25 per cent soap. It is more expensive than crude phenol preparations and should be used with economy. All Cresol and phenol preparations are potentially dangerous poisons even in dilute solution.

Chlorine derivatives of cresol and xylenol, chlorocresol and chloroxylenol, are less caustic than carbolic acid or lysol.

Aniline dyes. The flavine group of dyes is not used very widely now in surgical practice. Acriflavine was the preparation most frequently employed; proflavine is, however, more easily prepared and less irritating to the tissues than acriflavine. The flavine dyes have a specific action on staphylococci and streptococci and their activity is not decreased by the presence of serum. 5-Amino-acridine is a newer addition to the series and is practically non-staining. Other aniline dyes such as brilliant green and gentian violet are sometimes used in the form of skin paints.

Cationic detergents. These solutions, of which cetrimide and cetavlon are examples, have a detergent action removing grease and with it dirt and bacteria. They are not compatible with soap. Detergents are used for the cleaning of the hands, and of the skin of operation sites and for cleansing wounds. A proprietary preparation, Savlon, is a combination of cetrimide and chlorhexidine.

Another example of a cationic bactericide is domiphen bromide (Bradosol) which can be used for a number of different purposes, e.g. disinfection of linen and utensils, hand lotion and mouth wash.

Disinfectants, Antiseptics and Lotions

Substance	Uses	Strength
Benzalkonium chloride (Roccal)	Disinfection of skin Disinfection of linen and utensils, also deodorant	1:10 solution 1:40 solution
Chloroxylenol and similar preparations, e.g. Dettol and Osyl	These preparations are less irritating and less caustic than phenol or cresol Disinfection of linen and utensils Antiseptic hand lotion	 1:20 to 1:40 solution 1:40 to 1:100
Chlorhexidine (Hibitane)	Skin disinfection. Disinfection of instruments	1:100 solution or weaker
Chlorine, in the form of hypochlorite solutions, e.g. eusol, Electrolytic hypochlorite (Milton)	As a dressing or irrigating lotion in the treatment of sloughing or infected tissues For disinfection and storage of infants' feeding bottles and utensils	1:80 solution
Cetrimide (cetyltrimethyl ammonium bromide)	Cleansing the skin. Cleaning utensils	1:100 solution
Cresol in soap solution—lysol	Disinfectant lotion for general purposes Disinfecting linen and other fabrics	1:40 solution 1:80 (14 g to water 1 litre) if linen is left for at least 6 hr
Domiphen bromide (Bradosol)	Disinfection of utensils and linen Cleansing wounds and irrigations	1:500 solution (or weaker)
Flavine group, acriflavine, proflavine, euflavine and 5-aminoacridine	These dyes are used in the treatment of wounds and as antiseptics on the skin They may be combined with sterile liquid paraffin as an oily dressing	1:1000 solution in water or spirit proflavine is not soluble in spirit)

Disinfectants, Antiseptics and Lotions (*cont.*)

Substance	Uses	Strength
Formaldehyde and formalin (a solution of formaldehyde in water)	For disinfecting articles which cannot be treated with steam, e.g. books and leather articles, for fumigation of rooms	If used as a spray, 50 g of formalin to 1 litre of water for every 400 ft^2 of surface
Paraform tablets, these disintegrate slowly liberating formaldehyde	For the sterilization and storage of elastic gum articles and endoscopes	
Liquor boracis et formaldehyde	A solution of formaldehyde with borax and phenol for storing sterile surgical instruments	
Hydrogen peroxide	Used for the irrigation of wounds and cleaning septic mouth conditions. Is non-poisonous and in the presence of organic matter readily liberates oxygen and helps in the separation of sloughs	Stock solutions contain either 10 or 20 volumes of available oxygen. Diluted with warm water, as required for use, in 2·5, 5 or 10 volumes
Iodine	Used for skin preparation, it is more penetrating than most skin paints especially if the skin is dry	'Weak tincture of iodine,' 1 : 40
Mercurial preparations: Phenylmercuric nitrate	Used for sterilizing certain instruments, e.g. the telescopes and sheaths of non-boilable cystoscopes; for preserving fluids and suspensions prepared for parenteral injection	1 : 2000 to 1 : 10 000 solution
	For skin preparation	
	As a vaginal douche for non-specific infections	
	For mycotic infections	0·5 or 1 : 1000 in a water soluble ointment base
Phenol (carbolic acid)	Liquefied phenol, carbolic acid, *Poisonous and corrosive*, if splashed on the skin should be swabbed off at once with methylated or surgical spirit	
	Disinfecting linen, crockery and sanitary utensils	1 : 20
	Disinfecting excreta	1 : 10 for 1 hr
Crude phenolic disinfectants, i.e. 'black' and 'white' disinfecting fluids, e.g. Jeyes fluid, Cylin, Izal, etc.	Disinfecting excreta	1 : 10 solution mixed with excreta for 2 hr
	Disinfecting linen, 'white' fluids should be used for this purpose as the 'black' disinfectants may stain linen.	1 : 160 solution for 12 hr
	Scrubbing floors, laboratory or sluice room benches, etc.	1 : 160 solution
	For local pollution of floors, e.g. with sputum	Swab with 1 : 5 solution
Savlon 0·3 per cent chlorhexidine with 3 per cent cetrimide	Washing equipment, e.g. dressing trolleys.	1 : 40 solution
	Skin cleansing	1 : 20 solution

Disinfectants, Antiseptics and Lotions (*cont.*)

Substance	Uses	Strength
Sodium chloride solutions. Normal saline (Physiological Solution of Sodium Chloride B.P.)	Used for bathing and irrigating wounds and cavities: for rectal, subcutaneous and intravenous injection	9:1000 sodium chloride in water
Hypertonic salt solution	In the treatment of wounds as baths or irrigations	1 to 2:10 solution
Sudol (contains 50 per cent phenols	Disinfectant mop for theatre and dressing trolleys	1:120 solution
	Disinfecting utensils	1:40 to 1:60 solution
	Soaking linen	1:160 solution

Suggestions for Further Reading

Prevention of Cross Infection in Hospitals. Medical Research Council Memorandum no. 11.

Sterilization Practice in Six Hospitals. Nuffield Provincial Hospital Trust.

The Planning and Organization of Central Syringe Services. Nuffield Provincial Hospital Trust.

Staphlococcal Infections in Hospital. Ministry of Health. Her Majesty's Stationery Office.

Microbiology for Nurses (*Nurses' Aid Series*) 4th edn, Parker, M. (1972). Baillière Tindall

Central Sterile Supply Services. Nursing Times.

5

Admission and discharge of patients

HIS FIRST impressions of a hospital may colour the subsequent experiences of that hospital for a patient. He will be feeling apprehensive about his treatment, about the lack of privacy in the ward, and about leaving his family and friends. By considering his feelings, the hospital staff can help him to adjust quickly and easily to hospital life, and give him confidence in the treatment he will receive. A patient's first contact with a member of the hospital staff may well be with a porter at the gate lodge or administrative block, who will direct the patient to the ward. Sometimes necessary forms are filled in by a clerk in an admissions or reception office before the patient proceeds to the ward itself. Clear direction signs and ward names will help the patient; all members of staff should be encouraged to think of themselves as engaged in public relations as they walk along hospital corridors and in the grounds. Members of staff may well be stopped and asked the way to a ward by an anxious patient, and a friendly manner together with clear instructions can be a great help.

The ward staff will always have been notified of the patient's admission, and can help to make him feel welcome by turning back the bed and putting out water, glass and towels in readiness. When a ward is very busy, the staff may all be occupied in caring for their patients, and a new patient and his relatives can wait anxiously at the ward door for some little time before he is noticed. Sometimes it is the ward maid or orderly who is the first to greet the new patient. Good ward organization could ensure that one member of the ward nursing staff is free to coordinate ward activities and attend to visitors and new patients. Thus, a member of staff will be available to welcome the patient the minute he appears, instead of him nervously trying to catch the attention of a member of staff. A friendly welcome from the nurse as she introduces herself will help the patient to feel at home. He can then be seated, together with his relatives, whilst the nurse obtains any information that is required. If the patient and his relatives have had a long, exhausting journey to reach the hospital, they can be shown where the lavatory is and offered tea and food.

When the patient is shown to his bed, he should be introduced to the patients on either side. It is usual to ask the patient to undress and get into bed, but it is worth considering whether this is absolutely necessary for a little while, or whether it is possible for the patient to sit in the day room and get accustomed to his surroundings, the other patients, and the staff, before he is asked to put on, in the middle of the day, clothes usually worn at night. Of course, some people may feel happier in pyjamas and dressing gown, since then they will be less conspicuous amongst the other patients; but for others, their normal clothing will help them to feel at less of a disadvantage when dealing with the staff.

Some patients will need to get into bed straight away, because they are exhausted after the journey; because they are to be examined; or because observations and tests will begin straight away. It may be necessary for the nurse to help the patient to undress if he is unable to do this for himself and there is no relative who can help.

It is rare for suitable individual accommodation to be available for the patient's clothing. Commonly, a communal cupboard is provided and, since all patients' clothing in the ward is placed in this, it is necessary that each item of clothing is carefully labelled with the patient's name before it is put away. All the patient's belongings are carefully listed in duplicate, so a record of all property within the hospital is kept by the ward and a copy given to the patient. Patients are advised not to have valuables with them, and these are locked in the hospital safe after a careful record of them has been made. Many hospitals persuade the relatives to take home all but the bare essentials that the patient will need whilst in hospital. This absolves the hospital of responsibility for belongings not directly in the patient's own care.

Care of the Patient's Relative

When once the patient has been settled in bed, or shown the day room if he is to be up, he is allowed some time to say goodbye to the relative accompanying him. Before the relative leaves the hospital, a telephone number and address should be obtained so that contact may be made in emergencies. Information about visiting hours and the hospital procedure for telephone enquiries should be explained and, if there are likely to be difficulties in visiting at the stated hours, alternative arrangements can be made. Any information about the patient's course of treatment should be given before the relative leaves, and he can be asked to bring anything further the patient needs, during visiting hours.

Information the Patient Will Need

The patient will need information about the ward routine, the layout of the ward, and how to identify members of staff. So that he is not overburdened with information, this can be given a little at a time, during the admission procedure. To reduce his uncertainty, information about his treatment should be given as soon as it is known, and the reason for everything that is done should be carefully explained to him, and he should be carefully prepared for the way in which procedures will affect him.

Observation of the Patient

Whilst the nurse is admitting the patient to the ward, she can make many observations about him and his condition. What is his activity level? How well can he walk? Does he become breathless or exhausted on exertion? What is his mental state? How well does he adjust to admission to the ward? Is he apprehensive? What is his general health like? Does he show signs of neglect? What about his colour? Is he in any pain? Specific observations that will be made and recorded are: temperature, pulse, respiration rate and blood pressure. (Allow him to settle into the ward before recording these since pulse, respiration and blood pressure are affected by exertion and anxiety.) His weight is recorded, and his urine tested for abnormalities.

Before the patient is left to his own devices, he should be given a magazine or book to read, if he has none of his own with him. This gives him the security of appearing to be doing something, whilst he is getting used to his surroundings and assimilating the information he has been given.

Information Required from Patient

Name and address.
Age.
If married or single, widow or widower.
Occupation—in the case of a child the father's occupation.
Religion.
The address of the nearest relative (if not the same as the patient's
    address) and the telephone number, or the telephone number
    of a neighbour or friend willing to take a message.
The name of the physician or surgeon in charge of the case.
The name and address of the patient's general practitioner.
If the patient is a child, it is important to obtain full par-
ticulars, including the child's previous medical history, from the
parents before they leave the ward. They should also sign a form
giving permission for an operation to be performed, or for an
anaesthetic to be given if it is at all likely that these procedures will
be required.
Business telephone of relative.

Persons to be Notified of Admission

(1) The minister of the patient's particular religion.
(2) The porter dealing with the patient's post, telephone queries
    and directing visitors.
(3) The admissions office, if they do not already know.
(4) The house doctor in charge of the patient.
(5) The dietician, if the patient is on a special diet.

Emergency Admission

For a patient who is being admitted as an emergency, the most
urgent need will be for treatment of his physical condition. He will
no doubt also be very apprehensive about coming into hospital,
but his predominant feeling will be one of relief at being admitted
so that he can get expert care and attention. He may be feeling
very ill, or he may be in great pain. When the ward is informed
that such a patient is to be admitted, it is important that as much
information as possible is obtained about his condition, so that
the bed can be suitably prepared, and any equipment that may be

required for emergency treatment can be placed in readiness at the bedside.

Preparation of Bed and Equipment

The bed clothes are prepared into a 'pack' so that they can be removed in one operation from the bed when the patient arrives in the ward. This means that the patient can be lifted straight from the stretcher on to the bed; the pack can then be unfolded and the bed clothes placed in position over the patient and tucked in, in the usual way. If the patient has been involved in a road traffic accident, or has been vomiting, it may be advisable to protect the bed linen from being soiled.

Equipment needed in preparation at the patient's bedside will vary according to his condition, but examples are:

Bed blocks to raise the foot of the bed
Intravenous infusion trolley } if patient is shocked.
Injection tray

Anaesthetic instruments
Denture container
Suction apparatus with catheters } for unconscious patient.
Identification bracelet

Oxygen and equipment
for its administration } for patient in respiratory failure.
Extra pillows

Dressing trolley and shaving tray, if patient has an open wound.

Reception of Patient

When the patient arrives in the ward, the relative is asked to wait, whilst the nurse supervises the lifting of the patient from the trolley to the bed. If the patient's condition is critical, treatment may have to be instituted whilst the patient is still on the trolley. The nurse should assess the patient's condition, taking any emergency measures that are necessary, and she should also get a message sent to the doctor in charge that the patient has arrived, together with information about his condition. The patient's fears and apprehensions should not be forgotten, but the best way to reassure him is to ensure that he is safe and comfortable, as soon as possible.

Explanations of all that is being done should be given, although of course elaborate explanations are not required by a very ill patient. Ideally, another nurse should see the relative and reassure him that the patient is receiving treatment and attention. If no relative has accompanied the patient, steps should be taken as soon as possible to inform the next of kin of the patient's admission. After the patient's physical needs have been attended to, the admission details can be obtained and the relative allowed to see the patient. If immediate operation is planned, a consent form will have to be signed, and preparations for the operation carried out; this latter may include aspiration of the patient's stomach if he has had a meal recently.

Doctor's Examination of Patient

The doctor will carry out a full examination of the patient; when once the condition of the patient permits this in the case of an emergency admission; or at a mutually convenient time for a patient admitted from the waiting list. A lot of information about the patient's condition can be gained by the nurse who is present to look after the patient during the examination, by observing for any obvious abnormality that is revealed during the course of the examination. If she shows an intelligent interest, the doctor will probably be willing to explain to her the patient's signs and symptoms and their significance.

Equipment Required for Examination

Ophthalmoscope—to examine the optic disc.
Auriscope—to examine the ear drum.
Visual acuity charts.
Hat pins with coloured ends—to test visual fields and sensation to pin prick.
Cotton wool—to test sensation of light touch and corneal reflex.
Hot and cold water in test tubes—to test temperature sense.
Spatula and torch—to examine tongue, throat and palatal movement.
Patella hammer—to test tendon reflexes.
Tuning fork—to check hearing and vibration sense.
Tubes containing oil of cloves, peppermint, almond, salt, sugar —to test taste and smell.

Sphygmomanometer—to record blood pressure.
Stethoscope—to listen to heart and respiratory sounds.
Tape measure—to check for any bony or soft tissue deformity.
Glove and petroleum jelly—for rectal examination.
Note: In specialist wards, routine examination will include examination of special organs, e.g. vagina, ear, nose, throat.

When the doctor has completed the examination, the patient should be made comfortable and the bed straightened, before the curtains are drawn back. A word from the doctor to explain any further investigations or the line of treatment will help to reassure the patient.

Discharge of Patient

A great deal of thought and preparation should be directed towards ensuring continuity of care when once the patient has left the hospital. It is necessary to make a careful assessment of how well the patient can look after himself, and how much he will need to rely on other people. Is there a relative or friend who can carry out any care he will require? If not, arrangements for transfer to a convalescent home, or for visits from a home help or district nurse, will be needed. Education of the patient in caring for himself and carrying out any treatment is a part of the nursing staff's responsibility and should be undertaken early in his hospital stay. Diabetes and anaemia are conditions in which teaching of the patient is especially important; also where the patient is receiving hormone therapy or has a colostomy or ileostomy operation.

If the relatives cannot provide transport for the patient, or if he is being transferred to another hospital whilst he is still very ill, it will be necessary to order a hospital car or ambulance. Unless he is being transported by stretcher, the relatives will be asked to bring in his outdoor clothing. The time of his discharge must be discussed with his relatives, to ensure that someone is at home to greet him. Any drugs or dressings that he will require should be obtained, and appointments made for the outpatient, physiotherapy or occupational therapy departments, as necessary. It is usual for a final examination to be carried out by the medical staff just before discharge. Any clothing or valuables held by the hospital should be returned to him.

The patient's final impression of the hospital will be like his first, a lasting one, and although he will no doubt be anxious to get home, he may worry about his being able to cope without the support and security that having nursing and medical staff constantly available brings. If he has been encouraged to be as independent as possible during the whole of his hospital stay, it will facilitate his readjustment to normal life.

6
Basic nursing care
1. Patient's needs

INTRODUCTION

When a patient comes into hospital, the nurse is responsible for seeing that he receives the treatment that is ordered by the doctor; that all his physiological needs are met; and that he comes to no harm as a consequence of being in hospital. It is also most important that the nurse ensures that the patient's psychological and social needs are met, but this aspect of care has, traditionally, been emphasized less. One of the needs of the human individual, which manifests itself very early in life, is the need for independence and, although this need may vary in strength in different individuals, it is essential that it is not overlooked by the hospital staff. If one feels completely responsible for a patient, it is only too easy to encourage his dependence and to resent any signs of independence or initiative on his part. Passive dependence on the part of the patient makes him a 'good patient' whilst he is in the ward, but it ill equips him for assuming a normal, independent existence when once he is discharged.

Basic nursing care consists of helping the patient to carry out those health maintaining functions which he is unable to carry out for himself. The nurse's responsibility is to diagnose the exact amount of assistance required by each patient, and to supply that assistance. Physiological needs of individuals which the nurse must bear in mind in relation to her patients are: respiration, nutrition, excretion, activity and movement, sensory stimulation and comfort, sleep and rest, maintenance of body temperature within physiological limits, cleanliness and grooming.

NUTRITION

All organisms require food and water to maintain life. Food consists of several substances of different chemical composition, and there is a minimum amount of each of these compounds which must be taken in the diet to prevent deficiency disease. However, in highly developed countries, there is a great diversity of foods which will fulfil the basic needs, and what an individual actually eats will depend upon cultural and individual preference, as well as on the amount of pleasure the particular individual gets from eating.

Components of Food

Carbohydrates

The basic units of carbohydrates are the rather small sugar molecules, which are made of carbon, hydrogen and oxygen. Hundreds of sugar molecules may be combined to form the large molecules, starch and glycogen, whilst the molecular form in which other carbohydrates are found in the diet, is that of two sugar molecules combined together. In the body, carbohydrates are split into their component simple sugar molecules and are transported in the blood stream in this form. These substances are then oxidized by the body cells to form carbon dioxide and water, releasing some energy as heat and storing the remaining energy obtained to perform chemical or physical work. Some sugar molecules are incorporated into the body structure, but the majority contribute toward the total calorie (energy producing) content of food. Fruit, sugar, potatoes, flour, bread and rice are the main sources of carbohydrate. Cellulose, a large molecule carbohydrate, cannot be split into its component parts by the enzymes contained in the human digestive juices, and thus it passes unaltered through the alimentary tract. Cellulose is contained in fruit and vegetables, and it performs the useful function of stimulating peristalsis.

Fat

Fatty acids and glycerol, the component molecules of fat, also contain carbon, hydrogen and oxygen. Fat has the property of releasing more energy per unit weight than glucose. Any fat taken in excess of the calorie requirements can be stored in the fat deposits in the body. Excess glucose is also converted into fat and stored in this form. Fat is a component of cell membranes, and this is particularly important with regard to the cells of the nervous system. Butter, meat, some fish, milk and lard are good sources of fat, together with vegetable oils such as olive oil and nut oil which is converted into margarine.

Protein

This is the only source of nitrogen in food, and if adequate quantities of protein containing foods are not eaten, kwashiorkor may result. Proteins are very large molecules composed of many smaller compounds the amino acids, of which there are twenty. Some of these amino acids must be obtained from the diet (the essential amino acids), whilst others can be built up by the body, given adequate quantities of protein. Amino acids contain carbon, hydrogen, oxygen and nitrogen. They are used in the body to form enzymes, protoplasm, plasma proteins and hormones. Like fat, they are also essential components of cell membranes. Any amino acid taken in the diet in excess of the requirements for replacement and growth is converted to fat or glucose and used to obtain energy. The part of the molecule containing nitrogen is converted into urea and excreted in the urine.

Meat, fish, cheese, eggs and milk are good sources of protein in which can be found all the essential amino acids. Protein from a vegetable source (peas, beans, nuts, cereals) may not contain all the essential amino acids, so a variety of different protein foods is required daily if a vegetarian diet is strictly adhered to.

Mineral Salts

Small amounts of mineral salts are found in the body. Some of these help to maintain the osmotic pressure and pH of body fluids, some are structural components of bone, whilst others are combined in large organic molecules to form enzymes, coenzymes, haemoglobin, myoglobin and hormones. Mineral salts must be present in the diet to maintain health. Those required are: potassium, sodium chloride, calcium, phosphorus, magnesium, iron, copper, iodine and manganese. Iron, calcium and iodine are those most likely to be deficient in the diet. Meat, molasses, eggs, wholemeal bread and some green vegetables contain *iron*; milk and cheese contain *calcium*, and it is added to flour other than wholemeal. Iodine is found in fish and foods grown in iodine-containing soil (i.e. soil which is not too far distant from the sea). Table salt may have iodine added to it. *Fluorine* is found in variable amounts in drinking water and protects against dental caries in children. In large quantities, however, it causes mottling of the teeth.

Vitamins

'Vital amines' as their name implies are essential to life, although they do not provide energy and are required only in minute quantities. Some are soluble in fat and are absorbed from the digestive tract along with fat, whilst others are soluble in water.

Fat soluble vitamins. Absorption of these vitamins may be poor in the absence of bile or pancreatic lipase.

Vitamin A is a constitutent of the visual pigment retinene and is, therefore, essential for normal vision. It also maintains the epithelial tissue of the body. Foods containing vitamin A are: meat, fish, fish liver oils, butter and cheese. Carotene, found in tomatoes and carrots, is converted into vitamin A in the body. Excessive intake of vitamin A can occur, and leads to gastro-intestinal disturbance, scaly dermatitis and bone pain.

Vitamin D increases absorption of calcium and phosphorus from the digestive tract and, in its absence, rickets, a disease in which calcium is removed from the bone and teeth, may occur. Vitamin D is found in milk, butter, fish and fish liver oils. It is added to margarine. It is possible to take vitamin D in excess, leading to calcification of soft tissue.

Vitamin E: there is no evidence of the effects of deficiency of this vitamin in man, but in experimental animals vitamin E deficiency has been found to cause muscular dystrophy and foetal death. It is found in milk, eggs, meat and leafy vegetables.

Vitamin K is essential for the formation in the liver of prothrombin. Prothrombin, in turn, is an essential factor in the clotting of blood. Since bile and pancreatic lipase are necessary in order to absorb vitamin K, the clotting properties of the blood should be checked before an operation on a patient who has some biliary obstruction. Vitamin K is found in most green vegetables.

Water soluble vitamins. *Vitamin B* is a complex of different vitamins; thiamine, riboflavin, niacin, pyridoxine, pantothenic acid, biotin, folic acid and cyanocobalamine. These are essential components of enzymes or coenzymes concerned in intermediary metabolism. *Vitamin B_1 or thiamine*, is found in liver and unrefined cereals. Deficiency diseases associated with it are beri-beri and neuritis. Deficiency of *riboflavin or vitamin B_2* leads to glossitis and dermatitis around the mouth, nose, vulva and scrotum. It is found in liver and milk. The *niacin* deficiency disease is pellagra. Yeast, meat and liver contain niacin. *Pyridoxine or vitamin B_6* is also found in yeast and liver, and in wheat and corn. Its deficiency leads to mental confusion, depression and dermatitis. *Pantothenic acid* is found in eggs, liver and yeast; and dermatitis, enteritis, alopecia and adrenal insufficiency may occur if it is deficient in the diet. *Biotin* is thought to be synthesized by intestinal organisms. Deficiency has been produced in man, by the intake of large quantities of raw egg white. The symptoms were dermatitis, anaemia and muscle pain. *Folic acid* is essential for the formation by division of cells, and deficiency manifests itself by sprue and anaemia. It is found in leafy green vegetables. *Vitamin B_{12}* or cyanocobalamin is found in liver, meat, eggs and milk. Dietary deficiency is rare, but deficiency can occur due to malabsorption through the stomach wall, as in pernicious anaemia.

Vitamin C: the action of this vitamin has not been fully determined. It is concerned in the metabolism of some amino acids and it seems to be essential for the formation of collagen. It is found concentrated in endocrine glands, especially in the adrenal cortex, and depletion of ascorbic acid (vitamin C) from the adrenal gland occurs in physiological stress. Dietary deficiency of the vitamin results in scurvy, a disease in which there are subcutaneous bruises, haemorrhage from the gums, anaemia and delay in healing. Vitamin C is found in vegetables, fruit and milk, but it is very easily destroyed by heat and exposure to light.

Calorie Requirements

Neither mineral salts nor vitamins release energy for use by the body. Energy is needed to perform chemical, physical and muscular work within the body and to produce the heat which provides the optimum conditions for life processes in the human. If the energy-producing foods (carbohydrates, fats and protein) are taken in excess of requirements, fat is stored and the individual puts on weight. If fat, carbohydrate and protein are taken in insufficient quantities, then the body stores of these substances are used, and weight is lost. The measure used to estimate an individual's requirement of these foods is the Calorie, which is the amount of heat required to raise 1 kilogram of water through 1 degree centigrade. Calorie requirements vary with the amount of muscular work carried out, the size of the individual, the age, and the efficiency with which the body stores and uses energy. A patient lying in bed will require fewer Calories than an active, working individual, but very restless patients, for instance after head injuries, may use a great deal of energy and require a relatively high Calorie intake. The average diet should contain about 15 per cent of the Calories in the form of protein, 50 to 60 per cent in the form of carbohydrate, and 25 to 30 per cent in the form of fat.

Water

All tissues in the body contain water in varying proportions. For instance, the teeth contain 5 per cent water and bone 32 per cent water. Other tissues contain a greater proportion of water than this, the greatest being the lungs which contain 84 per cent. Urea and other waste products require water so that they may be excreted in solution. Water is required for the cooling of the body surface by sweat and for moistening inspired air. Digestive secretions contain a large volume of water, which is lost from the body if vomiting or diarrhoea occurs. Keeping fluid balance charts ensures that the patient gets sufficient fluid for his needs, and that fluid is neither retained nor excreted in excess.

FEEDING PATIENTS IN HOSPITAL

Patients' diets in hospital, other than those ordered individually from the special diet kitchen, are often classed as 'full', 'light' and 'fluid'. A patient taking full diet usually has three main meals, breakfast, midday dinner and supper, and the food served will be similar to that which he is accustomed to eat at home. Apart from therapeutic diets, some special diets may be needed for patients whose racial or religious customs may prohibit the eating of certain foods, for example, the kosher diet of the Jewish people and strictly vegetarian diets. Light diet commonly includes eggs, fish and chicken with additional milk drinks between main meals. Fluid diets, of which the basis is usually milk and sweetened fruit drinks, are generally served at 2-hourly intervals.

Some of the difficulties encountered in catering for large numbers are the distances which the cooked food has to travel between the central kitchen and the wards and the need to cook some food a considerable time before it will be eaten. The proper planning of kitchens and the provision of adequate equipment helps to solve this latter problem. Trolleys with separate compartments for hot foods and for cold foods are in general use for the transport of food to the wards. More recently a tray system whereby individual meals are served directly on to the patient's trays in the kitchen and then conveyed immediately to the ward has been introduced in some hospitals. Special plates are used to keep hot food at the right temperature (Fig. 3).

Fig. 3. A modern cafeteria system.

Most hospitals have a catering committee which considers all aspects of providing food for patients and staff, buying supplies, approving dietary scales and arrangements for cooking and serving meals. Special therapeutic diets, for example diabetic, reducing or low calorie, high protein, calcium balance diets, are planned and supervised by a qualified dietitian.

Serving Meals

The practice as regards serving meals may vary in different hospitals, but the nurse needs to be aware of the patient's preferences as regards food, and to observe the amount of food a patient actually eats. Eating is a pleasure for the great majority of people, and meals should be so presented that they are occasions which are looked forward to by the patients. Thus they should be served attractively and at the right temperature. Individual tastes should be considered so that, for example, gravy is not automatically put on to every plate regardless of whether a patient likes it or not. If the patient really cannot tolerate the meal sent from the kitchen, effort should be made to provide an alternative, even if this entails cooking a simple meal such as scrambled egg in the ward kitchen. The nurse should position her patients so that they can eat their meals in comfort. Dirty china should be cleared away immediately, especially if food scraps are left on the plate. Cold, congealed, half eaten food can be most unpleasant for sensitive but well individuals, let alone ill ones.

Feeding Patients

Skill, patience and gentleness are needed to feed another individual successfully with food or fluid. The speed with which a patient eats needs to be observed, so that the nurse matches this with the rate at which she presents the food. She needs to be able to place the spoon or fork accurately into the patient's mouth; if it is placed too far back it may produce gagging. If the movements of patient and nurse are not coordinated, the spoon or fork may hit against the patient's tongue or teeth and cause discomfort. Some people like to eat one kind of food at a time, whilst others like several different kinds of food mixed together. Patients may find it difficult to swallow unless they have frequent sips of water, whilst others do not like cold fluid whilst they are eating hot food. A sip of water can act as a boundary between two different types of food, and to go straight from a savoury food such as fish to a sweet food, or from a greasy food to a non-greasy food, without the opportunity to rinse the mouth with water, can be extremely distasteful. Such preferences must be taken into account. The nurse should sit down when she is feeding a patient so that this is made a pleasant social occasion for him.

If a patient with a neurological lesion is being fed, then careful observation must be made to detect any difficulty in swallowing. The swallowing reflex can be initiated by gentle pressure on the tongue with the spoon. Care must be taken to feed the patient from the side of the face on which there is no weakness or sensory loss, and to ensure that food does not accumulate in the cheek on the affected side.

When blind patients are being fed, it is important that they are told exactly what food is being given them, to avoid the shock of expecting one taste and getting a different type of food. If possible, even with blind patients, it is better if the patient can actually place the food in his mouth for himself, even though the nurse has placed the food on to the spoon or fork.

An angled straw, used with a cup or drinking glass may be used to give drinks to helpless patients. If a spouted feeding cup is used, then the patient should be told he can put his tongue over the end of the spout to control the flow; otherwise he may be afraid of choking. The best way to support his head whilst he is drinking is to put an arm under the pillow, raising the pillow and his head together.

When children are admitted into hospital, it is a good idea to ask about their special likes and dislikes with respect to food, and also about the way in which they normally eat their food. If their normal diet is totally unsuitable, they may be coaxed into eating more suitable food, but it must be remembered that the child will be returning to the environment from which he came.

Special Difficulties

Feeding patients following injuries or operations on the mouth and tongue often calls for special care and management. Examples of such conditions which are fairly commonly seen, are harelip and

BASIC NURSING CARE. 1   71

cleft palate in infants and operations for malignant disease of the
tongue.

Harelip Deformity

Infants with this type of congenital deformity may be able to
suck naturally, but if the condition of complete cleft palate is also
present he will need to be fed with a spoon or by an intragastric
tube. For spoon feeding the child should be laid flat on the lap of
the nurse or mother and the feed should be spooned into the hollow
of the cheek, well to the back of the mouth. After operation for the
repair of the lip, spoon feeding is continued using a small, narrow
spoon which will not stretch the mouth. Crying will put additional
strain on the stitches and it is therefore important that the infant
should have adequate nourishment and fluid so that he does not
cry from hunger or thirst. Water is given before and after each
milk feed.

Cleft Palate Operation

After this operation, which is usually performed at a later age
than the repair of the harelip but before the child begins to talk,
feeding may be given by an intragastric tube or from a spouted
feeding cup with a rubber tube attached. Cold liquids are usually
given for the first few days; later semi-fluid feeds and soft solids
given by spoon are allowed. A drink of water should be given before
and after each feed to clean the mouth.

Operations on the Tongue

Following operation on the tongue (including the insertion of
radium needles) the patient is given a fluid diet either by an intragastric tube or from a spouted feeding cup with a rubber tube
attached. The tubing should be put at the side of the mouth well to
the back. Gentle irrigation of the mouth is usually ordered before
and after feeds. If radium needles have been inserted their presence
and position must be checked at the end of any treatment. Careful
attention should be paid to thorough cleansing of the feeding cup
and tubing after use, using a bottle brush for the spout and tubing.
The cup and the rubber tubing should then be boiled and placed in
a sterile covered bowl in readiness for the next feed.

Infant Feeding

The natural food for the new-born infant is the secretion of the mother's mammary glands. The breasts first secrete a substance called colostrum which contains some protein. On the third day after delivery milk is produced; human milk contains the proteins lactalbumin and casein, carbohydrate (in the form of lactose) and fat. This milk also contains protective antibodies which give the new-born infant a degree of immunity to certain infections.

It is generally accepted that every infant should be breast fed, at least for the first few weeks of his life, unless there is some contra-

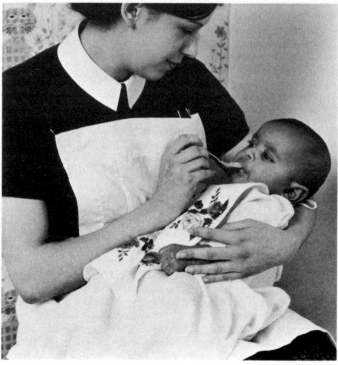

FIG. 4. Spoon feeding a new-born infant.

indication such as active tuberculosis in the mother. Many paediatricians, however, now hold that the infant can and should have additions to this food at an early age, some say from birth. The infant's diet may therefore include pounded meat, and fish, eggs, cereals, sieved fruits and vegetables; also given are cow's milk, fruit juices and, of course, water to drink. With this type of diet a feeding bottle can be dispensed with, since the infant, apart from feeding at the breast, takes all his food from a spoon or cup (Fig. 4). A mixed diet will usually provide the necessary vitamins; if the infant is fed on milk only, it is necessary to give orange or black-currant juice and fish-liver oil daily to ensure a sufficiency of vitamins C, A and D, since the vitamin content of both human and cow's milk is variable.

When an infant is admitted to hospital his feeding should if possible continue on the lines to which he is accustomed. His condition may, however, make this impossible. Milk is usually the basis of the feeds for a sick infant unable to take a mixed diet. Some addition, such as two teaspoonfuls of Farex, or one tablespoonful of Benger's Food to one pint of milk, may be suitable.

The management of feeding difficulties in young infants and premature babies is a specialized subject on which the student is advised to consult a textbook of paediatric nursing.

When feeding an infant either with a spoon or a feeding bottle, the nurse or the mother should sit in a comfortable position with the child in her lap supported on her left arm. A sick baby may have to be fed in his cot. If a feeding bottle is used, it may be either the upright or the boat-shaped variety; the latter has two openings with a rubber valve at one end and a teat at the other; the upright bottle has only one opening, which is usually kept covered with a rubber cap which is exchanged for the feeding teat immediately before giving the feed. The hole in the teat should be large enough to allow the fluid to drop through, but not big enough to allow the infant to gulp the feed too quickly.

After use the bottle should be well flushed through with cold water then washed in warm soapy water and either boiled or auto-claved, or completely immersed in a tank of solution such as Milton 1 in 80. Teats are cleaned first in cold water, then in hot water and are then kept in a small covered jar containing Milton 1 in 80 until required. Salt rubbed over both inside and outside surfaces of the teat will remove grease when necessary. Teats may be boiled, but repeated boiling tends to soften the rubber.

Tube Feeding

If a patient is unable to swallow, for any reason, he may be fed artificially using a tube passed down the oesophagus into the stomach. Conditions in which tube feeding may be necessary are:

(1) Coma.
(2) Paralysis of the soft palate or pharyngeal muscle.
(3) After operation on the mouth, pharynx or larynx.
(4) For premature or weak infants who are unable to suck.

Principles

(1) Great care must be taken before any fluid is given to ensure that the tube is correctly placed in the stomach, and is neither in the lungs, nor coiled in the mouth or pharynx. Two people should check the position of the tube, and in some hospitals it is required that one of these should be a qualified nurse or doctor.

(2) Air should not be allowed to enter the stomach whilst the feed is being given; therefore the apparatus should not be allowed to become empty until the entire feed has been administered.

(3) To avoid discomfort caused by the sudden stimulation of stomach nerve endings by cold fluid, the feed should be warmed to room or body temperature before it is given.

(4) Sudden distension of the stomach can also stimulate nerve endings and cause discomfort. This can be avoided by giving the feed slowly, either by the use of small apparatus or by pinching the tube slightly as the feed is given, to reduce its calibre.

(5) It is not necessary to remove the tube after every feed if it has been passed nasally, but it will require periodic removal for cleaning and to avoid a tissue reaction. A rubber tube should be changed every 24 hr, a polythene one every 7 days.

(6) Lack of skill in passing a tube into the stomach can cause damage to the mucous membrane of the nose, nasopharynx or oesophagus. If any difficulty is encountered, the attempt to pass the tube should be abandoned. A later attempt, by a different individual, or using different apparatus, may be more successful.

Apparatus Required for Tube Feeding

Mouthwash, *or* tray for cleaning the mouth, if the tube is to be passed orally.

Orange sticks and wool swabs; a gallipot containing sodium bicarbonate, for cleaning the nostrils if the tube is to be passed nasally.

A small glass or polythene funnel. (The barrel of a Dakin's syringe is suitable.)

An oesophageal tube (Fig. 5), size 6 to 18 (English gauge) or 14 to 22 (French gauge). (The larger sizes are used for the oral route, the smaller for the nasal route.)

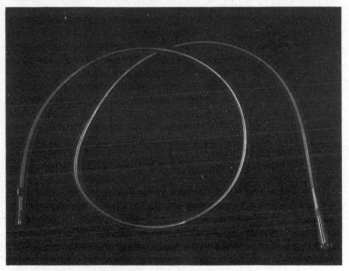

Fig. 5. Oesophageal tube.

A bowl for the apparatus.

A measure containing water, to clear the tube.

A measure containing the feed.

A lotion thermometer.

A protective cape and a towel.

Liquid paraffin *or* water to act as a lubricant.

A 20-ml syringe and an adaptor, *or* the rubber bulb of the Dakin's
syringe.

A measure and litmus paper, for gastric juice.

For an unconscious patient, a tray containing a tongue spatula,
tongue forceps and a gag should be provided, so that the mouth
may be opened to observe the position of the tube.

Passing the Tube

The nasal route. Position the patient, sitting him up well with
the head slightly flexed if possible. Clean the nostrils and observe
if the nasal septum is deviated from the midline. Note the approximate distance of 50 to 60 cm from the stomach end of the tube
before the tube is inserted as a guide. Pass the tube gently along
the floor of the larger nostril. Ask the patient to swallow as the tube
is passed down the oesophagus. Proceed slowly, and do not persist
if there is any resistance to the passage of the tube. A conscious
patient will cough if the tube enters the larynx, and the tube must
be withdrawn. A deeply unconscious patient will have no cough
reflex but he may become cyanosed if the tube enters the respiratory
system. The tube should be in the stomach when it has passed for
50 to 62 cm (19½ to 25 in.), depending upon the height of the adult.

The oral route. Any dentures should be removed. The procedure
is the same as for the nasal route, except that the tube is passed
over the tongue, not through a nostril. A mouth gag may be needed
to hold open the mouth of an unconscious patient.

Checking that the Tube is in the Stomach

There are two ways of doing this:

(1) A syringe is attached to the end of the tube and a specimen
of fluid obtained by suction. This is tested by litmus paper for
acidity, since gastric juice has a low pH (it contains hydrochloric
acid). If there is any difficulty in obtaining a specimen of gastric
juice, it may be helpful to place the patient in the left lateral
position with one pillow under the head, and the foot of the bed
on blocks. This helps the gastric fluid to gravitate to the fundus of
the stomach where it has been shown that the end of the tube tends
to lie.

(2) The other method of ensuring that the tube is in the correct place is by placing a stethoscope over the stomach and listening through the ear pieces whilst 5 ml air is injected through the stomach tube, using a Dakin's or 20-ml syringe. If the end of the tube is in the stomach, the air will be heard, by means of the stethoscope, as it enters.

Note: Another method for checking the position of the tube is sometimes proposed. This consists of connecting a funnel and tubing on to the tube, inverting the funnel into a bowl of water, and observing for the presence or absence of bubbles from the apparatus. The presence of bubbles signifies that the tube is in the respiratory tract. In my opinion, this is a very bad method to use for two reasons:

(1) If the tube is in the respiratory tract, the patient will be breathing in as well as out, and on inspiration the fluid will be sucked up into the apparatus. If a small funnel and short tubing is used, there is a real danger that this fluid may get into the patient's respiratory tract.

(2) A demonstration that the tube is *not* in the respiratory tract does not show that it *is* in the stomach. Thus the methods discussed above are safer as regards ensuring that the tube is in the stomach.

Administration of the Feed

The feed to be given is usually prepared in the diet kitchen to give the correct quantity of fluid, calories, and nutrients for the particular patient. Substances which may be used to prepare the feed are: 'Complan', 'Metercal', glucose water, egg and milk, and orange juice.

The 24-hr amount is divided so that a quantity may be given 2- to 4-hourly.

Method

Having checked the position of the tube, the temperature of the fluid is checked and a funnel is attached to the end of the tube. Some tubing may be interposed between the oesophageal tube and the funnel, if necessary. Half of the water is inserted into the funnel and allowed to enter the stomach before the feed, ensuring easier flow of the thicker liquid. The feed is run in slowly, pinching the tube if necessary. The funnel should not be allowed to empty or air will enter the stomach. At the end of the feed, the remaining water is used to clear the tube and the tube is either spigotted and attached to the patient's forehead or it is pinched, and gently withdrawn. If the tube is not pinched as it is withdrawn, any fluid remaining in it will empty, and may drop into the larynx causing choking or chest infection, depending upon whether the cough reflex is present or not.

Feeding by Gastrostomy Tube

When the operation of gastrostomy is performed for the purpose of feeding a patient, a catheter (usually a self-retaining one, such as a De Pezzer catheter) is put into the stomach through an incision made in the abdominal wall and the stomach wall. The tube is taken out periodically and replaced by a new one.

It is especially important in the first few days after the operation to notice if the tube slips out of the opening, as it should be replaced at once. If it remains out for any length of time it may be very difficult to replace. Should the nurse have to replace it, she should remember the danger of pushing it between the abdominal wall and the stomach wall into the peritoneal cavity. The tube should be inserted without force into the centre of the opening.

Apparatus

Funnel.
Piece of tubing.
Tubing clip.
Connector.
A catheter, if the gastrostomy tube has been removed and the opening closed by gastrostomy plug.
Mackintosh.
Clean dressing and bandage, if likely to be required.
Measure containing water.
Bowl for apparatus.
If the gastrostomy tube has not been removed and the outer opening is closed by a spigot, a clean spigot should be provided to close the tube after the feed has been given.

The Feed

As the usual reason for gastrostomy is a malignant stricture of the oesophagus, the patient is probably emaciated from months of starvation. It is important that he should receive a diet which is adequate in nutritive quality and also containing the necessary accessory constituents of a balanced diet. A diet with a Calorie value of 2500 to 3000 is desirable. The patient if properly fed, should regain some, at least, of his lost weight and strength. Feeding is begun as soon as he recovers from the anaesthetic and at first small quantities are given, but these are soon increased.

Method

The mackintosh is arranged to protect the dressing. The spigot is removed from the catheter or, if the catheter has been removed, the gastrostomy plug is taken out and the catheter required for feeding inserted into the opening.

The end of the connector is fixed to the catheter in the gastrostomy opening. The tubing is compressed to expel air. The feed is given slowly, finishing with water to wash through the catheter; if this is omitted the catheter may be blocked by coagulation of the milk as a result of the action of the gastric juice.

The connector tubing and funnel are removed and the spigot or the gastrostomy plug, whichever is used, is replaced. The gastric contents are very irritating to the skin should they leak through the tube; therefore a protective silicone cream or similar application is applied around the gastrostomy opening. As soon as possible the patient is taught to give his own feeds.

Care of the Mouth

Epithelial tissues line the mouth and cover the tongue, and the upper layers keratinize. Friction from the muscular movement involved in eating and talking, aids normal desquamation of the keratinized layer, and the saliva then helps to wash the shed cells away. Saliva also dilutes and washes away microorganisms, as well as having a mildly antiseptic action. Any condition, then, which reduces either the normal muscular activity of mouth structures, or the amount of saliva present, will predispose to mouth infection. Worse still, the presence of any instrument or appliance in the mouth can lead to a tissue reaction, or may allow the accumulation of debris. An airway, a Ryle's or oesophageal tube, dentures or an endotracheal tube all increase the risk of damage or infection of the membranes with which they are in contact.

Conditions which reduce the quantity of saliva:

(1) Dehydration due to insufficient fluid intake or to excess sweating, as in fever.

(2) Mouth breathing.

(3) Lack of reflex stimulation of salivary glands by food, e.g. when patient is being fed artificially.

(4) Administration of drugs which dry salivary secretions, e.g. atropine, scopolamine, antihistamines.

(5) In anxiety, when the sympathetic nervous system is over-active.

Lack of normal mouth hygiene leads to halitosis, collection of dried secretion, microorganisms and shed cells, and eventually to mouth infection. Infection can then spread to nasal structures, or the respiratory tract. Conversely, a pre-existent infection of nasal structures or respiratory tract will predispose to mouth infection. The importance of mouth hygiene in sick people cannot be over-emphasized and, where the patient cannot undertake this for himself, the nurse must assess the best method and the frequency of mouth care.

For the patient who is not seriously ill, the best method of caring for the mouth is by cleaning the teeth and the tongue, using a soft toothbrush and toothpaste. This removes debris and stimulates the blood supply, maintaining the gums in a healthy condition. An antiseptic mouthwash may be pleasant for the patient, but it is no substitute for cleaning the teeth, and it should be very mild or it will irritate the oral tissues.

When the patient is too ill to clean his own teeth, or for the nurse to do it for him, then the nurse must clean the mouth using swabs and lotions.

If a patient is able to sit up in bed to clean his own teeth he should be supported in a comfortable position with a towel to protect his jacket and the sheet. He needs a tooth glass or metal mug containing tepid or hot water according to preference, toothpaste, brush and a large receiver or basin. If the patient cannot sit up, he should be turned to his left side with the towel spread under his head and neck and the receiver on the towel conveniently placed for him to spit into.

A patient who is not able to assist himself should lie on his side. The teeth are cleaned by brushing systematically with a moist toothbrush and the dentifrice, beginning with the outer surfaces of the front teeth, then with patient opening his mouth widely enough to allow the brush to be inserted between the inner surface of the cheek and the teeth; clean first the teeth on the right side and then on the left side and finally brush the inner surface of the teeth. The teeth should be brushed by starting at the gum margin and working towards the edge of the tooth. The patient should be allowed to rinse freely during the process and, if he cannot raise his head sufficiently to use a tooth glass, an angled drinking tube should be provided. The state of the tongue and mouth should be noted during the tooth-cleaning process. False teeth must receive frequent attention; they should be scrubbed in clean warm water with a small brush, using bicarbonate of soda or a special dentifrice. The patient should be given a mouth wash after the dentures have been cleaned and replaced.

Cleaning the Mouth of an Ill Patient

Principles. (1) Dried secretions, keratinized cells, and micro-organisms are loosened and removed from the epithelial surface by the use of swabs soaked in sodium bicarbonate or hydrogen peroxide solutions.

. (2) A mildly antiseptic mouthwash solution is used to freshen the mouth.

(3) The salivary glands are stimulated by the action of swabbing the mouth. Lemon or glycerine may be used to increase the amount of salivary secretion.

(4) Dry, cracked lips may easily become infected and this infection could spread to the mouth. Petroleum jelly or the patient's own face cream applied to the lips will prevent the skin from cracking.

(5) If herpes simplex lesions are present on the lips, they should be treated by applying an appropriate antiseptic lotion, preventing the spread of this virus.

(6) Great care should be taken when cleaning the mouth of an unconscious patient that neither lotion nor a piece of swab is allowed to enter the nasopharynx, from whence it could enter the respiratory system. The use of hydrogen peroxide which froths, cotton wool and gauze from which small pieces may fray should be avoided. Stitched gauze strips, firmly clipped into artery forceps should be used instead (Fig. 6).

(7) The mouth should be cleaned frequently enough to keep the membranes pink and moist, and the breath odourless.

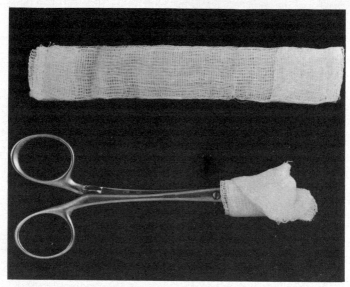

FIG. 6. Spencer-Wells forceps with stitched gauze strip applied ready for mouth care.

Apparatus required

A small bowl containing linen swabs or gauze strips.

A pair of artery forceps and a pair of dissecting forceps.

Gallipots containing hydrogen peroxide, 2·5 volumes *or* sodium bicarbonate, 1:60 solution; glycothymoline *or* some other suitable antiseptic solution; glycerine, lemon or glycerine and borax; petroleum jelly.

A disposal bag for soiled swabs.

A bag for soiled forceps.

Method

Secure the linen or gauze swabs in the forceps so that the ends of the forceps are completely protected by the swab. Moisten them with the hydrogen peroxide or sodium bicarbonate solution and gently swab the epithelial surfaces of the mouth and the surfaces of the teeth. Use the swabs once only, removing the dirty swabs from the forceps by means of the dissecting forceps. Swab the area again using the antiseptic lotion. Glycerine and borax, glycerine or lemon can then be applied, if desired.

Finally, apply petroleum jelly or cream to the lips by means of a swab held in the fingers.

7

Basic nursing care
2. General procedures

BEDMAKING

Skilled bedmaking, placing pillows comfortably, and correct positioning, contributes a good deal to the comfort of an ill person since he will spend the greater part of his time in bed.

Principles of Bedmaking

(1) Bedmaking should be carried out as often as is necessary to keep the patient comfortable and to make sure that the sheets are smooth and clean, but at the same time an ill patient should not be disturbed merely to ensure that the bed looks tidy.

(2) The quality of the mattress is to some extent beyond the nurse's control, but she should at least make sure that mattresses are replaced when they become worn, and that the patient gets the most suitable type of mattress for his condition.

(3) Cross-infection is a danger if bedmaking is carried out unskilfully. Movement of the bedclothes dislodges microorganisms from the bed into the air and also disturbs the air above the bed, increasing the area over which microorganisms may be airborne. Excess shaking and flapping of the bedclothes should be avoided, and smooth movements causing little disturbance of the air should be used.

(4) The bedclothes should be stripped on to a chair which is used exclusively for the patient, or on to a bed stripper attached as an integral part of the patient's bed. A bed stripper, carried from bed to bed, is a potential danger from the cross-infection point of view. Care should be taken to prevent the bedclothes from dragging on to the floor, picking up microorganisms; passers-by should be careful not to brush the bedclothes with their personal clothing.

(5) Bedclothes should never be stripped completely from over the patient, leaving him uncovered. A sheet should be left over him if the ward temperature is warm, or a blanket if it is cold. His comfort should be the prime concern whilst the bed is being made; if he is being turned, he should be moved very gently and a pillow left under his head for comfort.

(6) If the patient is hot and sticky, ensure that the sheets are replaced so that a cool, fresh area is in contact with the patient.

(7) All the equipment which may be required should be available at the bed side, before stripping the bed, and two people should work together so that the bed is made as efficiently and quickly as possible and the patient moved without causing him pain or excessive exertion.

(8) Removal of debris from the sheets and tautening creases from the sheets helps to prevent pressure sores.

To Make Up an Unoccupied Bed

(1) Collect washable blankets, sheets, pillow cases, counterpane and disposable polythene sheeting, and place them on the chair at the foot of the bed in the order in which they will be required.

(2) See that the mattress is pulled well up to the bedhead and spread out the bottom sheet over the mattress, ensuring sufficient to tuck well in at the bottom; tuck in at the sides and top of the mattress, mitring the corners.

(3) Place the polythene sheeting across the bed about 46 cm (18 in.) from the head and tuck in on either side. Over it, place the draw sheet, and tuck in about 30 cm (1 ft) of the sheet on one side; if it is a long draw sheet, neatly fold the other end and tuck it in smoothly and evenly under the mattress.

(4) Spread out the top sheet, allow a turnover of approximately 50 cm (20 in.) at the head end, and tuck in on either side whilst moving to the foot of the bed. Tuck it in at the foot.

(5) Take the first blanket to the top of the bed and place it in position. Fold over about 20 cm (8 in.) and fold in the corner diagonally so that there will be room for the patient to move. Move towards the foot of the bed, tucking in the sides of the blanket as you go, and tuck in at the foot, attending to the corners. Repeat for all blankets.

(6) Take the counterpane to the top of the bed and lay the top edge over the blankets. Turn back the sheet and, allowing the counterpane to hang loosely on either side of the bed, tuck in the bottom, mitring the corner to give a neat appearance.

(7) Place the pillows at the head of the bed on top of the bed-clothes.

To Make an Occupied Bed

(1) Explain to the patient that his bed is to be made.

(2) Place his chair at the foot of the bed if there is not a bed stripping area incorporated into the bedstead. Loosen the bed-clothes on either side and from the foot of the mattress.

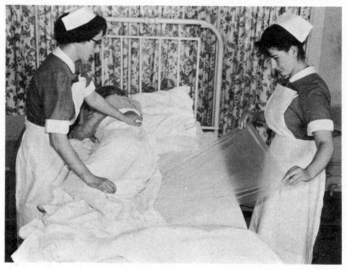

Fig. 7. A disposable waterproof sheet in use.

(3) Starting at the top of the bed, move towards the foot of the bed, taking the counterpane from the top and folding it neatly into three or four as you go, and finally lay it on the chair or stripper. If it is likely to drag on to the floor, fold the sides up neatly over the chair to prevent this.

(4) Repeat with the other top bedclothes except for a sheet or blanket.

(5) Remove all but one pillow and place on to a chair near the head of the bed, whilst one nurse supports the patient.

(6) Roll the patient to one side, placing one pillow under his head. The nurse towards whom he faces should stand close to the bed, so the patient does not feel afraid of falling out.

(7) Roll the drawsheet and polythene sheeting to the centre of the bed (Fig. 7).

(8) If the bottom sheet needs changing, roll this also to the centre of the bed and tuck in the new sheet on one side and halfway along the head and foot of the mattress. Use the folds laundered into the sheet to ensure that it is centred properly. Make sure that a good amount is tucked in at the bottom. Roll up the other half of the sheet lengthways in the middle of the bed. Bring back the polythene over the top of the roll and also the draw sheet unless a clean one is inserted. If the bottom sheet is not being changed it should be untucked, brushed clean with the hand and tucked in again, so that no creases remain, pulling it up well, before smoothing and tucking in the polythene and draw sheet.

(9) Roll the patient gently on to the opposite side, taking the precaution mentioned above. Warn him about any sheets rolled in the middle of the bed, since these will give the feeling of a big 'hump'.

(10) Remove all dirty sheets into a container at the bedside. Smooth the sheets, brush all debris away, and tuck them in as smoothly and tightly as possible; thus the making of the bottom of the bed is completed.

(11) Turn the patient back to the centre of the bed and support him whilst his pillows are 'plumped' and rearranged. Lift him into a comfortable position.

(12) As soon as the top sheet has been placed over him, the blanket covering him may be removed. Replace the top bedclothes as explained above (see section entitled 'To Make Up an Un-occupied Bed', p. 85.

(13) Ensure that the bedclothes are loose over the patient's feet. A bed cradle may be used to support their weight, but in the absence of this the bedclothes should be pleated over the feet, or the patient can be asked to cross one foot over the other whilst the bed is being made, ensuring plenty of room for his feet.

(14) Replace the patient's locker in a convenient position for him.

An Alternative Method

If the condition of the patient allows, it may be easier to lift the patient to the foot of the bed where he can be supported by one nurse. The bottom sheets at the head of the bed are straightened or changed. The patient is then lifted back on to the newly made part of the bed whilst the lower end of the bottom sheets are attended to.

To Make A Cot

A cot can be made easily by one nurse, since usually the child can be taken out of the cot and held on a nurse's knee. The procedure for making a cot is the same as that for making a bed, except that the counterpane is tucked in all round to allow the cot sides to be put up. A toddler may spend the greater part of the day on top of the bedclothes rather than in the bed, so he should be warmly clothed. For the child's safety, the cot sides must be fastened in position before he is left.

To Make the Top Bedclothes into a 'Pack'

This is done whenever the patient is to be moved directly from a stretcher to the bed. Circumstances in which this might happen are:
(1) Emergency admission.
(2) On return to the ward from the operating theatre.
(3) Following X-ray or any other examination in a separate department.

Method

Place the bottom sheet and draw sheet in position in the usual way. The top bedclothes are made up as usual at the head end of the bed but are left loose at the foot, allowing the usual amount for tuck in. When all the bedclothes have been replaced, the counterpane is folded back at the foot, the blankets are folded over it and finally the sheet. This allows for quick and easy tucking in when the patient is back in bed. The bedclothes are then folded so that they can be easily removed to allow the patient to be lifted onto the bed. An electric blanket may be placed in the bed to keep it warm.

Clean bed linen should be used when making up the bed for a patient in the operating theatre; the bed frame itself and the mattress should have been cleaned with antiseptic and dried.

In the case of an emergency admission, if the patient is admitted fully clothed, or has been involved in a road traffic accident, the sheets may be protected by blankets, but it is cheaper and easier to launder sheets than blankets so this is not a very logical procedure.

Modifications of Basic Bed Making in Special Conditions

After Tonsillectomy

After this operation the patient will be nursed in a semi-prone position, with no pillow under his head (Fig. 8). A pillow is placed under the mattress at the back of the patient to help maintain his

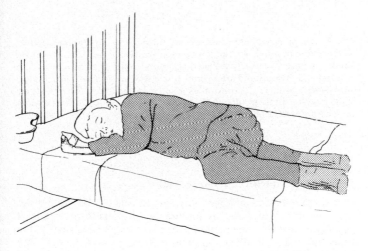

FIG. 8. Position following tonsillectomy. Any blood and secretions can easily drain out of the mouth and inhalation is prevented.

position, and the top of the bed is protected by a disposable polythene sheet and draw sheet. A bed elevator should be available.

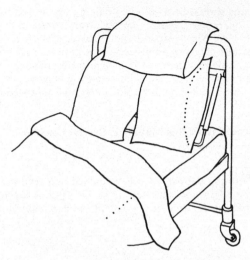

FIG. 9. Bed prepared with a bed rest and three pillows to support a patient in the sitting position. Two pillows on one end are placed against the bed rest and a third placed across them to support the head and shoulders. The bed rest and three pillows are a comfortable support and more economical in pillows and linen than are pillows only. In the bed illustrated, for a patient with a drainage tube in the thoracic cavity connected with a water seal bottle, a central gap left between the pillows prevents kinking or obstruction of the tube.

If Traction is Applied to a Lower Limb

A fracture board should be in position. The top bedclothes are made up in two sections, by folding the blankets to the required size within a sheet; one section is to cover the patient's body, the other covers his good leg and tucks in at the foot of the bed. The limb to which traction has been applied emerges from between the two sections and should be covered by a small blanket.

Following Amputation of the Lower Limb

A fracture board is required and a divided bed (as described for traction applied to a lower limb above) may be used, but more usually the bed is made up in the normal way over a bed cradle. A roller towel may be placed over the stump, and its ends anchored firmly by sandbags on either side of the limb to prevent flexion deformity of the hip in an above-knee amputation.

To Allow Drying of Plaster of Paris

A good circulation of air around the wet plaster of Paris aids drying. For an upper limb, no modification of the bed is required. The limb should be supported on a firm plastic covered pillow on top of the bedclothes.

In the case of a lower limb, a large bed cradle is used, and the bedclothes are turned back over it so that the bed end is open to the air.

BATHING PATIENTS

If possible the patient should bath in the bathroom, or better still, use a shower if one is available rather than have a bed bath. Practically any patient who can sit out of bed for long periods can be lifted into a bath, or can sit in a special chair whilst being given a shower.

Procedure for Bathing a Patient in the Bathroom

(1) Ensure that the air temperature in the bathroom is warm and that the bath has been cleaned and disinfected after the last patient. Take the patient's washing equipment and towels to the bathroom together with clean pyjamas or nightdress and place on the towel rail to warm.

(2) Fill the bath with water at a suitable temperature, e.g. 38°C. If the patient is to be lifted into the bath only about 20 cm (8 in.) of water should be drawn before he is lifted in.

(3) *If the patient can bath himself*, leave him whilst he is bathing. Since most ward bathroom doors have no lock, a screen can be placed around the bath to give a degree of privacy.

(4) *If the patient is to be lifted into the bath*, it is useful to place the wheelchair at the end of the bath, opposite the taps, with the

patient facing in the direction he will sit in the bath. At least two nurses will be needed to lift him on to the edge of the bath; from there he can be gently lowered into the water.

(5) Add more water, taking care not to scald the patient with water from the hot water tap (a mixer tap is best), and wash the patient thoroughly. Parts of the body not in the water should be rinsed and dried immediately.

(6) The water should then be let out of the bath, and the patient dried as much as possible before he is lifted back into the chair.

(7) A clean dry, warm towel, should be placed in the chair to dry the buttocks. Again, the patient can be lifted in two stages, first to the edge of the bath and then to the chair. He is then dried thoroughly, talcum powder applied, and his clean pyjamas, his slippers and dressing gown are replaced.

It is possible to get special bath lifts and hoists which are useful to help lift a heavy patient in and out of a bath.

Bathing a Patient in Bed

Principles

(1) Unless a patient is very ill, it is better if he can be bathed daily.

(2) Ensure the comfort of the patient throughout the procedure. Carry out as much of the bath as possible before moving him from his original comfortable position. Carefully arrange the procedure so that the minimum of movement and turning is required. Rinse and dry the washed areas thoroughly, and do not wet such a large area that the patient gets cold and uncomfortable before he can be dried. Keep the patient warm throughout the procedure.

(3) Let the patient carry out as much of the bath for himself as he is able. It may be necessary to hand him the flannel and towel. If possible place the bowl of water on a towel, on the bed, so he can place his hands and feet into it, to soak and wash them.

(4) Change the water as often as necessary so that it remains warm and clean, and always change it immediately after washing the pubic area. The water should be as hot as the nurse can tolerate on her hands, because considerable cooling of the water on the flannel will occur before it reaches the patient's skin.

(5) Make sure that everything needed for the bath is at the bed-

side before beginning so that the patient is not left during the procedure.

(6) The patient should feel refreshed as well as being clean at the end of the bath. Mouth care should be given, nails should be clean and smooth, talcum powder and/or deodorant should be applied; the patient's hair should be brushed, and in the case of a woman, make-up should be applied if she normally wears it. If the patient has been unable to take a bath for some time before coming into hospital, special attention should be paid to the cleanliness of the umbilicus and toes.

Requirements

These should be preferably placed on a trolley which can then act as a working surface and is better than using the top of the patient's locker.

(1) Clean bed linen, nightdress or pyjamas.
(2) Container for dirty linen.
(3) Bowl containing hot water.
(4) Jugs containing fresh hot water.
(5) Lotion or bath thermometer.
(6) Bath blankets.
(7) Tooth mug and receiver or mouth tray.
(8) Nail file, hair brush and comb.
(9) Flannels, soap and towels for face and body. Talcum powder.
(10) Bucket for dirty water.

Method

(1) Explain to the patient and offer him the opportunity to pass urine. Screen the bed.

(2) Strip the top bedclothes, leaving the patient covered with a bath blanket and one of the blankets from the bed as well if the day is cold. The bath blanket can be put in position simultaneously with the removal of the sheet so that the patient is never completely uncovered. Place the second bath blanket in position underneath the patient by rolling him from side to side.

(3) Remove the patient's nightdress or pyjamas.

(4) Wash, rinse and dry his face, or better still, allow him to do this for himself. Only use soap if this is the normal practice for the patient.

(5) Wash, rinse and dry the arm furthest away from you. (This is useful if another nurse is helping; she can then dry the limb whilst the one nearer to you is washed.)

(6) Wash, rinse and dry the other arm, the chest, the abdomen and the legs, making sure that the bath blanket covers the parts not actually being washed.

(7) The pubic area may be washed next; if the patient can do this for himself, the nurse can hold the bath blanket up as a 'tent' so the patient has room to work without being embarrassingly exposed. If the patient cannot manage by himself, the nurse must give the area a thorough wash.

(8) Remove all the pillows except one, and roll the patient on to the side so he faces away from the nurse who is washing him, and is supported by the other one. Using clean water wash the upper part of his back. Then his buttocks, anal region, and pubic area if this has not already been done. Treat his pressure areas and make this side of his bed.

(9) Roll the bath blanket to the middle.

(10) Turn the patient to the other side, wash and treat pressure areas as necessary. Attend to the bottom sheets and remove the bath blanket from under him.

(11) Put on clean pyjamas, position him comfortably, and re-make the bed. Attention to mouth toilet, nails and hair can then be given.

To Wash the Patient's Back

(12) *If the patient cannot lie flat*, or prefers to sit up: support him, sitting forward, so his back is exposed, and can be washed and dried. Put on his pyjama jacket. Attend to the bedclothes at the head of the bed whilst he is leaning forward, rolling in clean linen as necessary. Replace the pillows and allow the patient to lean back. One nurse can then support his buttocks free of the bed, whilst the other washes the area, carries out pressure area care, and makes the bottom of the bed.

CARE OF THE PATIENT'S HAIR

The patient's hair should be brushed and combed and put into his/her usual style each morning if he is unable to do this for himself. Any patient who is in hospital for a long time may need his hair washing and the nurse must be able to do this, although many hospitals have a hairdresser who visits the ward at regular intervals, and will wash and set the patient's hair.

To Wash the Hair of a Patient in Bed

Requirements

Waterproof sheeting for the floor, the bed, and to place under the washing bowl.

A mackintosh cape and towel to protect the patient's pyjamas.

Towels. Shampoo.

A small jug and two large ones containing water at 37°C (99°F).

A lotion or bath thermometer.

A washing bowl.

A hair dryer.

Extra pillows or sandbags may be needed.

Method

(1) If possible, pull the patient's bed away from the wall and remove the bed head.

(2) Arrange the empty bowl on a stool at the head of the bed on top of a waterproof sheet, and spread one waterproof sheet on the floor, the final one protects the bed linen.

(3) Put the mackintosh cape over the patient's shoulders; tuck the towel in around his neck to prevent water running down.

(4) Position the patient as comfortably as possible at the top of the bed with his head protruding over the bowl and his shoulders and neck supported.

(5) Rinse the hair with warm water into the bowl to wet it, and apply the shampoo, massaging it into the scalp with the fingertips. Rinse until all soap is removed, and repeat the application and rinsing if the patient wishes it.

(6) Put a warm dry towel around the patient's head and make him comfortable in bed.

(7) Use the hair dryer to dry the hair, having set the hair first if the patient is a woman and wishes it to be set.

(8) Brush out the hair, using a clean brush and comb.

Alternative ways of arranging the patient and the bowl are:

(1) The mattress may be turned under at the head, or pulled

down the bed, to expose the springs, and this space can be used for placing the bowl over which the hair is washed.

(2) The bowl may be placed on a bed table, in front of the patient, who sits up and leans forward over the bowl for the hair washing procedure.

ADMINISTRATION OF BEDPANS AND URINALS

Definite 'rounds' when each patient is offered a receptacle in which to void urine may be carried out after meals. During these rounds the wards are 'closed' and casual visitors and staff prevented from entering the ward. In addition, bedpans and urinals should be given as required. Each bed should be screened whilst the patient uses a bedpan.

Bedpans

These may be made of stainless steel, polypropylene or rubber, They are sterilized after use, by means of a bedpan sterilizer, and are warmed before use either in a heated trolley or by being held under the hot water tap and then thoroughly dried.

The bedpan is taken to the patient and she is seated comfortably on it, two nurses lifting her if she cannot help herself. She should be supported whilst using the bedpan if she is very weak or ill. When the bedpan is removed it should be covered by a paper cover and may be placed into an unheated trolley. The urine should be measured if the patient is having her fluid intake and output charted, and the amount should be recorded before the urine is emptied and the bedpan washed in the bedpan washer. It is then placed into the sterilizer to be sterilized before re-use. The patient is made comfortable and the curtains drawn back.

If the patient has his bowels open, *either* the nurse should clean the patient using cotton wool swabs, soap and warm water, following which the patient is thoroughly dried, *or* the patient may be provided with the equipment to carry this out for himself. He must be given the opportunity to wash his hands afterwards.

Whenever possible the patient should be allowed up to the toilet, being taken in a chair and helped by a nurse if necessary. A sanichair, into which a bedpan can be fitted, or a commode, may be used at the bedside, and the patient can be lifted on to it.

Urinals

There is much less formality about the use of urinals, since these can be used unobtrusively under the bed covers, and in general men seem much less self-conscious about passing urine than do women. It is very often the practice for male patients who are confined to bed to have a clean urinal at the bedside, which is emptied after use.

8

Basic nursing care
3. Positions used in nursing

Upright Position

This is a comfortable position for the patient who is in bed during the day time, when no other position is indicated (Fig. 10). It is also a useful position to aid breathing, and prevent chest complications.

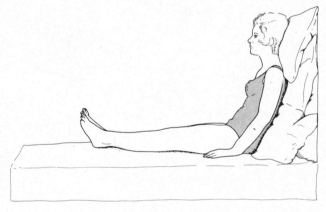

FIG. 10. Upright position.

Orthopnoeic Position

This position may be used in heart failure when the patient has great difficulty in breathing, unless he is sitting well upright (Fig. 11). He should be helped to stay in position by means of a foot support (see Fig. 12). This will help to prevent bed sores caused by a shearing force as the patient slips down the bed. An arm rest can be provided as illustrated by means of a pillow placed on a bed table, enabling the patient to lean forward.

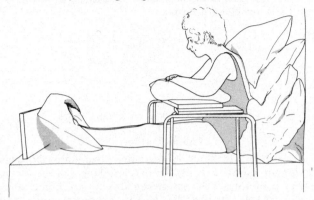

FIG. 11. Orthopnoeic position.

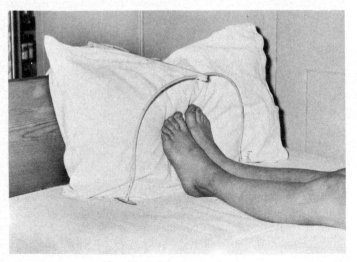

FIG. 12. A foot support in use.

Recumbent Postion

For this the patient lies flat with two pillows at the most (Fig. 13). This position is rarely used nowadays but may be employed if a patient has a low blood pressure.

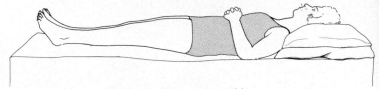

FIG. 13. Recumbent position.

Lateral Position

This is a position which is more commonly used if a patient must be flat for any reason (Fig. 14). There is less danger of chest infection or pressure sores if the patient can have his position changed from side to side. Besides this, he can see more of the ward activities in this position than in the recumbent position. Note that the lower arm rests in front of the patient and the upper leg rests on a pillow behind the lower leg.

FIG. 14. Lateral position.

Semi-Prone Position

This is the position in which an unconscious patient is often nursed (Fig. 15). It may also be used for gynaecological examination. In the case of an unconscious patient in whom the corneal reflex is absent, care should be taken to protect the eye from the pillow. Note here that the lower arm is resting on the bed *behind* the patient, thus, tilting the thorax and head so that fluid should drain from the mouth. The upper leg is supported on a pillow in front of the lower leg.

FIG. 15. Semi-prone position.

Prone Position

This position can be used to relieve pressure if the sacral area and hips show signs of pressure (Fig. 16). Note the supporting pillows beneath the upper abdomen preventing lordosis of the spine. The pillows support the patient so that no part of the body rests on the mattress. It is especially important to use a sufficient number of pillows under the shins to prevent foot drop.

FIG. 16. Prone position.

Dorsal Position

This position is used for gynaecological examinations (Fig. 17).

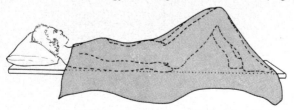

FIG. 17. Dorsal position (gynaecological).

LIFTING THE PATIENT

Figures 18 to 25 illustrate methods of lifting and moving patients.

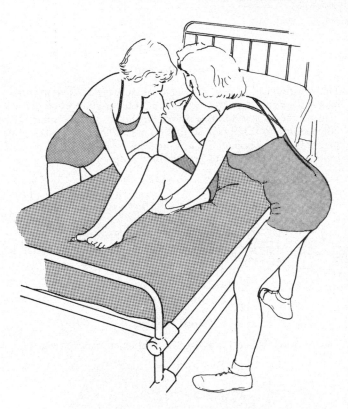

FIG. 18. Orthodox lift. Lifting the patient up the bed. I. Note the position of the lifters' hands under the patient's thighs.

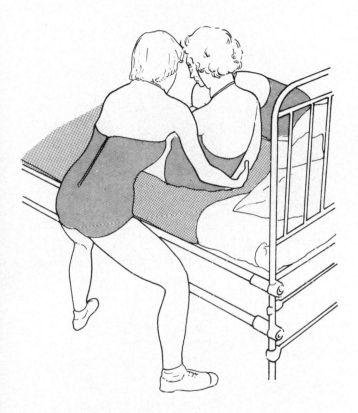

FIG. 19. Orthodox lift. Lifting the patient up the bed. II. Note the position of the lifters' feet and legs and the posture of the head and back. Also note the position of the lifters' hands in relation to the patient's sacrum. The patient is moved by the lifters straightening their legs a little and transferring their weight in the direction of the movement.

Fig. 20. Orthodox lift. Lifting the patient from bed to chair. Note particularly the bent knees of the lifters, and the positions of their feet. The lifters' hands support the small of the patient's back.

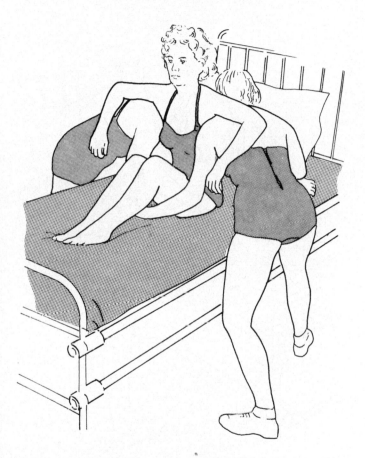

FIG. 21. Shoulder lift. Lifting the patient up the bed. I. Starting position. Note the general position of the lifters in relation to the patient. It is essential that the lifters stand level with the patient's hips. One lifter grasps the other's forearm under the patient's thighs, and each presses her shoulder into the patient's axilla. The patient should be asked to rest her arms lightly on the lifters' backs.

FIG. 22. Shoulder lift. Lifting the patient up the bed. II. The lift. Having pressed her shoulder into the patient's axilla, each lifter smoothly extends her hips and knees and transfers her weight on to the forward leg. Throughout the movement the lifters stand as close to the bed as possible. *Note that the shoulder lift cannot be used if the patient has injuries to the upper part of the trunk, shoulder or arms.*

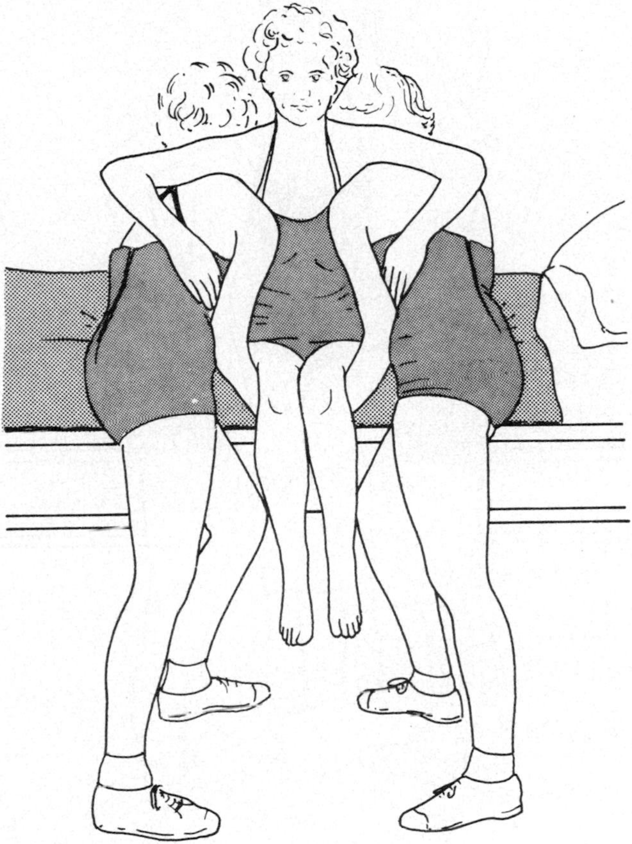

FIG. 23 Shoulder lift. Lifting the patient from bed to chair. I.

FIG. 24. Shoulder lift. Lifting the patient from bed to chair. II. The lift. Having lifted the patient from the bed, each lifter's free hand is placed to support the small of the patient's back. When necessary, one lifter can use this free hand to carry any object, such as a tube or an infusion bottle.

FIG. 25. Shoulder lift. Lifting the patient from bed to chair. III. After lifting, the lifters turn in an agreed direction to face the chair.

9

Prevention of complications due to bed rest

A HEALTHY man is ever active. He constantly changes his position in small ways, even when he is apparently sitting or standing still. Constant activity is necessary to maintain an adequate blood supply to all tissues. Deprived of blood, tissue cells die, the length of survival depending upon the particular type of cell. That activity is necessary to maintain the circulation is witnessed by the occasional fainting of healthy young guardsmen standing absolutely still on parade.

In hospital, a patient is encouraged to be as active as possible, but he may be incapable of changing his position for himself; activity may cause him pain, or being active may conflict with a specific need for rest as part of his treatment. Good nursing care ensures that the patient will not develop complications due to inactivity, which would delay his return to health.

Complications likely to develop as a result of inactivity in bed are bed sores, deep vein thrombosis, urinary complications and constipation.

PREVENTION OF BED SORES

Bed sores are caused by constant pressure on small blood vessels supplying the skin, which reduces the blood flow to the area and prevents the epithelial cells from obtaining the glucose and oxygen they need to maintain life. The blood vessels become compressed between the weight of the body and the bed surface, especially where there is very little protective tissue other than skin between bone and bed surface. Epithelial cells die and the skin breaks, leaving a raw area of tissue. New cells must be formed by division of existing cells, to replace the dead tissue. For this, a good blood supply is essential. Microorganisms can enter an area where the protective integrity of the skin is lost. They readily multiply in such an area, which provides ideal conditions for their growth (warmth, moisture and nutrients). The defences of the body against micro-organisms (antibodies, macrophages, white blood cells) are for the most part derived from the blood. Thus a good blood supply is necessary to combat infection. A poor blood supply, then, not only causes the sore but prevents it from healing when it occurs.

When once a bed sore has developed it may deteriorate very rapidly, due both to infection and the further death of cells; the sore increasing in area and depth. Eventually bone may be exposed, grafting is required to cover the area, and the patient is seriously ill. It can be seen how essential it is that pressure does not build up for a sufficient length of time to interfere with the blood supply to an area of skin.

The Responsibilities of the Nurse

Prevention of pressure sores is the responsibility of the nurse, and involves the assessment of both the type of care most suitable for the patient and the frequency with which it needs to be carried out. For this it is necessary to have a thorough knowledge of the factors predisposing to bed sores and of the areas most subjected to pressure, in different positions. Other factors which must be taken into account in deciding the particular measures necessary are the activity level of the patient and the nutritional state of the tissues.

Factors which Predispose to Pressure Sores

Nutritional State of the Patient

Very thin individuals in whom there is little tissue overlying the bone are at greater risk than the more well nourished. A high protein diet may be ordered to improve the condition of such a patient. On the other hand, a very obese, heavy patient subjects his skin to greater pressure than does a person of normal weight.

The Pathological Condition

Oxygen is essential to the life of cells and, if the oxygen content of the blood is reduced in any way, the cells will be much more susceptible to the effects of a reduction in blood flow. Two conditions in which the oxygen content of blood may be reduced are respiratory failure and anaemia. Patients with diabetes mellitus are also more prone to develop pressure sores since the blood vessels in this condition are particularly liable to small occlusions. Paralysis renders the skin of an affected area especially vulnerable, since reflexes involving minute muscle changes and changes in blood flow are lost. Thus patients with any of these conditions are at special risk as far as pressure sores are concerned.

Minor Breaks in the Skin

A break in the skin can very readily become infected, and is likely to develop into a pressure sore if it occurs in an area subjected to pressure. It is most important that such breaks in the skin are prevented. There are two main ways in which the skin may become broken: (a) due to trauma to the skin, and (b) because of the condition of the skin itself.

The nurse must be very careful not to scratch the patient's skin when she is changing his position. It is partly for this reason that she should take care of her own hands, keeping them soft and supple, with short, well filed, smooth nails. She should never, of course, wear a watch on her wrist whilst attending to a patient.

Dampness of the skin may cause it to crack. This can occur if the skin is not dried properly after washing, if the patient is incontinent of urine, or if he sweats excessively. The use of harsh substances on the skin may cause dryness; soap which is not rinsed off and spirit applications can both dry the skin excessively. If the patient is excessively restless, dryness of the skin can be caused by friction. Applications of lanolin, zinc and castor oil cream, or barrier cream will help to counteract dryness of the skin and prevent moisture from causing it to break down.

Pressure Exerted on a Very Small Area of Skin or by Hard Objects

Crumbs in the bed or creases in the sheet can cause damage to skin. Careful and frequent bed making eliminates the possibility of this happening. Hard metal bed pans should never be left in position for any length of time as they exert a great deal of pressure on the skin. Rubber bedpans can be used instead of metal ones.

for patients whose skin is especially liable to break; for instance, they are particularly useful for paralysed patients.

Areas at Special Risk

Skin areas particularly subjected to pressure when the patient is lying supine are the heels, the area overlying the sacrum, the skin over the shoulder blades, the back of the head and the elbows. The sacrum and heels are also subjected to considerable pressure when the patient is in the sitting position. In the lateral and semi-prone positions, the tips of the shoulder, the hips, the inner aspect of the knees, and the ankles are the areas most at risk. Careful placing of sorbo pads or pillows and the use of a bed cradle can prevent pressure on knees and ankles. The areas of skin over the anterior superior iliac spines, and over the knees needs careful inspection when the patient has been lying in the prone position.

Methods by which Pressure may be Relieved

Frequent Changes of the Patient's Position

The greater the number of different positions which are available for use, the better, since pressure on a given area will be relieved far longer if, say, four positions can be used in rotation than if only two positions are used alternately. Frequency of the position changes needs to be determined individually for each patient, and depends both upon any predisposing factors which may be present and the activity level of the patient, but in any case it should not be less than 4-hourly during the day time. If signs of pressure are noted when the patient is turned, this means that the patient's needs have not been accurately assessed and more frequent attention must be instituted.

The first sign of pressure is redness of an area of skin on which the patient has been lying. If this redness does not disappear rapidly when the patient is turned, then tissue damage has already occurred and the area must be given time to recover before the patient is allowed to lie on it again.

Momentary Relief of Pressure

The patient's condition may be such that he must be nursed in one particular position and it is not possible to turn him. Pressure may be relieved by lifting him up from the surface of the bed for a second. This must be carried out very frequently, even ½-hourly.

Use of Pressure Relieving Devices

It is possible to ease the pressure upon the skin by using one of several devices available for this very purpose. These include ripple beds, air rings, water beds, sorbo pads and sheepskins. However, certain precautions are necessary in the use of some of these or they will do more harm than good. Pressure can be com-

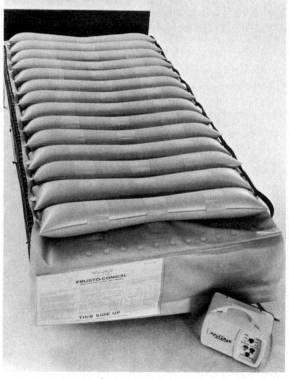

FIG. 26. A ripple bed (*Talley Surgical Instruments Ltd*).

pletely relieved by the use of a hovercraft bed, where one is available, and staff have been specially trained in its use.

A *ripple bed* consists of a double layer of plastic which is sealed into tubes (Fig. 26). Every other tube has air pumped into it; these tubes are then deflated whilst the remainder are inflated; thus the areas of skin subjected to pressure are alternated. The ripple bed is placed on top of the ordinary mattress, and it is essential that it is covered with one sheet only, or its efficiency is reduced.

Air rings must be inflated with the correct amount of air; too much will exert pressure upon the patient's skin, too little will enable the patient's body to displace the air at the areas of greatest pressure and rest upon the bed; a situation worse than the situation the air ring is designed to remedy. The nozzle of the air ring is a source of danger and the patient must not be allowed to rest on it. Air rings may be too small for very obese patients. There is, similarly, an optimum amount of water required for filling a *water pillow* if it is to relieve pressure as intended.

Sorbo pads which can be made individually for each patient, and *sheepskins* are both very helpful in the prevention of pressure sores.

It is important to remember that these appliances are aids only, and not substitutes for frequent changes of position.

Treatment of a Pressure Sore

Good nursing care will ensure that pressure sores do not occur. If one should develop, it is treated in the same way as any other wound. Infection is treated; dead tissue is removed using an aseptic technique; and sterile dressings are used to cover the area. Under no circumstances should the patient be allowed to lie on the broken area. Ultraviolet light locally and a high protein diet may be ordered to aid regeneration.

DEEP VEIN THROMBOSIS

One very important protective mechanism of the body is the ability of the blood to clot, given certain conditions which are present in injury, but along with that ability other mechanisms have evolved which prevent the blood from clotting within the blood vessels themselves. These mechanisms include the property of the platelets to repel each other, thus preventing large aggregates of solid material. Certain substances essential for the clotting process are contained within platelets and tissue cells, and only become available in quantity when there is damage to these cells. The smooth endothelial lining prevents particles from adhering to it, and the flow of blood in the vessels is such that under normal circumstances the larger solid particles tend to remain in the centre of the stream. In addition, small amounts of heparin (an anti-clotting agent) are carried in the blood stream.

However, given changes in the equilibrium between the anticoagulant and the clotting mechanisms, it is possible for blood to clot within the blood vessels. When an individual remains still in bed for a period of time, changes may occur in blood flow and the lining of the veins of the lower limb.

Blood flow in the veins of the lower limb is aided by the pumping action of the calf muscles on movement, and the sucking action of the changes in pressure in the inferior vena cava, consequent upon breathing. Inactivity in bed results in a slowing of the blood flow from the lower limbs, since not only are the calf muscles less active but respiration may be less deep than normal. In the supine or sitting positions the veins may become compressed between the bed and the bones of the lower limb; this further slows the circulation and may damage the delicate lining of the vessel. Solid particles of the blood, especially the platelets, come into contact with the lining of the vessel and an aggregation of these forms a thrombus.

An individual undergoing surgery is at even greater risk, partly due to compression of the deep veins of the calf during the operation. and partly due to the changes which occur in the blood following surgery. The plasma becomes more viscous, its fibrinogen content increases, and the platelets cease to repel one another, tending to aggregate.

The thrombus may be firmly adherent to the blood vessel, the wall of which is inflamed, and acute pain in the calf and swelling of the limb are present. More dangerous is the thrombus which is not firmly adherent to the vessel wall, because symptoms and signs are difficult to detect and the thrombus may loosen from the wall of the vessel and be carried along with the flow of the blood. Between the leg veins and the heart the calibre of the vessels increases, but the vessels branch and decrease in diameter as the blood is distributed to the lungs. The thrombus may get lodged and occlude the blood vessel, causing a pulmonary infarction. If the infarction is sufficiently large, death may be instantaneous.

Prevention of Deep Vein Thrombosis

(1) Leg exercises must be carried out frequently, at least 1-hourly during the day. These consist of dorsi-flexion and plantar-flexion of the foot, against resistance. If the patient is unable to carry these out for himself, the ankle and knee joints should be taken passively through a full range of movement.

(2) Deep breathing exercises should be taught to the patient, and the nurse must encourage him to carry them out every hour during the day.

(3) The patient should not lie in one position for any length of time.

(4) Any device which could further slow the blood flow in the veins must be avoided. Pillows should never be placed under the knee or calf.

To Prevent Pulmonary Emboli

The prevention of a pulmonary embolus depends upon the prevention of deep vein thrombosis. If the latter should occur, its early detection and treatment will help to prevent an embolus.

Signs of deep vein thrombosis are:

(1) A slight rise in temperature.

(2) A slowly increasing pulse rate, with or without a temperature rise.

(3) Tenderness of the calf on local palpation.

(4) Tenderness of the calf, if the foot is suddenly dorsiflexed. This is called Homan's sign.

If deep vein thrombosis should occur, anti-coagulants may be given, and if the physician considers that the danger of embolus formation is very great, then the vein may be occluded above the site of the thrombosis.

URINARY COMPLICATIONS

In the normal, active, healthy adult, urine is formed continually by the kidney and passes down the ureters to the bladder. The bladder, a hollow muscular organ, fills from its empty, collapsed state until pressure stimulates the stretch receptors in its wall and initiates micturition. This reflex is initiated in the adult when there is a volume of approximately 300 ml of urine within the bladder, but from infancy the act of micturition can be inhibited or facilitated at will. However, this inhibition and facilitation is greatly influenced by emotional factors.

The use of a bedpan or urinal by a patient confined to bed involves passing urine in what is, for persons of our culture, an unnatural position. There are still very few hospitals which supply single rooms for the patients and so, for vast majority, the voiding of urine is carried out within sound of other patients and hospital staff. Bed curtains ensuring privacy have a disadvantage from the patient's point of view, in that persons wishing to enter the bed space cannot knock before doing so, and therefore do tend to enter without warning. There is a great deal of individual variation in the interval between the urge to pass urine, as well as variation in the tolerance of this urge if it cannot immediately be relieved. A patient who wishes to micturate and cannot do so immediately may become very anxious and be unable to control the bladder sphincter, wetting the bed as a result. On the other hand, powerful inhibition of the act may mean that he is unable to pass urine when the opportunity to do so does arise. Not all patients, therefore, can regulate their bladders so that they only pass urine during a 'sanitary round' dictated by the convenience of the ward staff. This problem is less acute for male patients since there is usually an 'up' patient who is willing to fetch a urinal if asked, and this can be used discreetly. Sensitive female patients may be unwilling to ask an apparently busy nurse for a bedpan between rounds, because it involves an interruption of whatever task the nurse is carrying out. Indeed, the occasional female patient, confined to bed, finds the whole business such an embarrassment that she will voluntarily restrict her fluid intake so that she will not need to use the bedpan so frequently. This, in a patient lying still in bed, could lead to urinary infection or the formation of renal calculi. Thus the urinary complications of enforced bed rest may be: (1) wetting the bed (a very shameful thing to an adult patient), (2) retention of urine, (3) urinary infection, or (4) renal calculi.

The Prevention of Urinary Complications

(1) One of the most important ways in which a nurse can prevent urinary complications is by developing the capacity to appreciate the patient's embarrassment and fears, occasioned by the use of the bedpan. Her attitude toward this problem will be betrayed in her behaviour. She should ensure maximum privacy for the patient and respect that privacy. To reduce embarrassment to a minimum, the nurse should be relaxed and matter of fact when attending to the sanitary needs of the patient. It is essential that the bedpan or urinal should be at a comfortable temperature and scrupulously clean. The nurse must always be willing to supply a bedpan or urinal to the patient when he asks, and the patient must be aware of the nurse's willingness in this respect. It is here, particularly, that the nurse's attitude is all important, since a verbal willingness accompanied by feeling that the patient is a nuisance may appear false to the patient, since facial expression and movements of the body can reveal true attitudes to the on-looker. If possible, the nurse should be sensitive to the facial expression of patients so that she can anticipate the patient's need to pass urine, and offer a receptacle before being asked.

(2) Observation of the urinary output is necessary. This does not necessarily have to be formally charted on a fluid chart, but an assessment of the amount passed and the frequency with which the bedpan or urinal is used can be made in the light of the nurse's experience. The nurse should always bear in mind the possibility that the bladder is not being emptied completely, even though urine is passed; a situation very likely to result in urinary infection. If it is suspected that urine is being retained, then measurement of the patient's fluid intake and output will be necessary and the bladder should be examined to see if it is distended.

(3) Unless the fluid intake is being restricted as part of the treatment, the nurse should ensure that the patient takes sufficient fluid to prevent the complications of infection, or calculi from occurring.

(4) Observation of the colour, smell and turbidity of the patient's urine should be carried out every time a urinal or bedpan is

emptied. If any abnormality is suspected, it should be reported and a specimen should be saved for inspection, so that any urinary infection is detected as soon as it occurs.

The Nurse's Responsibility if Urinary Complications Should Occur

(1) If *urinary infection* is present or suspected, a specimen of urine will be needed for microbiological examination, and this must not be contaminated with microorganisms from the container or the external genitalia. The specimen may be collected by means of catheterization but, more usually, a clean midstream specimen of urine is obtained, since there is always a danger of introducing microorganisms into the bladder whenever catheterization is carried out. It may be difficult to obtain a midstream specimen of urine when the patient is confined to bed.

(2) If the patient has *difficulty in passing urine*, attempts may be made to help by using suggestion. Running taps near the patient's bed or, in the case of a female, pouring warm water over the vulva, may initiate the act of micturition. A plain muscle relaxant, such as carbachol (0·2 to 0·5 mg) may be prescribed by the doctor, but this drug does have unpleasant side effects (pallor, sweating, defaecation, vomiting and faintness in some patients). If retention of urine develops, then catheterization will be necessary.

Preventing Complications when an In-Dwelling Catheter is Used

If a patient develops retention of urine, the pressure may be relieved gradually, rather than decompressing the bladder suddenly and completely, when the catheter is passed. In either case, it may be necessary to leave the catheter in position and, for this reason, the initial catheterization for retention of urine is often carried out using a self retaining catheter.

Other reasons for inserting a self-retaining catheter:

(1) To keep bladder empty during and after gynaecological operations.

(2) To ensure careful observation of the urine after operations upon the bladder itself or in its vicinity, and to allow bladder washouts to be carried out if required.

Complications of a Self-Retaining Catheter and their Prevention

(1) Inflammation of the urethra may occur, simply as a tissue reaction to the presence of a foreign substance. This reaction can be kept to a minimum by the use of polythene catheters rather than rubber, and the use of disposable ones rather than ones which have been used before, causing the surface of the catheter to be damaged. Gibbon's catheters are very useful in preventing a tissue reaction. The catheter should be changed at intervals which are not greater than seven days.

(2) The presence of a tube within the bladder sphincter and the urethra provides a direct pathway into the bladder for micro-organisms. Thus the risk of urinary infection is a very real one when a self-retaining catheter is used, even though the catheterization technique itself is aseptic. Indeed, the danger of infection is such that intermittent catheterization may be preferred to the use of self-retaining catheters for patients with retention of urine in paraplegia. If the catheter is spigotted and released intermittently, a newly sterilized spigot must be inserted on each catheter release; the previous one must never be re-used without first being sterilized. Releasing the catheter must be carried out using aseptic precautions. Should the catheter be attached to the tubing of a disposable urine bag or a tidal drainage apparatus, then the whole apparatus must be sterile and a strict aseptic technique used whenever the tubes are disconnected in any way. Routine toilet of the catheter and the urethral orifice should be carried out 4-hourly, unless the patient is able to get into the bath daily.

(3) For a patient who has a self-retaining catheter for urinary retention, there is a great danger that the muscular tone of the bladder wall will be lost if the bladder is allowed to drain continually, so that it remains empty and contracted. This is especially likely to happen if the retention of urine was caused by a neurological lesion. To prevent this, a method must be used which allows the bladder to fill for between 2 and 4 hr before it is emptied. There are two methods which allow this. One is to spigot the catheter and release it at prescribed intervals. It is important that the catheter is released on time so that the intervals during which the bladder is allowed to fill are equal ones. The other method is to use a tidal drainage apparatus, which allows filling of the bladder to a prescribed pressure determined by the height of the

siphonage tube in relation to the bladder, before automatic emptying occurs.

To Collect a Midstream Specimen of Urine

Principles

(1) Contamination of the urine specimen by organisms from
the urethra and genital organs is avoided: (a) by thorough cleaning
of the urethral orifice and the area around it, and (b) by allowing
any organisms within to be washed away by the first part of the
urine stream before the specimen is collected.

(2) The cleansing agent used should be mild, to avoid trauma
to delicate mucous membranes. If it should contaminate the urine
specimen, it should not be strong enough to kill delicate infecting
organisms.

Requirements

A sterile, wide necked container.
A bedpan or urinal.
Sterile wool or gauze swabs.
Sterile water, or a mild sterile antiseptic lotion, e.g. Hibitane
    1 : 5000.
Normal saline.
Soap and warm water.
Sterile absorbent towels.

Procedure

For a female patient. The procedure, and the reasons for it,
should be explained very carefully to the patient. If possible, the
patient should be allowed to carry out the cleaning of the area for
herself and an ambulant patient can carry out the whole procedure
for herself. The vulva is washed thoroughly with soap and water,
using the sterile swabs and working from front to back. The area
is thoroughly rinsed with clean water and dried. Next, the area
around the urethral orifice is swabbed with the particular lotion in
use in the hospital, and dried. The bedpan is placed in position,
with the patient leaning forward as far as possible. The first part
of the urine flow is collected in the bedpan, then the sterile container is placed in position, the 'midstream' urine is collected, and

the bottle is sealed. Any remaining urine is passed into the bedpan. After the procedure, the patient should be dried thoroughly and made comfortable. The nurse must wash her hands and ensure that the specimen is taken to the laboratory straight away, accompanied by the appropriate request form. Speed is essential or delicate organisms may die whilst less delicate ones multiply, giving a false picture of the infecting agent.

For a male patient. Again the patient should carry out the procedure for himself as far as is possible, so careful explanation is very important. The penis and especially the area around the urethra should be washed thoroughly with soap and water, rinsed and dried. The prescribed lotion should then be used to cleanse the area immediately around the urethral orifice, the foreskin being pulled back to ensure thorough cleansing. The patient then passes urine into a urinal before stopping the stream in order to pass the second part of the stream into the sterile container. He must be warned not to let the penis touch the inside of either the urinal or the sterile container.

Note: For female ambulant patients the 'Specitest' collector may prove a satisfactory method of collecting a midstream specimen of urine, but it does involve the installation of a special lavatory into the ward.

Catheterization

Catheterization of the urinary bladder may be required: (a) to empty the bladder before operation, (b) to keep the bladder empty after operation, (c) to obtain a specimen of urine, and (d) to relieve distension.

Principles

(1) Precautions are taken to avoid introducing microorganisms into the urinary system.

(2) Trauma of the urethra and bladder is avoided by means of skilful technique, a knowledge of the anatomy of the area, and the use of catheters made of smooth, atraumatic material.

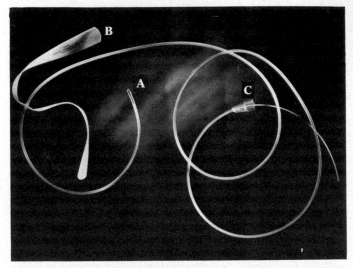

FIG. 27. Polyvinyl Gibbon's in-dwelling catheter. (A) Tip of catheter with three side holes; (B) wings of soft material cemented 12 in. from lip which are strapped to the patient's abdomen; (C) graduated adapter which fits the tube of the collecting bag or bottle.

Varieties of Catheter in Common Use

Most varieties of catheter are available in pre-sterilized, individual packs, and are disposable (Figs 27, 28 and 29). The central sterile supply department of most hospitals also supplies individually wrapped sterile catheters which are re-sterilized by them after use. Prepacked catheters are usually made of polyvinyl varying in stiffness and are sterilized by gamma rays.

For female catheterization. (1) Jacques catheters made of soft rubber or polythene, (2) soft polyvinyl disposable female catheters (Fig. 30), and (3) Foley's self-retaining catheter.

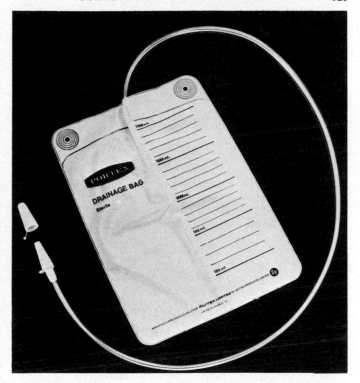

FIG. 28. Disposable urine collecting and measuring bag for use with
Gibbon's or other types of in-dwelling catheters (*Portex Ltd*).

For male catheterization. In general a stiffer catheter is used for
male catheterization than for female. (1) Whistle tip; (2) Tieman's;
(3) Gibbons (self-retaining); (4) Foley catheter (self-retaining);
(5) Kinder (for bladder irrigation) (Fig. 31); and (6) Coudé or
bicoudé catheters which are made of semi-stiff polyvinyl and are
angled once, or twice, near the eye.

Size 14 (French gauge) is the size most commonly used, although
catheters are obtainable in sizes 1 to 30 (French gauge).

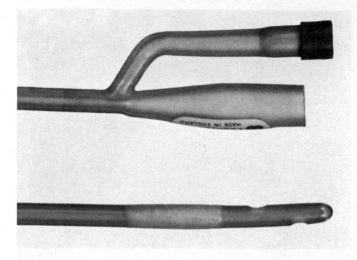

FIG. 29. Foley's urethral catheter.

FIG. 30. Female disposable catheter.

Catheterization of a Male Patient

Requirements

The required, prepacked catheters.

A lubricant, such as sterile glycerine or liquid paraffin, chlor-hexidine cream, KY jelly *or* Anaesthetic gel.

Sterile gloves.

Two pairs dissecting, dressing or Spencer Wells forceps.

Container for used instruments.

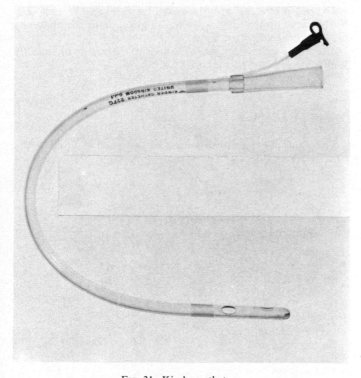

FIG. 31. Kinder catheter.

Disposable bag for dirty dressings.
1 pair of sterile scissors to cut pack containing catheters.
Sterile towels and swabs.
Bowl of warm lotion for swabbing, e.g. Hibitane 0·1 per cent,
    Bradosol 1:2000 solution.
Large receiver for urine.
Waterproof sheet
(If a 'clean' specimen for examination is required, a sterile screw-
top bottle to receive the urine must be provided.)

The bed is screened and the bedclothes arranged so that they can be easily turned down over the thighs, leaving the abdomen and chest covered with a blanket.

After the trolley is brought to the bedside the nurse is not usually required to give any further assistance.

If the catheter is to be tied in. the following should also be provided:

Tape.

Adhesive strapping.

A pair of scissors.

If urethral bougies are to be passed these are sterilized in the same way as catheters. The same trolley should be set as for catheterization.

Catheterization of a Female Patient

Requirements

Prepacked sterile catheter.

Sterile gloves *or* 2 pairs sterile dressing forceps.

Pair of sterile scissors.

Container for used instruments.

Disposable bag for dirty dressings.

A bowl of lotion for swabbing.

Sterile swabs and towels.

Waterproof sheet.

Large receiver for urine.

A hand lamp.

A lubricant is not as a rule required.

(When a sterile specimen is required a sterile screw-top bottle should be provided, and all traces of antiseptics should be removed by swabbing with sterile water.)

The bed should be screened and the bedclothes turned down from the patient's knees, leaving her covered with a blanket. A waterproof sheet is placed under the patient's thighs and buttocks and a receiver or a porringer between her legs. The hand lamp should be adjusted so that it gives a good light; it is absolutely essential that the nurse should be able to obtain a clear view of the area when swabbing the external genitalia and when actually passing the catheter.

The nurse then prepares her hands by washing and drying them on a clean towel. When she returns to the bedside she turns back the covering blanket with her elbow, or asks an assistant to do this for her.

Using swabs well moistened with the antiseptic lotion she swabs the external genital region beginning with the labia majora, then swabbing the labia minora and lastly the area around the urethral orifice. Each swab should be used once only and the direction of swabbing should be from the anterior aspect of the vulva towards the posterior margin. The nurse should then wash her hands and apply sterile gloves, if she prefers to handle the catheter with gloves rather than forceps. The sterile towels are arranged to cover the patient's thighs and then, separating the labia minora, using the first finger and thumb of the left hand, the catheter is passed, using either the gloved right hand or a pair of dressing forceps. It is important that the tip of the catheter is not allowed to touch the patient before entering the urethral orifice. The urethral orifice should be clearly seen and a good light is essential; the opening is situated immediately in front of the vaginal orifice and at the base of the triangular area known as the vestibule. The tip of the catheter is passed into the urethral orifice and then the instrument is pushed on in an upward and backward direction for about 5 cm (2 in.), leaving the open end in the receiver between the patient's thighs. If the catheter should accidentally touch any adjacent part before it is safely inserted in the urethra it should be discarded as probably contaminated and the second sterile catheter should then be used.

If a catheter specimen is required for laboratory examination, it is collected in a sterile screw-top glass bottle.

When urine ceases to flow the nurse should make gentle pressure over the pubes and withdraw the catheter for about 1 cm (0·5 in.); when she feels sure that the bladder is empty the catheter is withdrawn and placed in the receiver provided. The porringer is removed, the vulva dried and the bed remade. The amount of urine withdrawn should be measured and a specimen saved if required.

Catheterization is a procedure that should be carried out with the utmost care, since by introducing the catheter through the urethra microorganisms could also be introduced, and the procedure itself may damage the delicate urethral lining.

Catheter Toilet

This is carried out whenever a self-retaining catheter is used and the patient is unable to get into the bath.

Principle

Cleaning of the urethral orifice and the external surface of the catheter at its insertion is carried out to prevent accumulation of dried secretions at this point which could provide a good medium for the multiplication of microorganisms.

Requirements

Sterile wool or gauze swabs.
Sterile towel.
Sterile water, saline, or Hibitane 1:5000.
Disposable bag for dirty dressings.
Pair of sterile gloves.

Method

The procedure is explained to the patient and the bedclothes turned back. The nurse should wash her hands and place the sterile towel in position beneath the catheter. She then applies the sterile gloves and carefully swabs the urethal orifice with the prescribed lotion. The exterior of the catheter at its insertion is also swabbed and then the whole area is carefully dried using the remainder of the sterile swabs.

Tidal Drainage

Tidal drainage may be used to maintain or to restore bladder tone, where there has been retention of urine (Fig. 32). A large receptacle for the irrigating lotion is connected to a drip outlet which in turn is joined by a piece of rubber tubing to one arm of a Y-shaped glass connection. The stem of this connection is attached to a catheter in the patient's bladder, the remaining arm to a length of rubber tubing which is looped to form a U-shaped manometer 35·5 cm (14 in.) high with the centre at the level of the patient's bladder. The end of this long piece of tubing opens into a pail on the floor which collects the fluid. The lotion is allowed to drip slowly into the bladder via the catheter; as the bladder fills with the lotion and with urine the pressure in the U loop rises, and when the fluid reaches the top of the U it empties by siphonage into the pail. The bladder then begins to fill again.

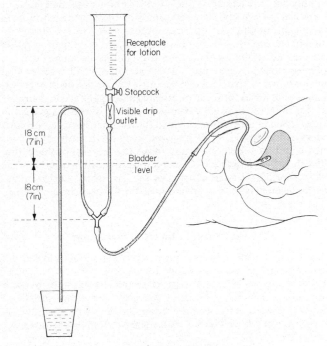

Fig. 32. Tidal drainage.

BOWEL COMPLICATIONS DUE TO BED REST

When one is healthy, the exercise involved in day to day activities helps to maintain the tone of skeletal muscles used in the act of defaecation. Peristalsis is aided by the upright posture in walking or standing, which avoids compression of internal abdominal organs. Most individuals establish very regular bowel habits, involving the use of the lavatory at much the same time each day, often after breakfast. Their diet too, though changing in detail from meal to meal, probably contains fairly constant quantities of roughage, carbohydrate, protein, fat and fluids. When the patient is confined to bed in hospital, he is denied exercise, his daily routine is modified to suit the hospital, and his diet is changed in both content and timing. All of these factors may cause a change in bowel habit, and usually the change is towards constipation rather than diarrhoea. Given the inhibiting conditions under which a patient confined to bed must defaecate, it is small wonder that constipation is often a problem. Because the use of a bedpan entails an unnatural position, some physicians allow patients on complete bed rest to be lifted on to a commode. Some of the drugs used in the treatment of the patient can lead to constipation, e.g. morphine and its derivatives. A lot of gas producing foods in the diet, combined with lack of exercise, may make flatus a real problem too. All of these problems may become more acute after surgery, since peristalsis will have been affected by the anaesthetic during operation, and wound pain may postoperatively seriously impede straining at stool.

The Prevention of Bowel Complications

(1) The diet of the patient is very important and should contain as much fresh fruit and vegetables as possible.

(2) If at all possible, the patient should be allowed to use a commode rather than a bedpan. A request for either should be dealt with immediately, and the nurse should try to maintain the patient's normal bowel habits with regard to timing. Privacy must be ensured.

(3) Laxatives may be given as prescribed.

(4) Suppositories or enemata may be administered if constipation does arise. A flatus tube may be passed to relieve wind if this is a problem.

Administration of Suppositories

Suppositories used to evacuate the bowel are made of glycerine or dulcolax. Some drugs which can be absorbed through the bowel wall are administered in the form of suppositories. It is important in the latter case that the bowel is empty before the drug is administered and that the reason for the administration of the suppository is carefully explained to the patient so that the suppository is retained.

Requirements

Prescribed suppositories, together with the prescription sheet.
Rubber gloves *or* two finger stalls.
Petroleum jelly and swab, *or* bowl of hot water.
Waterproof sheet and towel, *or* incontinence pad.

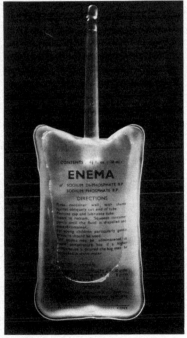

FIG. 33. Disposable enema.

Procedure

The waterproof sheet and towel are put in position, to protect the bed, and the patient is positioned, if possible in the left lateral position, with knees and hips well flexed. The procedure should have been very carefully explained to the patient. The glove or finger stalls are applied and the suppository is lubricated, either by using petroleum jelly or by dipping it into hot water, thus causing the surface to melt slightly. The suppository is inserted through the anal sphincter as far as possible into the rectum. The sheet is removed and the patient is re-positioned. An evacuant suppository should be retained about 20 min if possible, but the patient may get agitated for fear that the nurse will not get the bedpan or commode to the bedside in time. It is useful, then, to leave one at the bedside to reassure the patient.

Administration of Evacuant Enemata

Solutions Which May be Used

Sodium phosphate disposable enemata (Fig. 33).
Water 280 to 1120 ml.
Soap and water 280 to 1120 ml.
Magnesium sulphate 25 per cent solution approximately 224 ml.
Glycerine and water 25 per cent solution approximately 118 ml.

Principles

(1) The patient is positioned so as to take advantage of the natural curvature of the rectum. Therefore, if at all possible, the patient should either lie on his left side or on his back with the pelvis raised slightly.

(2) All air must be expelled from the tubing, or it will cause acute discomfort to the patient.

(3) The fluid must be measured before and after administration, as it is possible for fluid to be absorbed from the mucous membrane, upsetting the electrolyte balance.

(4) The rate of flow of the fluid can be regulated by pinching the tubing with the finger or by altering the height of the funnel above the patient's rectum—the higher it is, the greater the flow rate. The size of the apparatus will also affect the flow rate; thus small, narrow bore tubing and catheter should be used if only a small amount of fluid is to be administered or if the fluid is to be administered very slowly.

Requirements

For large quantities of fluid, a douche can, or large funnel, a piece of tubing about 60 cm (24 in.) long, a connector and a rectal tube or catheter size 18 to 26 (French gauge) or 14 to 16 (English gauge).

A Higginson's syringe with a rectal tube attached is occasionally used, and in this case the solution to be used is placed in a bowl.

For small quantities a glass funnel or the barrel of a glass syringe is connected to a rubber catheter size 12 to 14 (French gauge) or 8 (English gauge).

Linen swabs.

A clip to control the flow of fluid.

A jug containing a measured amount of solution to be administered.

A lotion thermometer.

A disposal bag for soiled equipment.

A bedpan with toilet paper or cheap cotton wool.

A waterproof sheet.

Procedure

It is important that the procedure is explained in terms the patient will understand. He is positioned on the sheet and towel. The temperature of the liquid which is to be administered is checked. This should be at a temperature of 38°C (100°F). Next, the apparatus is filled with fluid, ensuring that there is no air remaining in the tubing. The catheter is lubricated and gently inserted through the anus into the rectum, until 10 cm (4 in.) have been inserted. The catheter must not be forced if there is any resistance, as this may harm the patient. Whilst the liquid is running in at the prescribed rate, the nurse must never allow the funnel to become empty of fluid until the completion of the procedure, or air will enter the apparatus. If the patient complains of nausea or faintness at any time, the procedure must be discontinued. The catheter is withdrawn gently, and disconnected from the rest of the apparatus so that it can be washed separately. The patient is placed on to the bedpan or commode, and supported if necessary. On emptying the bedpan, the fluid must be measured to ensure that the whole amount administered has been returned.

Careful observation and reporting of the faecal and flatus result of the enema should be carried out.

Passing a Flatus Tube for the Relief of Distension

Requirements

(1) A rubber rectal tube. This tube has thick walls and the eye is at the end. (In this respect it differs from a catheter which has a lateral eye.) A connector attaching the rectal tube to a length of tubing with a funnel at the other end.

(2) Petroleum jelly, or other lubricant and swabs.

(3) A bowl of water.

(4) A receiver for soiled swabs.

(5) A waterproof square and pad to protect the bed.

The tube is lubricated and passed into the rectum to a depth of about 5 cm (2 in.). The funnel is placed under the surface of the water in the bowl which is placed at the bedside. The advantage of attaching the tube to a funnel placed in a bowl of water is that the bubbles of gas can be readily seen as they escape from the funnel.

10

Observation of the patient
1. General

THERE is always a nurse on duty in a ward whereas the doctor only visits at intervals. Between his visits he relies on the nursing staff to keep him informed of any deterioration in the patient's condition which might require surgical intervention, a change of treatment, or even resuscitation of the patient. To carry out this nursing function adequately, the nurse must observe her patient, keep records of her observations, interpret them, and make a decision as to whether or not any action is required.

Proper *observation* of her patient requires not only that the nurse should observe the patient's conscious level, colour, temperature, pulse rate, respirations and blood pressure at intervals as required, but that whilst working in the ward she remains receptive, or sensitive to stimuli emitted by her patients. Thus she notices a change in the respiratory rhythm of a patient whose respirations are noisy, even though it occurs in the interval between formal observations. Similarly she notices that a patient has become restless, or is in pain, even though she is merely walking past the patient's bed to attend to someone else.

Each nurse is off duty for approximately 16 out of 24 hr, and task allocation rather than total patient care is the usual method of ward organization in this country. It is important, therefore, that observations made of patients are accurately *communicated* from the nurse making the observation to other members of staff. Written *records* are kept of many of the observations that are made. These aid communication, ensure continuity of care, and provide a permanent record of the condition of the patient over a period of time.

Interpretation of observations that are made requires two kinds of knowledge. Firstly, a knowledge of how this observation compares with the normal value for the population of which the patient is a member, and secondly a knowledge of how this observation compares with the normal values for this particular patient. For instance, to interpret the significance of a patient's pulse rate one needs to know not only the normal pulse rate for people of the patient's age group and activity, but also to know this patient's previous pulse rate. The normal or average pulse rate

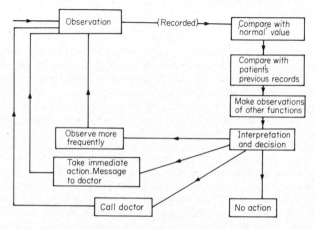

FIG. 34. Flow diagram of observation–decision process.

of an adult at rest is 72 per min. A pulse rate of 50 per min would cause disquiet if observed in a patient with an intracranial lesion, whose previous pulse rate was higher than this. It could, however, be the normal rate for a trained athlete, and would merely reflect a physiological adaptation. A pulse rate rising to 80 per min in the trained athlete at rest should be investigated further however, although it would be considered normal if one had no previous recordings with which to compare it.

An observation of a single bodily function, although better than nothing, gives little information, and the greater the number of different functions assessed at the same time, the more pieces of evidence are obtained to allow correct interpretation. A pulse rate of 50 per min is of no special significance in an individual who looks healthy, is alert mentally, is active physically, and whose blood pressure, temperature and respiratory rate is normal. The same pulse rate in an individual who is very drowsy, who is developing some paralysis, and whose blood pressure is rising, should cause concern.

Thus, interpretation of individual observations depends upon comparison with the normal for a given group of individuals; a knowledge of the result of previous observations of this particular patient; and the sum total of observations on several different parameters at the time of the present observation.

The interpretation of any given sign or symptom involves a *decision*, as to its significance in the light of the nurse's knowledge (Fig. 34). This decision determines whether or not the nurse must take immediate resuscitative action herself, whilst getting a message to the doctor, whether she should inform the doctor of the patient's condition but take no other action herself for the moment, whether she should wait but observe the patient more frequently, or whether no action is required.

OBSERVATION ON ADMISSION

From this, it can be seen how important it is to observe the patient very carefully when he is admitted. The interpretation of observations made on admission is difficult, however, since there is no baseline of previous observations of this patient for comparison, and a good knowledge of normal values is especially important.

Examples of the kind of observations which may be made on admission are as follows:

(1) *Activity level.* Is the patient able to walk? If so, is his gait normal?

If he is confined to a wheelchair, can he stand unaided?

If he is on a stretcher, is he lying or sitting?

Does his position cause him distress?

(2) *Mental state.* Is he anxious or worried?

Is he talkative or quiet?

What is his educational level?

(3) *Conscious level.* If he is conscious, is he orientated?

Does he show mental confusion?

Is his memory good?

(4) *Colour.* Is he pale? jaundiced? or cyanosed?

(5) *Nutritional state.* Is he thin? obese? dehydrated? oedematous?
(6) *Deformity.* Does he show joint deformity? weakness of limbs?
(7) *Skin.* Has he any skin lesions? e.g. ulcers or bed sores.
  Are there any bruises? Is there a wound?
  Is there a skin rash present?
  Temperature or moistness of the skin.
(8) *Respirations.* Is there any difficulty in inspiration or expiration?
  Are the respirations noisy?
(9) *Eyes.* Is there any jaundice? redness? swelling?
(10) *Pain.* Is pain present on movement? At rest?
(11) *Vomit.* Is the patient nauseated or vomiting?

In addition, the temperature, pulse, respiration and possibly blood pressure are recorded on admission, and repeated at intervals throughout the patient's stay in hospital. His urine is tested for abnormalities on admission.

Observation and Recording of Temperature, Pulse, Respirations and Blood Pressure

Temperature and Its Measurement

The temperature of a body is a measure of its warmth or coldness compared with a standard, such as boiling or freezing water. On the centigrade scale the boiling point of pure water at standard atmospheric pressure (760 mmHg) is marked as 100°C (212°F), and the freezing point as 0°C (32°F). The scale between these points is divided into 100; thus each centigrade degree is a measure of 1/100th of the difference between the heat energy of boiling water and freezing water. A thermometer, used to record temperature, is based on the principle that matter expands on heating and contracts on cooling, and it is constructed so that coloured liquid of some kind, held in a reservoir, can only expand along a narrow glass stem which is marked with an appropriate scale to indicate temperature. Measurement of the temperature of the human body is carried out using a clinical thermometer, which most frequently has mercury in its bulb. In the stem immediately above this is a constriction which causes a break in the thread of the mercury when the thermometer is removed from contact with the body. Thus it remains at the level of temperature reached whilst it was in equilibrium with the body temperature and can be read. It must be shaken down each time before a new temperature is recorded.

Body Temperature

The healthy human body, far from reflecting the temperature of the environment, remains within rather narrow limits of 35·5° to 37·2°C (96° to 99°F). This narrow range of temperature is maintained by a controlling system of cells in the hypothalamus. Mechanisms for conserving, producing or losing heat are brought into use according to the temperature of the blood circulating through the hypothalamic heat centre, together with less important information from temperature receptors in the skin.

Both muscular and metabolic activity of the body produces heat energy as a side product, and this heat is dispersed rapidly throughout the body by means of the blood stream. Vascular changes at the skin surface help in the control of body temperature, heat conservation being increased by the constriction of the blood vessels which reduces the flow of blood through the skin; whilst heat loss is increased by the dilatation of peripheral blood vessels. The greater blood flow which results allows loss of heat, not only by radiation, but also by evaporation of sweat. Heat is lost unavoidably in expired air and in excreta. Control of temperature in infants and the aged is less efficient than in children and adults.

Normally, there is a diurnal variation in body temperature, the temperature being higher in the evening and lower in the morning.

Pyrexia is the term denoting a body temperature raised above the normal range, and this may occur either if the metabolic rate is increased or if the hypothalamic centre is affected by 'pyrogens' from microorganisms or broken down tissue cells.

Hyperpyrexia is used to describe a body temperature of 40°C (104°F) or more. A patient with a body temperature above normal may be said to have a *fever*. Terms such as continuous fever, remittent fever (an exaggeration of diurnal variation), intermittent fever (where pyrexia and normal temperature alternate but less frequently than diurnally), have been used to describe the patterns seen on the temperature charts of patients with particular types of infection. Antibiotics usually suppress these patterns today. Crisis was a term used to describe the sudden drop of temperature to normal levels within a few hours after severe fever. During a crisis the heat loss is greater than heat production.

Hypothermia is the term used for a state where the body temperature is below the normal range, and it may accompany shock, or be brought about by prolonged exposure to cold, or to cold, wet, windy conditions. It also accompanies an excessively low metabolic rate.

Any deviation of the patient's temperature from normal should be reported. Particular care should be taken when recording the temperature of patients who might be suffering from hypothermia, since the usual clinical thermometer does not record subnormal temperature, and a special thermometer may be needed.

To Record the Patient's Temperature

Principles

(1) A clinical thermometer is reserved for the individual use of the patient whilst he is in hospital.

(2) It should be dried before use, and the mercury should be shaken below the markings on the thermometer.

(3) It should be placed in the selected position and left there for a minimum of 3 min and preferably for 6 min before being removed and read.

(4) Care should be taken that the temperature recorded by the thermometer is not affected by conditions peculiar to the particular area used to take the temperature so that the temperature as recorded is an accurate reflection of the core temperature.

Equipment required

(1) The patient's clinical thermometer.
(2) Swabs for drying the thermometer before use.
(3) A disposal bag for used swabs.
(4) A watch with a second hand.
(5) The patient's temperature chart and a pen.
(6) Petroleum jelly if the rectal temperature is to be recorded.

Areas Which May be Selected for Recording the Temperature

The mouth. This is the most commonly used area for taking the patient's temperature. There are many situations and conditions in which it is best to avoid using the mouth, however; these include: if the patient has recently swallowed hot or cold fluid or food; if he cannot close his mouth for any reason; if his breathing is diffi-cult or rapid; if his mouth is inflamed or sore; or if he is confused, or comatose. Oral temperatures should not be recorded in infants and young children.

The patient is asked to hold the thermometer under his tongue, closing the lips but not the teeth. He should be requested not to talk whilst the thermometer is in position.

The axilla or groin. This method should be avoided in patients who are very thin so that two skin surfaces cannot be in contact with the thermometer at the same time. It will not reflect core temperature in a patient who is in a state of shock, or whose peripheral blood vessels are constricted for any other reason. The skin surfaces must be dry whilst the thermometer is in position.

Fig. 35. Monitoring apparatus including ECG monitor, ratemeter, sphygomanometer and electrical thermometer.

The rectum. It can be very embarrassing for a patient to have his temperature recorded per rectum, therefore other methods should be used if possible. Rectal temperatures are sometimes recorded in babies and young infants whilst they are being bathed or having their nappies changed.

To record a baby's temperature, he is placed, lying on his back, on the nurse's knee, with the hips flexed and the knees straight so that the legs are at an angle of 90° to the body. The lubricated thermometer is then passed through the anus for about 1·3 cm

(0·5 in.) and held in position by the nurse, who holds his legs in position with the other hand.

For adults, the procedure must be carefully explained, and the thermometer is lubricated with petroleum jelly before use. The patient should be in the lateral position with knees and hips flexed, and the thermometer should be held in position by the nurse. It is inserted through the anus about 3·5 cm (1·5 in.).

When the thermometer has been in position for a minimum of 3 min, and preferably for 6 min, it is withdrawn, the temperature is read, and the thermometer is returned to an antiseptic solution, so that it is disinfected before being shaken down. The temperature should be charted.

Sometimes very accurate or frequent records of 'core' temperatures are required. An electric thermometer (Fig. 35) may be used, the lead of which is placed into the oesophagus or rectum and left in position. The machine is then switched on to record the temperature.

The Pulse

A pulse is the wave of expansion felt in artery walls when the heart pumps blood into the aorta which, because it contains elastic tissue in its wall, is thus distensible. This distension, when the aorta accommodates the blood from the left ventricle, spreads rapidly along the walls of the whole arterial system, but dies out before reaching the capillaries. A pulse can be felt wherever a superficial artery runs over a bone, e.g. radial, facial, temporal, posterior tibial and dorsalis pedis arteries. Pulsation can also be felt in the carotid arteries in the neck.

In normal individuals, the pulse rate accurately reflects the heart rate, and is recorded mainly as an indication of heart rate. Pulse may also be recorded at the extremities, expecially in the lower limbs, to observe the adequacy of the blood supply to distal parts when there is disease of the arteries.

The normal pulse rate of a resting, healthy, individual varies with age. In infancy it is 120 to 140 per min; at 3 years of age it falls to about 100 per min, whilst the average rate for an adult is 72 per min. In old age, the rate slows further. For adults, rates between 50 and 90 per min can be regarded as within normal limits, although a pulse rate of 50 in a patient whose pulse is normally 90, and vice versa, requires investigation. Exercise and emotion both increase the heart rate above the resting values quoted.

Disorders of Heart Rate

Recordings of the pulse rate are made to detect changes in the heart rate associated with disease, or changes in the patient's condition.

Tachycardia is the term used to denote an increase in heart rate. This may occur in the following conditions:

(1) Pyrexia, and its accompanying increased metabolic rate. The heart rate increases by 10 beats per min for every 0·5°C (1°F) rise in body temperature above normal.

(2) Increased metabolic rate due to thyrotoxicosis.

(3) A decrease in the effective circulating blood volume (shock).

(4) Heart muscle which is failing.

(5) Nervous disorder of the heart beat, called paroxysmal tachycardia.

(6) Due to some drugs, e.g. atropine, amyl nitrite.

Bradycardia refers to a heart rate which is slower than normal, and this may be associated with the following conditions:

(1) Excessive stimulation of the vagus nerve, as when the vagal nucleus is compressed due to increased intracranial pressure.

(2) Disease of the conducting tissue of the heart, leading to 'heart block', where the ventricles contract at their own intrinsic rate.

(3) When the metabolic rate is decreased, as in myxoedema.

(4) When excessive amounts of digitalis are given. Not only slowing of the heart rate but also coupling may occur in which two beats of unequal force are followed by an extra long pause in a regular pattern. The pulse rate and rhythm should always be checked immediately before giving a dose of digitalis, and the presence of coupled beats, or a pulse rate of 60 per min or less, should be reported, and the dose then omitted until medical orders have been given.

Disorders of the Rhythm of the Heart Beat

The heart beat is normally regular in rhythm except that occasionally the condition of sinus arrhythmia may be present, especially in children and young adults. In sinus arrhythmia the heart rate increases on inspiration and decreases on expiration; it is physiological and of no pathological significance. Whenever the pulse rate is being counted the rhythm should also be noted, and if it is irregular the pulse rate should be counted for a whole minute. In this case the apex beat should also be counted simultaneously by a second person using a stethoscope, and both rates recorded on the chart. Any irregularities in the strength of the beat should also be noted.

Extrasystole is a condition in which an extra beat of the ventricles of the heart follows rapidly on the previous beat and is followed by an abnormally long pause. The patient may be aware of this and it may cause him some anxiety since subjectively it seems as if his heart 'stops'. In young people extrasystole is often associated with excessive smoking, strong coffee, fatigue or a septic focus. In an older individual it may indicate some damage to the heart muscle.

Atrial Fibrillation

Fibrillation occurs when the atrial muscle no longer contracts as a whole, and a series of small and inadequate contractions pass over the muscle at a rapid rate, only some of these stimulating the ventricular muscle. Not all of the ventricular contractions eject sufficient blood to be reflected in the arterial pulses, thus the ventricular contraction rate will be greater than the pulse rate, the difference between the two being known as the pulse deficit. Atrial fibrillation may occur in mitral stenosis, coronary artery disease and thyrotoxicosis.

Recording the Pulse Rate

This may be counted wherever a superficial artery runs over a bone and also at the carotid artery in the neck; the radial and temporal arteries being the most convenient. The patient should have been resting for a quarter of an hour and his arm should be in a comfortable position, either at his side, or more conveniently palm down across his chest. This latter position allows his respirations to be counted either immediately before or immediately after the pulse rate is counted, whilst the nurse appears to be recording the pulse rate. By this means an alteration in the respiratory rate or rhythm due to self-consciousness on the part of the patient may be prevented.

To record the pulse the nurse's fingers should be placed along the course of the radial artery on the thumb side of the anterior surface of the wrist. She should observe the regularity of rhythm and the force of the pulse before beginning to count the rate. The arterial pulsations must be counted for a minimum of half a minute and the result doubled. If there is any irregularity present, the pulsations must be counted for a minute or the rate will be recorded inaccurately.

Blood Pressure

Blood pressure is the pressure exerted by the blood upon the walls of the blood vessels. It is usually recorded in the arteries, where it is greater during the contraction of the ventricles (systolic pressure) than during the period in which the heart is relaxed (diastolic pressure).

Arterial blood pressure depends upon several factors:
(1) The force of the ventricular contractions.
(2) The heart rate.
(3) The quantity of blood returned to the heart.
(4) Resistance to blood flow in the arterioles.
(If the plain muscle in the walls of these vessels contracts, then the calibre of the vessels decreases, the resistance to blood flow increases, and so does the arterial blood pressure.)
(5) The state of the arterial walls. If their normal distensible state, associated with the elastic fibres, is lost, then there is an increase in arterial blood pressure.
(6) The quantity of effectively circulating blood. An increase in this volume causes an increase of blood pressure, whilst a reduction causes a low blood pressure, unless homeostatic mechanisms compensate effectively.
(7) The viscosity of the blood.
Note. The force of the ventricular contraction, the quantity of blood returned to the heart and the heart rate together determine the *cardiac output* in terms of amount of blood per minute.

Blood pressure is recorded in millimetres of mercury (mmHg) and the normal arterial systolic pressure of a healthy adult at rest is sufficient to support a column of mercury 120 mmHg in height. Thus, normal arterial systolic blood pressure is quoted as 120 mmHg whilst the average arterial diastolic pressure of an adult at rest is 80 mmHg. Blood pressure tends to rise with age, so average arterial systolic pressure is 30 to 40 mmHg at birth whilst in the elderly it may rise to 140 to 150 mmHg.

Since the cardiac output increases with exercise, so does the blood pressure, and it should be recorded only when the subject has been at rest for some time, unless a record of the pressure during exercise is required. Emotions such as fear and anxiety cause an increase in blood pressure. *Hypertension* is the name given to the condition where the blood pressure of the individual at rest is increased above normal, an increase in diastolic pressure being of greater significance than an increase in systolic pressure.

This may be due to:

(1) Prolonged constrictions of arterioles.

(2) Loss of elasticity of the arterial walls.

(3) An increase in viscosity of the blood as in very severe polycythaemia.

(4) Hypertension may be associated with renal disease. It is postulated that the rise in blood pressure is mediated by a hormone called renin, released from tissue near the glomerulae of the nephron if the glomerular blood pressure falls. Renin increases the amount of circulating angiotensin, which causes an increase in blood pressure.

(5) Prolonged increase in the quantity of certain hormones which raise blood pressure, e.g. adrenaline and noradrenaline in phaeochromocytoma; serotonin in carcinoid; aldosterone in Conn's syndrome; and cortisol in Cushing's syndrome.

Hypotension refers to a condition in which the blood pressure is lower than normal. It may be associated with:

(1) Haemorrhage

(2) Burns — All resulting in an actual loss of circulating fluid.

(3) Severe dehydration

(4) Vagal inhibition, resulting in a reduction in cardiac output.

(5) Reduction in cardiac output due to sudden failure of the heart muscle.

(6) In severe infective states and anaphylactic shock, where fluid is not lost from the body but is effectively lost from the circulation by stagnating in dilated vessels and/or by collecting in tissue spaces.

(7) Adrenocortical insufficiency may increase the effects of the loss of circulating fluids in injured individuals who have been receiving corticosteroids over long periods of time.

Recording of Blood Pressure

Principles. Blood pressure is estimated by using a sphygmo-manometer, which consists of a glass manometer containing mercury, and calibrated in millimetres. An inflatable rubber cuff, attached by a piece of tubing to the manometer, is enclosed in a cotton bag, and when applied around a limb, and inflated, acts as a tourniquet, constricting the blood vessels of the limb to which it is applied. When the pressure of the inflatable bag just exceeds the systolic blood pressure the pulsation in the artery disappears. On its return, a tapping sound can be detected by listening over the vessel wall through a stethoscope. The height of the mercury in the manometer at the point of the first sound gives the arterial systolic blood pressure in millimetres of mercury. As the air is let out of the bag, the sounds change in character and then disappear. Either the point at which the sounds change, or at which they disappear, may be taken as the diastolic pressure according to the convention in the hospital. All persons recording the blood pressure of a particular patient should use the same criteria to determine the diastolic blood pressure.

Do not allow the patient to see the mercury whilst his blood pressure is being recorded, or it may cause him anxiety which could increase his blood pressure.

Procedure. Unless otherwise stated, it is usual to record blood pressure with the patient relaxed and at rest, with his arm resting on a pillow at the side of his body, palmar surface of the hand uppermost and with the elbow flexed very slightly. The cuff of the sphygmomanometer should be placed firmly but smoothly around the arm just above the elbow, and secured, with the inflatable bag lying over the brachial artery. Both the tubing and the lower border of the cuff should be well clear of the antecubital fossa (front of the elbow). Locate the site of the brachial pulse on the ulnar side of the antecubital fossa and note its position. Palpate the radial or brachial pulse and keep the fingers lightly in position over one of these pulses whilst inflating the cuff with air. Note the height of the mercury in the manometer at the point at which the pulse disappears and continue to inflate the cuff for a further 10 to 20 mmHg. Place the stethoscope over the location of the brachial pulse (it cannot of course be felt now) and listen for the onset of the blood pressure sounds, the change in their character, and the point at which they disappear, whilst slowly deflating the sphygmomanometer cuff. Note the height of the mercury column when each of these phenomena occur. Remove the cuff from the patient's limb, leave him comfortable and chart the blood pressure. If for some reason (e.g. very low blood pressure), the blood pressure sounds cannot be heard through a stethoscope, the systolic blood pressure may be charted at the point at which the pulse can no longer be felt; although by using this method the systolic blood pressure is very slightly underestimated.

The technique of taking blood pressures should be practised on normal individuals before taking the blood pressure of ill people, since the inflated cuff can cause great discomfort.

Observation of Respiration and Recording of Respiratory Rate

Respiration is the diffusion of gases between the air contained in the alveoli and the blood contained in the alveolar capillaries. The main gases involved in the exchange are oxygen which diffuses from the alveolar air to the blood, and carbon dioxide which diffuses from the blood to the alveolar air. The composition of the alveolar air is kept constant by the movements of respiration which ensure that the lungs alternately inflate with extra air from the environment and then deflate, expelling some of the alveolar air into the environment.

Muscles of respiration (the main ones are the intercostal muscles and the diaphragm) are voluntary muscles, but the movements of respiration are automatic. Their rhythm may be altered consciously, but not arrested deliberately over any significant period of time. However it is important that the patient should not become self-aware whilst his respirations are being observed, or the rhythm or the rate may change.

At rest, respirations are regular, effortless and quiet, breathing out, or expiration, being merely a relaxation of the inspiratory muscles. During rest the greater proportion of the expansion of the thoracic cavity may be due to diaphragmatic contraction rather than contraction of the intercostal muscles. At each inspiration the anterior abdominal wall moves outward slightly to allow descent of the diaphragm into the abdominal cavity. Average rates of respiration at rest are:

Infants: 34 to 40 per min;
Children aged 5: about 25 per min;
Adults: 14 to 20 per min.

Respirations are quiet, slow and shallow in sleep, and rapid, deeper and more noisy during and after exercise, and in emotion.

Abnormalities of Respiration

(1) Rapid, shallow respirations may occur postoperatively if deep breathing increases the pain of an abdominal or chest wound.

(2) An increase in the rate can occur in pneumonia or other infections of the respiratory tract where the volume of air entering into the lungs is restricted, or if the total alveolar surface available for gas diffusion is curtailed.

(3) Increased intracranial pressure can cause either an increase in rate, the respirations assuming an automatic character, or the respirations may become very slow and shallow. Either of these phenomena should be reported, but the latter type of respiration, particularly, is a poor prognostic sign.

(4) An increase in the acidity of the blood (as in diabetic coma) or in the carbon dioxide content of the blood can cause a great increase in the depth and rate of the respirations (hyperpnoea).

(5) Respirations become noisy, or stertorous, if there is some mechanical obstruction to the passage of air in the respiratory tract. Urgent action is required to relieve the obstruction, especially if respiratory *stridor* is present, indicating laryngeal spasm as the cause.

(6) Difficulty in expiration occurs in asthmatic attacks. Respirations become noisy because of bronchiole constriction and great expiratory effort is required. Accessory muscles of respiration are used.

(7) Cheyne–Stokes respirations occur when the respiratory centre itself is affected by lack of oxygen. The respirations become cyclical in character. A period without breathing (apnoea) is followed by shallow, slow respirations which increase in depth and rate to reach a crescendo following which they get slower and shallower until apnoea occurs again.

(8) Respirations become very slow and shallow when an overdosage of a depressant drug affects the respiratory centre.

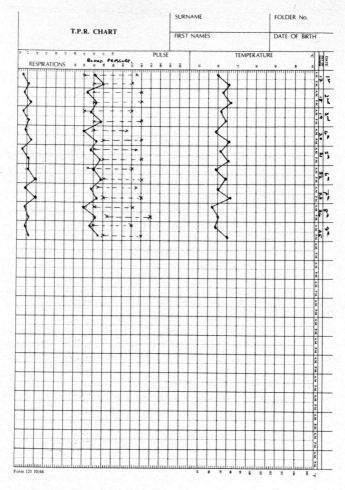

FIG. 36. Temperature, pulse and respiration chart.

Dyspnoea means difficulty in breathing. Orthopnoea is the term used to describe the symptom in which there is difficulty in breathing except when the individual is sitting up.

To Record Respiratory Rate

The number of respirations is counted for half a minute and the quantity doubled to give the rate per minute. A respiration consists of both inspiration and expiration. The respirations should be counted for a full minute if there is any abnormality present of rate, rhythm, depth or if there is any difficulty in breathing. Any of these abnormalities should, of course, be reported. Avoid letting the patient know that his respirations are being counted.

Charting. A record of the temperature, pulse and respiratory rates and blood pressure is kept for each patient in the form of a graph on specially printed charts. The observation of these functions should be charted immediately, so that not only the possibility of forgetting the correct value is eliminated, but also so that the chart is always up to date. Points on the graph should be made clearly and unambiguously and joined together neatly. Observations should be made as often as necessitated by the patient's condition. It may only be necessary to record the temperature, pulse, respirations and blood pressure daily, or it may be necessary to do it as frequently as quarter hourly (Fig. 36).

Cardiac Monitoring

Following cardiac infarction, or cardiac surgery, continuous observation of the electrocardiogram may be requested, so that cardiac arrhythmia may be detected the moment it occurs. This continuous observation of the ECG is made possible by its display on an oscilloscope. The electrical changes of the heart during the cardiac cycle are picked up by electrodes attached to the anterior chest wall or the limbs, and are amplified and converted into a visual picture on the screen (Fig. 37). Nurses looking after a patient whose heart beat is being 'monitored' in this way should be capable of detecting any changes in the oscilloscope display, and of looking after the electrodes.

Electrodes may be attached to the limbs by means of straps, but more commonly they are attached to the anterior chest wall, since

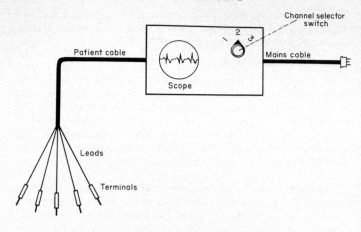

FIG. 37. Diagram of the basic features of a monitor.

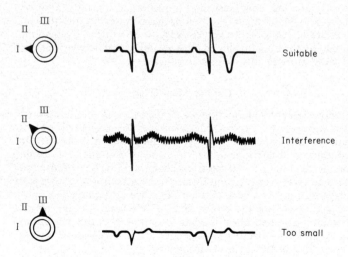

FIG. 38. Select the channel that shows the waves of ECG trace most clearly.

this gives the patient greater freedom of movement. Intimate contact between the skin and electrode is necessary to obtain a clear trace, and so all oil must be removed from the skin. The area selected is shaved, and may be on either side of the sternum, or below the nipples. It is then thoroughly cleaned by some fat solvent, such as ether, methylated spirit or acetone. Since the skin will become reddened and abraded by this thorough cleaning, the site must be changed frequently thereafter to prevent a sore. KY jelly is then spread on the electrode, which is placed on the prepared area and taped in position. It should then be connected up, and a trace displayed to ensure that it is clear (Fig. 38), otherwise it may have to be moved. When once the trace is adequate, a loop of lead should be taped to the patient's abdomen to give freedom of movement without endangering the connection of electrode to skin.

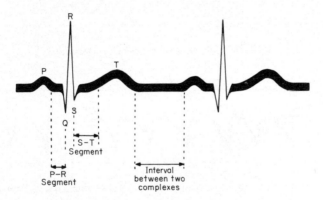

FIG. 39. Normal ECG trace. P wave + QRS complex + T wave = one complex. QRS complex + T wave = one QRS–T complex.

All members of the staff should acquaint themselves with the controls on the particular oscilloscope model in use in their ward. The oscilloscope should be placed so that it can be seen easily by the nursing staff. Sometimes a second monitoring screen is placed near the nurse's station, with several channels, so that the ECGs of four or five different patients may be displayed simultaneously.

Observations Which Should Be Made

(1) *Rate of heart beat.* This can be readily counted by observing the number of complete cycles traced on the screen per minute.

(2) *Any change of rhythm.* In the normal ECG each trace (Fig. 39) is identical with any other trace and they occur at completely regular intervals. Any change from the rhythm previously displayed should be reported.

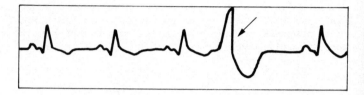

FIG. 40. ECG trace of ventricular extracystole.

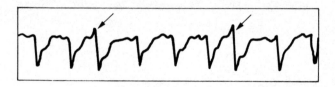

FIG. 41. ECG trace of a ventricular extracystole falling near a T wave.

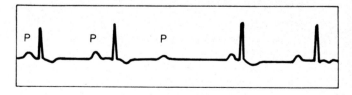

FIG. 42. ECG trace of the Wenckebach phenomenon (P = P wave).

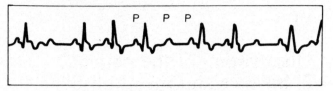

FIG. 43. ECG trace of second degree heart block (P=P wave).

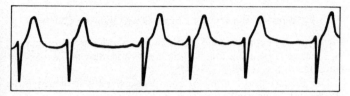

FIG. 44. ECG trace of atrial fibrillation.

Changes Which Should be Reported

(1) *Ectopic beats.* An extra, early heart beat, leaves the heart muscle refractory, so the next normal beat does not occur (Figs 40, 41, 42 and 43). The ectopic beat is then followed by a long pause and the trace is irregular.

(2) *Fibrillation.* The atria contract irregularly, and the contraction may not be strong enough to trigger the ventricles into contraction. The RST complex will occur less frequently than the P waves and the whole trace will look irregular (Fig. 44).

(3) Any change in the general condition of the patient must be reported.

11

Observation of the patient
2. Balance and metabolism

Fluid Intake and Output Charts (Fluid Balance Charts)

These may be kept as an aid to diagnosis, a guide to treatment, or as a means of ensuring that a patient gets adequate fluids when he is unable to help himself (Fig. 45).

The following are some of the circumstances in which fluid charts may be needed:

(1) If there is a risk that the patient may become dehydrated, as in vomiting, diarrhoea, excess sweating or malabsorption of tube feeds.

(2) As a guide to the treatment of dehydration.

(3) To assess the effectiveness of treatment in oedema.

(4) To keep a careful record of fluid balance in kidney failure.

(5) Whenever a patient is receiving intravenous fluids, since overhydration can occur if care is not exercised.

(6) Whenever the regular aspiration of gastro-intestinal contents is being carried out.

(7) When artificial drainage of the bladder is carried out by urethral catheter or suprapubic cystotomy.

Procedure

Fluids should be measured before they are administered to the patient and the amount he drinks should be charted straight away.

It is conventional to chart the quantity of intravenous fluid in each new container, as the bottle (or polythene bag) is changed. If for some reason the infusion is discontinued before it has all been used, the remaining quantity should then be subtracted from the total amount. This method ensures that the chart is always up to date and is accurate, since all members of staff use the same convention.

INTAKE AND OUTPUT CHART

NAME ..*M. D. Brown*.....

DATE ..*10-1-62*..   WARD....*X.X*.............   CASE No.................

TIME	IN		OUT				NOTES
	ORAL	INTRAVENOUS	ASPIRATION	URINE	VOMIT	DRAINAGE	
1 a.m	— ml (cc)	*1000* Dextrose/Saline ml (cc)	30 ml (cc)	ml (cc)	ml (cc)	ml (cc)	*Clear fluid aspirated*
2 a.m	Water 30 ml	ml	24 ml	200 ml	ml	ml	"
3 a.m.	— ml	ml	20 ml	ml	ml	ml	"
4 a.m.	— ml	ml	15 ml	ml	ml	ml	"
5 a.m.	— ml	ml	10 ml	ml	ml	ml	"
6 a.m	Water 30 ml	ml	20 ml	250 ml	ml	ml	"
7 a.m.	— ml	ml	36 ml	ml	ml	ml	"
8 a.m.	Water 30 ml	ml	30 ml	ml	ml	ml	"
9 a.m.	Water 30 ml	ml	36 ml	150 ml	ml	ml	"
10 a.m.	Water 30 ml	*1000* Dextrose 5% ml	24 ml	ml	ml	ml	"
11 a.m.	Water 30 ml	ml	16 ml	ml	ml	ml	"
12 noon	Water 60 ml	ml	18 ml	360 ml	ml	ml	"
1 p.m	Water 60 ml	ml	20 ml	ml	ml	ml	"
2 p.m.	Water 60 ml	ml	10 ml	ml	ml	ml	"
3 p.m.	Water 60 ml	ml	24 ml	ml	ml	ml	"
4 p.m.	Water 60 ml	ml	16 ml	500 ml	ml	ml	"
5 p.m.	Water 60 ml	ml	18 ml	ml	ml	ml	"
6 p.m.	Water 60 ml	ml	14 ml	ml	ml	ml	"
7 p.m.	Water 60 ml	*1000* Dextrose/Saline ml	10 ml	ml	ml	ml	"
8 p.m.	Water 60 ml	ml	10 ml	460 ml	ml	ml	"
9 p.m.	Water 60 ml	ml	12 ml	ml	ml	ml	"
10 p.m.	— ml	ml	— ml	ml	ml	ml	—
11 p.m.	— ml	ml	10 ml	ml	ml	ml	*Bile stained fluid*
12 midn't	— ml	ml	— ml	ml	ml	ml	—
24 Hour Totals	780 ml	3000 ml	423 ml	1920 ml	ml	ml	

Na.	K.	Cl.	HCO₃	Hb			
							TOTAL IN 3780 ml
							TOTAL OUT 2343 ml
136-146 mEq/1	3.8-4.6 mEq/1	98-108 mEq/1	24-28 mEq/1				BALANCE 1437 ml

FIG. 45. Intake and output chart.

All fluid lost from the body should be observed, measured, and the quantity charted (e.g. vomit, urine). If the patient is suffering from diarrhoea it may not be possible to measure the volume of fluid lost but an estimate should be made, so that an equivalent quantity may be replaced. It is necessary to check whether or not the patient's fluid intake and output is to be recorded before throwing away any excreta.

At the end of each 24-hr period the individual quantities of fluid taken in and lost from the body are added up, and attention should be drawn to any imbalance, making due allowance for fluid lost in sweating and expired air. The addition should be carried out at the same time each day, but the actual time will vary from hospital to hospital, the most common times being 24.00 hours or 08.00 hours.

NAUSEA AND VOMITING

Vomiting is a reflex action which results in the contents of the stomach being ejected through the mouth. It is usually accompanied by a feeling of nausea, and possibly faintness. Subjectively, the victim may suffer from extreme distaste and embarrassment, especially if his night clothes or the bed linen become soiled in the process.

Since nausea is usually experienced prior to vomiting, it may be possible to prevent vomiting by taking note of complaints of nausea, and reporting these to the doctor, who can then decide if an anti-emetic drug is required. Care with diet and fluids, and the prevention of excessive stimulation, such as sudden movement of the patient, may also help to prevent vomiting. A vomit bowl and tissues should be placed within easy reach of him, since fear of soiling the bed may increase his anxiety level, thus increasing the likelihood of vomiting.

If the patient vomits despite all precautions, the wound should be supported by the nurse, or if there is no wound, she can support the patient's forehead. A clean vomit bowl should be provided when once the vomiting attack is over, and the patient should be given a mouth wash. Any soiled clothing must be changed, and the patient's hands and face washed if possible. He will probably be feeling ill, so a balance must be struck between disturbing him as little as possible and leaving him clean and comfortable.

Observations of the Patient

(1) Any preceding nausea or retching.

(2) Whether the vomiting was associated with the intake of a particular kind of food.

(3) Any regularity in the pattern of vomiting.

(4) Any pain present.

(5) Whether vomiting is forcible in character (projectile).

Observations of the Vomit

The quantity of fluid should be measured and recorded on the fluid chart.

Appearance of Vomit

The presence of certain substances in vomit can be detected by its appearance. (This method is not infallible but does give a guide.)

Poorly digested food may be seen and recognized. If the patient has been swallowing secretions from the respiratory tract, mucus may be present in the vomit. Bile, from the duodenum if present, gives vomit a brown-green colour. Frank blood can be recognized easily, whilst partially digested blood becomes dark brown in colour and unevenly distributed through the fluid due to coagulation. In intestinal obstruction, fluid which contains foul smelling, partially digested fluid, may be vomited from the intestine. This is termed faecal vomiting. If poisoning is suspected the vomit must be saved for analysis.

The vomit of patients with suspected or actual peptic ulceration should be tested for occult blood.

Causes of Vomiting

(1) *Conditions local to the gastro-intestinal tract:* (a) local irritation of the stomach mucosa due to drugs, irritating foods, infective states, bleeding; or (b) obstruction of gastro-intestinal tract causing dilatation of the tract above the site of the obstruction.

(2) *Excessive or unusual stimulation of peripheral nerves:* (a) severe pain, especially in visceral muscle, as in renal or biliary colic; or (b) disturbance of the organs signalling one's position in space, as in travel sickness.

(3) *Stimulation of the vomiting centre:* (a) in severe emotion, especially if occasioned by unpleasant sights or smells; (b) in

increased intracranial pressure; or (c) if the vomiting centre is affected by disturbance of the blood chemistry, as by bacterial toxins in the blood stream.

OBSERVATIONS OF URINE AND URINE TESTING

All urine should be measured and recorded if the patient is on a fluid chart, and even if he is not, the nurse should notice and report any difficulty in passing urine, any frequency, incontinence or abnormally small or large quantities being passed.

Normal urine is a clear, amber coloured liquid, usually slightly acid in reaction and with a specific gravity of 1004 to 1030. Urine which is very dilute owing to a large fluid intake has a low specific gravity, whilst highly concentrated urine has a high specific gravity. The specific gravity of urine is the weight of a litre of the urine, compared with the weight of a litre of water. (Weight of 1 litre of pure water at $4°C = 1000$ g.)

The quantity of urine passed in 24 hr depends on the fluid intake, but the average for an adult is 1500 ml. Urine consists of water, urea, uric acid, creatinine, various ions (e.g. sodium, potassium, hydrogen, chloride, ammonium and bicarbonate ions), urates, phosphates and urochrome, a pigment which gives urine its colour. An unusual appearance of urine may be due to abnormal or excessive amounts of constituents.

A sediment may settle out when urine stands and this may consist of urates or phosphates in large quantities. Urates form a pink deposit, whilst phosphates form a white one. Pus, mucus and renal tubule casts may also form a sediment when urine stands, and may render the urine cloudy. Very concentrated urine looks dark in colour. Frank bleeding may give the urine an appearance of dilute blood, whilst small amounts of blood in the urine give it a smoky, dark appearance. Urine may also appear brown or green, due to the presence of bile pigments. Thus, visual inspection may reveal the presence of some abnormalities; other abnormalities of the urine may alter its smell. Acetone in the urine gives it a sweet smell, likened to the smell of new mown hay, whilst infection with *Escherichia coli* is associated with a fishy smell. Urine often has a smell of ammonia which may be due to microorganisms breaking down urea to ammonia when the urine is left to stand.

Inspection of the urine may lead one to suspect that abnormalities are present, but this should always be confirmed by chemical or microbiological tests.

Simple testing of urine for the presence of abnormal constituents is carried out in the ward by nursing staff, using a specimen of urine, in the collection of which no special precautions have been taken. Such testing of urine is carried out routinely when patients are first admitted to hospital, and before general anaesthetic is administered or an operation carried out.

Ward Urine Testing

General Principles

(1) Urine should be fresh, collected in a clean, detergent-free receptacle, and carefully labelled with the patient's name.

(2) All test tubes and apparatus should be clean and dry and preferably have been rinsed with distilled rather than tap water.

(3) Urine should not be acidified before testing.

(4) Lids should be replaced on all reagent bottles when they are not in use.

(5) Reagent tablets should be handled with forceps and reagent strips should be handled only by the non-impregnated end.

(6) Testing should be carried out methodically, and carefully. The results of each test should be charted immediately it has been carried out.

Tests

(1) *The appearance* of the urine is noted and recorded.

(2) *Reaction.* Litmus paper is used to determine whether the urine is alkaline or acid. A drop of urine is placed on to a piece of red and a piece of blue litmus paper. Acid urine turns blue litmus red, whilst alkaline urine turns red litmus blue. Urine is normally acid since the slightly alkaline reaction of the blood (pH 7·4) is maintained by adjustment made in the blood vessels surrounding the renal tubules. Excess acid or alkaline ions pass into the tubule to be excreted in the urine. The reaction of the urine varies with the diet.

(3) *Specific gravity* is recorded by a urinometer which is placed into the urine and allowed to float freely. The stem of the urinometer is calibrated, and the mark at the level at which the stem

emerges from the urine gives a reading of the specific gravity; the lower level of the meniscus of the fluid should be taken. If there is insufficient urine to allow the urinometer to float free, then add an equal quantity of water, and double the final two figures of the reading obtained.

(4) *Test for albumin.* Albumin is a large molecule protein found in the blood, and under normal circumstances it is too large to pass through the glomerulus, and into the glomerular filtrate. Occasionally it does pass into the urine in some individuals when they stand, so that urine formed in the standing position contains albumin, whilst that formed whilst the individual is lying down contains no albumin. Protein can also be found in the urine as a contaminant from vaginal secretions, or from infections of the urinary tract. However, albumin does appear in the urine in kidney damage, as in nephritis, and heart failure. Albuminuria may be an early sign of toxaemia of pregnancy.

To test for the presence of albumin in the urine, 'Albustix' reagent strips are used. The test end of the strip is dipped into the urine and removed immediately. A change of colour to green or blue-green, developing straight away, shows the presence of albumin. This colour can be compared with the chart provided to indicate the amount of albumin present.

Esbach's albuminometer can also be used to get an estimate of the quantity of albumin present. Urine should be clear, with a specific gravity of less than 1020, and acid in reaction. Thus it may be necessary to add acetic acid until it turns blue litmus pink; filter, or dilute the urine with a known quantity of distilled water. The tube of the albuminometer should be filled to mark U with urine, and to mark R with Esbach's reagent. It is then corked, mixed by inversion several times, and left undisturbed for 24 hr, after which time the height of the precipitate which forms at the bottom of the tube is read off on the graduated scale indicating grams of protein per 100 g of urine.

(5) *Test for glucose.* Glucose appears in the urine when the blood level of glucose exceeds the renal threshold for glucose, i.e. approximately 180 mg per 100 ml. The renal threshold for glucose may be exceeded in normal individuals immediately after meals with a heavy carbohydrate content, if their renal threshold is on the lower side of normal. Glucose also appears in the urine of individuals suffering from diabetes mellitus, whose blood sugar

level rises and remains high for a considerable time after a meal. Small amounts appear in the urine in pituitary and thyroid disease, head injury and subarachnoid haemorrhage.

Glycosuria can be detected by the use of 'Clinistix' reagent strips. The test end of one of these should be dipped into the specimen of urine and then removed. A positive result, indicating the presence of glucose, is shown by a blue colour developing at the moistened end of the strip within 10 sec.

A quantitative estimation of the glucose present can be obtained by using 'Clinitest' reagent tablets. These tablets must be fresh for accurate results. Five drops of urine are placed into a clean test tube, using a pipette. The pipette should be rinsed with distilled water, and then 10 drops of water added to the urine, followed by the Clinitest tablet. The latter will cause agitation of the solution. Fifteen seconds after the agitation has ceased the test tube should be shaken gently, and the resultant colour matched with one of the colours on the chart provided to indicate the quantity of glucose in the specimen. Whilst 'Clinistix' react only with glucose, 'Clinitest' tablets react with other sugars, such as lactose (may be present in the urine of pregnant women), galactose and fructose, and other reducing substances such as ascorbic acid and salicylate metabolites.

(6) *Test for 'ketones'* (acetone and aceto-acetate). Ketones accumulate in the blood stream when excess quantities of fat are being metabolized, in the absence of the metabolism of adequate quantities of glucose. This may occur in diabetes mellitus and in starvation; in both of which conditions acetone and aceto-acetate will be excreted in the urine as the blood level increases. The presence of ketone in the urine of a diabetic patient should be reported, since diabetic coma occurs as a result of large quantities of ketone bodies in the blood stream and not as a result of the high blood glucose.

'Acetest' reagent tablets are used to test urine for the presence of acetone and aceto-acetate. One tablet is placed on a clean surface, such as a white tile or piece of paper, and one drop of urine is added. A colour change at the end of 30 sec exactly should be matched with the scale provided, a positive result being shown by a pale lavender to a strong mauve colour.

'Ketostix' reagent strips also react with acetone and aceto-acetate. The test end of the strip should be dipped into a fresh specimen of urine, and removed immediately. Excess moisture should be removed by touching the strip briefly on the side of the container. Fifteen seconds later, the colour should be compared with the chart provided. The presence of aceto-acetate or acetone is indicated by a lavender or purple colour.

(7) *Test for the presence of blood in urine.* Large quantities of blood in the urine will be obvious to the naked eye, but it may be necessary to test for the presence of blood in the urine which may be present in small quantities in infective lesions and nephritis.

'Hemastix' reagent strips react to haemoglobin. The test end should be dipped into the urine and removed immediately. Thirty seconds later the test end should be matched with the colour chart. A positive result is shown by the development of a blue colour.

(8) *Test for bilirubin.* Bilirubin is a product of the metabolism of haemoglobin. It is conjugated in the liver, and in this form it can pass through the glomerulus into the glomerular filtrate. Since it is normally secreted from the liver in the bile it does not appear in the urine in this form, but in the form of urobilin and urobilinogen which are formed from the further breakdown of conjugated bilirubin. The blood concentration of conjugated bilirubin rises if the flow of bile is obstructed in any way, and bilirubin appears in the urine.

'Ictotest' reagent tablets are used to test for bilirubin in urine. Five drops of urine should be placed on a special test mat, and the reagent tablets placed in the middle of the moist area. Two drops of urine are then flowed over the tablet. The colour of the test mat *around* the tablet should be observed 30 sec later. A positive result is indicated by a bluish-purple colour on the paper around the tablet.

OBSERVATION OF SPUTUM

Excessive secretions from the respiratory tract are coughed up, a process called expectoration, the expectorated secretions being called sputum. A patient should be discouraged from swallowing sputum, and a disposable sputum carton should be provided for him, together with tissues to wipe his mouth. The quantity and type of sputum should be noted and the ease with which it is coughed up. If there should be any difficulty in expectoration, then physiotherapy, inhalations or expectorants may be ordered by the doctor to help liquefy the sputum.

Sputum may be predominantly *mucoid* in character, as in the early stages of inflammatory conditions such as pneumonia or bronchitis. *Mucopurulent* sputum may be coughed up in bronchiectasis, or if a lung abscess ruptures. The sputum may be *blood-stained* in pneumonia, in pulmonary infarction, tuberculosis, and carcinoma of the bronchus. If a large amount of blood is present it may be bright red and frothy. The coughing up of fresh blood is termed *haemoptysis*. Sputum may be very *frothy* when the pulmonary blood pressure is raised, giving pulmonary oedema.

OBSERVATION OF RATES OF INFUSION

Infusion tubing incorporating a special 'drip chamber' allows fluids to be administered slowly over long periods of time at a constant rate of drops. Infusions may be used to administer fluids into the following tissues or areas: (1) intravenous, (2) subcutaneous, (3) intragastric, or (4) rectal.

Since there is a greater risk of complications from intravenous infusion than any of the others, the observations required whilst an intravenous infusion is in progress will be described. If blood is administered by this means, then it is termed a blood transfusion.

Observation of the Patient Having a Blood Transfusion

(1) Careful checking is needed to ensure that the bottle of blood being transfused is the bottle of donor blood which has been cross-matched with the patient's blood and found to be compatible with it.

(2) The patient's temperature, pulse and respiration rates should be recorded at frequent intervals, and a fluid intake and output chart kept. A mild incompatibility reaction may be reflected in a rise of temperature.

(3) Empty blood bottles should be returned to the laboratory unwashed.

Observation of the Patient Whilst an Intravenous Infusion or Transfusion is in Progress

(1) Frequent observation of the rate of administration is needed. This should be regulated if necessary to match the prescribed rate in terms of drops per minute.

(2) Inspection of the site of the insertion of the needle or

catheter should be made to ensure that it is securely within the vein and that no fluid is leaking subcutaneously. Some intravenous fluids can cause damage if allowed to get into subcutaneous tissue, e.g. blood, noradrenaline, urea.

(3) The level of fluid within the bottle or infusion container must be watched to ensure that it never completely empties; or air will get into the tubing and this is very difficult to remove. An exchange should be made for a full container whilst there is still a very small amount of fluid left in the old one. Tubing must be clipped off whilst the bottle is changed, and sterility must be preserved.

(4) Care must be taken that the fluid given is that which has been prescribed.

(5) The infusion may stop completely. Among the reasons why this should happen are the following: (a) accidental clipping off of the tubing; (b) blood clot blocking the needle or catheter; (c) occlusion of the needle because it is displaced in the vein and its lumen is resting against the vein wall; and (d) spasm, or compression of the vein above the infusion.

In general, the nurse deals with factors affecting the tubing, whilst the doctor deals with factors involving adjustment of the needle within the vein.

(6) When once the infusion has been discontinued, the vein site should be observed for signs of inflammation.

WOUND DISCHARGES AND DRAINS

Bleeding immediately postoperatively may stain the dressings of the wound, which should be repacked. A drain may have been inserted into the wound at operation to allow for the drainage of any anticipated collection of fluid which could delay healing. The drain is often shortened before it is removed, and observation of the type and amount of discharge should be made whenever the wound is dressed. Discharge will usually consist of stale blood unless the wound becomes infected, in which case it may be purulent.

Occasionally some kind of suction is needed to help the drainage of discharge from a wound. This may be provided by apparatus such as a Roberts' low pressure pump or by some form of vacuum drainage such as a 'Redivac' bottle. Whatever apparatus is used the amount of drainage should be measured, sterility being ensured whilst the apparatus is changed.

Special types of drains may be inserted into deep tissues. Following an operation on the common bile duct, a T-tube may be inserted with the short arms of the 'T' lying within the lumen of the common bile duct and the long arm emerging from the wound, and draining into a sterile, closed, container at the side of the bed. The quantity of bile should be measured carefully and the tubing replaced into a fresh sterile container; the colour of the drainage should also be noted. This T-tube is removed when drainage stops, and an X-ray following the use of a radio-opaque dye shows the common bile duct to be functional. The use of an analgesic is needed before its removal.

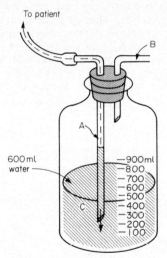

FIG. 46. A drainage bottle with underwater seal. (A) Tube connected to drainage tubing; (B) air inlet tube; (C) water seal.

Water-Seal Drains

If the visceral and parietal pleural membranes are separated from each other by a collection of fluid or air, a drain may be inserted to drain these off by gravity and allow re-expansion of the lung. The free end of the drain must be sealed under water placed in a container well below the level of the patient, otherwise air would be sucked into the pleural cavity at each inspiration. Provided the tubing is patent and the lung has not fully re-expanded the level of the water in the tubing (as it passes down into the bottle) rises, as the patient breathes in, and falls again as he breathes out.

This 'swinging' of the water level is, therefore, a good guide as to whether the tubing is patent and the reason should be investigated if the rise and fall cannot be seen. The amount of fluid draining in should be measured as necessary. A known and accurately measured quantity of fluid is placed in a fresh, sterile, bottle (Fig. 46). To change the bottle the tubing must first be clamped with two pairs of Spencer Wells forceps placed near to the insertion of the tubing, to prevent air getting into the pleural cavity. Careful technique is essential to prevent microorganisms from getting into the apparatus. At no time must the water seal bottle be lifted higher than, or even at a level with, the patient. The drainage tube is removed by the medical staff when the lung is fully re-expanded.

12

Nursing care of the unconscious patient

NURSING an unconscious patient can be a most satisfying experience for a nurse. Her nursing care can both preserve life, where death would otherwise occur, and prevent tissue damage or deformity which would severely incapacitate the patient on recovery from the coma. Caring for an unconscious patient allows her to exercise to the full her skills in the physical care of people, although until such time as the patient regains consciousness, she cannot use the other skills so important in nursing, such as those of communicating with her patients, and encouraging them back to independence. She will, however, need to give a great deal of help and support to the relatives during this most difficult time.

An unconscious patient has lost the ability to attend to his own nutritional and toilet needs, together with the ability to request that these needs are attended to; he has also lost the ability to swallow, and all control over his sphincters. In deep coma, protective reflexes, such as the cough reflex, and the blink reflex, are also lost. The patient is unable to change his position for himself, or exercise his limbs, and cannot protect himself from harmful stimuli.

Prevention of Airway Obstruction

The first essential in caring for an unconscious patient is to *ensure that he has a clear airway,* thus allowing adequate ventilation of the lungs, so that the essential exchange of gases can take place between the alveolar surface and the blood. *Obstruction of the airway* may occur in several ways:

(1) The tongue may be flaccid and can fall to the back of the throat.

(2) Secretions from the mouth, throat or respiratory tract may accumulate in the tract itself.

(3) False dentures may become displaced.

(4) Vomit or regurgitation from the alimentary tract can be inhaled, causing obstruction of the airway.

To prevent obstruction of the airway, the patient may be nursed in the semi-prone or lateral positions. These positions prevent the tongue from falling back, and allow vomit and excessive secretions to drain from the mouth, preventing their inhalation. Dentures should be removed from any unconscious patient, labelled and kept safely. Secretions can be removed from the back of the throat by means of gentle suction, using a sterile catheter. *Noisy respirations are signs of an obstructed airway*, and the airway must be cleared immediately.

A rubber or polythene airway may be employed to keep the tongue in position and to prevent it from falling back. It should not be employed over long periods of time, however, or ulceration of the mucous membrane will occur. If an airway of this type is employed, very frequent mouth toilet is essential, together with changing the airway and cleansing and sterilization of the used one. An endotracheal tube (see p. 181) may be inserted to maintain the patency of the respiratory passage, but this, too, can cause ulceration of the mucosa, with stricture due to scar tissue at a later date. For this reason, it is unusual to leave an endotracheal tube in position for longer than 48 to 72 hr, at which point a tracheostomy may be performed if the breathing remains difficult. A tracheostomy not only ensures a clear airway, but it allows secretions to be sucked out more easily, and cuts down the ventilatory dead space, allowing better ventilation of the lungs (see p. 178).

Prevention of Chest Infection

In the absence of the cough reflex, normal bronchial secretions accumulate within the chest, and are very likely to give rise to chest infection. This can be prevented by changing the patient's position from side to side, 1- or 2-hourly, so that each lung in turn lies uppermost, aiding its expansion on inspiration, and draining secretions. If allowed, the foot of the bed should be raised from time to time, further helping the secretions to drain, and the physiotherapist should be asked to carry out frappage to the chest wall, loosening thick mucus, which can then be sucked from the back of the throat. The physiotherapist should be asked to teach her technique to the nursing staff, so that this treatment can be continued at intervals throughout the 24 hr. She can advise as to how frequently it should be carried out. If chest infection does occur, in spite of these precautions, a sputum specimen should be obtained, so that the appropriate antibiotic can be administered to the patient.

Artificial Feeding

Since the patient is unable to swallow, an alternative method of feeding him is essential. Initially, this may be by the intravenous route, but prolonged administration of intravenous fluids is likely to cause thrombosis in the vein being used. Fluids that can be administered easily by this route do not supply the full nutritional requirements. Intragastric feeding is, therefore, the method of choice for any patient who is unconscious for any length of time. Careful checking of the tube to ensure that it is in the stomach should be carried out before each feed is given, since the tube can enter the respiratory tract without any telltale coughing and choking. Before each feed is given, the nurse should make sure by aspirating the tube, that the previous feed has been absorbed or emptied from the stomach, as vomiting may occur if the stomach becomes excessively distended. The times at which the patient is turned should be calculated carefully, so that he is turned before intragastric feeding. Regurgitation or vomiting might occur if he is turned immediately after a feed. With the help of the dietician, the feeds must be carefully calculated to give the full nutritional, calorie, and fluid requirements needed by the patient in the 24-hr period, allowing for small amounts of water to be used to clear the tube before and after each feed. The amount and frequency of each individual feed can then be determined according to the size of the patient and his individual food habits. Frequent, small feeds, may be needed for a patient who is used to small, frequent meals, whilst another patient may tolerate larger quantities, less frequently. The type of food used may need changing if the patient is not tolerating his feed well, or if he develops diarrhoea (for example, glucose and water may be absorbed better then Complan, until digestive function improves).

Sometimes unconscious patients require a higher calorific content in their feeds than would be expected from their activity level.

Restless patients, patients with pyrexia, or an increased metabolic rate from other causes, may lose weight whilst unconscious, unless their needs are very accurately estimated, and the Calorie content of their feeds increased. A naso-gastric tube should be changed daily, whilst one passed through the mouth should be removed after every feed. In general, the nasal route is more satisfactory, but the oral route should be used in head injury, nasal injury, or patients with a grossly deviated nasal septum.

Mouth Toilet

Frequent mouth toilet must be carried out for unconscious patients. Salivary secretions will not be stimulated by eating, mouth breathing is common in unconscious patients, and this not only dries the membranes, but also abolishes the changes of pressure which occur in normal breathing and stimulate the circulation of the mucous membrane. The presence of chest infection increases the need for frequent mouth cleaning, whilst a dirty mouth increases the likelihood of chest infection. Mouth toilet should be carried out 1- to 4-hourly.

Special precautions are required when cleaning the mouth of an unconscious patient. The swabs should be of gauze with stitched ends, so that no wisps of cotton can find their way into the respiratory system. They should be firmly clipped onto Spencer Wells forceps, and hydrogen peroxide should not be used as a cleansing agent, since it froths and could be breathed in. Petroleum jelly may be needed on the lips to prevent dryness and cracking.

Care of the Skin

A daily blanket bath should be carried out, and if the patient is incontinent of urine, or perspires a lot, the bed linen must be changed, and the skin washed and dried frequently, to prevent excoriation of the skin. Frequent turning of the patient, use of sorbo pads, and careful positioning of limbs, should prevent pressure sores from occurring. The use of an alternating pressure point mattress may be of value. When attending to the patient's needs, it is important to prevent abrasions or scratches of his skin; thus watches and rings must not be worn by the nurse. She should place pens securely in her pockets so that they do not fall out. Her nails should be short and smoothly filed.

Management of the Bladder

It is likely that an unconscious patient will be incontinent of urine, and that the urine will endanger his skin. Wet beds may be prevented, in the case of a male patient, by placing a urinal in position, although care must be taken to prevent it from pressing on the skin. There is less chance that a urinal can be successfully used in the case of a female patient, and catheterization may be necessary to prevent bed sores. However, it is possible to prevent wet beds by placing a patient on a bed pan at frequent intervals, or by changing the bed linen very frequently. If catheterization is carried out, great care must be taken to prevent urinary infection.

Occasionally, retention of urine may occur, and careful observation of the urinary output, and the state of distension of the bladder is needed, especially if retention of urine with overflow, is present. Careful recording of the estimated urinary output should be carried out by all members of staff when changing a wet bed. If retention of urine should occur, then catheterization is essential. If a self-retaining catheter is inserted, by intermittently releasing it, 2- to 4-hourly, the bladder tone may be maintained. This method is preferable to open drainage for an unconscious patient.

Management of the Bowel

Careful recording when the patient has a bowel action is important, to observe the occurrence of diarrhoea or constipation. If severe constipation should occur, there may be some faecal overflow, simulating diarrhoea. The administration of suppositories, every 2 to 3 days, is a useful way of preventing constipation.

Care of the Limbs

Deformity of the limbs and joints should be prevented by massage of muscles, careful positioning of limbs, and daily passive movements of all joints, through a full range of movement. A bed cradle is very useful for preventing the pressure of bed clothes upon the patient's limbs.

Care of the Eyes

Since the corneal reflex may be lost, bathing of the patient's eyes should be carried out 4-hourly. If the eyelids remain open, a tarsorraphy may be necessary to prevent corneal damage by the pillow when the patient is in the semiprone position. Corneal damage can also occur from excessive drying if the patient is being fanned for pyrexia. Half strength normal saline solution should be used for bathing the eyes. Liquid paraffin or antibiotic drugs, may be ordered by the doctor if the eyes become dry or infected.

Assessment of the Level of Consciousness

Careful observation of the patient's condition will help to establish the diagnosis, assess the effectiveness of treatment, and allow timely intervention if the patient's condition should deteriorate. Observations that should be made and recorded, include assessment of the patient's conscious level. Does he rouse when spoken to? Does he obey commands? Does he respond to painful stimuli? The presence of any paralysis should be noted. If he moves his limbs spontaneously, is the movement equal on each side? Is the response to painful stimuli equally brisk on either side? If brain damage is suspected, the pupillary size, equality and reaction to light should be noted. A urine specimen must be obtained on admission and tested. The blood sugar may also be estimated. Frequent recordings of temperature, pulse, respiratory rate and blood pressure will be necessary. The temperature should be recorded from the axilla or rectum, *not* orally, and particular attention must be paid to the respiratory rate; any rise or fall should be reported, since respiratory infection is such a likely complication, and in brain damage an early sign of deterioration may be a change in the rhythm or rate of the respirations.

The Patient's Relatives

Since it is difficult to estimate the exact extent to which sensory function (especially hearing) is lost by any given patient, care must be taken about what is said within his hearing, and relatives should be warned about this. As with any other patient, the unconscious patient should be warned before he is moved in any way. For the relatives' sake great care should be taken with the patient's appearance, so that he looks well cared for and as attractive as possible. The hair should be regularly combed and brushed and washed at intervals if he is in hospital for a long time. Male patients should be shaved regularly.

The patient's relatives will need a great deal of information, help and support, whilst the patient is unconscious, and they should be allowed to visit freely. However, if the nurse feels that it is causing them distress to be present at the bedside, she can suggest less frequent visiting, so that they reserve their strength for when he regains consciousness, for then he will need and appreciate their presence. If the nurse intends to suggest less frequent visiting, she should be sure that the motive is for the good of the relatives and not because the relatives are in the way, or because she finds it difficult or embarrassing to talk to them, and give them the help and comfort they need. Relatives should be kept informed of any change in the patient's condition, so that they can be present at the bedside when the patient regains consciousness. They will also wish to be present if the patient's condition deteriorates and death is likely. It can cause them a great deal of unnecessary grief, and possible guilt, if the patient should die alone, even though he cannot be aware at the moment of dying

13

Tracheostomy care, and care of patient with respiratory failure

TRACHEOSTOMY

A tracheostomy is an artificial opening into the trachea, which is kept patent by the insertion of a metal or portex tube (Fig. 47).

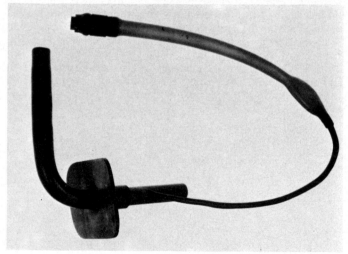

FIG. 47. Cuffed tracheostomy tubes.

Reasons for Tracheostomy

(1) In respiratory obstruction if the obstruction is above the tracheostomy site.

(2) If there is paralysis of the vocal cords.

(3) To aid suction of secretions from the respiratory tract, in respiratory tract infection.

(4) To reduce the respiratory dead space so that more efficient exchange of respiratory gases can occur.

(5) To ensure maximum efficiency of the system if the patient is being artificially respired with a positive pressure respirator.

Types of Tracheostomy Tube

A Silver Tube

This has both an outer tube, and an inner tube. The latter can be removed for cleaning at frequent intervals. The outer tube may be removed every 7 days by a member of the medical staff, and replaced by a new, sterile set.

A Portex Inflatable Tube

This is a disposable tube which does not have an inner tube. It does have an inflatable cuff around the lumen. When inflated, the cuff makes for an airtight fit in the trachea, preventing leakage of gases when a respirator is being used. To prevent ulceration of the trachea the cuff should be deflated at intervals, such as 5 min in every hour.

A Portex Tube, With No Inflatable Cuff

This is a plain tube which fits into the tracheostomy.

Apparatus which should be kept at the bedside

Suction machine or piped suction; the tubing should be fitted with a polythene 'Y' connection.

Oxygen cylinder or piped oxygen.

A pair of sterile dressing forceps.

Suction catheters of the correct size.

A bowl of sterile sodium bicarbonate solution.

Disposable gloves.

Sterile tracheal dilator forceps.

A sterile tracheostomy set of appropriate type and an introducer.

A syringe and adaptor if a cuffed tracheostomy tube is in use.

For a conscious patient, a bell and writing materials.

Care of the Airway

It is vital that the patient's airway should be kept clear. Signs that the airway is becoming blocked are as follows:

(1) In the early stages, the respirations become noisy. This is the stage at which the situation should be detected and dealt with.

(2) The patient may become cyanosed in colour.

(3) If the hand is placed directly in front of the tube, no air can be felt on expiration.

Action to be Taken

For partial blockage, suction may be employed to clear the airway. If there is an inner tube present, it should be removed for cleaning, and suction should be carried out through the outer tube. If neither of these measures work then the patient should be positioned with the head retracted and the neck extended, and the outer tube should be removed. Tracheal dilators should be inserted to maintain the opening and suction should be carried out, through the neck incision. Medical help will be required to insert another tube. Oxygen can be given, and artificial respiration may be necessary. The obstruction must be relieved as rapidly as possible.

Routine Maintenance of the Airway

Since it will be extremely difficult for the patient to cough, suction should be carried out at intervals sufficiently frequent to prevent distress of the patient.

Suction of a Patient with a Tracheostomy

(1) Have the patient lying on his back with his head retracted and his neck extended. Full explanation should be given.

(2) Choose an appropriate suction catheter which is only half the diameter of the tracheostomy tube. It should have an opening in the end, across the diameter of the catheter.

(3) Use disposable gloves.

(4) Open the pack containing the catheter and connect the end to the 'Y' connection of the suction apparatus.

(5) Withdraw the catheter from the packet, using the left hand to hold it at the connection and a pair of sterile forceps in the right hand to grip the catheter near the other end.

(6) Pass the catheter into the trachea, using the forceps.

(7) Switch on the suction and occlude the open arm of the 'Y' connection.

(8) If suction does not proceed smoothly, switch off the machine, withdraw the catheter, and clear it by sucking sterile sodium bicarbonate solution through.

Repeat from Step (6).

Continue the procedure until the patient's airway is clear.

(9) Disconnect the catheter and dispose of it, together with the gloves. Make the patient comfortable.

Throughout the procedure observation should be made of the patient's colour. Oxygen should be given if he becomes at all distressed.

Frequent turning and chest physiotherapy will help to loosen secretions.

Positive Pressure Respirators

If artificial aid to breathing is required over a long period, some form of respirator is used, and most commonly this is a positive pressure respirator where gas is forced into the lungs under pressure at regular intervals, through a mask, an endotracheal tube, or a tracheostomy tube. Expiration either occurs passively, or by negative pressure. Types of respirator in common use include the Beaver, Radcliffe, Cape Wain, Bird and Smith Clarke. A nurse, asked to work on a ward where one of these respirators is available for emergency use, should ensure that she understands how it works at the beginning of the ward experience.

Observations to make on taking over the care of a patient being artificially respired include:

(1) Observe the patient's colour and chest movement. The chest should inflate equally on either side.

(2) Test all tubing for air leaks, and make sure that it is not kinked.

(3) Check that you know how to operate the machine by hand in an emergency, and that you know how to give artificial respiration manually, if necessary. [An Ambu bag or similar apparatus should be available.]

(4) Check that you are fully conversant with all the controls of the machine, then check that the readings all conform to those ordered by the doctor. These readings include the maximum and

minimum pressure to be exerted by the machine, the respiratory rate required, tidal volume required, and possibly the expired minute volume.

(5) If oxygen is being used, ensure that a supply is available, and check the rate of flow.

(6) If humidification of the air or oxygen is needed, check the temperature and that the humidifier is filled.

All these observations should be repeated at prescribed intervals of time.

In addition, the following points should be kept in mind:

If the patient should make respiratory movements which are out of phase with the machine the doctor must be informed.

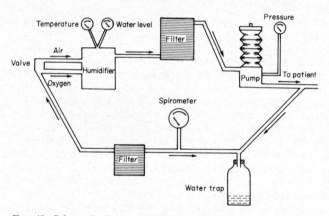

FIG. 48. Schematic diagram of artificial ventilation (*Nursing Times*).

Great care must be taken not to disconnect the tubing when carrying out nursing care. After suction, make sure that the ventilator is properly reconnected (Fig. 48).

If the pressure readings change the cause should be traced and dealt with.

A rise in pressure may be due to obstruction to the flow of gas. This may be kinked tubing, an obstructed airway requiring suction, or if the humidifier is in use, water may accumulate in the tubing. A fall in pressure is usually due to loss of gas from the system, so the tubing must be checked for leaks. The doctor should be notified if the situation cannot be corrected.

ADMINISTRATION OF OXYGEN

Oxygen benefits the patient whose respiratory capacity is diminished, as is the case following chest injuries or operations on the lung, in pneumonia, acute pulmonary oedema, cardiac failure and many other conditions.

Oxygen Cylinders and Fittings

For purposes of identification oxygen and other medical gas cylinders are painted in distinctive colours and the name and/or symbol of the gas is stencilled on the cylinder. Oxygen cylinders are painted black with a white valve end.

Oxygen is compressed into cylinders of different sizes at 132 atm (atmospheres), which is an equivalent of approximately 1940 lb per in^2. This pressure must be reduced prior to administration to a patient. Wherever possible an automatic oxygen regulator should be employed for this purpose, but when not available a fine adjustment valve may be used with care. A litre gauge or flowmeter is necessary in order that the prescribed rate of flow may be maintained. These gauges may be of the dial or the bobbin type. In the latter a bobbin inside a graduated glass tube rises as the oxygen passes through and the height of the bobbin against the scale shows the amount of oxygen being delivered. The flowmeter is usually incorporated in the cylinder fitting with the pressure gauge and regulator.

Before attaching the regulator to the cylinder the cylinder valve should be opened slightly, so that any grit or dust that may have accumulated may be blown out. The regulator is then fitted into the head of the cylinder by inserting the threaded end into the valve opening and tightening it by means of the winged nut. The litre gauge should be turned off and the cylinder opened slowly until the cylinder contents gauge shows 'full', the cylinder is then opened completely by giving the key one more turn. The cylinder is then ready for use.

In some wards the oxygen supply may be delivered by a pipeline to each bed, but every ward should possess at least one oxygen outfit ready for immediate use. The cylinder, in a wheeled stand with the fittings and the apparatus for delivering the oxygen to the patient, should be regarded as emergency apparatus which must always be kept in working order. An empty cylinder should be clearly marked 'EMPTY' when removed from the stand and should be replaced at once by a full cylinder.

Fire Precautions

Although oxygen itself does not burn, any material which burns in atmospheric air will burn much more easily if the concentration of oxygen in the air is increased. Therefore certain precautions should be strictly observed.

Patients and visitors should be warned against smoking or lighting matches in the vicinity. No electrical bells, lights or heating pads should be allowed inside an oxygen tent and children should not be given mechanical toys. The patient must not be rubbed with oil or spirit whilst the tent is being operated; should such procedure be necessary the oxygen flow must be discontinued during the time that the treatment is being carried out.

Oil or grease of any description must not be used on the oxygen cylinder or fittings. The nozzle of the cylinder must be cleaned before attaching the regulator.

Administration of Oxygen

Oxygen may be given by means of a mask, an oxygen tent or through nasal tubes or fine catheters. Whenever a patient is having oxygen therapy he must be under continuous observation. The apparatus must be frequently and carefully checked; should the supply of oxygen run out, the patient may be unable to obtain sufficient air. In certain cases, for example in patients suffering from chronic bronchitis and emphysema who develop pneumonia, carbon dioxide may build up in the blood when the anoxia, which has been the respiratory stimulus in these patients, has been relieved. This can lead to carbon dioxide narcosis, the symptoms of which are a full bounding pulse, muscular twitchings, mental confusion and eventually coma. For this reason intermittent rather than continuous oxygen is usually ordered for bronchitic subjects, or oxygen may be administered by 'Venti mask' (see p. 186).

Masks

Disposable polythene mask (*Oxygenaire*) (Fig. 49). This type of mask is light in weight and as it is inexpensive it can be destroyed after use and so presents no problems of sterilization. When the

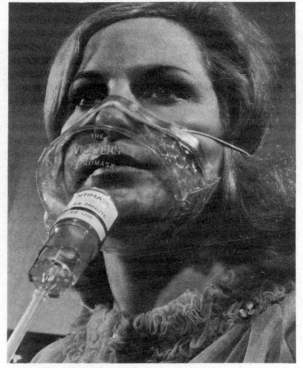

FIG. 49. Disposable face mask (*Oxygenaire*).

mask is connected to the oxygen supply, the flow of oxygen inflates a cuff round the edge of the mask, which then fits closely and comfortably. Should the oxygen supply accidentally run out the cuff will deflate, thus calling attention to the failure; in the meantime the patient can continue to breathe atmospheric air.

The 'Venti' mask (*Oxygenaire*) (Fig. 50). The Venti mask is designed to give accurate control of the oxygen concentration so that it does not rise high enough to cause respiratory depression, but is sufficient to relieve anoxia. The range of controlled concentration is 24 to 35 per cent. The disposable face piece is edged with foam rubber so that it fits closely and comfortably round the patient's nose.

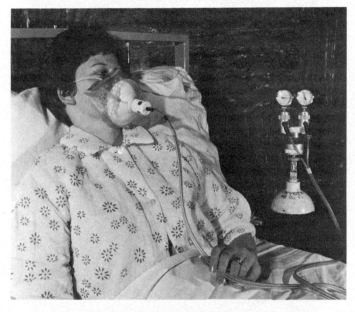

FIG. 50 A 'Venturi' mask (*Oxygenaire*).

Tracheostomy mask (*Oxygenaire*) (Fig. 51). If a patient has had a tracheostomy performed it is obvious that he cannot benefit from oxygen given through a face mask. The tracheostomy mask shown in the illustration is made of perspex and fits over the tracheostomy opening; an opening with a peardrop cover in the front of the mask, over the tube, allows suction to be carried out with the mask in position. There are perforations at the side of the mask; these allow excess carbon dioxide to be removed and enable the patient to breathe atmospheric air, should the oxygen supply fail.

If a mask is not available, oxygen can be given by means of a catheter passed through the opening of the tracheostomy tube.

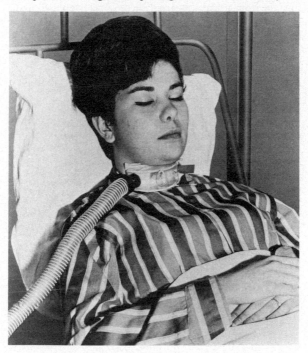

Fig. 51. A tracheostomy mask (*Oxygenaire*).

Oxygen Tent

There are several types of oxygen tents in use, but the general principles of construction and the management of the patient in the tent are very similar (Fig. 52).

The aim is to have an oxygen content of 40 to 60 per cent (average concentration 50 per cent) inside the tent. The excess carbon dioxide must be removed, and the air prevented from becoming over-hot and excessively humid. The tent is made of transparent plastic material attached to a frame; the whole is mounted on wheels, enabling the tent to be easily moved. The windows in front are transparent in the other types of tent. The canopy has openings, through which the nurse's arms can be put to give attention to the patient. Cooling of the air inside the tent is effected by passing the air through an ice box or through a refrigeration unit, and in some types of tents the carbon dioxide is removed by passing the air through a container of soda-lime.

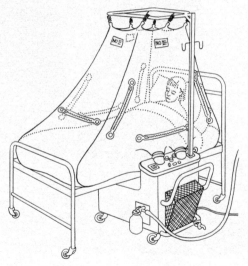

FIG. 52. An oxygen tent.

A full cylinder of oxygen ready for use, as described above, and a supply of ice should be obtained before erecting the tent. A wall thermometer will also be required. This is hung in the tent when it is erected, at the opposite end to the ice cabinet.

The ice is broken into pieces about the size of a man's fist and the ice container filled to capacity. About 90 cm (3 ft) of rubber tubing is then connected to the water outlet of the ice cabinet and a pail is placed under the rubber drain pipe. The ice cabinet is raised so that it will be clear of the ground when the canopy is fitted; the lid of the cabinet must be securely fastened otherwise there will be a leak of oxygen. A water seal is provided in the cabinet to prevent oxygen leaking through the drain pipe.

The head of the canopy must be securely attached to the openings provided on the ice cabinet, this is done by means of rubber inserts or rubber corrugated tubing. The back of the canopy has a nozzle marked 'oxygen inlet' to which the rubber tubing from the cylinder regulator is attached. This should be done and the flow adjusted to 5 litres per min before the canopy is placed over the patient. The temperature control should be set to 'cold'. Two persons are needed to fit the canopy over the patient's bed. The height of the tent and cabinet must be adjusted so that the head of the canopy will be from 15 to 30 cm (6 to 12 in.) above the patient's head. The skirt of the canopy is lifted and spread out so that it covers the bed and can be tucked in on both sides and at the back. The free end at the foot of the bed may be rolled into a sheet across the patient's knees. Alternatively, if a rubber sheet is placed over the frame of the bed the canopy is tucked in all round between the rubber sheet and the mattress. The openings of the canopy are closed with zip fasteners by rolling them up and securing the flaps with bulldog clips.

Once the tent is set up the oxygen flow should be turned on until the needle of the litre gauge registers 'flush' and this full flow is then allowed to continue for about 5 min, after which time the flow is reduced to the dosage ordered, which may be from 4 to 8 litres per min.

When the canopy has been opened to allow access to the patient the tent should be flushed with oxygen as soon as the openings are closed again. The temperature in the tent should usually be maintained at $18°$ to $21°C$ ($65°$ to $70°F$).

In some cases the patient may not be nursed continually in the tent; as already mentioned, certain patients suffering from respiratory disease may develop carbon dioxide narcosis if they are continually breathing a high concentration of oxygen. An example of the routine that may be followed in such cases is 10 min in the tent and 20 min with the tent open.

Caution is needed in the use of an oxygen tent for premature infants since high concentrations can lead to a condition known as retrolental fibroplasia and blindness. The minimum concentration of oxygen that will relieve cyanosis and respiratory difficulty should be given.

When an oxygen tent is dismantled after use the canopy should be mopped with a disinfectant, such as Savlon 1:20 solution, and then washed with soap and water.

Nasal Tubes

This method is used if a tent is not available or a face mask is not suitable, as, for example, where there are facial injuries. It is much less efficient than either the tent or the mask as it is wasteful of oxygen and the patient cannot as a rule tolerate a rate of flow greater than 4 litres per min. Disposable nasal tubes are used.

When giving oxygen by nasal tubes it is necessary to moisten the oxygen by passing it through a humidifier before it reaches the patient, as dry oxygen is irritating to the nasal passages.

Before the tubes are inserted the nostrils should be cleaned with warm sodium bicarbonate lotion and wool swabs. A cocaine spray or cocaine ointment may be used in order to make the treatment less uncomfortable for the patient. The two nasal tubes should be passed about 5 cm (2 in.) along the floor of the nostrils. The tubes should be removed and cleaned if left in for more than 24 hr.

USE OF STEAM

In respiratory infections it may be helpful to humidify the inspired air. If a tracheostomy has been performed a humidifier will be used. When sophisticated equipment is not available, steam can be used instead.

Steam Tent

A steam kettle which has a very long spout can be used to saturate the atmosphere with steam. If the patient is being nursed in the open ward, a special frame or screen may be attached to the corners of the bedstead, supporting a canopy above the bed to prevent loss of steam from the immediate vicinity of the bed (Fig. 53). Friar's Balsam may be added to the water in the kettle, to produce a soothing vapour. Precautions must be taken so that there is no danger of the patient being scalded. The kettle should not be allowed to boil dry.

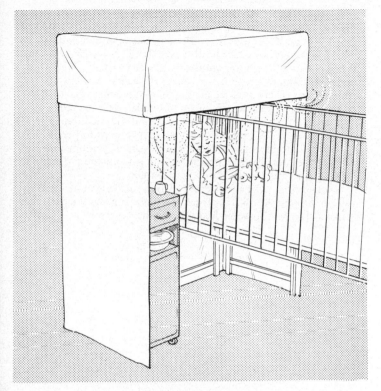

Fig. 53. A steam tent.

Extra attention should be given to the patient or he may feel very isolated, since his view of the world is severely curtailed. The temperature within the steam tent must be observed and not allowed to go above 21°C (70°F). The patient should be encouraged to cough and expectorate.

Steam Inhalation

When a patient has an upper respiratory tract infection such as laryngitis, pharyngitis or a head cold, a steam inhalation may relieve his symptoms. The treatment can be given by means of a Nelson's inhaler. It should be half filled with boiling water to which a prescribed quantity of Friar's Balsam or menthol can be added. A flannel hot water bottle cover should be wrapped around the inhaler, and the latter should be placed in a bowl. The whole apparatus should be on a firm surface, such as a table, for the patient's use. There must be no danger that it might tip, and if the patient cannot cooperate, he must not be left with the inhaler.

A gauze swab should be fixed in position with Sellotape round the glass mouthpiece, and the patient is instructed to put his lips to the mouthpiece and breathe in through the mouth and out through the nose. The treatment is continued until the water cools. Mouthpieces must be sterilized between use.

A satisfactory substitute for a Nelson's inhaler can be made by using a litre jug. A towel is placed round the rim and the patient is instructed to lean forward and breathe the steam.

14

The care of patients with pyrexia

PYREXIA

An increase in body temperature occurs when there is an initial increase in heat production and a decrease in loss of heat from the body.

Factors which increase heat production are:
(1) Increased secretion of adrenaline.
(2) Increased secretion of thyroxine.
(3) Increased muscular activity, as in rigor.

Factors which decrease heat loss are:
(1) Vasoconstriction of peripheral blood vessels.
(2) Diminished sweating.

Control of body temperature is a function of the hypothalamus. Disease processes which may be associated with pyrexia are:
(1) Infection and inflammation due to microorganisms.
(2) Tissue infarction.
(3) Haemorrhage.
(4) Collagen disease.
(5) Malignant disease.
(6) Reaction to foreign protein.
(7) Lesions of the brain stem and hypothalamus.

In all of these conditions, with the exception of the last named, cells in the hypothalamic centre are depressed by circulating 'pyrogens' and act as if they are 'reset' to control the temperature at a higher level than normal.

As well as the conditions listed above, an increase in the amount of circulating thyroid hormones will cause a rise in body temperature by a direct effect on metabolism.

The Effects of Pyrexia Upon The Body

(1) The basal metabolic rate is increased by 7 per cent for each half Centigrade degree (one Fahrenheit degree, approximately) rise of temperature above the normal.

(2) There is an increase in the pulmonary ventilation rate and the cardiac output.

(3) Since the basal metabolic rate is increased, there may be excessive protein breakdown, a tendency to ketosis and negative nitrogen balance, unless the Calorie intake is adequate to counteract this. If protein breakdown does occur, body wasting may result from prolonged pyrexia.

(4) An increase in sweating may occur after the initial rise of temperature and this may be sufficient to cause sodium and fluid depletion.

Hyperpyrexia is a particularly dangerous condition, since above a body temperature of 41°C (106°F), the temperature controlling centre itself may fail, and death may ensue if the high temperature is prolonged.

Hyperpyrexia may occur in:

(1) Very severe infections.

(2) Excessively hot or humid climates (heat stroke).

(3) Brain stem or hypothalamic damage.

Nursing Care of Patients with Pyrexia

The nursing care should be directed toward preventing the possible side effects of pyrexia, the prevention and treatment of excessively high temperatures, and the administration of drugs which have been ordered.

Much of the nursing care relates directly to the excessive sweating which may occur. Plenty of fluids should be given, and drinks should be nourishing. Frequent baths, and change of clothing, are necessary, as is frequent mouth care. Unfortunately the patient may have lost his appetite, but efforts should be made to maintain his Calorie intake, especially when pyrexia is prolonged. The temperature, pulse, respiration rates and blood pressure should be recorded frequently.

Pyrexia may be accompanied by headache, due to intense constriction of blood vessels of the head. Photophobia and irritability may also be present. As far as possible, noise should be reduced to a minimum, bright lights should be avoided in the patient's vicinity, and the patient should be moved very gently when treatments are carried out. Analgesics may be necessary for the headache.

Measures to Prevent Excessively High Temperatures and Their Treatment Should They Occur

(1) The amount of bedclothing over the patient should be the minimum which is compatible with his comfort, and the use of a bed cradle helps the circulation of air around the patient's skin surface.

(2) An electric fan may be employed to cool the air around him. Care must be taken to ensure that the eyes are not dried excessively by the fan, especially in the case of unconscious patients.

(3) Drugs which reduce temperature may be ordered by the doctor, e.g. acetylsalicylic acid, chlorpromazine, paracetamol.

(4) Tepid sponging may be carried out to reduce temperature if other measures fail, or it may be used to increase the comfort of the patient.

(5) In hyperpyrexia ice packs may be used, if ordered by the doctor.

Tepid Sponging

Aims of Treatment

(1) To increase loss of heat from the body surface by evaporation, thus reducing body temperature.

(2) The treatment should not cause shivering, since shivering causes a rise in body temperature.

Principles

(1) Long sweeping strokes using a sponge soaked in tepid water leave drops of water on the skin surface, to be evaporated by the body heat.

(2) Wet sponges placed in axilla and groin help to reduce the temperature.

(3) A sponge which is not in use is cooled by placing it in water at a lower temperature than that being used for the procedure.

(4) The temperature of the water being used for the sponge is gradually reduced during the procedure.

(5) The body temperature of the patient should be recorded frequently throughout, and after the procedure, and unless specific instructions are given by the doctor, the patient's temperature should be reduced by only one degree Centigrade (two degrees Fahrenheit, approximately).

Requirements

A supply of hot and cold water.
A bath thermometer.
Six sponges.
A face towel.
Two compresses for the forehead, soaked in iced water.
Polythene sheeting.
Two bath blankets (thin ones).
Two large washing bowls, one containing cold water, and one containing water at the prescribed temperature (which is usually between 26° and 18°C [79° and 65°F]).

Procedure

The bedclothes are removed, and the polythene sheeting and a bath blanket are rolled into position beneath the patient. His face and hands are washed and dried, and a cold compress left over his forehead. Sponges soaked in water at the prescribed initial temperature are placed in axillae and groins, and using one of the remaining sponges, the patient's arms, trunk and legs are sponged gently, leaving beads of water on the skin. Both the sponges and the cold compress must be changed from time to time, the used sponges being placed in the bowl of cold water and then transferred to the bowl of water at the correct temperature before being re-used. The patient is finally turned on his side, and his back is sponged.

The procedure should take approximately 15 to 20 min unless otherwise stated, and should be discontinued if the patient's temperature falls drastically, or if he complains of feeling worse.

Occasionally it may be necessary on the doctor's instruction, to rub the skin surface whilst sponging, in order to dilate the peripheral blood vessels, since if they are constricted no evaporation of fluid by heat from the blood will take place.

At the end of the sponging, the patient should be left dry and comfortable and light clothing replaced on his bed.

15

Care of the dying

THE PROVISION of comfort for the dying is a great challenge to nursing skill, since nurses may find that their own emotional reactions to the dying patient prevent them from carrying out their role to the best of their ability. So that they may overcome these reactions, it is important that staff have insight and understanding into their origin and operation.

One common reaction to the presence of a dying patient in the ward is avoidance of that patient. On the overt level, the patient may be placed in a side room, and the staff may then avoid entering this room unless it is absolutely necessary. If the patient remains in the main ward, staff may hurry past his bed, avoiding his eye. On the other hand a semblance of interaction may be maintained; his physical needs being met, and time spent in talking to him, but staff can still fail to give the emotional support he needs, by keeping the conversation on a superficial level, talking themselves rather than letting the patient talk, evading direct questions, or giving light, flippant answers.

There are differing reasons for this avoidance reaction. Undoubtedly caring for a dying patient can be a stressful experience. Staff may feel a sense of failure that they have not cured the patient. They may feel embarrassed at the idea of death, since death is not freely discussed in our society. To watch someone whose death is imminent can upset the onlooker, who is brought full face with a sense of his own mortality and can project himself into the situation only too easily.

A young nurse may not know how to help the patient and will feel very inadequate and inexperienced. Sometimes inexperienced members of staff conform to the example set them, and expect that time spent with the patient just talking will gain them strong disapproval from senior staff.

One particularly distressing situation for a student nurse may arise when she knows the patient is dying but the patient has not been told, and it is the policy of the consultant that he should not be told. The patient may ask the student directly if he is dying. She is then faced with the dilemma of telling a lie, or being evasive, with the result of increasing or even confirming the patient's suspicions. One way of dealing with this situation is to tell the patient that the doctor is the correct person to deal with questions of that kind, and to promise that she will ask the doctor to come and talk to the patient. This is probably the best way in which a young inexperienced person could deal with the situation. For a more experienced person, the question could be used for getting the patient to talk and express some of his fears, which might be unrealistic and ill-founded. She might therefore reply: 'What makes you ask that?' or 'What makes you think you are dying?' If the patient has good grounds for his fears, again the doctor should be brought in to deal with his questions.

The Needs of the Dying Patient

A patient who knows he is dying may feel afraid of death, or he may resent that this disaster has fallen on him. He may feel it is punishment for some episode in his past, or be bewildered as to why he should be singled out. He may feel regret that his life is being cut short with things left undone, goals unachieved, opportunities lost. He may feel tired of life, and thus welcome death, or regard it as an end to pain and unhappiness. He may simply accept the idea of death as a culmination of goals achieved, ambitions realized, or a life enjoyed to the full. More likely, his feelings will vacillate between fear, resentment and acceptance.

Regardless of his particular reactions he will need to talk about his reactions and his feelings and to feel free to talk about death, which after all, is probably the most significant event of anyone's life. A minister of religion is an ideal person to visit and listen to the patient and give him comfort. Many patients do not hold a religious belief, however, and do not wish to be visited by a chaplain. These patients particularly need to feel free to express themselves to a member of the nursing staff. Those to whom religion is important also need to be able to talk to a nurse, since the chaplain will only be able to visit infrequently.

The patient needs to feel that he is still a valued and useful person. He will feel valued if members of staff can spare the time to talk to him and to get to know him as a person. His relatives can help him to feel useful still by bringing family problems to him for his help and advice. Unless this is done he will feel that no one bothers about him and he is useless. He can be helped by being brought into contemporary life as much as possible.

If it is at all possible, it is better that just one or two nurses are responsible for his care, so that he can develop a close relationship with them, and not have to keep getting to know a lot of new faces. Experienced nurses rather than inexperienced should be assigned to his care, since inexperienced ones may find it acutely disturbing to spend long periods of time with a dying patient. The question then arises as to how they are to learn to help patients who are dying. It is impossible to teach communication skills in an abstract way. Students can best learn by listening to conversations between experienced nurses, social workers, priests and the patient. Later, they can begin to talk with the patient themselves, with the situation being discussed afterwards with an experienced individual, who points out other ways in which the student could have helped the patient.

Unless the patient himself wishes to be in a single room, or requires such a lot of nursing care that his presence is disturbing to the other patients, it is better that he should stay in a ward with other patients so that he is surrounded by activity and can participate in the ward life with the others.

Nursing care is very important to keep the patient clean and comfortable, and to help him to look as attractive as possible, maintaining both the relatives' and the patient's morale. One of the most crucial aspects of nursing care is the prompt administration of drugs prescribed by the doctor to keep the patient pain free. A great deal of the fear of dying is really a fear of pain and suffering, and the patient will be spared much anguish if he can be confident of being kept pain free. Some patients develop the attitude when they know that they are dying that time spent by a nurse in washing or caring for him is time wasted which could be better spent on others. The nurse must make him feel that she enjoys giving him care and attention and that he is equally as important as the other patients. Touch may begin to assume comparatively more importance than the other senses to an ill person and the nurse who can sit quietly and hold the patient's hand will help him considerably. She should not feel guilty about sitting when there are other jobs to be done; and neither should she feel inadequate because she is not talking to the patient, and 'taking his mind off his troubles'.

A visit from the medical social worker may be needed so that the patient can discuss arrangements for the future of his family, and he may wish to see his solicitor or financial adviser.

Support of Relatives

The patient's relatives will need continual support and advice during this time. If the patient hasn't been told about his imminent death, the relatives will find the situation stressful and will need to be able to discuss the situation with the doctor. They may seek advice about how to talk to the patient and how often to visit. A wife (or husband) may need advice on maintaining a balance between the needs of the patient and the needs of any children of the marriage. A greater dilemma will be created if the relative finds the strain of visiting continually over long periods of time too much, so that his/her health is affected. Full and frank discussions will be needed so that both the patient and the relative see the need to give priority to the relative's health. The great danger is that the relative will feel both guilt and remorse, especially if the death of the patient occurs when he is not there. He must be helped to overcome these feelings of guilt, which are very normal and natural.

Discussion with the nursing staff after visiting will help the relative.

As death becomes imminent, the relatives should be notified, as well as the priest in certain religions. The relative should be asked if he wishes to stay at the hospital overnight to be present at the moment of death. If he wishes to stay at home, does he want to be called in the night if there is any deterioration in the patient's condition?

Care of Bereaved Relatives

It often happens that death occurs in a patient who was not known to be dying, and then the notification of the relatives needs special care. Relatives should, of course, be informed of any deterioration in a patient's condition, but if they are not available, or if the patient dies suddenly, it may become necessary to inform the relative of the fact of death with no prior preparation. If the relatives are actually present in the hospital they can be asked to sit down before the news is broken to them. Occasionally, there is no telephone number by which to contact the relatives, and a local policeman may take a message. In this case, he will ensure that the news is broken gently, and that there is someone to look after the relative before he is left. A difficulty does arise if the news has to be given over the telephone to the relative who happens to be alone in the house. He should be asked to sit down before being given the news. If it is possible for him to fetch a neighbour to be with him, this should help. It is not really practicable to get him to fetch the neighbour before the news is broken as he will realize something dreadful has happened and uncertainty will increase his agitation. The nurse should make sure that the relative is all right before ringing off.

In the case of the sudden death of a Catholic patient, the priest must be informed as soon as possible.

The relative should be given the opportunity of seeing the patient after death. For this visit, the patient should be made to look as peaceful as possible; the area in the vicinity of the bed should be cleared of apparatus and tidied.

If the relative wishes to see the deceased when once the latter has been taken from the ward, the nursing staff can arrange for the body to be placed in the mortuary chapel and, if possible, a member of the ward staff will go with the relative to show the way and give comfort and support by her presence.

The location of the main hospital chapel should be pointed out so that the relative may spend some time there if he wishes. Tea and food should be provided as necessary.

A relative may experience shock, or feelings of guilt. He will need reassurance that everything possible was done for the patient and that the patient did not suffer at the end. An appointment should be made for the relative to see the medical social worker if he needs advice about the social agencies available to help him. Before the relative leaves the hospital the staff should see that there is someone at home on whom the relative can call for help and support. It is best if arrangements can be made for a friend or relative to spend the night with the bereaved, or to take the bereaved into their own home for the night. If there really is no one who can be called upon in this way, it might be possible to get in touch with a local health visitor or district nurse, who can call in the near future to see that the bereaved relative is all right. Quite often the number of formalities to be attended to before the funeral will prevent the individual fully realizing his loss. It may only be after the funeral when the guests have all gone that the full sense of loss and grief is experienced.

Administrative Details Associated with the Death

Shock may impair an individual's attention to, understanding and recall of what is said to him. So it is important that instructions are given to the relative very clearly, and that efforts are made to check that he has understood them. He will be asked to come to the hospital to see the doctor in charge, who will be able to explain all the details of the diagnosis to the relatives. He may seek consent for a post-mortem examination, and he will give the relative the death certificate, so that they can get on with organizing the funeral. The nursing staff should ensure that the patient's property is handed over to the relative, and a signature obtained for it. This may be done by the administrative officer of the hospital. If there should be a coroner's enquiry into the death, the coroner's officer may interview the relatives at the hospital.

Last Offices

The fact that death has taken place should be certified by the medical officer. Notification of death is sent to the nursing administration offices, the porter's lodge, and the lay administrator's office. When the relatives have left the bedside, the top bedclothes are stripped from the bed, leaving a sheet covering the body. Airrings, cradles and pillows should be removed; the body should be straightened into the supine position and one pillow left under the head. The gown and any jewellery should be removed, but false teeth and the wedding ring should remain unless the relatives request otherwise. Small pledgets of damp cotton wool may be placed on the eyelids to keep them closed. The mouth should be cleaned and then closed before the jaw is bandaged into position, protecting the skin from discolouration by a tight bandage by using cotton wool or plastic foam padding. If the body cannot be attended to straight away it should be left for no longer than an hour.

Equipment Required

(1) Gown and mortuary sheet.
(2) Washing bowl, with warm water, soap, flannel and towels.
(3) Brush and comb. Shaving equipment in the case of a male patient.
(4) Disposal bag for soiled dressings.
(5) Bin for dirty linen.
(6) A name card on which is written the patient's name, time of death, date and ward. Sellotape for attaching this to the mortuary sheet.
(7) An identification band for the patient's wrist, if there is not one already in position.
(8) Adhesive strapping.

[It may be the practice to plug the rectum and vagina with cotton wool, in which case a supply of cotton wool and disposable forceps should be available.]

Method

The body should be thoroughly washed, rinsed and dried. Nails should be cleaned, and the hair brushed out and arranged neatly. A male patient should be shaved if necessary. Any dressings should be left undisturbed. If discharge has seeped through them, fresh dressings should be placed over the existing dressings. Drainage tubes, catheters, tracheostomy tubes should be left in position. Intravenous infusion tubing should be cut near the needle insertion and strapped into position.

The gown should be put on, the body wrapped in a mortuary sheet, and the card attached to the latter with the Sellotape, so that it can be read from the head of the patient. A nurse should supervise the lifting of the patient when the porters come to take the body to the mortuary.

All bed linen, blankets and pillows should be sent for cleaning or washing. The bed and locker should be washed with antiseptic and dried.

The patient's possessions must be carefully packed, and checked against the list of possessions recorded on admission. Possessions acquired during the patient's stay should be added to the list, so that an accurate and up-to-date list of contents is placed with the parcel. Arrangements should be made for relatives to collect any valuables which have been placed in the safe.

The Other Patients

It is usual for the ward to be screened in such a way that the other patients do not get a glimpse of the dead patient, either in the ward, or during the time he is being taken to the mortuary.

If the death occurs in the daytime, it will be obvious to most patients what has happened, unless the dying patient is in a side room. When the death happens during the night, the majority of patients may be unaware that anything has happened, but they may miss the patient in the morning and enquire about him. On the whole, it is better to be frank about what has happened, since the patients may get to know the truth by other means.

16

Barrier nursing

BARRIER nursing is the term used whenever special precautions are taken to avoid carrying microorganisms from one patient, or a member of staff, to infect another patient. Such precautions are used either when a patient has an infectious disease, or is infected with antibiotic-resistant organisms, to prevent spread to other patients. They may also be used to protect a patient whose natural defence mechanisms to microorganisms are deficient in some way. This latter procedure is often called 'reverse barrier nursing'.

Principles of Barrier Nursing in Infectious Diseases

(1) The patient should be nursed in a single room which has a wash-hand basin or sink, and a source of hot and cold water. All surfaces in the single room should be washable.

(2) The number of people entering the room should be reduced to a minimum. Only close relatives or intimate friends should be allowed to visit, and these should be carefully instructed in putting on protective gowns and masks should masks be necessary. Two or three nurses should be assigned to look after the patient, as 'his' special nurses, so that others have no need to come into his room.

(3) Protective clothing, preferably disposable gowns, should be worn by all who visit or attend to the patient.

(4) There must be some kind of working surface, such as a table or trolley, in the room, to give facilities for nursing treatments.

(5) If disposable gowns are not available, then there should be hooks just inside the door on which the linen gowns can hang.

(6) A clinical thermometer, pulsometer and sphygmomano-meter should be left inside the room for the whole of the patient's stay. His charts should be kept outside.

(7) Any toys should be washable or disposable and paperbacks which can be incinerated should be provided for adult patients.

(8) The room should contain one big foot-operated bin, lined with a polythene bag, so that all articles which are to be incinerated may be placed within it. A second polythene lined bin should be provided for soiled linen.

(9) Cleaning of the room must be carried out under supervision of the nursing staff. All surfaces should be washed in an antiseptic solution advised by the microbiological department, using a paper towel, and then dried with another paper towel. The room should either be vacuum cleaned with a special vacuum cleaner kept just for this room, or it should be mopped with the prescribed disinfectant solution, if no special vacuum cleaner is available. A gown and disposable gloves should be worn by the member of staff carrying out this cleaning, and a mask as well, if necessary. If there is a vacuum cleaner available, the dust bag should be lined with a paper bag so that the dust can be removed for incineration and the external parts must be washed over. The vacuum cleaner must be thoroughly cleaned when once the patient has been discharged.

(10) Nothing from the patient's room should be removed and put into general use without first being sterilized. Staff must know the methods advocated by the microbiology department for the sterilization of equipment, excreta and linen. Any instructions as regards the strength of disinfectants and length of time required for their action must be followed precisely.

(11) If possible, all equipment should be disposable. Items which can be obtained in disposable form include flannels, sputum containers, bedpans, urinals, cutlery, plates and dishes, cups, instruments, syringes, draw sheets, waterproof pillow cases and gloves. Paper towels, medical wipes and toilet paper should be provided. A washing bowl should be used exclusively for the patient and left in his room throughout his stay.

(12) Recommended cleaning materials and antiseptics should be available in the room and kept exclusively for the patient, as should lotions, creams and mouthwashes to be used for caring for him.

The most important thing is that staff assigned to look after the patient should be fully conversant with the ways in which the disease is spread, and should be conscientious in carrying out all procedures so there is no risk of cross-infection. A good knowledge of microbiology will help nurses to care intelligently for a patient who has an infectious disease.

Protective Clothing for Nurses, Doctors and Visitors

Ideally, disposable gowns should be worn when attending to the patient. These can be left outside the room, so that people can put one on before coming in. Masks should be worn as well if the infection is airborne. To remove the gowns, individuals should first wash their hands and dry them on disposable towels. Then the gown is removed, taking great care not to contaminate the clothing underneath. The gown should be put straight into the bin so it can be incinerated, and the hands are then washed again, before leaving the room. Care should be taken not to contaminate either surface of the door of the room in any way.

If linen gowns are used, they should be hung just inside the room, with the outer surface outermost and the inside, which touches peoples' clothing, protected. These gowns can be handled by the inside of the neck band or the inside of the gown, and the individual should slide their arms into the sleeves, and then, grasping the inner surface, pull the gown around then and do up the tapes. To remove, the hands should be thoroughly washed, the tapes untied, and then the arms slid out of the sleeves. Holding the gown by the inner shoulders, it is slipped on to the coat hanger, as it was found. The hands must be washed again.

Provision of Meals

Disposable containers and cutlery should be used, but if this is impossible, clean china and cutlery should be used. The food is served in the kitchens and then taken to the single room where it is handed to a nurse wearing protective clothing. She gives the patient his food, and washes the dishes in the room, then takes them and sterilizes them. Any food scraps should be placed in the bin for incineration.

Washing the Patient and Other Basic Nursing Procedures

There should be a washing bowl in the room which can be used, together with disposable flannels, the patient's own soap and a hospital towel. When the patient has been washed, the water should be poured down the wash basin drain, and the bowl cleaned with the materials available in the room. It is then dried and left ready for use again. For mouth toilet, disposable cups and forceps can be used. Any additional lotions required can be prepared outside the room, and handed to the nurse in disposable cartons. If barrier cream or other cream is used, a specially dispensed supply can be used for the patient and thrown away for incineration when he is discharged.

If the patient should require tepid sponging, polythene foam sponges can be used, since these can be incinerated after use.

Care of Excreta

It is particularly important that the nurse should know whether or not excreta is contaminated with the infecting organism. In enteric diseases both urine and faeces may be contaminated. In respiratory infections, the sputum is likely to be contaminated. Any contaminated excreta should be incinerated immediately, disposable containers being used. If incineration is not possible, then sterilization of the excreta before it is placed into the sewerage system is best. If disinfectant is used, the instructions of the microbiologist as regards the strength of the solution and the time of immersion must be followed. Excreta must be completely immersed in disinfectant, and the time at which this was done recorded. Gloves, and a gown, should be worn by the member of staff dealing with infected excreta, and a special area of the sluice must be isolated for this purpose.

Care of Linen

Linen is unlikely to be heavily contaminated except in enteric disorders, when it should be disinfected according to instructions before being sent to the laundry. Otherwise the linen should be placed in a polythene lined bin. The polythene bag is sealed in the room, and then placed in a special linen bag which the hospital staff knows is used for linen from infected patients.

Terminal Cleaning of the Room

This must be carried out under the supervision of staff from the microbiology department. All linen, blankets and pillows should be autoclaved. Surfaces, including walls, must be washed with a recommended antiseptic. Radio earphones should not be forgotten. The room may be fumigated.

REVERSE BARRIER NURSING

This may be used for patients whose immunological mechanisms have been suppressed following transplant surgery, in leukaemia, or following treatment with cytotoxic drugs. It may also be used following head injury, if there has been tearing of the dura mater beneath a fracture, so that there is direct communication between the meninges and the outside air.

The patient is protected from the microorganisms in the environment.

Principles

(1) The air entering the room should be filtered and should come from outside not from an inside corridor.

(2) The room should have been thoroughly cleaned before the patient moves into it.

(3) The number of people allowed into the room should be kept to a minimum.

(4) All those who are allowed in must wear a mask, and protective gowns. They should be in good health and should be meticulous about their personal hygiene.

(5) Equipment and other articles supplied to the patient should either be brand new, or have been sterilized.

17

Prevention of complications due to surgery and administration of anaesthetic

GENERAL anaesthetics not only prevent the sensation of pain, but also abolish the natural protective reflexes. During operation, muscle relaxant drugs are usually given, and these may affect the respiratory muscles as well as the postural muscles.

Complications which may occur during or after the administration of a general anaesthetic are:

Respiratory:
 Asphyxia.
 Atelectasis.
 Chest infection.
Cardiovascular:
 Hypotension.
Alimentary:
 Vomiting, or regurgitation of stomach contents.
Tissue damage:
 Skin or nerve damage, due to pressure whilst the patient is unconscious.

Surgery interrupts the continuity of tissues of the body; the skin, connective tissue, blood vessels and muscle are affected, as well as the particular organ to be operated upon.

Complications which may occur include:
 Infection.
 Haemorrhage, leading to shock or anaemia.
 Non-healing of the wound.
 Depressed activity of an organ.

Both the preoperative preparation and the postoperative care that the patient receives are directed toward preventing these complications from occurring.

Preventive Measures

Respiratory Complications

Careful preoperative examination ensures that any pre-existing disease of the respiratory tract itself or the structures nearby can be treated. A chest X-ray will be taken, and the house surgeon or anaesthetist will listen to the chest sounds to make sure that these are normal. Any chest infection is treated with appropriate antibiotics and physiotherapy. Mouth care is important, to ensure cleanliness of the mouth and teeth; and urgent dental treatment should be carried out. Any head cold or sinusitus is allowed to subside before operation is undertaken.

Postoperatively, breathing exercises are necessary, and these are usually taught preoperatively, since the patient will be in no condition to learn a new skill in the immediate postoperative period. Smoking, which irritates the mucosa, should be discouraged. Steps are taken to ensure that the stomach is empty at operation, all food and drink being withheld from the patient for 4 to 6 hr before the scheduled time of operation, depending on the emptying time of the stomach of the individual patient. This prevents both vomiting and excess secretion of saliva, either of which could get into the respiratory tract, whilst the cough reflex is abolished during the anaesthetic. As an extra precaution, to dry up salivary and respiratory tract secretions further, an anticholinergic drug such as atropine or hyoscine, is administered by intramuscular injection $\frac{1}{2}$ to 1 hr before operation, along with an analgesic drug.

Asphyxia could occur during anaesthetic or immediately afterwards, due to:

(1) The flaccid tongue falling back, obstructing the upper respiratory tract.

(2) Loose dentures displaced during the passage of the endotracheal tube or airway, may get into the upper respiratory tract. (Small plates containing one or two teeth are especially dangerous.)

(3) Spasm of the vocal cords, following the removal of an endotracheal tube, can limit the air entry very considerably. If this should occur, the respirations will become very noisy with a rasping character. Immediate action is required by the anaesthetist;

either the passage of an endotracheal tube or a tracheostomy may be needed.

These complications are prevented or dealt with as follows:

(1) By the removal of any dentures before operation.

(2) By ensuring that loose natural teeth are taken out pre-operatively or, if that is impossible, that the anaesthetist knows about them.

(3) When once the endotracheal tube has been removed, and before the patient has regained consciousness, the tongue must be prevented from falling back. This is helped by the presence of an airway lying over the tongue and protruding through the lips and teeth, thus ensuring a free passage of air to the pharynx. To prevent the tongue from falling back if the patient is lying in a recumbent position, the jaw should be held up and forward. If possible, the patient should lie in a semi-prone position; this will both prevent the tongue from falling back and help any vomit or excessive secretions to run out of the mouth, rather than back into the respiratory passages.

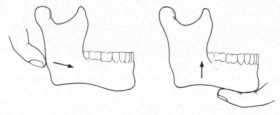

Fig. 54. How to hold the jaw of an unconscious patient.

(4) The character of the respirations should be observed carefully and, if laryngeal spasm occurs, oxygen should be given until the anaesthetist arrives, an immediate message having been delivered to him. Another nurse can be collecting together the equipment for intubation, so that it is available.

(5) If his face shows any cyanosis, the patient will need oxygen so his colouring should be observed. Whenever oxygen is to be given, the first essential is to ensure a clear airway (i.e. a clear respiratory tract). A high concentration of oxygen in the air available for inspiration is useless, unless it can get to the alveolar membrane for exchange with the blood gases.

(6) 'Anaesthetic instruments', which are useful in any respiratory emergency, should accompany the patient to the operating theatre, so that they are available during the journey back to the ward. These instruments are: tongue depressor, tongue clips, mouth gag and gauze swabs (with bound edges) clipped firmly into sponge holding forceps. Using these instruments, it is possible to open the mouth of the patient, pull the tongue forward, and remove any secretions accumulating in the back of the throat (Fig. 54).

Postoperatively, the important thing is to encourage full inflation of the lungs, so the patient is sat into a position allowing good descent of the diaphragm as soon as his condition will allow. Deep breathing exercises are encouraged shortly after operation. If necessary, expectoration is aided by the use of inhalations, physiotherapy to the chest wall and postural drainage. The patient's temperature and respiratory rates are recorded to detect the onset of chest infection, so that antibiotics may be started and vigorous treatment instituted. If the throat has been sprayed during the operation, fluids and food must be withheld until the effects of the anaesthetic spray have worn off. Postoperative vomiting should be prevented by cautiously reintroducing foods and fluids, and the use of anti-emetic drugs, if necessary.

Cardiovascular Complications

Pre-existing cardiovascular disease could endanger the patient during the operation. Thus, careful examination of the cardiovascular system is part of the preparation for operation; special attention being paid to the functioning of the heart, the blood pressure, and the haemoglobin content of the blood. A preoperative course of digoxin may be necessary in elderly patients and, if the haemoglobin level is below normal, this will need correction, probably by transfusion before operation. Blood is routinely grouped and cross-matched before any but the most minor of operations, and blood ordered in the quantity appropriate to the expected blood loss at operation. The patient's pulse and blood pressure should be recorded by the nursing staff preoperatively to provide a comparison for the postoperative recordings. This is especially important for a hypertensive patient in whom a blood pressure of say 120 mmHg systolic may appear normal, unless a preoperative record is available, when it is revealed to be very low for that particular patient.

Many drugs which are given to individuals over a long period of time can cause cardiovascular disturbances, either by potentiation of drugs given during anaesthesia, or because they are withdrawn suddenly before anaesthesia. The anaesthetist should be aware of all medication that the patient has been receiving, so that suitable precautions may be taken. Drugs which may affect the cardio-vascular system in either of these ways include corticosteroid, whose sudden withdrawal may be associated with hypotension; monoamine oxidase inhibitors, whose presence may cause either hypertension or hypotension: diuretics, which can cause severe hypotension; and anti-hypertensive drugs, which can also cause hypotension.

Careful postoperative observation of the patient is necessary to detect the early signs of shock; shown by an increasing pulse rate, a low blood pressure, restlessness or an increasing pallor. Shock may arise as a result of bleeding, and the dressings covering the wound should be carefully observed for this. The only satisfactory treatment of shock is to increase the circulating blood volume by the intravenous administration of fluid. Any bleeding, of course, must be stopped, and the foot of the bed should be raised to aid the maintenance of the blood supply to the brain.

If a blood transfusion is in progress when the patient returns from the operating theatre, careful observation of the body temperature to detect an incompatibility reaction is necessary; also careful recording of the pulse rate, the rate of infusion, and inspection of the infusion site to ensure that it is not running subcutane-ously. Similar observations will be necessary if the patient is receiving an infusion of fluid other than blood. A fluid intake and output record will be needed if the patient is receiving intravenous fluid, to ensure that the vascular compartment is not being over-loaded; in any case, careful observation of the urinary output is necessary, since kidney damage and anuria can result from a low blood pressure.

The risk of deep vein thrombosis is increased by operation; partly due to increased blood viscosity after tissue damage during surgery, and partly due to the showing of the venous flow in the calf veins whilst the patient is on the operating table. Thus, lower limb exercise should be encouraged very early after operation, and the patient is allowed out of bed for bed making, as soon as possible. A slight rise in temperature and/or pulse rate may be the first clue that this complication has occurred. Anticoagulation may then be necessary to prevent a pulmonary embolus.

Wound Infection and Delayed Healing

The patient will be carefully examined for the presence of any infective lesion before operation and, if possible, the operation should be delayed until the patient is infection free. A course of antibiotics may be started preoperatively. The patient should be as healthy as possible, before and after operation, to allow him to resist infective organisms, so a good nutritious diet should be given; high protein, or vitamin supplements may be necessary. Before operation, the skin at the operation site and for a wide surrounding area should be shaved clear of hairs, which are a source of microorganisms, especially of staphylococci. The patient should then have a bath; further preparation of the skin by painting with an antiseptic lotion may be carried out in the ward, but in any case will be carried out in the operating theatre before the incision is made. If collection of body fluids or stale blood within the wound is foreseen, either of which could exert pressure upon the suture line, or act as a focus for inflammation, delaying healing, the surgeon will insert a drain before closing the wound. Stitches, or clips, are used to keep the wound edges in apposition to one another; the amount of regenerated tissue needed to fill the gap is thus kept at a minimum and healing takes place rapidly (by 'first intention').

Clean blankets are used to cover the patient as he is taken from the ward to the operating theatre; thus there is a reduced possibility of carrying microorganisms from the ward to the operating theatre. Whilst the patient is being operated on, his bed is cleaned and remade with clean linen into a 'pack' ready for his return. The use of clean linen helps to prevent the contamination of his dressings with microorganisms.

Postoperatively, the wound should be kept dry and clean, by means of dressings or Nobecutane. It should be uncovered only when absolutely necessary. As soon as possible, the drains and stitches are removed, using an aseptic, atraumatic technique; the longer these are left in position, the greater the chance that they will initiate an inflammatory reaction, since they are 'foreign' to the patient's tissue, yet they must remain long enough to allow healing to take place. The interval for which the stitches or clips are left in position depends on two factors: (a) the site of operation, e.g. the scalp heals very rapidly and stitches can be removed within 48 hr of operation, whilst the stitches following laminectomy will be removed only after 10 to 14 days; and (b) the rapidity with which the individual patient's skin heals. Healing may be delayed if there is a poor blood supply to the area, or if in the presence of infection. The prevention of postoperative shock will help to maintain a good blood supply to the area. Careful observation and the judicious use of intravenous fluids will thus be necessary. It is important to observe for signs or symptoms of wound infection. Pain, throbbing or local heat in the area may be the symptoms complained of by the patient, whilst redness of the area or pyrexia will indicate the presence of infection.

Prevention of Damage to the Patient

The patient is unconscious during the administration of a general anaesthetic, and therefore unable to care for himself in any way. Normal protective reflexes are abolished, and the hospital staff must ensure that he comes to no harm in this time. Some means of identification must be attached to the patient; the skin should be marked on the side of operation when operation is planned on one of paired organs; these measures ensure that only the operation needed by the patient is carried out. Notes, X-rays, and prescription sheet should accompany the patient to the operating theatre.

Before the operation is carried out, the patient must have given written consent. In the case of a minor, or an unconscious patient, the next of kin is asked to sign the operation consent form. For some gynaecological operations, it is usual to ask for the husband's consent, as well as the patient's. Immediately before operation, anything that could cause damage by pressure or in the presence of diathermy is removed from the person of the patient, including hairgrips and all jewellery except the wedding ring. An operating gown which is secured by tapes is substituted for the patient's own night attire. Great care must be taken to prevent nerve damage whilst the patient is unconscious; positioning of limbs must be done with care. The eyes must be protected by the lids, to prevent corneal damage, and the patient's hair should be covered by a cotton turban, so that there is no risk of it getting into the eyes.

Pain

Preoperatively, an analgesic such as morphine, Omnopon or pethidine is administered by injection together with the anticholinergic drug. This helps to prevent immediate postoperative pain. Further analgesia may be needed when its effect has worn off. Ideally, the patient is kept pain free. Pain is very unpleasant for the patient and it will curtail his movement, possibly affecting his respirations. If the wound is in the abdominal or chest area, the respirations will become shallow, and he will be unable to cough or expectorate in the presence of pain. It can be seen how other complications may occur if pain is not adequately treated.

Alimentary Tract

Peristalsis ceases during the general anaesthetic, and the stomach is empty at the time of operation. The return to a full diet should proceed gradually, or vomiting may occur. Sips of water only are given in the immediate postoperative period, then a light diet, and usually not until the first postoperative day or later does the patient return to a full diet. One cannot lay down any hard and fast rules about this however, the site and severity of the operation must be taken into account, as well as the reaction of the individual patient.

Constipation may occur postoperatively as a result of the administration of morphine, lack of exercise, lack of solid food, or a change in diet. Aperients or enemata may be necessary if the patient's normal pattern of bowel action is grossly upset.

Flatus, accumulating in the bowel, may be extremely uncomfortable for the patient. A flatus tube passed via the anus will usually relieve this satisfactorily.

Complications of the alimentary tract are most likely to occur when the operation is on the tract itself, or in its vicinity (e.g. gynaecological operations). Prolonged administration of drugs such as morphine, which depress peristalsis, can also give rise to complications of the tract. The main danger is of cessation of peristalsis, with accumulation of fluids or gas within the tract causing gross distension. This is prevented in high risk patients by keeping the alimentary tract empty in the immediate postoperative period. A Ryle's tube is passed immediately before operation, and either continuous or intermittent gentle suction keeps the stomach empty after operation. Carefully measured sips of water may be allowed postoperatively but an intravenous infusion is maintained until bowel sounds are heard. A fluid balance chart must be kept. If paralytic ileus should arise as a postoperative complication, it is treated by the passage of a Ryle's tube, stomach aspiration and the use of an intravenous infusion. Antibiotics are usually given.

Urinary Tract

The urine of every patient is tested on admission to hospital, and the result of that test usually accompanies the patient to theatre. It is important that not only metabolic disorders such as diabetes mellitus are revealed by urine testing, but that abnormalities of the urinary system itself are detected. In an elderly patient, the blood urea may be estimated.

Immediately before the operation the patient should empty his bladder, but if the operation is to be carried out on the bladder or in its vicinity (e.g. gynaecological operations), a self retaining catheter is inserted and the bladder is drained.

A sustained low blood pressure affects the renal blood flow, and anuria may result. Shock must, therefore, be prevented and careful observation will ensure that, should it occur, it is detected very early and can be treated before any renal damage occurs. If the blood pressure was low during operation, a fluid balance chart should be recorded postoperatively. If anuria does occur, then a self retaining catheter will be inserted to allow the urinary output to be recorded accurately. Fluid and dietary restriction, peritoneal dialysis, or an artificial kidney will be necessary until kidney function returns.

If a patient does not pass urine postoperatively, it may be due to retention of urine or anuria, and it is important to observe for both these conditions and to distinguish between them. Thus, careful observation and reporting when the patient micturates postoperatively will save a lot of anxiety. If the patient fails to pass urine within about 18 hr of operation, the fact should be reported so that his bladder may be examined. If it should be distended, then he may be allowed to stand (male patient) or use a commode (female patient) in the hope that a more natural position will help. An injection of carbachol (0·2 to 0·5 mg) may be needed to relax the urethral sphincter but, since this substance has unpleasant side effects, catheterization may be preferred. The patient will usually be able to pass urine later, when he is more mobile.

Psychological Effects

If the patient is to have complete faith in the surgeon who is carrying out the operation, full explanation must be given of the diagnosis, and the operation necessary to relieve the condition. The patient must have complete trust in the surgeon if he is to put himself at the surgeon's mercy whilst he is unconscious and unable to know what is happening. If there is the slightest doubt of the diagnosis, the possibility of a more radical operation than the planned operation should be mentioned, since if the patient recovers from the anaesthetic to find that he has lost a greater amount of his body than he expected, this can have a profound effect upon him, causing acute depression and lack of trust in the hospital staff. This in turn could delay his physical recovery. The operation consent form usually includes a clause to cover this eventuality, but not all patients read the form carefully before signing. Their attention should be drawn to this clause, and steps should be taken to ensure that the patient has fully understood the implications.

As with everything else that is done to him in hospital, the way in which the preparation, the operation itself, and the postoperative care will affect him must be carefully explained to the patient. The reduction of uncertainty thus afforded will not only help the patient's subjective feelings, but adequate explanation related to specific aspects of the effects of operation actually reduces the incidence of complications which occur. Thus, the way in which a nurse is able to reduce the anxiety of a patient is a valuable measure of her nursing skill.

18

Dressing technique

DRESSINGS are carried out for the following reasons:

(1) To remove soiled and wet dressings (which may encourage the multiplication of microorganisms) and to replace them with clean, dry, sterile dressings.

(2) To place a protective cover over a broken area of skin.

(3) To remove stitches or clips; to shorten or remove drainage tubes.

Dressing a wound is a potential source of cross-infection, since, by definition, a wound is an interruption in the continuity of the protective surface of the body (skin). Microorganisms can, thereby, gain direct access to the body, which provides ideal conditions for their growth. An understanding of microbiology and a scrupulous technique is needed if infection is to be avoided. Infection delays wound healing at the very least, and may even cause the death of the patient at the worst.

General Principles Involved in Performing Dressings

(1) Since there is a danger from airborne organisms in carrying out a dressing, however good the technique, dressings should never be carried out unnecessarily. An operation wound which has been sutured or clipped with no drain inserted should heal well with no complications. Such a wound need be dressed only when the sutures and clips are to be removed.

(2) All instruments and dressings which will come into contact with the wound must be sterile.

(3) Since the wound will be uncovered during the procedure, the number of microorganisms in the air and the disturbance of the air should be reduced to a minimum. At least 1 hr should have lapsed after ward cleaning, bed-making or furniture moving activities, before dressings are carried out.

(4) The technique should be such that the wound is exposed for the minimum time possible.

(5) Movement of staff within the ward, and movement of staff and visitors in and out of the ward must be curtailed whilst dressings are carried out, unless there is a special clinic room in which dressings can be done.

(6) Unused dressings should be placed for autoclaving and must not be carried from bed to bed.

(7) Anything which is taken from bed to bed (e.g. the trolley, the lotion bottle) should be washed over with antiseptic lotion and thoroughly dried between each dressing, so that possible contamination is reduced to a minimum.

(8) Any wound known to be infected should be dressed last of all if a series of dressings is being carried out.

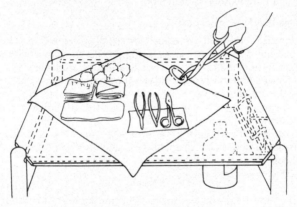

FIG. 55. Basic dressing pack opened out. Equipment arranged using handling forceps.

Basic Dressing Trolley

Requirements

The trolley should be made of light, washable material, and it should be smooth running and quiet in use. It should be thoroughly washed before starting the dressings and after each dressing, with an antiseptic detergent solution (e.g. Savlon). If possible, this solution should be sprayed on, then the trolley should be dried thoroughly with clean, absorbent, paper towels.

Top Shelf

A sterile pack which contains sufficient material to carry out the dressing is placed on the top shelf of the trolley. A basic dressing pack will contain wool balls, gauze swabs and sterile towels (Fig. 55). A gallipot and four pairs of forceps (Spencer Wells, dissecting or dressing forceps can be used) may be included, or supplied in separate packs. Larger packs may include more dressings and a roll of cotton wool. Other instruments which may be required, such as stitch scissors, clip removers, safety pin, large bandage scissors, may be included in the appropriate pack, or may be supplied in individual containers.

Bottom Shelf

A bottle of lotion, if prescribed for the dressing, will be taken to the bedside. The outside of the bottle should be washed with antiseptic solution and dried, as described for the trolley above.

Sufficient adhesive tape, bandage, tubular gauze, elastic net, etc., to fix the dressing in place, should be placed on the trolley.

A disposal bag for dirty dressings and a container for dirty instruments will be required.

Note: If the dressings are sterilized and stored in a bag, this may be used as a container for the dirty dressings when once the pack has been opened.

Masks

Masks are commonly worn to filter microorganisms from the expired air, both during the preparation of the trolley, and to carry out the dressing. These masks may be made of paper or gauze. Cellophane paper may be inserted into the gauze masks to provide a more adequate filter of the expired air.

Certain precautions are necessary when wearing a mask to prevent it from being a positive danger to the patient, rather than a safeguard for him:

A paper mask should be worn only for a maximum of 15 min at a time or it will become so dampened from the water vapour content of the expired air that it is no longer efficient.

The mask must be adjusted correctly, so that it covers the nostrils and the mouth.

Care is needed in removing the mask. It should be handled by the tapes or elastic, and the body of the mask should not be touched. The mask should be placed directly into the pedal action bin provided for it, and the hands washed straight away.

Basic Dressing Procedure

Two nurses should carry out this procedure, one to do the dressing (dresser) and one as assistant (assistant).

(1) Prepare the trolley, making sure that everything which will be needed is on it.

(2) Take the trolley to the patient's bedside, and explain the procedure to the patient, in terms he will understand.

(3) Screen the bed, and position the patient so that the wound is accessible and he is as comfortable as possible. Then turn back the bedclothes, and place a flannelette sheet or bedjacket over the patient to keep him warm.

(4) The nurses who are to carry out the dressing should wash and dry their hands thoroughly.

(5) The assistant then opens the dressing pack. If the dressings are contained in a bag, they are slid gently within the towel wrapping from the bag, on to the trolley, and the bag is placed either on the bottom shelf, or attached to the side rail with the adhesive tape from the pack, so that it can be used as a disposal bag.

(6) Whether there is an outer bag or not, the towel wrapping the dressings should be carefully opened, and spread out on the top shelf, touching the outer surface only. This forms a sterile working surface on the trolley, when once it is spread, so that the previously outer surface is in contact with the trolley surface, and the inner surface is facing upwards and has been kept sterile. Next, a pair of forceps should be picked up. If they are in a separate container the assistant can open this, whilst the dresser extracts them very carefully, touching only the handle. If they are in the main pack, the dresser picks them up by the handle, ensuring that she does not contaminate the pack contents in the process. She can then use these forceps to arrange the pack contents on the sterile surface as she wishes. It is a good idea to have a well-defined surface on which she can rest forceps which she has used once, and

which will be needed again. This can be a gauze swab, or better still, a kidney dish.

(7) The assistant now pours any lotion, and opens the packs containing extra instruments which are needed. Great care must be taken that the assistant touches only the outside of the pack. The dresser can take the contents and place them on the sterile working surface, using the first pair of forceps.

(8) Now the assistant removes any bandages, or loosens the adhesive tape, holding the dressing in position, so the dressing can be removed by the dresser, using two pairs of forceps, which she then discards.

(9) Two fresh pairs of forceps are used to arrange a sterile towel over the skin near the wound, and then the dressing is carried out.

Principles of Dressing a Wound

(1) Lotion should not be used unless it is absolutely necessary. Microorganisms require moisture for growth and division. Antiseptics provide moisture, and few are effective against all organisms.

(2) If antiseptic lotion is used, wring the swab out with the forceps to remove as much moisture as possible. Swab from the wound out. Never swab in toward the wound, since this sweeps microorganisms which are harmless on the intact skin into the wound where they can do harm.

(3) Dry the area, using wool swabs.

(4) If dressings are to be placed over the wound, place them so that they completely cover and protect the wound. If strapping is used to hold the dressings in position, it should be applied so that the patient can move freely without dislodging a corner of the dressing. Whenever a dressing is being performed, it should be carried out as gently as possible. The patient's facial and vocal expressions can be noted to ensure that he is not being hurt unnecessarily, since it is more difficult to estimate the exact amount of pressure to be exerted using forceps, than when a procedure is carried out using one's fingers or hands.

When the dressing has been completed, any old plaster marks can be removed, and the patient is repositioned by the assistant whilst the dresser takes the trolley, disposes of all the used articles, and cleans it thoroughly, ready for the next dressing.

Removal of Stitches

The exact technique for removing stitches depends upon the way in which they have been inserted.

(1) Cut the stitch so that, in withdrawing it, no part of the stitch which was exposed to the air, is dragged through the tissues.

(2) Ensure that the cut is made in such a way that no piece of stitch is left in the tissues.

(3) It is easier, if all the sutures to be removed are cut, holding the stitch scissors, or stitch cutter (Fig. 56), in the right hand, and a

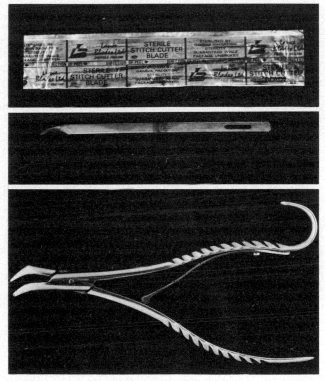

Fig. 56. Stitch cutter and clip removers.

pair of dissecting forceps in the left hand, to lift the knot of the stitch so the stitch can be cut between the knot and the skin.

(4) The scissors can then be discarded and a second pair of dressing or dissecting forceps are taken into the right hand for removing the stitch from the skin. Gently lay the dressing forceps, held in the left hand, over the skin area, in the same plane as the skin to prevent the skin from being pulled when the stitch is withdrawn.

(5) Commonly, half the stitches (alternate ones) are removed on one day, and the rest the following day.

Removal of Clips

Special clip removing forceps are used. Take the clip removers in the right hand and a pair of dissecting or dressing forceps in the left hand. Steadying the clip with the dressing forceps, insert one blade of the clip removers under the centre of the clip, and one blade over the centre of the clip. Ensure the blades are inserted for a sufficient distance. Gently squeeze the blades together. This straightens the clip metal, lifting it from the skin on either side.

To Shorten A Drain

(1) Using forceps, open the sterile safety pin and place it on the sterile area, ready for use.

(2) Clean the area around the drain, using wool swabs and lotion if necessary.

(3) Remove any stitch holding the drain in position.

(4) Gently turn the drain within the wound, to loosen it, if it is a Portex tubular drain.

(5) Grasp the protruding end of the drain with a pair of artery forceps and clip them into position.

(6) Using these forceps, gently ease the drain out of the wound for the prescribed distance, e.g. 13 to 25 mm ($\frac{1}{2}$ to 1 in.).

(7) Take another pair of artery forceps and pick up the sterile safety pin. Grasping the pin firmly in the forceps, pass it through the tube, and out the other side, as near to the skin surface as possible. Great care is needed not to injure the patient; the pin should be directed in a slightly upward direction away from the skin. The

second pair of forceps can be used to steady the tubing. Close the pin, using two pairs of forceps.

(8) Cut excess tubing off, using sterile bandage scissors.

Removal of A Drain

The method is as above, except that the drain is removed completely at Step 6.

Note: A different technique is required for the removal of a water seal drain or T-tube. These are usually removed by a medical officer.

Dressing Technique when there is only One Nurse Available

If one individual has to carry out a dressing by herself, it is far more difficult to achieve an aseptic technique. The nurse should have a good knowledge of microbiology, and carry out the dressing as conscientiously as possible.

The trolley is prepared as previously described, and taken to the bedside. Explanation is given to the patient, the bed is screened, and the patient positioned. The bedclothes are turned back and the patient is kept warm with a flannelette blanket.

Next, the dressing is loosened, but left in position to protect the wound. The nurse washes her hands, and then opens the pack as described previously, arranging the contents on the sterile surface with a pair of forceps. Any extra forceps or equipment required must be taken out of the packs and arranged on the sterile area. If lotion is required it should be poured out. Using a second pair of forceps if necessary, the dressing is removed from the wound into the disposal bag, and the forceps discarded. Using fresh forceps, the wound is dressed as described above.

Vulval Swabbing and Jug Douching

When there is a wound in the vulval, vaginal or perineal area, a dressing of the type described above is not very practicable. Usually, a sterile maternity pad is used to cover the area, and it is held in position by a sanitary belt or T-bandage. The area is cleaned by means of swabbing or jug douching after the patient has passed urine or has had her bowels open, and before a new sterile pad is applied.

Requirements

Sterile bedpan, on which the patient sits. (*Note:* the one into which she has passed urine should be removed.)
Sterile gloves.
Sterile maternity pad.
Lotion.
Thermometer.
Lotion bowl (or jug), containing warm, mild antiseptic lotion at 39°C (102°F), e.g. Savlon 1:1000, Hibitane 1:1000, Bradosol 1:2000 (domiphen bromide).
Sterile wool swabs.
Disposal bag for used swabs and pad.

Procedure

Help the patient into a comfortable position on the sterile bedpan, with her knees flexed and hips abducted, so that the vulval area is accessible. Wash and dry hands, and put on the sterile gloves. Using a lotion soaked swab, clean the labia majora on one side. Swab from front to back, using each swab once only and then discarding it. Clean the other side similarly. Then with the fingers of the left hand, part the labia majora to expose the labia minora, and clean each side as before. Finally, part the labia minora and swab the clitoris, urethral and vaginal orifices, and perineum. Using the remaining solution, pour it gently over the labia and into the bedpan.

Dry the area, using dry swabs. Apply the sterile pad; remove the bedpan, turning the patient on to her side at the same time. Dry the perineal area thoroughly and fix the pad into position.

19

Administration of drugs

DRUGS are substances obtained from vegetable, mineral and animal sources and used for medicinal purposes. They may be introduced into the body in various forms and by various routes. Drugs may be dispensed in liquid form as solutions, tinctures, infusions, emulsions or oils, or in solid form as pills, powders, tablets or capsules.

Drugs may be administered by mouth, occasionally by the rectum, or parenterally, that is to say they may be introduced by other routes than the alimentary tract, such as subcutaneous, intramuscular or intravenous injections, or by inhalation.

Medicines for administration by mouth must be stored in a cupboard reserved for this purpose, and substances intended for external application only must be kept in a separate cupboard.

Drugs Controlled by the Dangerous Drugs Act

The Dangerous Drugs Act (D.D.A.) controls the sale and use of substances liable to cause drug addiction. Opium and its alkaloids, notably morphine, cocaine and Indian hemp were the drugs controlled by the original Act; more recent additions are pethidine hydrochloride, methadone hydrochloride (Physeptone) and phenadoxone hydrochloride (Heptalgin). These drugs may be supplied to the public only on the written prescription of a medical practitioner. Hospital wards and departments are, however, authorized to keep a stock of certain preparations, such as morphine and pethidine, but they must be ordered on a duplicate form signed by the authorized responsible person, i.e. the sister or charge nurse who is responsible for the safe storage of the drugs and for ensuring that they are used only in accordance with written orders of the medical staff. D.D.A. drugs must be kept in a locked cupboard reserved for the storage of these drugs the key of which is kept by the sister or charge nurse; the containers must have the letters 'D.D.A.' written on the label. All prescriptions and order forms must be kept by the hospital for a period of 2 years from the date of issue.

The Poisons and Pharmacy Act

The Poisons and Pharmacy Act controls the sale, prescription and use of a very large range of substances which are potentially toxic or dangerous. There are sixteen schedules under the Act which list a great number of poisonous substances and the regulations to be observed in their use. The two schedules which are of particular importance in medical and hospital practice are Schedules I and IV.

Schedule IV is now divided into Part A and Part B. Part A drugs are subject to the same controls as Schedule I drugs. Part B lists drugs which are to be used only on prescription and under medical supervision. In hospitals Schedule I and Schedule IVA drugs can be obtained from the pharmacist's department only on the written order of a medical officer or the sister or charge nurse of the ward or department. They must be clearly labelled Schedule I and stored in a locked cupboard. It should be noted that the toxic and addiction forming drugs controlled by the Dangerous Drugs Act are also listed in Schedule I. The usual practice with regard to storage is to have a drug cupboard for Schedule I and IVA poisons with an inner cupboard fitted with a separate lock and key for D.D.A. drugs. It is important to remember that the 'poisons cupboard' must be reserved solely for the storage of D.D.A. and Scheduled drugs.

Examples of drugs on Schedules I and IV of the Poisons and Pharmacy Act are the toxic alkaloids such as atropine and hyoscine and the barbiturates.

Each ward and department should keep a Dangerous Drugs and Poisons record book in which the patient's name, the drug, the dose, the date and the time of administration are entered and each entry signed by the nurse giving and the nurse checking the drug.

The Therapeutic Substances (Prevention of Misuse) Act, 1956

The Therapeutic Substances Act controls substances which are capable of causing danger to the health of the community if used without proper safeguards. The form of prescription is the same as Schedule IV drugs which may only be prescribed by a medical practitioner, dentist or veterinary surgeon. Drugs controlled by this Act include antibiotics, cortisone, prednisone and isoniazid.

ADMINISTRATION OF DRUGS BY MOUTH

Drugs must be given punctually, and the standard times for giving 4-hourly, 6-hourly drugs, and those given twice, or three times a day, should be known and adhered to by all members of staff. In this way errors can be avoided. It is important for many drugs that the blood concentration is not allowed to fall below a given level, so an interval longer than that prescribed must not be allowed to lapse. For other drugs, two doses closer together than prescribed might increase the blood concentration to a dangerous level.

Method of Pouring Medicine

(1) Shake the bottle.

(2) Hold the bottle with the label uppermost to prevent soiling the label. (*Note:* a bottle with a label which does become soiled, or illegible for any other reason, must be returned to the pharmacy.)

(3) Remove the cork, holding it in the little finger of the left hand.

(4) Measure the dose into the medicine glass, holding the glass at eye level.

(5) If there is a sediment, provide a glass rod to stir the medicine, immediately before the patient takes it.

Pills, tablets, capsules or cachets should be placed into a special disposable container, a spoon, or a medicine glass, before being taken to the patient.

Procedure for Administration of Medicines and Other Oral Drugs

(1) Collect the patient's prescription sheets and a container for the drug, and check that the dose has not already been given.

(2) Select the correct drug from the cupboard. Check the name of the drug and strength supplied against the prescription sheet.

(3) Measure the correct dose.

(4) Take the dose to the bedside with the prescription sheet.

(5) Check the patient's name, the drug and the dose against the prescription sheet.

(6) Give the drug to the patient. Ensure that he swallows it, and give him some water.

(7) Record that the drug has been given if it is an antibiotic, night sedation or a drug prescribed p.r.n. (pro re nata).

Note: if the drug is a scheduled poison, the whole procedure must be checked by a second person, who must witness that the correct drug is given to the right patient.

The prescription sheet referred to above must be the one on which the order signed by the doctor is written.

Administration of a Dangerous Drug

Two persons must witness the collection of the correct dose and its administration; one of these should be a state registered nurse or a medical practitioner.

(1) Collect the prescription sheet with the written order signed by the doctor, and the D.D.A. book.

(2) Check that the patient has not been given the drug.

(3) Select the correct drug from the D.D.A. cupboard.

(4) Find the entry for this drug in the D.D.A. book and check the total quantity of the drug against the quantity which has been previously administered as recorded in the D.D.A. book.

(5) Check the dose into a container or syringe and lock up the unused ampoules or tablets.

(6) Enter the patient's name, the dose of the drug and the date in the D.D.A. book.

(7) Take the drug and the prescription sheet to the bedside, and check the patient's name, the name and dose of the drug against the prescription. Make quite certain the dose has not been given.

(8) Give the drug.

(9) Enter the time of administration and the signatures of the two nurses into the D.D.A. book. Record the administration of the dose into the Kardex and on the prescription sheet.

General Remarks

Many medicines have an unpleasant taste, and the majority of patients can be allowed a drink of water, a piece of fruit or a sweet to take away the taste.

Holding the nose while drinking is sometimes a help, as taste depends to some extent on smell.

A medicine containing iron, stains the teeth and should be taken through a glass drinking tube or a straw. The mouth should be washed out afterwards and the teeth cleaned.

Powders are most easily swallowed if put upon the tongue and washed down with a drink of water. They may be put into a rice-paper cachet, which should be moistened with some water in a spoon, as it can then be more easily swallowed.

Pills and capsules are swallowed with a drink of water.

Oily substances are difficult to take, not only on account of the flavour, but also because of the disagreeable taste of oil in the mouth. Liquid paraffin has no distinct flavour and is fairly easy to swallow if a little soda or plain water is added. Castor oil is extremely unpleasant to take, both on account of its taste and the thickness of the oil. Infants, however, will usually take castor oil from a spoon quite readily, and older children will often take it beaten up in warm milk. For an adult patient the oil must be prepared so that the patient can drink it all at once without tasting it. One method is to warm a china measure or medicine glass in hot water; about 2 teaspoonfuls (10 ml) of lemon or mixed lemon and orange juice are poured into the measure and the prescribed dose of the oil floated on top of this. More fruit juice is poured on to the top of the oil. A slice of lemon or orange may be taken to the bedside with the dose. The patient is told to bite the piece of lemon, then swallow the dose at one gulp and bite the slice of lemon again.

The disadvantages of giving drugs by mouth are:

(1) The patient may not be able or may refuse to swallow the dose.

(2) The drug may be only partially absorbed.

(3) It may irritate the alimentary tract, causing vomiting or acting as a purgative, so that the desired effect is lost.

ADMINISTRATION OF DRUGS BY THE RECTUM

Drugs may be administered per rectum, either in the form of suppositories (e.g. aminophylline) or as solutions. The method is the same as for the administration of other types of suppository or retention enema (see Chapters 9 and 21).

GIVING DRUGS BY INHALATION

Drugs given by inhalation may be used for their general effect or for their local action on the respiratory tract. The drug must be either in the form of a vapour, or a liquid which readily vaporizes, or a fine spray, such as an aerosol spray. Anaesthetic gases are examples of drugs exerting a general effect when inhaled. Aromatic substances, such as menthol, and tincture of benzoin, may be added to steam inhalations for their local effect in the treatment of upper respiratory tract infections, such as acute sinusitis and laryngitis (see Chapter 13). An aerosol spray of an antispasmodic drug may be ordered in the treatment of asthma.

LATIN WORDS AND ABBREVIATIONS USED IN PRESCRIPTION WRITING

Latin and its abbreviations are falling into disuse because of the ease with which terms can be misread. The following list is included for reference because some doctors still use these terms.

Word or abbreviation	*Meaning*
āa, āna	of each
ad lib., ad libitum	as much as is desired
b.i.d., bis in die	twice a day
B.P.	*British Pharmacopoeia*
c., cum	with
cataplasma	a poultice
cibus	food
a.c., ante cibum	before food
p.c., post cibum	after food
collun., collunarium	a nasal wash
collut., collutarium	a mouth wash
collyr., collyrium	an eye wash
co., compositus	compound
cras.	tomorrow
emplastrum	a plaster
flavus	yellow
G, g	gram
gtt., gutta, guttae	a drop, drops

Word or abbreviation	*Meaning*
h., hora	an hour
lb, libra	a pound
mane	in the morning
mist., mistura	a mixture
mol., mollis	soft
nocte	at night
ol., oleum	oil
om., omnis	all, every
o.h., omni hori	every hour
o.m., omni mane	every morning
o.n., omni nocte	every night
p.r.n., pro re nata	occasionally, repeat as the need arises
qq., quaque	each or every
qq.h., quaque hora	each hour
qq. a.h., quaque quarta hora	every four hours
q.s., quantum sufficit	as much as is sufficient
s.o.s., si opus sit.	if necessary (once only)
ss., semis	a half
stat., statim.	immediately
ter.	thrice
t.d. or t.i.d., ter die, ter in die	three times a day
t.d.s., ter die sumendum	to be taken three times a day

20

Parenteral administration of drugs

WHENEVER a drug is given to a patient by injection, the dose should be checked and the whole procedure observed by a second nurse.

Drugs may be given by injection when rapid action is required, if the drug is destroyed by intestinal secretions, if it is not absorbed from the alimentary tract or if the patient is unable to take the drug orally for some reason.

Hypodermic Injection

Hypodermic (or subcutaneous) injection is the method commonly used when only a small volume of fluid is to be injected and when the solution is not likely to damage the superficial tissues. Drugs which may be irritant in the subcutaneous tissue must be injected either into muscle, which has a good blood supply, or into a vein. It should also be noted that, if the superficial circulation is depleted, absorption of a substance injected hypodermically is likely to be slow and uncertain. Therefore morphine for example, should be given intravenously to a patient suffering from severe shock.

Drugs for hypodermic injection are usually dispensed in solution, either in single dose ampoules, which provide a considerable safeguard against accidental over-dosage, or in multidose containers. Tablets which are dissolved in sterile water immediately before use are also obtainable and, although not often seen in hospitals now, they may be used in private practice. The usual sites for injection are the outer aspect of the upper arm or the thigh.

Syringes of 1 or 2 ml capacity are used, with size 17 to 20 needles. Before giving the injection the nurse must make sure that the needle is not bent or blunt. A bent needle may snap during the injection, a blunt needle will cause the patient unnecessary pain.

Where a central service deals with all syringes and needles, every needle is inspected and sharpened after each use. Disposable needles, used for one injection only, are supplied in some hospitals.

The syringe in its container should be placed on a tray, together with a spray bottle of skin cleansing antiseptic and sterile wool swabs.

The tray with the drug, and the patient's prescription sheet should be taken to a second person to be checked. If the drug is one covered by the Dangerous Drugs Act the book should also be taken to the second person who should be an S.R.N.

Solutions for hypodermic injections may be dispensed in multi-dose rubber-capped bottles. The bottle should be held so that the cap is not handled. After wiping the cap of the bottle with a swab moistened with alcohol, the needle should be pushed through the centre of the cap and a little air injected to facilitate the removal of the fluid. Slightly more than the required quantity of the solution should be taken up, and then, holding the syringe with the needle vertical, the piston is pushed up until the edge is on a level with the line showing the required number of millilitres.

When using drugs in tablet form a small amount of water should be boiled in a spoon and a convenient amount, 0·5 to 1 ml taken up in the syringe. The excess water in the spoon is then discarded, the tablet placed in the spoon, and the water from the syringe expelled into it. The tablet dissolves readily and the solution is drawn up into the syringe.

If the drug is in a glass ampoule, a file is required to make a mark on the neck of the ampoule where it is to be broken. The outside of the glass is washed with a swab, moistened with alcohol and, holding the ampoule in a piece of sterile gauze to prevent splintered glass from cutting the nurse, the neck is then broken at the file mark.

If the patient is not familiar with the procedure, the nurse should explain to him what she is about to do and that he will feel a small prick. An injection made with a sharp needle is scarcely felt.

The site of the injection should be rubbed fairly vigorously with a swab moistened with alcohol, in order both to cleanse the skin and to increase the blood supply. A small piece of skin and subcutaneous tissue should be taken up between the thumb and first finger of the left hand, pulling the skin fairly taut. The needle is inserted quickly and firmly into the fold of subcutaneous tissue at an angle of 45° and the piston pushed steadily down. The mop should be pressed on the skin while the needle is withdrawn.

Among the drugs commonly given by hypodermic injection are adrenaline and insulin.

Intramuscular Injection

This method is used when larger amounts are required to be injected than can be given by hypodermic injection when more rapid action is needed, and is also chosen when the drug would be irritating if injected superficially. The sites usually chosen are the vastus externus muscle of the outer aspect of the thigh, the gluteal muscles of the buttock, or the deltoid muscle in the upper part of the arm (Fig. 57). It is essential to avoid giving the injection into a

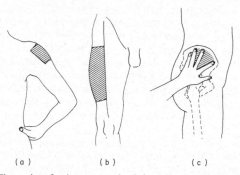

(a)   (b)   (c)

FIG. 57. Three sites for intramuscular injections. (a) Outer aspect of the shoulder; (b) antero-lateral aspect of the thigh; and (c) anterior part of the upper and outer quadrant of the buttock.

blood vessel, nerve or periosteum. To ascertain that the needle is not in a vein the plunger should be withdrawn a little; if blood is drawn up into the syringe, then a vein has been punctured and the needle must be withdrawn, reinjected and the plunger once more withdrawn before giving the injection. When making an injection into the buttock the upper and outer quadrant should be chosen, as there is a risk of stabbing the sciatic nerve if the needle is inserted too near the sacrum. The periosteum can be avoided by giving the injection into a site where there is plenty of muscle covering the bone and by not stabbing too deeply.

The injection and the skin over the site are prepared in the manner described for the giving of hypodermic injections. The size of syringe and needles required will depend on the amount and type of the drug to be injected and on the site of the injection, 1-, 2- or 5-ml syringes may be needed and needles 5 to 6 cm (2 to $2\frac{1}{2}$ in.) long.

The needle should be long enough to penetrate the muscle without inserting it up to the mount as, should the needle break, there is a better chance of removing it if a piece of the shaft projects above the skin surface.

The skin over the selected site is stretched with the left hand. The syringe and needle are held in the right hand and directed at a right angle to the skin surface, then the needle is inserted quickly and firmly deep into the muscle. If a large quantity of drug is to be given by one injection it must be given very slowly or it will cause pain.

Many drugs may be given by intramuscular injection. Some common examples are penicillin, streptomycin, vitamin B_{12}, Imferon, morphine and atropine.

Sensitization Dermatitis

Dermatitis, particularly of the hands, arms and face, may occur in nurses and doctors who come into frequent contact with penicillin, streptomycin and chlorpromazine when giving injections. An investigation into this problem has shown that spraying of the drug occurs when the air is expelled from the syringe and when the needle used for withdrawal of the drug from the container is changed for another needle for giving the injection. Contamination of the hands is also likely if there is a leakage at the junction of the needle and the nozzle of the syringe. In order to minimize the risk of dermatitis it is recommended that the air should be expelled from the syringe into the container before the needle is withdrawn and that the same needle should be used for giving the injection. Care should also be taken to ensure that the needle is firmly attached to the syringe. Wearing rubber gloves gives added protection and the gloves, hands and arms should be thoroughly washed under running water when the procedure is completed. The syringe and needle should also be washed under water.

Prolonged testing has proved that the needle is not blunted by puncturing the rubber cap of the container.

Disposable Injection Units

Disposable drug containers and injectors are available which have the advantages of providing sealed sterile equipment ready for immediate use. The use of these injector units for antibiotic drugs reduces the risk of sensitization dermatitis for doctors and

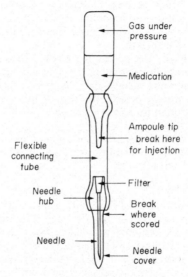

FIG. 58. An automatic injector.

nurses who have to give large numbers of these injections. The apparatus consists of a glass ampoule containing the solution to be injected, an inert gas and a needle protected by a glass sheath. A flexible plastic tube covers the neck of the ampoule and the mount of the needle. When using the injector the glass sheath is given a quick snap and removed, the needle is then inserted into the tissues and the flexible tube squeezed and released. If the needle has entered a vein blood will be seen on the filter pad round the needle. If no blood appears the neck of the ampoule is broken by bending the plastic tube and the solution flows through the needle under the pressure exerted by the gas in the ampoule (Fig. 58).

Intravenous Injection

This method of introducing drugs or fluid into the circulation is performed by the doctor.

The usual reasons for using this route are:

(1) When a very quick action is required in an emergency.

(2) When the drug used would be irritating to the tissues if given intramuscularly or hypodermically, e.g. arsenical preparations.

(3) When it is desired to introduce a drug into the circulation for diagnostic purposes, e.g. the various opaque media used in X-ray examinations, such as pyelography and angiography.

(4) When it is desired to produce local clotting in the treatment of varicose veins.

Intravenous injection is also used as a route for the administration of anaesthetics such as thiopentone sodium (Pentothal).

The usual site for the injection is one of the large superficial veins on the front of the elbow.

Note: when large amounts of fluid are to be administered intravenously this is termed an infusion (see Chapter 21).

Requirements

The drug for injection.

A sterile 10- or 20-ml syringe and needles.

A tourniquet or a sphygmomanometer.

A waterproof pillow to support the patient's arm.

Sterile swabs and a sterile towel.

Ether, surgical spirit or cetrimide.

A small adhesive dressing.

A disposal bag for dirty swabs.

The skin should be cleaned round the site of the injection, and the tourniquet or the cuff of the sphygmomanometer placed round the arm well above the elbow and then tightened or inflated sufficiently to distend the veins. The cuff of the sphygmomanometer is more convenient than a tourniquet, as it is easier to regulate the pressure so that the venous, but not the arterial, circulation is stopped. Also the wide cuff of the sphygmomanometer is more comfortable for the patient than a narrow rubber tourniquet.

The patient, if able to do so, may help by opening and closing his fist several times.

The nurse will be required to assist by steadying the patient's arm while the needle is being inserted and by releasing the tourniquet or deflating the cuff when the needle is in the vein and before the drug is injected.

21

Special procedures—infusions

AN INFUSION allows fluid to be administered slowly over long periods of time, directly into a tissue, or a cavity of the body. The apparatus used incorporates a 'drip' chamber which slows the flow of fluid, the flow being maintained by gravity. A gate clip, attached on the outside of the tubing, is used to compress the tubing and by adjusting the screw, can be used to slow the flow into discrete drops, regulated to a prescribed number per minute.

The tissues and cavities into which fluid may be administered by this method are:

(1) The venous system.
(2) Subcutaneous tissue.
(3) The stomach (milk feed).
(4) The rectum (administration of some drugs).
(5) The bladder (bladder washout and tidal drainage).
(6) The peritoneum (peritoneal dialysis).
(7) The extradural space (epidural analgesia).

Principles of Administration

(1) The apparatus should be completely filled with fluid, to exclude all air, before it is attached to the needle or catheter.

(2) To prevent air entering the system when once it is in use, the tubing should be intact and all connections should be tight.

(3) The patient's fluid intake and output should be recorded.

(4) With the exception of the stomach and rectal infusions, the apparatus and fluid must be sterile, to prevent microorganisms from gaining access to the body.

Intravenous Infusion

Many different fluids may be administered by this route.

(1) Substances to correct or maintain serum electrolyte levels, or to correct dehydration, e.g.:

Normal (physiological) saline (NaCl 0·9 per cent solution).
Potassium chloride.
Calcium lactate.
Sodium bicarbonate 1·3 to 8·4 per cent.
Dextrose 4·3 per cent, NaCl 0·18 per cent.

(2) Substances to maintain nutrition, when the patient is unable to take nutrients by other routes, e.g.:

Dextrose solution 10, 20 or 40 per cent.
Amino acids. Fructose 5, 10, 20 or 40 per cent
Intralipid. Galactose 5 per cent.

(3) Substances to maintain blood pressure, e.g.:

Plasma.
Dextran solution (10 per cent Dextran in normal saline or 10 per cent Dextran in dextrose).

Note: Dextran solution is commonly used to improve the capillary circulation in shock and burns. It is also used to improve the circulation in thrombosis.

(4) As a vehicle for the administration of drugs. Normal saline is the fluid used, and the drugs which may be administered in this way include antibiotics, noradrenaline.

Sites which may be used for intravenous infusion are superficial veins over the internal malleolus, over the back of the hand, in the antecubital fossa of the elbow, and scalp veins in babies.

If necessary, the skin should be shaved before the infusion is set up.

Apparatus Required

Giving set (no filter is required unless blood is to be administered) (Fig. 59).
The needle, cannula or intracath (Fig. 60), for insertion into the vein, and an adaptor if necessary.
Gallipot for cleaning lotion.
Cotton wool, gauze swabs and towels.
Syringe and needles for local anaesthetic.
Intravenous fluid.

} All sterile

The local anaesthetic.
A drip stand.
Sphygmomanometer.
Pillow with a waterproof cover.
Adhesive tape.

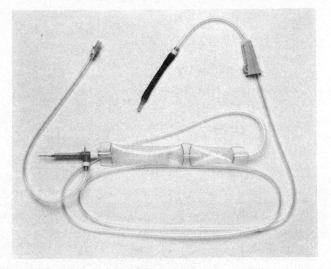

FIG. 59. Disposable polythene 'giving' set.

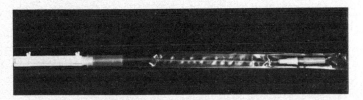

FIG. 60. An intracath.

Splint and bandage.

Bandage scissors.

Very rarely the venous system may be collapsed, and the skin will have to be incised and the vein exposed in order to puncture it. In this case a 'cut-down' set is used, containing:

Scalpel and blade.

Two curved blunt hooks.

An aneurysm needle, and thread size 60, or catgut size 00.

A cannula.

One pair of toothed, and one part of non-toothed dissecting forceps.

Needle, needle holder and skin suture.

Two pairs of fine artery forceps.

Syringe, needle and local anaesthetic.

Method of Setting up the Infusion

(1) The procedure and the reasons for it must be carefully explained to the patient, since his co-operation will be needed in keeping his arm still whilst it is in progress. He should be offered a urinal or bedpan and be made comfortable before it starts.

(2) The connector needle at the upper end of the giving set is exposed, and inserted into the container of intravenous fluid. Air entry must be provided for if the container is not collapsible. If an air entry tube is an integral part of the giving set, it must be clamped off if the fluid is in a collapsible container. The container must be held upright whilst the connector needle is inserted.

(3) The container of fluid is hung on the drip stand, and fluid is allowed to drip rapidly so that the apparatus is filled with fluid and all air is excluded. If the container is a plastic one, it can be gently squeezed to start the flow of fluid. The tubing is clamped when all air has been excluded and the needle adaptor should remain covered until it is connected to the needle.

(4) The sphygmomanometer cuff is applied to the limb above the site of the chosen vein, and is inflated to the level of the patient's diastolic blood pressure. The skin over the vein is cleaned with antiseptic lotion, and the selected needle or cannula is inserted by the doctor into the vein. Local anaesthetic may be infiltrated into the area before this if the patient is very nervous, or there is difficulty in getting the needle into the vein. As soon as blood flows from the needle, the sphygmomanometer cuff is released, the giving set is connected to the needle, and the intravenous fluid is dripped in at the prescribed rate.

(5) A dressing is placed in position over the needle and the tubing is also strapped to the limb so that small movements do not dislodge the needle by pulling on the tubing. The limb may be splinted.

(6) Clear, written instructions as to rate of flow and the fluid to be given should be obtained from the doctor; the fluid chart should be completed and the patient left comfortable.

(7) Frequent observations of the patient and of the infusion will be required.

Blood Transfusion

Blood is given directly into a vein as described above, but the procedure is called a transfusion when blood is given, and additional precautions are required.

Whole blood is required when the patient has lost a quantity of blood from the body over a short period of time. It may also be administered in anaemia, where there is a deficiency of red blood cells, or it may be given to increase the clotting power of the blood. Special precautions are required when transfusing blood to ensure that the donor blood is compatible with the recipient's blood. In particular, the donor's red blood cells must be unaffected by the recipient's plasma. Incompatibility between the donor and recipient blood may result in agglutination or clumping of the donor red cells, with consequent danger of blocking capillaries. A further danger is that of haemolysis of the red cells in large quantities releasing haemoglobin and potassium into the blood stream.

Investigation has shown that red blood cells may carry an agglutinogen (two major agglutinogens are classified A and B) whilst blood plasma may contain agglutinins which on contact with a red cell carrying the appropriate agglutinogen causes a reaction of that red cell (see table below).

The ABO blood grouping system

Blood group	Agglutinogen present on RBC	Agglutinin present in plasma
A	A	Anti-B
B	B	Anti-A
AB	A and B	None
0	None	Anti-A and anti-B

Note: It is the effect of the recipient's plasma on the donor cells which is important in transfusion.

Other antibody–antigen systems may be present, the most important of these being the Rhesus system. About 85 per cent of

Europeans carry an antigen, the Rhesus factor, on their red blood cells (these people are called Rhesus positive), whilst the rest of the population do not have this factor (called Rhesus negative). If a Rhesus negative individual is transfused with Rhesus positive blood, antibodies capable of reacting against red blood cells carrying the Rhesus factor may be formed, so that a second or third contact with Rhesus positive blood at a later date may result in some kind of reaction.

Note: Agglutinins to AB agglutinogens are present in the blood without any contact with the agglutinogen, whilst Rhesus antibody is formed as a *result* of contact with Rhesus positive blood.

It is vital that the patient should receive only that blood which is compatible with his own; for this reason, a specimen of the individual's blood is grouped, and cross-matched with a specimen of the blood from the container of donor blood. This means that the two specimens of blood are mixed in the laboratory and their behaviour is observed. The serial numbers of the units of blood which have been cross-matched against the patient's blood are recorded, and these numbers must be checked against the numbers on the unit label, before the blood is administered. Donor blood is marked with the date at which it was collected, and the date beyond which it should not be used. It should be stored at 4° to 6°C (39° to 41°F) and should neither be heated nor cooled before use.

Setting up a Blood Transfusion

The procedure is very similar to that for setting up an intravenous infusion of other fluids, except that a giving set with a filter must be used. Normal saline is used to start the infusion and then the checked unit of blood is substituted for the saline. Observations of the patient are especially important whilst a blood transfusion is in progress, to detect any complications which may arise.

Complications Which May Arise During a Blood Transfusion

Difficulty in maintaining the flow of blood. There are many different reasons why this might occur; the nurse should be capable of diagnosing the particular cause, some of which she can deal with, whilst others must be dealt with by the doctor.

(1) The vein may go into spasm. Warming the limb may help.

(2) The tubing may become kinked, which is easily put right by the nursing staff.

(3) The needle may become dislodged, so that its lumen is obliterated by the vein wall, in which case, lifting the mount of the needle to depress the point may be successful.

(4) The needle, or tubing, may become blocked by air. If this happens the apparatus should be disconnected from the needle, and the blood should be allowed to run freely through the tubing before it is reconnected again. This should be carried out by a doctor.

(5) The needle or tubing may become blocked by blood clot. If it is the tubing which is blocked, it can be dealt with as described in (4) above. If it is the needle, then the doctor may attempt to remove the clot by attaching a syringe to the needle and sucking the clot into the syringe. A new needle may have to be inserted.

Overloading of the circulatory system. The introduction of large volumes of blood, or any other fluid, into the blood stream can give rise to cardiac and respiratory distress as a result of over-loading the circulatory system if cardiac or renal function is insufficient. This danger is greatest when large quantities of fluid are rapidly introduced. Signs and symptoms of this complication are: rising pulse rate; rapid, shallow respirations; pain in the chest, and oedema. If this should occur, the transfusion should be stopped and the doctor informed.

Incompatibility reaction. This will usually occur soon after the transfusion has started. The symptoms are: shivering; rise in temperature; pain in the lumbar region; nausea and vomiting. The transfusion must be stopped immediately. Later jaundice and oliguria may occur.

Allergic reaction. Blood is a very complex liquid and may contain substances to which the patient is hypersensitive. The symptoms may be mild, such as irritation of the skin and urticaria; or severe, with difficulty in breathing, and laryngeal oedema. In the latter case, the transfusion must be stopped and the doctor informed. Adrenaline will be given in severe reactions, antihistamines in mild ones.

Febrile reactions. These may result from the introduction of contaminants with the blood. These usually occur some time after the transfusion has been started, or even after it has been completed. Symptoms are of an increase in temperature and pulse rate. If this should occur whilst the transfusion is in progress, the rate should be slowed and the doctor informed.

Thrombosis of the vein. This is a fairly common complication, and if it is extensive may be very painful for the patient. There may be a rise in systemic temperature. The doctor should be informed, the transfusion may be stopped, and warmth applied to relieve the pain.

Haematoma. A haematoma may form at the site of entry of the needle into the tissues, if the needle becomes dislodged from the vein. The transfusion should be stopped and the limb elevated. Hyaluronidase may be infiltrated into the area to help disperse the blood.

Changing the Blood Bottle or Polythene Unit

A new unit of blood which has been cross-matched with the patient's blood should be obtained and carefully checked before the previous unit has been completely administered. The fresh unit is taken to the bedside and its number, and the patient's name, are carefully checked to ensure that the blood is correct for this patient. A new unit should be substituted for the old one before the old one is completely empty, but as little blood as possible should be left in the old container, or blood will be wasted. Mix plasma and cells in the new unit by inverting gently. Do not shake. Clamp the tubing of the giving set to stop the flow from the old unit. This unit is then removed from the drip stand, the piercing connector needle is removed from this unit and quickly inserted into the new one. Care should be taken not to contaminate the connector needle. The new unit is then suspended from the 'drip stand', and the tubing clip adjusted to allow the blood to flow at the prescribed rate.

Subcutaneous Infusion

Subcutaneous infusion of clear fluids is more commonly used to supplement fluid intake in infants and young children than adults. Only small quantities of fluid will be absorbed by this route, and none will be absorbed if fluid loss has been so great that compensatory peripheral vaso-constriction has occurred (shock).

Requirements

Container of sterile solution for infusion, e.g.:
Sodium chloride 0·5 per cent.
Glucose 2·5 per cent.
Sodium chloride 0·9 per cent (normal saline).

An intravenous 'giving set' into which a Y connector has been inserted and an extra piece of tubing and a giving needle fitted (Fig. 61). Fine subcutaneous needles, 5 to 7·5 cm (2 to 3 in.) long, are used.

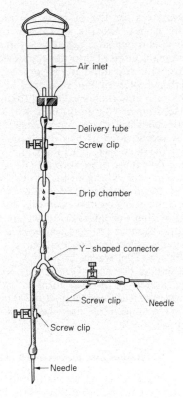

FIG. 61. Subcutaneous infusion apparatus.

Ampoules of hyaluronidase.
Syringe and hypodermic needle.
Sterile towel, swabs and gauze.
Dressing forceps.
Skin cleaning antiseptic, sterile gallipot.
Adhesive tape and scissors.
Containers for used instruments and dirty dressings.
Drip stand.

Method

Possible areas for the infusion are the outer aspects of the thighs, the axillae, and the area below the breast; the infusion being given into two sites near one another simultaneously.

The tubing is inserted into the container of fluid, which is suspended from the drip stand and all air is expelled from the apparatus, and then the flow of fluid is stopped when it fills the apparatus. A suitable skin area is cleaned and a fold of tissue is pinched up, and the needle inserted into the base of the fold and pushed along in the subcutaneous tissue for almost the whole length of the needle. A second area of skin is cleaned and the other needle inserted in the same way. The tubing clip is then adjusted to allow the fluid to flow at the prescribed rate. Hyaluronidase, 0·5 ml, may be injected into the tubing on each side, when once the infusion is under way, to aid absorption of the fluid. Adhesive tape is used to hold the tubing in position. Careful observation of the area is necessary during the infusion, to ensure that the fluid is being absorbed, so the area should be covered in such a way that the site is readily accessible for observation, but at the same time the patient must be kept warm.

If the fluid is not absorbed, it may leak from the site on to the skin surface, or it may form a hard swelling within the tissues, together with blanching of the skin over the area. Further hyaluronidase injections may help, or the infusion may be discontinued.

Infusion Into the Stomach (Milk Drip)

This is used rarely, but occasionally milk is administered by this method in severe peptic ulceration. The milk is placed in a vacuum flask, suspended from a drip stand, and is administered by means of an infusion set which is connected to an oesophageal or Ryle's tube, passed into the stomach. The end of the tube is strapped into position on the patient's cheek. As with all infusions, a fluid balance chart should be maintained, the rate should be observed, and regulated as prescribed. All air should be excluded from the apparatus. (For method of passing tube into the stomach, and checking its position, see Chapter 6.)

Rectal Infusion

This is another procedure which is rarely used, but drug solutions or substances to be retained in the rectum for some time before being returned might be given by this method, e.g. olive oil, cortisone solution, magnesium sulphate solution.

A cleansing enema may be administered before setting up the infusion. The apparatus is assembled as for other infusions but it need not be sterile. A small size, rectal catheter is inserted through the anus and the infusion tubing filled with the liquid to be administered is connected to the catheter, and the rate adjusted.

Bladder Washout and Tidal Drainage

The basic apparatus used for intravenous infusion may be modified to allow sterile solutions to drip slowly into the bladder through a self-retaining catheter. For tidal drainage a Y connection should be inserted between the infusion tubing and tubing from the catheter, to allow drainage tubing to be looped up before emptying into a urine container, syphonage of the bladder contents then occurs when the bladder has filled (see Chapter 9). (For bladder washout see Chapter 24.)

Peritoneal Dialysis

This may be used in kidney failure if no artificial kidney is available. Fluid is run into the peritoneal cavity, where any small molecular substances in the blood or tissue fluid at a concentration higher than in the introduced fluid will pass from the tissues and into the fluid. The fluid can then be drained from the peritoneum.

By introducing fluid which originally contains none of the substances to be removed from the blood, but which does contain small molecular substances needed by the body in a concentration equal to their blood concentration, the procedure compensates to some extent for the work of the kidney in maintaining the constant composition of body fluids. To prevent hydration from occurring because of absorption of the fluid from the peritoneal cavity, the solutions may be very slightly hypertonic, compared with the blood. If oedema is present, a solution which is more hypertonic may be used to remove the oedematous fluid.

Apparatus Required

   (1) A small dressing pack containing sterile dressings, forceps, swabs and a gallipot.
   (2) Lotion for cleaning the skin.
   (3) Disposal bag for dirty swabs.
   (4) A peritoneal dialysis set. This will consist of one or two containers of dialysis fluid at body temperature.

A giving set which is similar to an intravenous giving set but with modifications. There may be two pieces of tubing with clamps and connecting needles above the drip chamber. Below the drip chamber the tubing will terminate in a Y connection. Tubing on one arm of this Y connection is designed to be connected to an intraperitoneal catheter, whilst tubing from the other arm is a syphonage tube which runs into a collecting bottle or bag. Clamps are placed on both these tubes.

   (5) Drip stand.
   (6) Apparatus for the insertion of an intraperitoneal catheter.
       Local anaesthetic, syringe and needles.
       Paracentesis trocar and cannular.
       The intraperitoneal catheter.
   (7) Adhesive tape.

Dialysis Fluid

   This is specially prepared fluid and the particular fluid used depends to some extent upon the requirements of the individual patient. Examples of the content (in g per litre) of two different dialysis fluids are given in the following table:

	1. A slightly hypertonic solution	2. A markedly hypertonic solution
Dextrose	13·6	63·6
Sodium lactate	5·0	5·0
Sodium chloride	5·6	5·6
Calcium chloride	0·39	0·39
Magnesium chloride hexahydrate	0·15	0·15
Sodium metabisulphite	0·05	0·12

Procedure

(1) Explanation should be given to the patient, and his bladder should be empty at the start of the procedure. He should be placed lying on his back, with one pillow under his head. Mild sedation may be ordered if he is very nervous.

(2) The piercing, connecting needles of the giving set are inserted into the fluid containers and the containers are hung on drip stands. The syphonage tube is inserted into a collecting bag or bottle, and the apparatus is filled with fluid to exclude all air.

(3) By means of the trocar and cannula, the intraperitoneal catheter is inserted into the abdomen, the trocar being introduced into the midline of the anterior abdominal wall, about two-thirds of the distance from the symphysis pubis to the umbilicus. The catheter is passed in toward the right or left side of the pelvis.

(4) The protective cover should be removed from the end of the giving set to be connected to the intraperitoneal catheter, and the two should be connected. The tubing should be taped to the patient's abdomen, to prevent it from being pulled out.

(5) Input clamps are opened, and the clamp on the syphonage tubing is closed, and fluid is run into the peritoneal cavity at the prescribed rate. This is usually rapid; 2 litres of fluid may be run in, within 10 min, and all tubes are clamped off.

(6) The solution is left in the peritoneal cavity for some time, whilst equilibration with body fluids takes place. This may be for up to 1 hr.

(7) Clamps from the catheter and on the syphonage tube are opened, and the fluid is allowed to run out.

(8) Further containers of fluid should be available, warmed to body temperature, to repeat, as necessary.

Observations During the Procedure

(1) Sterility of the apparatus must be maintained.

(2) Careful observations of the patient's condition should be made, including conscious level, pulse, respiration rates and blood pressure. This is particularly important whilst fluid is being syphoned out, especially if a markedly hypertonic solution has been used, since it can drastically reduce the patient's blood volume.

(3) Careful records must be kept of the amount of fluid run into the peritoneal cavity and of the amount syphoned out. Normally the latter will exceed the former. Weighing the liquids is more accurate than measuring them.

22

Drainage and aspiration of body cavities

BODY cavities may be drained, or fluid may be aspirated from them, for several different reasons:

(1) To rest the area, e.g. stomach, bladder.

(2) To relieve pressure exerted by the fluid, e.g. pleural aspiration, abdominal paracentesis, bladder catheterization.

(3) To measure the pressure of fluid in the cavity, e.g. lumbar puncture.

(4) To obtain a specimen of fluid or tissue, e.g. pleural aspiration, tissue biopsies, sternal and lumbar puncture, stomach aspiration, bladder catheterization.

(5) To introduce drugs into the cavity, e.g. lumbar puncture.

Many of these procedures are carried out by the doctor in the ward, under local anaesthetic. Since there is a danger of introducing infection directly into the body with most of these procedures (the exception being stomach aspiration) all apparatus used must be sterile and the technique must be aseptic. The nurse's role is usually confined to the preparation of the patient and the equipment, assisting during the procedure, and looking after and observing the patient during and after the procedure.

General Requirements

(1) Skin cleansing agent, e.g. 1 per cent cetrimide; iodine; spirit solution.

(2) 2- or 5-ml syringe and needles for local anaesthetic.

(3) Local anaesthetic, e.g. 0·5 per cent lignocaine.

(4) Instrument handling forceps.

(5) Sterile towels, swabs and dressings.

(6) Sterile disposable gloves of suitable size.

(7) Sterile dressing, forceps and scissors.

(8) Scalpel for some procedures.

(9) Sterile containers for laboratory specimens.
(10) Pathological examination request forms and labels.
(11) Protective polythene sheeting.
(12) Collodion, adhesive strapping and scissors, or small adhesive dressings.
(13) Receptacles for used instruments and dressings.

Exploration and Aspiration of the Chest for Fluid in the Pleural Cavity

Exploration and, where necessary, aspiration of the pleural cavity are used in diagnosis and the treatment of a pleural effusion. Such an effusion may be an inflammatory exudate as in pleurisy accompanying pneumonia, or a transudate such as the fluid which collects as part of a generalized oedema in congestive heart failure.

Requirements

General requirements as listed above.
10- or 20-ml exploring syringe and long needles.
Two-way tap to fit the syringe.
Tubing to fit the tap.
Two sterile measure jugs.
Martin's syringe is one type of two-way syringe used for aspiration of the chest. This syringe has a bayonet fitting and is supplied with a trocar and cannula and a sharp needle. A piece of rubber tubing is attached to one arm of the nozzle through which the fluid drawn up into the syringe is ejected into the measure jug.

Preparation of the Patient

The patient should sit well forward in the bed with his head flexed and his arms resting on a pillow placed on a bedtable in front of him. The pillows behind him must be removed so that the doctor has easy access to the patient's back. The skin over the area where the puncture will be made is cleaned and the local anaesthetic injected.

Pleural Biopsy

Biopsy of the parietal pleura is most commonly undertaken in order to determine whether a pleural effusion is of tuberculous or malignant origin.

Requirements

    General requirements as listed on page 257.
    Abram's pleural biopsy needle (Fig. 62).
    Aspirating syringe.
    Two-way tap to fit the syringe.
    Skin suture.

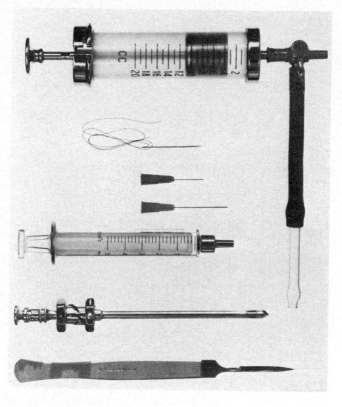

FIG. 62. Pleural biopsy set.

Preparation of the Patient

The biopsy needle is usually inserted into the posterior chest wall, the actual site of the puncture being determined by physical and radiological examination. The patient should sit forward in the bed in the position described under 'pleural aspiration' (Fig. 63). No preparation other than cleaning the skin and the injection of a local anaesthetic is usually required and there are usually no

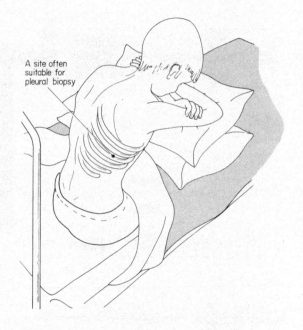

A site often
suitable for
pleural biopsy

FIG. 63. Position of the patient for pleural biopsy.

after effects, although the patient may experience some aching pain in the chest.

The small skin incision is closed with a single suture and a small sterile dressing is applied.

Tapping the Peritoneal Cavity (Paracentesis Abdominis)

Tapping may be needed in order to withdraw fluid from the peritoneal cavity (ascites) in cases of cardiac or liver diseases and in malignant conditions.

Requirements

General requirements as listed on page 257.
Ascites trocar and cannula (Fig. 64).
Tubing to fit side outlet,
   or Southey's trocar and cannula with fine rubber tubing.
Many-tailed bandage or abdominal binder.
Pail or other receptacle to stand at the side of the bed for the
   fluid.

FIG. 64. Thompson's ascites trocar and cannula.

When the Southey's tube is used the trocar should have the small shield screwed into place and the tubing should be attached to the end of the cannula. The trocar should be pushed through the rubber tubing (holding this stretched) so that its end protrudes just below the end of the cannula.

It is important that the fine tubing should be new and in good condition; if at all perished it will lose its elasticity, and therefore the small hole made by the trocar will not close up when the trocar is removed.

Preparation of the Patient

Immediately before the tapping the bladder must be emptied and catheterization may be needed.

The patient should sit upright supported with pillows. The bandage or binder should be placed in position so that it can be applied as soon as the trocar and cannula are inserted. If a large trocar and cannula are used, the fluid drains quickly and the nurse should tighten the binder frequently. If a Southey's tube is used the fluid drains much more slowly. Two small pieces of adhesive strapping will be required to keep the small shield in position.

Lumbar Puncture

Lumbar puncture is carried out in order to obtain samples of cerebrospinal fluid and to measure the pressure of the fluid. The procedure is also used when drugs are given by intrathecal injection.

Requirements

General requirements as listed on page 257.

Lumbar puncture needles. If the pressure of the cerebrospinal fluid is to be measured, a needle with a tap and side piece is used (Fig. 65). A small piece of rubber tubing to fit the side piece and the glass manometer will be required.

FIG. 65. Barker's needle for lumbar puncture.

If drugs are to be injected a large record syringe and an adaptor to fit the lumbar puncture needle will be required.

A general anaesthetic may be required if the patient is restless or likely to have fits.

Position of the Patient

Usually the procedure is carried out with the patient lying on his side near the edge of the bed. The spine and the legs are flexed as far as possible in order to separate the intervertebral spaces. The usual site for the puncture is between the third and fourth lumbar vertebrae. In some cases the patient may be sitting up with the knees and spine flexed.

After the procedure the patient should be kept quiet and lying flat for several hours, as headache is likely to occur. This may be treated by raising the foot of the bed and giving plenty of fluids.

When specimens of the cerebrospinal fluid are required for pathological examination, these should be taken to the laboratory immediately.

Cisternal Puncture

The requirements are the same as for lumbar puncture, except that a special needle with the shaft marked in centimetres may be used.

The site for this puncture is the junction of the skull with the spine, and the skin over the area will usually require shaving.

Bone Marrow Biopsy (Sternal Puncture)

In the investigation of some diseases of the blood a specimen of the red bone marrow is required and this is obtained either from the sternum or the iliac crest.

Requirements

General requirements as listed on page 257.

2-ml aspirating syringe.

Sternal puncture needle with stilette. This is a hollow needle with a short bevelled point and an adjustable 'stop' or guard (Fig. 66).

The patient is usually given a sedative, e.g. Seconal, 200 mg, or Physeptone, 10 mg, $\frac{3}{4}$ to 1 hr before the procedure is carried out.

The patient should lie flat with the head extended and a small pillow under the shoulders.

FIG. 66. Sternal puncture needle.

Splenic Aspiration

Splenic aspiration is sometimes performed in cases of unexplained splenomegaly and in some blood diseases. For this a fine-gauge Harris's lumbar puncture needle may be used, and a syringe for aspirating the specimen.

Liver Biopsy

Biopsy may be required in the investigation of liver disorders where physical and laboratory examinations have failed to give a diagnosis.

Requirements

General requirements as listed on page 257.

Liver biopsy needle, e.g. Silverman's or a modification of this type (see Fig. 67), or Menghini's needle (Fig. 68).

Fine injection needle, 7·6 cm (3 in.) in length.

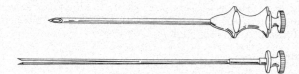

FIG. 67. Silverman's liver biopsy needle, adult size.

Preparation of the Patient

The patient's blood group is ascertained and his blood is cross-matched. The haemoglobin content, bleeding and clotting times and the prothrombin content of the blood are estimated. The examination is not usually carried out if the prothrombin content is below 70 per cent of the normal.

Procedure

The patient lies on his back well over to the right side of the bed, the trunk is then slightly tilted to the right by placing a pillow under his left side.

Following the biopsy it is important to keep a close watch on the patient's condition as haemorrhage may occur. A pulse chart should be kept for at least 12 hr.

Renal Biopsy

Renal biopsy may be useful in elucidating some cases of renal disease when other methods have failed to give a definite diagnosis.

The biopsy specimen is obtained by using a modified type of Silverman's liver biopsy needle.

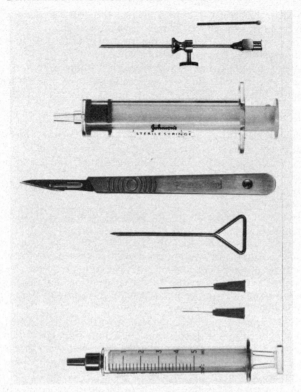

FIG. 68. Mcnghini's liver biopsy set.

Preparation of the Patient

An X-ray examination is carried out in order to determine the size and position of the kidneys. The patient's blood group is identified and his blood is cross-matched in case a transfusion is needed. The haemoglobin is also estimated.

The site of the biopsy is usually the lower pole of the right kidney. The patient lies in the prone position with a sandbag under the abdomen, this fixes the kidney against the dorsal surface of the body and helps to reduce the risk of haemorrhage.

The position of the kidney is determined after the injection of a local anaesthetic, by a fine exploring needle.

After renal biopsy has been performed it is important to keep a close watch for bleeding; a certain amount of haematuria is common, but even if slight it should be reported immediately.

Assisting with these Procedures

(1) Ask the doctor who is to carry out the procedure if he requires any apparatus not included in the special pack.

(2) Wash the trolley with antiseptic lotion, dry it and lay it ready for the procedure.

(3) Ensure that the patient has been informed what is to be done and why.

(4) Screen the bed, and give the patient the opportunity to empty his bladder.

Note: It is *essential* that the patient should have an empty bladder before an abdomino-paracentesis is carried out, to remove the danger of the trocar and cannula piercing the bladder wall.

(5) Instruct the patient into the correct position for the procedure and assist him as required. Place a flannelette sheet over any part of the body likely to get cold.

(6) Wash hands and take the trolley to the bedside. Open any packs required by the doctor and pour the lotion. Hold the local anaesthetic bottle so that he may read the label; clean the rubber cap if it is a multidose bottle, or break the ampoule, so that the doctor can then draw up the correct dose.

(7) Support and observe the patient during the actual procedure. If the doctor does not explain as he goes along, the nurse should do this. The patient needs to know just before the skin is cleaned that this will happen and that the lotion will be cold. He then needs to be told that local anaesthetic will be injected and that he will feel the injection, but that this will prevent pain during the passage of the needle into the cavity. If he is likely to feel pressure as the needle is pushed through connective tissue, as in lumbar puncture and sternal puncture, he should be warned about this, so that he does not move suddenly. If the patient is very nervous it may help if he can squeeze the nurse's hand. When the procedure is one which is carried out behind the patient, such as lumbar

puncture or chest aspiration, he should be reassured at the start that he will be kept informed when things are about to happen to him, so that he does not lie tensed and worried, expecting pain at any moment, whilst the apparatus is being prepared.

(8) Hold a specimen jar in position for the doctor if a specimen is to be collected to be sent to the laboratory.

(9) Perform any special manoeuvre required, such as a Queckenstedt test during the course of a lumbar puncture.

(10) Warn the patient when the needle is about to be withdrawn, since he will feel pulling. Provide a dressing to seal the puncture.

(11) Place the patient in an appropriate position.

(12) Clear the trolley. Measure the quantity of any fluid withdrawn, report on its appearance and send any specimen to the laboratory with the correctly filled in request form.

(13) Continue to observe the patient at intervals after the procedure, as requested.

For catheterization of the urinary bladder: see Chapter 9.

Aspiration of the Stomach

This is a procedure which is carried out by the nursing staff, and is not a sterile procedure, although sterile equipment may be used. The stomach may be aspirated hourly to rest the alimentary tract in paralytic ileus or after an operation on the alimentary tract.

The technique for passing a tube into the stomach is detailed in Chapter 6. When once the tube is in place it may remain in position for 24 hr at a time, provided it has been passed nasally.

Requirements for Aspiration

20-ml syringe and an adaptor.
A measure for the aspirated fluid.
A sterile spigot.
Adhesive tape.
Fluid chart.
Polythene sheet and paper towel.

Method

Protect the patient's chest. Remove the tube from the patient's cheek. This should have been fastened to the cheek by adhesive tape but so that the tube can be slipped away without the tape having to be removed from the skin every time, e.g.

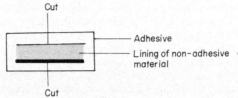

Cut

Adhesive

Lining of non-adhesive material

Cut

This side to the patient's face

Remove the spigot and attach the syringe to the end of the tube, using the adaptor. Apply suction to the tube by drawing on the piston of the syringe. Pinch the tubing and disconnect the syringe when it is full. Empty into the measure, re-attach and repeat until no more fluid is obtained. Insert the fresh spigot, re-attach the tube to the cheek and leave the patient comfortable. Record the amount and nature of the aspirant.

23
Washouts

A BODY cavity may be washed out as a method of removing or diluting secretions or other contents, and cleaning the area. Areas which may be washed out include the stomach, the rectum, bladder, ear, and vagina. Usually washouts are carried out by the nursing staff. Bladder and vaginal irrigations are sterile procedures, whilst stomach and rectal washout and ear syringing are not.

STOMACH WASHOUT, RECTAL WASHOUT

Apparatus Required

Rectal Washout Only
Rectal tube or catheter size 14 (English gauge)

Stomach Washout Only
Oesophageal tube, size 18 (English gauge) 22 (French gauge)

Length of tubing.
Tubing clip.
Connector for tubing and catheter/oesophageal tube.
Lubricant.
Swabs.
Jug containing washout solution at 37·5°C (100°F).

Water, N/saline.
Lotion thermometer.

Sodium biocarbonate 1:160 solution.

Irrigating can, or funnel and pint measure.
Container for soiled swabs.
Polythene sheets to protect bed and floor.
A pail to receive returned fluid.

Mouthwash if patient conscious.
Post-anaesthetic instruments if patient unconscious.

Stomach Washout

This may be done in cases of poisoning, to remove all traces of poison from the stomach. A large bore oesophageal tube is passed, orally. The patient may be in a semiprone or prone position during the washout, especially if loss of consciousness has occurred. The contents of the stomach are completely removed and kept for examination. The stomach is then washed out using an appropriate solution, such as sodium bicarbonate solution. Sometimes the washout fluid is required for analysis.

Stomach washout may also be carried out in gastritis, pyloric stenosis and preoperatively.

Rectal Washout

This may be carried out to remove faeces, or to prepare the area before a barium enema or operation. The procedure is continued until the fluid is returned clear.

Syphonage as a Method of Washout

In the case of both stomach and rectal washout, syphonage can be used as a method of removing the fluid from the organ when once it has been run in. A length of rubber tubing and a funnel should be attached to the tube which is passed into the cavity. The bed and floor should be well protected with polythene sheeting, and a bucket should be placed on the floor to receive the washings. The procedure for passing the tube is different in each case.

Passing the Rectal Tube

It is important not to allow air into the rectum as it is most uncomfortable for the patient and interferes with syphonage. The apparatus should be completely filled with the washout fluid at the correct temperature and clipped off when all air has been excluded. The rectal tube is then lubricated and passed for 10 cm (4 in.) into the rectum, with the patient in the left lateral position. Approximately 500 ml of fluid is allowed to run in, keeping the funnel filled at all times, so that air does not get into the apparatus. Whilst there is still some fluid in the funnel it is quickly inverted over the bucket and the fluid is allowed to run out. This is repeated until the fluid is returned clear. Both the quantity of fluid introduced and that returned should be measured to check that all fluid is returned.

Passing the Stomach Tube

This is done in the usual way (see Chapter 6). A check is made that the tube is in the stomach and the stomach contents are aspirated. Fluid is then run in through the funnel and tubing, and syphoned out again, as described above. Only 250 ml of fluid should be run into the stomach at a time.

Other Methods of Washout

It is possible to carry out a stomach washout by using a Senoran bottle, which enables suction to be used to aspirate the fluid back by depressing the rubber bulb and putting a finger over the small hole in the side of the syringe. The fluid should be allowed to run in at its own rate. A larger 50-ml syringe can also be used, using the barrel as a funnel to allow the fluid to run in, and then using the piston to aspirate the fluid back.

An alternative method of rectal washout is to allow 500 ml of fluid to run in to the rectum and then to allow the patient to pass the fluid back into a bedpan, commode or lavatory before further fluid is run in.

VAGINAL IRRIGATION (DOUCHING)

The vagina does not have a tight sphincter like the rectum, so there is no problem about the return of the fluid when douching is carried out.

Vaginal irrigation is ordered for cleansing purposes, e.g. before gynaecological operations, for patients wearing vaginal pessaries or for patients who have a vaginal discharge.

Requirements

An irrigation can, 3-pint capacity (about 2 litres).
A long piece of tubing to fit the outlet of the can and the irrigation nozzle.
Soft rubber catheter or irrigation nozzle, which may be glass, rubber or plastic.
Tubing clip.

Jug containing the lotion as ordered; lotion thermometer.
Bowl with lotion for swabbing, e.g. Hibitane 0·1 per cent.
Sterile swabs and pads.
'Douche' pan or large 'perfection' type bedpan.
Receptacles for soiled swabs and for soiled nozzle.

The apparatus may be sterilized by boiling and is then placed in a large sterile bowl. The lotion is prepared at a temperature of 40°C (105°F). As a general rule only mild lotions are used for cleansing, e.g. normal saline solution, 1 per cent lactic acid or domiphen bromide (Bradosol) 1:2000 solution.

The lotion is poured into the irrigating can and the tubing is clipped. The can should be hung about 30 cm (12 in.) above the level of the patient's pelvis so that the fluid will run in gently at low pressure.

The douche pan or bedpan is placed under the patient, who should lie on her back with one or two pillows under the head and shoulders. A square of waterproof material can be used to protect the bottom sheet.

Before the nurse washes her hands the bedclothes should be so arranged that the patient's thighs and legs are covered by a blanket and sheet while her chest and abdomen are covered by a folded blanket. When the nurse returns from washing her hands and drying them on a clean towel, she pushes the lower half of the divided bedclothes down using her elbow. Taking a swab in her right hand she first swabs the labia majora with the antiseptic lotion provided and then parting the labia with the first finger and thumb of her left hand she swabs the labia minora and the area of the vaginal orifice. The swabbing should be carried out from above downwards and each swab should be used once only. The tubing clip is released allowing the lotion to flow through the apparatus. The nozzle or catheter is then inserted gently upwards and backwards into the vagina for about 7·5 cm (3 in.).

When the irrigation is completed the patient should sit up on the douche pan for a few moments to allow the fluid to drain out of the vagina. The vulva is then dried with sterile swabs and a sterile pad applied.

A glass douche nozzle should always be carefully inspected before use to make sure that it is not cracked or chipped. In all cases where stitches have been inserted into the perineum or vagina it is safer to use a rubber catheter.

BLADDER WASHOUT

This may be performed after operations in the vicinity of the bladder, such as prostatectomy. An in-dwelling catheter will have been inserted and connected to a urine drainage bag. Great care should be taken to avoid the introduction of microorganisms into the bladder during this procedure.

Requirements

A sterile 50-ml syringe, Dakins, or Bladder Syringe.
An adaptor.
Sterile antiseptic cleansing lotion and swabs.
Sterile clip for catheter (a pair of Spencer Wells forceps is best).
Irrigating solution, at 37°C (99°F), e.g. normal saline (0·9 per cent), sterile water, Hibitane 1:5000 solution.
Lotion thermometer in antiseptic solution and sterile water to rinse it.
Sterile towels.
Polythene sheeting to protect the bed.
Sterile measuring jug for used irrigation fluid.
Sterile disposable gloves.
A sterile polythene connection.

Method

Explain to the patient, help him into position and arrange the bedclothes and bed curtains. Wash the hands and open the packs. Arrange a sterile towel under the catheter and clip it off, using the sterile forceps, and touching only their handle. Put on the sterile gloves, and swab the end of the catheter and the polythene connection so that the outside of these is clean. Draw up a measured quantity of irrigating fluid into the syringe, ensuring that all air is excluded from the syringe (a maximum of 50 ml fluid should be used) and attach the syringe to the catheter using the adaptor if necessary. Unclip the forceps so that the catheter is patent and gently syringe the fluid into the bladder, or allow it to flow in by gravity. Aspirate it back; clip the catheter; disconnect and empty the syringe into the empty measure. Check that the fluid put into the bladder has all been returned. Repeat the procedure from attaching the syringe to the catheter until the fluid is returned clear. Using a sterile polythene connection, reconnect the catheter to the drainage bag. Leave the patient comfortable and report the amount of fluid used and the initial amount of debris, or degree of blood staining.

Continuous, or Frequent Bladder Irrigation

If the bladder is to be irrigated frequently, the above method is very time consuming, as well as carrying a high risk of introducing infection into the bladder. A better method is to use a method of irrigation in which the apparatus is left in place, and the catheter does not have to be disconnected.

Apparatus

An intravenous infusion set is connected by a Y or T connection to a piece of tubing from the catheter on the one hand, and a piece of tubing leading to the urine bag on the other. All tubing and connections must be sterile. The infusion set is inserted into a bottle of normal saline 0·9 per cent solution, suspended from a drip stand. All air must be excluded from the apparatus by filling it with the saline before it is connected to the catheter. Spencer Wells forceps, or gate clips, are used as clamps.

To irrigate the bladder. The tubing leading from the catheter to the urine bag is clamped off and a small measured quantity of the normal saline is allowed to drip into the bladder. The tubing leading from the normal saline bottle is then clamped, the other clamp removed, and the irrigating fluid flows out into the urine drainage bag. This can be repeated as frequently as necessary, and is much less disturbing to the patient than the method described above.

EAR SYRINGING

The ear may be syringed following the instillation of wax softening drops if the external auditory meatus contains a lot of wax, causing deafness or obscuring the ear drum to auriscopic examination. It may be carried out by either a doctor or a nurse.

To Syringe an Ear

Requirements

An aural syringe. A metal syringe may be used, or a Higginson's bulb syringe with a straight Eustachian catheter attached.

Lotion, e.g. sodium chloride 0·9 per cent (normal saline) or
sodium bicarbonate, 1:160 solution.

Lotion thermometer. The lotion should be prepared at 38°C
(100°F) and injected at body temperature; if it is not the
correct temperature the patient is likely to feel giddy and
nauseated.

Angular aural forceps.

Wool swabs, and dressed wooden applicators.

Polythene sheet.

Towel.

Kidney-shaped receiver.

Receptacles for soiled swabs and instruments.

Head mirror and lamp.

Method

The patient's clothes should be protected by the polythene sheet
and towel placed round his neck. He should sit upright if possible
and hold the kidney dish under the ear (Fig. 69).

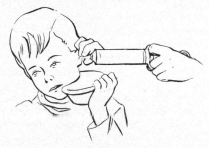

FIG. 69. Syringing the ear, showing method of holding the syringe.

The nurse should wear the head mirror and arrange the lamp so
that it will shine on the mirror.

The syringe is filled with the lotion and air expelled.

The pinna of the ear should be pulled upwards and backwards
to straighten the meatus and the flow of the lotion directed along
the floor of the canal. When a piece of wax has been removed, the
ear should be gently cleaned with a piece of wool on the angular
forceps and the meatus examined to see if it is clear.

If the wax is hard, drops may be ordered to soften it; sodium bicarbonate or oil may be used.

After syringing a little ointment may be wiped round the meatus to prevent soreness.

At the end of the procedure the ear should be examined to make sure that all the wax has been removed. A metal ear syringe should be handled with care. If dented, this will interfere with the smooth working of the plunger and there is danger that if force is used in pushing the plunger home, damage to the ear may result. The syringe should always be examined before use, to make sure that the plunger is working smoothly and evenly.

Examination of the Ear

Requirements

Forehead mirror and lamp, or illuminating headlight.
Aural specula of various sizes.
Angular forceps.
Probes, e.g. Jobson–Horne ring probes.
Dressed wooden applicators.
Small wool swabs.
Receptacle for soiled swabs.
The patient should sit sideways with the ear to be examined opposite the doctor. If a forehead mirror is used the light from the lamp is directed so that it shines on the mirror.
If the auditory meatus is full of wax, the doctor will order the ear to be syringed before the examination can be completed.

EYE IRRIGATION

This is a nursing procedure which may be carried out if a patient has an inflamed eye, to remove loose foreign bodies from the eye, to dilute splashes of liquid likely to damage the eye, and to maintain the cornea and conjunctiva of the eye in an unconscious patient.

Requirements

A special glass irrigator known as an undine which should be sterile.

Lotion at a temperature of 37°C (100°F) 0·9 per cent sodium chloride, e.g. normal saline solution.

Sterile cotton wool or lint swabs.

Polythene sheeting.

Towel.

A receiver for the lotion.

A receptacle for used swabs.

Method

If the patient is in bed, all the pillows but one should be removed so that the patient lies flat with the head tilted back. If he is sitting up in a chair, the head should be tilted back and inclined a little towards the affected side. The towel and polythene sheet are arranged to protect the patient's clothing and the receiver arranged to catch the lotion. The patient may hold this himself.

The lotion from the irrigator may be allowed to flow over the cheek first, so that the patient becomes accustomed to it and is then directed in a steady stream from the inner towards the outer canthus of the eye, taking care that the undine does not touch the eye or the eyelashes. It should be held 4 cm (1½ in.) above the eye. The lids should be separated. If they are glued together with sticky discharge, this should be done very gently after well moistening the edges of the lids with lotion. The lids and the surrounding skin should be dried with swabs when the irrigation is completed. An antiseptic ointment for the lids, to be applied after the treatment, may be ordered, such as yellow oxide of mercury. This is applied to the edges of the lids by means of a glass rod.

In all cases where the eye is acutely red or there is any purulent discharge the nurse should observe the following precautions:

(1) She should not directly touch with her fingers either the eye or any articles soiled with the discharge.

(2) If both eyes are to be treated, the cleaner eye should be attended to first.

(3) The nurse's hands must be very thoroughly washed after completing the treatment, the nurse being especially careful not to touch her own eye before doing this.

(4) The patient should be warned not to touch his eyes, and to keep all washing utensils, handkerchiefs and towels separate.

24

Laboratory investigations

Collection of Material for Laboratory Investigation

Examination and analysis of body fluids, excreta and tissue may be carried out in order to detect the presence of abnormal substances, an increase or decrease in normal constituents, or following the administration of diagnostic material, to measure its concentration in tissue, or urine, or the concentration of its end product.

In a number of conditions, microbiological examination of urine, blood, sputum, serous fluids and swabs from wounds, or from the nose or throat, is required in order to identify the infecting microorganism.

In many cases the collection of specimens and the preparation of the patient is part of the nurse's responsibility. She should fully understand her part in the investigation and carry out all instructions implicitly and accurately. Should it become impossible to follow the instructions, or if an error is made, this should be reported to the ward sister or medical officer immediately.

The Collection of Specimens

All specimens sent to the laboratory should be as fresh as possible, for in many cases even a few hours delay will render the specimen unsuitable for examination, due to bacterial decomposition, or other causes.

All specimens must be clearly labelled to prevent loss or error. Some specimens should be collected first thing in the morning, before breakfast; the taking of a meal may materially affect the level of some substances in the blood or urine.

Specimens of Blood

When sending blood for examination, care must be taken to avoid haemolysis of the specimen, for haemolysis renders the specimen useless.

To avoid haemolysis, the needle used for venepuncture should have a short bevel, the syringe and needle must be dry, and the container into which the specimen is placed must be dry.

For some tests whole, clotted blood is required, whilst for others it should be anti-coagulated, so that the laboratory may obtain the fraction of the blood for examination that they require. Each laboratory should issue specimen bottles containing the correct anti-coagulant for each test, with instructions as to the quantity of blood required. Heparin, potassium oxalate and sodium citrate are fairly common anti-coagulants. For blood sugar estimation fluoride is added to the tube to prevent the disappearance of the sugar from the blood. Once the blood has been added to the anti-coagulant, it must be inverted gently so that it is thoroughly mixed with the specimen. Shaking causes haemolysis.

Some Estimations Which May be Made of Blood Contents

Blood urea. The blood urea level may be increased in renal failure.

Serum cholesterol. This may be increased in nephrotic syndrome.

Plasma sodium. May be increased in water depletion, and may be decreased in diarrhoea and vomiting, shock and diabetic coma.

Plasma potassium. This may be increased in renal failure, and diabetic coma. It may be decreased in diarrhoea and vomiting, and during the treatment of diabetic coma. A deviation from the normal level of potassium in the plasma may affect the heart beat.

Plasma chloride. This is likely to be decreased in shock, diarrhoea and vomiting and diabetic coma.

Plasma bicarbonate. May be increased in metabolic alkalosis (caused, for example, by excessive intake of antacids), gastric vomiting, or excessive inhalation of carbon dioxide. The level may be decreased in renal failure, diabetic coma, or when inadequate quantities of carbon dioxide are breathed (hyperventilation).

10

Serum enzymes. Intracellular enzymes may be released into the blood stream from damaged tissue cells. Their presence in the blood in greater than normal quantities indicates that tissue damage has occurred.

Alkaline phosphatase. The level of this enzyme in the blood increases in obstructive jaundice (from the liver) and in any disease where there is a breakdown in bone.

Acid phosphatase. Released into the blood stream from the prostate tissue in carcinoma of the prostate.

Amylase. Found both in saliva and pancreatic juice. Its blood level is increased in pancreatitis, and salivary duct obstruction.

Glutamic-oxaloacetic transaminase. Found both in heart muscle and liver cells. It is released to raise the blood level considerably when cardiac infarction has occurred. The blood level is also raised in liver damage.

Glutamic-pyruvic transaminase. Found in liver cells and heart muscle. Its blood level is raised in liver damage and also in cardiac infarction.

Lactic dehydrogenase. Found in liver cells and its blood level is raised in liver damage.

Blood Counts

Blood counts are used to estimate the number of red blood cells, white blood cells, or platelets in a given quantity of blood (usually 1 mm^3). They may be made by drawing blood directly from a finger prick, into special pipettes, or venous blood may be collected into a specially anti-coagulated tube. A blood smear is taken onto a microscope slide for identification of the cell types. (Normal values of blood counts are given on p. 295.)

Erythrocyte Sedimentation Rate

The sedimentation rate measures the distance which the red cells fall in 1 hr when a column of blood is allowed to stand vertically in a glass tube of fine uniform bore. Several different methods are used, and the normal values vary with each method. It is not a diagnostic test as most infections cause an increase in the rate but it is very useful in following the course of a disease, e.g. in rheumatic fever and tuberculosis. The greater the activity of the disease the higher is the sedimentation rate.

Method. Wintrobe's method is the one most commonly used. 3 ml of blood are placed in a tube containing ammonium and potassium oxalate, and well mixed. A special Wintrobe sedimentation rate tube is then filled and allowed to stand vertically undisturbed for 1 hr, and then the height of the column of clear plasma above the sediment of cells is measured.

Another method is the Westergren method, where 0·4 ml of a 3 per cent sodium citrate solution is used for the anti-coagulant and a different size tube is used.

Normal Readings

	Men	*Women*
Wintrobe	0 to 9 mm	0 to 20 mm in 1 hr
Westergren	3 to 5 mm	4 to 7 mm in 1 hr

Bone Marrow Specimens

Samples of bone marrow may be required in cases of pernicious anaemia and leukaemia. These are obtained by puncturing the manubrium sterni or the iliac crest (see Chapter 22), and aspirating the bone marrow.

Plasma Proteins

Disturbances of the serum proteins occur in many conditions. Abnormally low levels of serum albumin may give rise to oedema and may be the result of liver diseases, loss of albumin in the urine in the nephrotic syndrome or a diet deficient in proteins.

Serum protein levels are often low in patients with chronic infections or extensive burns.

Microbiological Examinations

In many conditions specimens are required for microbiological examination in order to identify the microorganism responsible.

Materials required for such examinations include:

Throat and nose swabs.

Swabs from wounds.
Sputum.
Urine.
Faeces.
Blood.
Pleural and ascitic fluid.
Cerebrospinal fluid.

These specimens must always be collected under strict aseptic conditions and in sterile containers. When taking swabs for bacteriological examination care must be taken to ensure that no antiseptic is applied to the surface for several hours prior to the swabbing. If the patient is under treatment by any chemotherapeutic agent at the time this should be stated.

Specimens will be examined by direct smear and by culture; information can also be obtained with regard to the sensitivity of organisms to the various antibiotics.

Swabs from the Throat and Nose, Wound Swabs

The necessary apparatus ready sterilized is usually obtained from the laboratory and consists of a swab fixed to a short stiff wire or stick, placed inside a test tube and sterilized. For nasopharyngeal examination special swabs in curved glass containers for passing behind the soft palate are supplied.

No antiseptic lotions should be used for swabbing or for gargles for four hours before the swab is taken.

Sputum

The best method is for the patient to expectorate directly into a sterile flask or small container with a screw lid.

Urine

A catheter specimen of urine or a 'clean' specimen collected in a sterile container is usually required (see Chapter 9).

Twenty-Four-Hour Urine Specimens

These may be needed for estimation of the amount of certain hormones being excreted in metabolized forms.

Twenty-four-hour urine specimens are usually started at 08.00 hours. The patient is asked to empty his bladder at this time and the urine is then discarded. All urine passed during the next 24 hr is put into a clean container provided by the laboratory. At 08.00 hours, 24 hr later the patient again passes urine. This is added to the collection which is now complete and should be accurately labelled and sent to the laboratory with a request form.

Faeces

A freshly passed stool uncontaminated by urine, is required. The specimen is placed in a container which should have a small scoop incorporated in the stopper.

Cerebrospinal Fluid

For complete routine examination 10 to 20 ml of cerebrospinal fluid should be sent to the laboratory. The fluid is collected by lumbar puncture (see Chapter 22).

Serous Fluids

Pleural effusions, pericardial effusions and ascitic fluid are formed in a number of conditions.

Microscopic, bacteriological and chemical investigations of these fluids are used to determine the nature of the underlying disorder.

Cell content. In transudates only a small number of cells is present. In pyogenic infections pus cells are present in large numbers, while in tuberculous infection there is a high percentage of lymphocytes. Red blood cells are often present in malignant disease.

Bacteriological investigations. In infective conditions culture for pyogenic organisms or the *Mycobacterium tuberculosis* may reveal the organism responsible for the infection. For the detection of tuberculous infection the fluid may be injected into guinea pigs.

Chemical examinations. The protein content is increased in infective conditions, but may also be raised to a lesser extent in transudates.

Specimens of Tissues for Histological Examination

Specimens removed at operations should be sent to the laboratory as soon as possible.

Small fragments such as scrapings should not be allowed to become dried.

If the specimen cannot be despatched at once it should be placed for the time in a solution of 10 per cent formalin in normal saline. Surgical or methylated spirit should not be used.

If sent through the post the nature of the contents should be stated on the label (i.e. material for clinical examination) and the parcel marked URGENT. There are special regulations relating to the despatch of specimens through the post, and special containers must be used.

Tests of Gastric Function

Tests of gastric function are used to estimate the hydrochloric acid in the gastric juice and also the amount of residual gastric contents after 12 hr fasting.

Aspiration of Gastric Residuum ('Resting Juice')

This test is carried out in the early morning after the patient has fasted for 12 hr. A Ryle's or Rehfuss's tube is passed (see Chapter 6) and the entire contents of the stomach are aspirated, measured and saved. Gastric contents are aspirated at 10- or 15-min intervals over a stated period, e.g. 1 hr. The fluid aspirated on each occasion is placed in a labelled test tube; each test tube is numbered consecutively. A hypodermic injection of histamine, 0·3 to 0·8 mg, may be ordered. Histamine stimulates secretion of hydrochloric acid, but in some types of anaemia there is no response to histamine. The patient's blood pressure should be recorded before the histamine is given. An anti-histamine and adrenaline should be available and careful observation of the patient should be carried out after the histamine has been administered.

'Tubeless' Test for Hydrochloric Acid

This test depends on the hydrochloric acid in the gastric juice effecting an exchange of hydrogen ions with a dye, azure A, contained in the test substance. Azure A resin (Diagnex) is absorbed and excreted in the urine.

No preparations containing aluminium, iron or magnesium may be given for at least 24 hr prior to the test; the patient fasts for 12 hr before the test begins and nothing but water may be given by mouth until the test is completed.

Procedure

06.00 hours

The patient empties his bladder; this urine is discarded. He then swallows two capsules of a gastric stimulant, caffeine sodium benzoate, with a glass of water.

06.45 hours

If ordered a hypodermic injection of histamine is given.

07.00 hours

The patient empties his bladder, the entire amount of urine is saved for the laboratory and labelled 'control urine'. The patient is given the Diagnex blue granules suspended in 60 ml of water. The granules do not dissolve and the patient is instructed that they must be swallowed and not chewed. A further 60 ml of water is given in the same glass to ensure that no granules are left.

09.00 hours

The patient empties his bladder and the entire amount of urine is sent to the laboratory labelled 'test urine'.

The directions issued by the laboratory should be carefully followed and the timing must be accurate; if a repeat test has to be done at least a week must elapse before the second test. The patient will continue to pass blue or green urine for some days.

Fractional Test Meal

The preparation of the patient is the same as for the gastric residuum test. A series of specimen bottles or test tubes, one marked 'R J' (resting juice) and the remainder numbered from 1 to 12, will be needed. An intragastric tube is passed and the resting juice is aspirated, measured and saved. With the tube in position, *either* the patient is given a meal consisting of gruel made by boiling 60 g (2 oz.) of fine oatmeal with 1 litre (1 quart) of water until the volume is reduced to 0·5 litre (1 pint); *or* alcohol (200 ml of 5 per cent or 100 ml of 7 per cent alcohol) is injected down the tube.

At the end of 15 min the first sample of gastric contents is aspirated (5 to 10 ml is sufficient), thereafter a sample is aspirated every 15 min until no material can be obtained. This procedure will take 2 to 3 hr. Each sample is placed in a numbered test tube specimen bottle and the whole series, with the resting juice, is sent to the laboratory.

During the process the intragastric tube may become blocked; it can be cleared by pumping a little air down, using the aspirating syringe. The syringe should be rinsed after collecting each specimen. In the intervals the tube should be clipped and may be fastened to a towel round the patient's neck. If the patient is salivating freely he should be told not to swallow the saliva, but to spit it out into a receiver; he should be given paper handkerchiefs, or pieces of old linen, to wipe his mouth. This is a long and rather tedious process for the patient and he may be kept occupied by acting as time-keeper and given a bell to ring every 15 min. Make sure that the patient gets his breakfast at the earliest possible moment after completion of the test.

Examinations of Faeces

Occult Blood

Meat, extracts and soups and very green vegetables, e.g. spinach, should be withheld for 3 days before collecting faeces for this examination; the administration of a purgative on the first of these days is recommended. Patient should not brush his teeth if this is liable to cause bleeding of the gums, but may use a moistened swab and a mouth wash. A sample of 15 to 30 g ($\frac{1}{2}$ to 1 oz.) of faeces is required.

The report states the result of the benzidene or guaiac test, a positive test indicates the presence of blood.

A quick test for the detection of blood in faeces is 'Hematest'. A thin smear of faeces is placed on the test paper provided, one 'Hematest' tablet in the middle of the smear and two drops of water added. A positive result is shown by a diffuse area of blue colour developing around the tablet within 2 min.

Analysis of Faeces for Fat

It is of the greatest importance to inspect specimens of faeces before submitting them for quantitative analysis. The highly fluid stools obtained by means of purgatives and enemas are useless, as also are specimens which are non-homogeneous, unless these are thoroughly mixed to uniform consistency before sending the sample for analysis. It scarcely need be said that oily purgatives and liquid paraffin must not be used for several days before a specimen is sent for fat estimation. On occasions when the whole stool cannot conveniently be forwarded, the material available must be mixed to a uniform consistency and a 30-g (1-oz.) sample sent in an airtight container.

The report states the percentage of water present, the percentage of the total solids which consists of fat (i.e. neutral fat, fatty acid and fatty acid as soap) and the percentage of the total unsplit fat.

Fat Balance Test

The patient is given a standard diet, containing 50 g fat per day during the test and for at least 48 hr prior to its commencement. It is important that all the food should be eaten, but if any is left it should be returned to the diet kitchen. Liquid paraffin and oily drugs must not be given during the test, or for at least 3 days prior to its commencement.

Procedure

07.00 hours
   1st day. The patient is given two capsules of carmine (i.e. 1·0 g) on an empty stomach.
07.00 hours
   6th day. The patient is given 60 g (about 2 oz.) of charcoal water (i.e. 120 hr later).

Collection of faeces. The stools are examined as passed and those coloured by carmine are saved, as are subsequent stools until the charcoal appears; stools containing charcoal are discarded. The stools are collected in a sheet of cellophane placed in a bedpan and covering the rim. The edges of the sheet are brought together and the whole stool in the cellophane wrapping is deposited in a large waterproof container.

In place of the full fat balance test, fat excretion on a normal diet may be measured over a period of several days. Normally, 91 to 99 per cent of the ingested fat is absorbed.

Pancreatic Function

The internal secretion of the pancreas, insulin, is disturbed in diabetes mellitus, but is not usually affected by other diseases of the pancreas unless the organ has been extensively destroyed. This aspect of pancreatic function is considered under 'Carbohydrate Metabolism' on pp. 291 to 292.

The external secretions of the pancreas may be tested either by estimating the amylase content of the blood or urine or by analyses of the duodenal contents for pancreatic enzymes and bicarbonates.

Urinary Amylase

A 30 g (1 oz.) sample from a specimen of urine collected over several hours is desirable. When, however, it is a matter of urgency, as for example for the confirmation of a diagnosis of acute pancreatitis, examination of a smaller casual specimen is permissible. If the urine has to be sent some distance to the laboratory it should be preserved with benzene.

The normal range of urinary amylase is from 6 to 30 units per ml. A value of 200 or more units in a patient with acute abdominal signs is almost certainly due to acute pancreatitis. Intermediate values between 30 and 200, if found regularly may indicate pancreatic duct obstruction.

Duodenal Drainage

A more detailed examination of the pancreatic function may be carried out by examination of the duodenal juice obtained by duodenal drainage. A weighted tube (Rehfuss duodenal tube) is passed into the stomach and a specimen of gastric juice is withdrawn. The patient then lies on his right side to promote the passage of the tube into the duodenum. If necessary the position of the tube can be checked by X-ray. When the tube is in the duodenum the contents are aspirated and tested for sodium bicarbonate and the pancreatic enzymes, trypsin, amylase and lipase. Pancreatic secretion may be stimulated by a hypodermic injection of Mecholyl, or an intravenous injection of Secretin.

Liver Function

Tests of liver function are less satisfactory than function tests of some other organs because the liver has numerous functions, any single one of which may be deficient, whilst the others remain relatively intact. Also the liver has a large reserve and has to be very extensively damaged before any of the tests show an abnormal result. No test has yet been devised which tests the liver as a whole, but there are innumerable tests which depend on the different individual functions of the organ. The commonest of these tests are given below.

Bile Pigments

Failure of the liver to excrete bile pigments leads to the accumulation of these in the blood and their excretion in the urine.

Bilirubin. The normal level of bilirubin in the blood serum varies from 0·2 to 0·75 mg per 100 ml. Increased serum bilirubin is found in liver damage, obstructive jaundice and haemolytic jaundice.

Bilirubin will be present in the urine in all cases of jaundice except haemolytic jaundice.

Urobilinogen. This pigment will be present in the urine in cases of incomplete obstructive jaundice, in diffuse liver damage, for example infective hepatitis and in haemolytic jaundice. In cases of complete obstructive jaundice urobilinogen is absent from the urine.

(For urine tests for bile pigments see p. 166.)

Serum Protein Tests

These tests are designed to show variations from the normal ability of the liver to synthesize serum proteins. They are not specific tests for liver damage since alterations in the serum proteins may be found in many other diseases.

In liver diseases the serum albumin level is low and the serum globulin is raised. The abnormal composition of the serum proteins is also reflected in the so-called 'empirical liver function tests', for example the thymol turbidity and cephalin-cholesterol tests. These become positive when liver function is impaired, e.g. in cirrhosis of the liver and infective hepatitis.

Not less than 5 ml of whole blood is required for each of these tests.

Measurements of serum enzymes, released from liver cells, gives information of any damage to liver cells. It is not a specific test of liver damage, however, since many of these enzymes are also released from other damaged tissue cells, especially in cardiac infarction (see 'Blood Tests', p. 280).

Prothrombin Concentration Test

Prothrombin is formed in the liver from vitamin K absorbed from the intestine. A low prothrombin may be due to liver damage, or to the non-absorption of vitamin K resulting from biliary obstruction. If the prothrombin concentration is low, the test may be repeated after an injection of vitamin K, and if it then returns to normal it is suggestive of biliary obstruction.

Liver Biopsy

This method of examination is described on p. 264.

Renal Function

Chemical and microscopic examination of the urine, although valuable, gives only limited information as to the condition of the kidneys. Proteinuria, for example, may be met with apart from any nephritic condition, and in nephritis it is not always possible to form an opinion merely from a simple chemical urinary examination, whether the kidneys are functioning properly. Tests have therefore been devised with the object either of directly estimating renal efficiency or of investigating the severity and following the progress of events in a nephritic lesion.

Blood Urea Estimation

Procedure. Breakfast may or may not be taken according to instructions.

Eight millilitres of blood are collected from a vein into a tube containing potassium oxalate to prevent coagulation.

If this test is done in conjunction with a urea concentration test the blood must be taken before the urea is given.

The normal range of variation of blood urea is from 20 to 40 mg per 100 ml. Some authorities allow up to 60 mg in elderly patients. Very high results of 100 mg or more nearly always indicate serious renal impairment.

Urea Concentration Test (Maclean)

The intake of fluids should be restricted as much as possible from the afternoon preceding the test. No breakfast is given on the morning of the test.

The object of the test is to estimate the amount of urea excreted in the urine after giving a known quantity of urea by mouth.

A sample of blood for urea estimation is taken first. The patient is given 15 g urea dissolved in 60 to 100 ml of water.

The patient passes urine 1, 2, 3 and sometimes 4 hr, after taking the urea. The total amount of urine passed on each occasion is sent to the laboratory in bottles marked, '1', '2', '3' and, if required, '4'.

Some authorities prefer to discard the urine passed during the first hour after the urea is given and consider only the results for the second, third and fourth hours.

A figure of 2 per cent or over in one or more of the hour specimens is regarded as evidence of satisfactory renal function. Diuresis sometimes prevents this concentration being reached and if the volume exceeds 113·4 g (4 oz.) (about 120 ml) a concentration of urea below 2 per cent does not necessarily indicate poor function. The restriction of fluids is designed to prevent diuresis and ignoring the first hour specimen (in which diuresis is often most marked) also aims at overcoming this difficulty.

Urea Clearance Test

The aim of this test is to estimate the efficiency of kidney function in relation to the average normal function.

Two methods are used, one without and one with urea, the idea of the latter being to impose a load on the kidneys to provoke maximum efficiency. The need for this is denied by some authorities.

At a stated time, e.g. 08.00 or 09.00 hours, the patient empties the bladder. The whole amount of urine is placed in a bottle and marked '1'. A sample of blood is then taken for urea estimation.

If urea by mouth is ordered, this is now given.

One hour after the first urine has been passed the patient again empties his bladder and the whole amount is placed in a bottle marked '2'.

Tests for Carbohydrate Metabolism

Tests of carbohydrate metabolism are mainly used where diabetes is suspected or to check the diet and insulin dosage in patients with established diabetes.

Estimation of Blood Sugar

The specimen of blood is taken in the early morning before breakfast; 0·5 ml of blood is collected into a tube containing a preservative mixture of sodium fluoride and thymol.

Where repeated estimations are required for a diabetic patient, all blood samples should be collected at the same time each day, the actual time being related to insulin administration and meals.

Normal fasting blood sugar levels are between 80 and 120 mg of glucose per 100 ml of blood.

Glucose Tolerance Test

If at all possible, the test should be carried out in the morning before food is taken. Smoking is forbidden. The patient empties his bladder; a specimen of this urine is saved and labelled with the time of collection and the date.

Fifty grams of glucose in 100 ml of water is given by mouth (the quantity will be less for a child, depending on age).

At $\frac{1}{2}$-hourly intervals thereafter five more samples of blood are collected.

One and 2 hr after taking the glucose solution the patient empties his bladder. These specimens are labelled with the time of collection.

The normal effect of a large dose of sugar is to raise the blood sugar level in the first hour, but this returns to fasting level in 2 hr and no glucose appears in the urine. The diabetic patient may or may not have a raised blood sugar level before taking the glucose solution; after taking it his blood sugar will rise to above 180 mg per 100 ml and will remain above the fasting level for more than 2 hr. Although in the majority of cases glucose will not be present in the first specimen of urine, it will appear in the second and third specimens. Some people have a low renal threshold for glucose and in these cases glucose will appear in the urine after drinking the glucose solution, although the blood sugar remains within the normal range.

Calcium Metabolism

The commoner causes of disturbed calcium metabolism are diseases of the parathyroid glands and failure of absorption of calcium due to steatorrhoea or vitamin D deficiency and chronic renal disease.

In the condition of hyperparathyroidism due to tumours of the parathyroid glands calcium is lost from the bones leading to osteomalacia and a raised serum calcium level. In these cases the blood phosphorus is low and the alkaline phosphatase level in the blood is raised. In tetany due to absence of the parathyroid hormone blood calcium is low.

In steatorrhoea there is failure of absorption of calcium from the gut which gives rise to low blood calcium and osteomalacia.

The administration of vitamin D aids calcium absorption, but excessive dosage can cause a raised level of the blood calcium.

Laboratory tests used in disordered calcium metabolism include the following:

(1) Estimation of the blood calcium.
(2) Estimation of the blood phosphorus.
(3) Estimation of the blood alkaline phosphatase.
(4) Calcium balance estimation.

This latter test involves a somewhat complicated routine as detailed in the following instructions.

Calcium Balance Routine

The patient is on a weighed and analysed diet. The tray is delivered to the patient and collected by the dietitian, who weighs any uneaten food. The diet is the same throughout the test. Nothing extra is allowed.

The water is distilled for drinking. As much as the patient likes may be given. All food is cooked in distilled water in utensils kept solely for this purpose. No toothpaste may be used, distilled water mouthwashes are substituted.

The patient is on this routine for 6 days before collections are begun. This is the equilibrium period during which time small alterations may be made in the diet to suit the patient's taste.

At 06.00 hours on the first day of the specimen collection, the patient empties the bladder. This urine is rejected. All subsequent specimens are collected in 24-hourly bottles, the last specimen of each 24 hr being obtained at 06.00 hours after which a new bottle is begun. Each bottle contains 10 ml toluol to preserve the urine.

The evening before the start of the collections a carmine cachet is given to colour the faeces. This is given the evening before the end of each balance period. Following this all stools are saved in individual containers and the balance periods are considered to be from the end of the marked (red) stool to the end of the second marked stool.

Urine and faeces must be collected separately. The bedpan is rinsed in distilled water before being used by patient. After use it is cleaned in the normal way and rinsed in distilled water again. All the faeces passed must be saved. The bedpan is lined with cellophane to facilitate this.

No drugs may be given unless charted. All drugs given must be analysed. The advisability of giving any drug should be checked before administration.

This routine may be modified to allow balance tests on other substances to be carried out.

Phosphatase

Two forms of phosphatase enzyme are present in blood serum, the alkaline and the acid. The former is increased in bone diseases, such as hyperparathyroidism bone tumours and Paget's disease; the latter is frequently increased in carcinoma of the prostate gland with secondary deposits. The laboratory should be told which form is required when sending the specimen.

Either form of phosphatase can be determined on the serum obtained from 5 to 6 ml of blood. The normal ranges vary with the method used for determination, and information will be given by the laboratory.

Tests of Thyroid Gland Function

Basal Metabolic Rate (BMR)

At complete physical and mental rest a healthy individual consumes a given volume of oxygen per minute, the actual amount depending mainly on the sex, age, height and weight.

During the test the patient lies quietly on a bed and breathes through wide rubber tubes into a special apparatus which records the respirations over a measured period of time, usually 6 min and collects the expired air.

From the recording so made the volume of oxygen used by the patient can be measured. This is compared with the volume used by a normal subject of the same sex, age, height and weight.

Endocrine disorders, more especially those involving the thyroid and pituitary, profoundly alter this basal metabolic rate, and hence its determination is not infrequently of considerable value in detecting the existence and assessing the severity of these conditions.

The BMR is considered normal if the figure obtained is within -10 to $+15$ per cent of the value predicted for the individual in question. Success depends almost entirely on the patient being perfectly quiet and at ease; he must go without breakfast and should relax completely for about $\frac{1}{2}$ hr before the test is begun. This must be achieved without fuss about the test itself. In order to allay apprehension the simple nature of the procedure and its object should be explained, or, better still, demonstrated beforehand.

Radioactive Iodine

A tracer dose of radioactive iodine (^{131}I) is given orally or occasionally intravenously, and the amount of 'take up', or concentration of the radioactive material by the thyroid gland, is recorded by a Geiger counter sited over the thyroid area.

The results of the test may be invalidated if the patient is given radiological contrast media or food containing iodine, such as fish, thyroid preparations, perchlorates or thiocyanates, or radioactive isotopes. Some of these preparations may affect the result of the test even if a considerable time elapses between their discontinuation and the test, as for example Lugol's iodine and X-ray contrast media; it is therefore advisable to have an interval of 4 weeks if at all possible before carrying out the test.

The following instructions are usually given to the patient:

(1) No fish should be eaten for at least 2 days before coming for this test.

(2) Iodized throat tablets, cough linctus and any proprietary food said to have a high iodine content should also be avoided. If these have been taken during the past month, will you please inform the department at the time of making the appointment.

(3) A light breakfast may be taken on the morning of test.

Normal Blood Count Values

Red Cells, per mm^3

Men	4·5 to 6 $\times$ 10^6
Women	4·3 to 5·5 $\times$ 10^6

Haemoglobin, in grams per 100 ml

Men   15 to 16
Women   13 to 15

White Cells, per mm^3

5000 to 10 000
Neutrophils   40 to 60 per cent
Lymphocytes   20 to 40 per cent
Monocytes   4 to 8 per cent
Eosinophils   1 to 3 per cent
Basophils   0 to 1 per cent

Platelets, per mm^3

200 000 to 500 000

25

Some diagnostic procedures

SOME body tissues (bone for example) have a greater density than others, and throw a shadow on X-ray which allows their structure to be seen. Air and other gases, which are less dense than body tissue, also show up on X-ray. So when present within an organ may show up that organ. Air, present within the lungs enables X-rays of the chest to be helpful in diagnosing disorders of the lungs and heart. Where tissues are of a uniform density, however, an individual tissue cannot be seen on X-ray and some kind of 'contrast' medium may have to be used to outline the organ. Contrast media usually contain iodine, but barium or air may be used for this purpose.

Straight X-rays

X-rays in which no contrast medium is introduced are called straight X-rays, and are useful mainly in examination of bony structures; to show up thoracic structures, and to examine the abdomen since there may be gas present in the intestine. Any structure in which calcification has taken place will also show up on straight X-ray. Thus, gall stones, or kidney stones may be seen, or the pineal body in an adult, when straight skull X-rays are taken. A great deal of information can be obtained from a straight X-ray by a radiologist who is trained to identify structures and their abnormalities.

If a patient is sent for X-ray, he should be informed of what is involved, since for some X-rays unusual positions may be demanded of him. Ill, unconscious and nervous adults should be accompanied by a nurse, and children must always be accompanied, preferably by their mothers.

Metal objects, such as brassiere fastenings, buttons, hair grips, zips, show up on X-ray, so the part to be X-rayed must be free of these objects. It is far more satisfactory if a patient wears a plain cotton gown or pyjamas with tapes to fasten them. Elastoplast, kaolin and plaster of Paris show up on X-ray.

Special X-rays

These are X-rays in which some contrast media is used. Preparation of the patient before the X-ray, or special nursing care or observation afterwards, may be necessary. Since preparation and after care may vary in detail in different hospitals, only a broad outline is given below.

Examination of the Renal Tract

There are two ways in which contrast medium may be introduced into the renal tract:

By intravenous injection (intravenous pyelogram). The iodine compound is excreted from the blood by the kidney and provided the kidney is functioning normally the contrast medium becomes concentrated in the urine, outlining the renal tract. It can be seen that some indication of renal function as well as structural detail is obtained by this method.

By retrograde pyelogram. A cystoscope is passed into the bladder, and a catheter is passed into the ureter of the kidney to be examined. The opaque medium is then injected through this ureteric catheter into the kidney.

Preparation for Renal X-ray

Faeces, or gas, in the intestine obscure the kidney shadow, so the aim of preparation is to prevent either from accumulating. An aperient such as Dulcolax is given 48 to 36 hr before the X-ray is due, and the diet should be adjusted to avoid flatus or bulk-producing foods. (A low residue diet is given.) If at all possible the patient should be walking about as this helps peristalsis. No food or drink should be given from midnight on the day of the X-ray. Charcoal biscuits may be given to absorb any flatus or an injection of 'Pituitrin' may be ordered $\frac{1}{2}$ hr before the X-ray to help the expulsion of flatus. There is no special care after the X-ray.

Examination of the Gall Bladder

Cholecystogram

An opaque medium taken by mouth is absorbed from the intestinal tract and becomes concentrated in the gall bladder, outlining it on X-ray. As with renal X-rays, the gall bladder picture can become obscured if faeces or flatus are present in the intestine. Thus an aperient and a low residue diet is given, as described above. The evening before the X-ray the prescribed radio-opaque substance is given orally to the patient, and following this he should either have nothing by mouth until the X-rays are taken, or water only may be given. When a picture of the gall bladder has been obtained, a fatty meal, or drink, may be given in X-ray to stimulate the emptying of the gall bladder, before further films are taken.

Angiography of Gall Bladder and Bile Ducts

Intravenous biligrafin may be given to be concentrated in the bile to outline the gall bladder. The preparation for this is exactly as for cholecystogram except that the oral dose of contrast medium is omitted.

If the bile ducts are to be outlined after the gall bladder has been removed, the investigation is called a cholangiogram, and the procedure is as for cholecystography, but no fatty meal is given in X-ray.

Biligrafin may be injected into the T-tube inserted into the common bile duct at cholecystectomy before the T-tube is removed, about 12 to 14 days postoperatively. The only preparation here is that the T-tube is usually clamped some hours before the injection is made and X-ray pictures are taken.

Examination of the Alimentary Tract

The opaque medium used for outlining the alimentary tract is barium sulphate and this may be given orally as a suspension (barium meal) or rectally (barium enema).

Barium Meal

Medicines containing bismuth must be omitted for 3 days before the X-ray and no aperient should be given within 24 hr of the X-ray.

Nothing should be given by mouth for 6 hr prior to the barium meal. When once the barium has been drunk, its progress through the alimentary tract may be followed by taking X-rays at intervals. This is one-X-ray examination in which the patient may be tipped into odd positions, and he should be warned about this. Food is allowed when once the stomach is empty of barium, but aperients, antacids and enemas must be avoided until the X-ray films are complete.

Barium Enema

The bowel should be empty for this examination. A faecal softener may be administered by mouth, some days before the X-ray, and this is followed by a mild aperient, such as Dulcolax. A low residue diet is given. The evening before the X-ray, an evacuant enema is administered and this is followed by a rectal washout in the morning, before the patient goes to X-ray. Barium sulphate solution is administered as a retention enema in X-ray. Obviously careful explanations must be given to the patient.

Examination of the Bronchi

By injecting opaque medium into the respiratory tract, the bronchi and their branches are outlined on X-ray. The X-ray medium may be inserted over the back of the throat, or by means of a broncho-scope.

Preparation of the patient includes intensive chest physiotherapy and starving him for the 6 hr immediately before the X-ray to prevent vomiting. A mild sedative and a drug which will inhibit bronchial secretions may be given within 1 hr of the examination. A local anaesthetic will be given to the throat, so the patient must not be allowed to eat and drink until the effects of this have worn off after the X-ray (i.e. not until the cough reflex returns).

Intensive chest physiotherapy must be given after the X-ray to remove the contrast medium from the respiratory tract.

Salpingography

The aim is to outline the Fallopian tubes to show up any stenosis of the tubes which might be a cause of sterility. The medium is injected into the uterus, and from there it gets into the Fallopian tubes. Both bowel and bladder should be empty at the time of the injection. So an aperient may be given 36 hr before the X-ray, and the patient should empty her bladder at the last minute. Further X-rays are taken 24 hr after the injection, and no aperient or enema should be given in the interval.

Examination of the Central Nervous System

Ventriculography

Air is inserted into the lateral ventricles of the brain. By careful positioning of the patient on the X-ray table the air can be made to show the shape and position of the lateral and third ventricles. In order to inject the air into the ventricles, burr holes must be made in the skull in the post-parietal region. This involves an operation which may be carried out under local or general anaesthetic. Preoperatively the post-parietal scalp area must be shaved, and the patient is prepared as for a general anaesthetic even if the procedure is to be done under a local anaesthetic, since operation may be urgent if the films show up some abnormality. After ventriculography, the patient must be observed carefully, particular note being taken of conscious level, limb movements, pupillary reflexes, pulse rate, respiratory rate and blood pressure.

Lumbar Air Encephalography

Air may be inserted into the ventricular system of the brain by means of a lumbar puncture. This latter is carried out with the patient in a sitting position and under a general anaesthetic. When once the air has been injected into the lumbar subarachnoid space it rises within the cerebro-spinal fluid and by manipulation of the patient's position can be made to enter the ventricular system. This method outlines the 4th and 3rd ventricles particularly well. Lumbar puncture might be dangerous in the presence of increased intracranial pressure, when ventriculography would be the method of choice.

For lumbar air encephalography, the patient is prepared as for a general anaesthetic. Afterwards the patient must be carefully observed as after ventriculography. Headache may be severe, and can be relieved by analgesics, fluids and keeping the patient lying flat.

Myelography

An oily, radio-opaque substance, Myodil, is injected into the lumbar subarachnoid space, by means of a lumbar puncture. Careful positioning of the patient enables it to run to any particular area of thoracic or lumbar subarachnoid space, outlining any abnormality. No special preparation of the patient is required, apart from careful explanation.

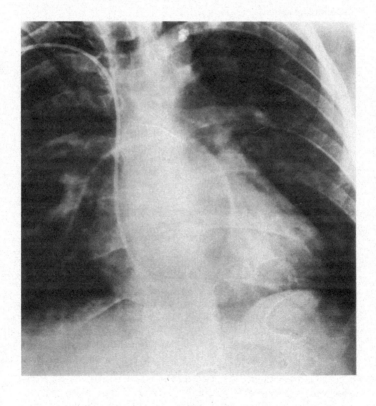

FIG. 70. Cardiac catheterization of the normal heart.

Examination of the Cardiovascular System

Cardiac Catheterization

This is carried out to measure the blood pressure in the chambers of the heart, and to withdraw samples of blood from the chambers to estimate its oxygen content. Defects of the heart can be shown, using this technique. A long opaque catheter is introduced into a vein in the right arm and is passed through the venous system into the right atrium, right ventricle, and pulmonary artery. Its progress can be watched on a television screen (Figs 70 and 71).

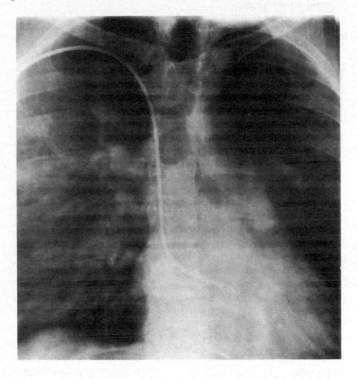

FIG. 71. Cardiac catheterization of heart with atrial septal defect.

Angiography

A radio-opaque dye is injected through the cardiac catheter.

No special preparation of the patient is needed. An adult is given a sedative before going to X-ray. A child may require a general anaesthetic.

Arteriography

An opaque medium is injected directly into arteries to outline the arterial wall, or the blood supply to a particular area.

Femoral Arteriography

This may be used to outline the blood supply to the lower limbs, the placenta or the kidneys (Fig. 72). The investigation is carried

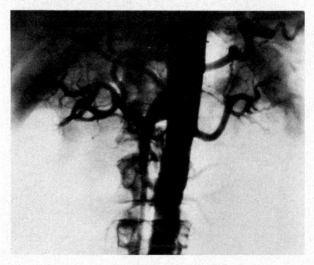

FIG. 72. Renal arteriogram.

out under general anaesthetic and the patient must be prepared accordingly. The area near the femoral artery must be shaved (pubic shave). A guide wire is introduced into the artery and a catheter is fed over it to the required position. When the guide wire has been withdrawn, the catheter can be used to inject the contrast medium.

Carotid Arteriography

This is used to demonstrate the cerebral blood vessels and is carried out under general anaesthetic. If it should be carried out under local anaesthetic, sedative drugs are given to the patient beforehand (Fig. 73). After the investigation, the site of injection

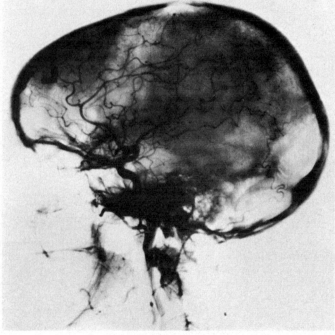

FIG. 73. Carotid arteriogram.

in the neck must be observed carefully to note any haematoma formation which could lead to asphyxia. If this should happen a tracheostomy would be required as an emergency. The patient's conscious level, limb movements, pupillary reflexes, pulse rate, respiratory rate and blood pressure must be observed as well.

Subclavian Arteriography

This procedure is used to outline intracranial blood vessels supplied by the vertebral arteries. It is carried out under general anaesthetic. Postoperatively the patient must be observed as described above, but it is particularly important to watch for signs of respiratory distress, since the subclavian artery is very near to the pleural cavity.

26

The medical use of ionizing radiation

X-RAYS and radioactive materials are used in medical science both as an aid to diagnosis, and in the treatment of disease. Radioactive materials emit γ-rays (which are very similar to X-rays), and they also emit subatomic particles. X-rays, γ-rays and subatomic particles have similar effects to one another upon biological tissues, X-ray plates and other matter through which they penetrate.

Their effect upon the molecules comprising gases through which they penetrate gives these radiations the name *ionizing radiation* since they convert molecules with which they collide into ions of gas. An ion is an electrically charged molecule.

The effect upon an X-ray plate is to blacken the photographic emulsion; thus any matter which obstructs their passage shows as a light area, whilst a black area indicates that the radiations have passed unobstructed to the plate.

Ionizing radiation has an effect on certain inorganic crystals causing them to emit light. This principle is used in scintillation counters, and in 'scanning' an organ, following the use of diagnostic doses of radioactive isotopes.

Damage to developing biological cells which can be caused by radiation, depends upon several factors:

(1) The intensity of the radiation.

(2) The rate at which the radiation decreases in intensity. (This is usually determined in the case of radioactive isotopes by means of their 'half-life'. The half-life of an isotope is the time it takes to decay to half its original activity.)

(3) The penetrating power of the radiation.

(4) In the case of radioactive material taken into the body the rate at which it is excreted from the body is important.

(5) When the source of the radiation is outside the body, the tissue must be in the path of the radiation to be affected by it. In

general the greater the distance from the source the less the radiation to which an individual is subjected. As far as the biological effects of radiation is concerned, the effects on both staff and patients must be considered.

The Uses of Ionizing Radiation

X-rays are used in low doses and short exposure times for diagnostic purposes. By passing the rays through a part of the body on to an X-ray plate; an X-ray film of the part can be developed. X-rays are also used in high doses for treatment. The rays are focussed so that their maximum effect occurs at the affected organ or tissue. Radioactive isotopes may also be used as an aid to diagnosis. A suitable preparation of an isotope is ingested by the patient in a carefully calculated tracer dose. Its presence and its approximate concentration in a tissue or organ can be detected later by means of a scan. Radioactive substances may be placed within the body in therapeutic doses so that an effect upon the disordered tissue occurs. An example of this is the insertion of radium into the vagina in the treatment of carcinoma of the uterus.

Whenever patients are exposed to ionizing radiation, it is done under carefully controlled conditions, so that there is no danger of any untoward effects upon them. It is possible, however, for staff to be exposed to radioactivity accidentally, unless simple precautions for their safety are observed.

Protection of Nursing Staff

Radioactive sources within a hospital are shielded by means of concrete or lead, which absorb radiation. Both the X-ray and radiotherapy departments are constructed of protective materials, and radium and other radioactive sources are carefully shielded.

Staff are normally protected from diagnostic X-rays by protective screens. If a nurse should be required to support a patient, whilst an X-ray is being taken, then she should wear a protective apron and gloves. Protection of staff during the treatment of patients by high doses of radiation from an external source, is ensured by allowing no-one into the treatment room except the patient, whilst the treatment is being given. The source is shielded before staff are allowed to enter the room. When nursing a patient who has been given a therapeutic dose of a radioactive source or in whom a radioactive source has been implanted, the nurse must ensure that she both knows the rules laid down within the hospital for her protection, and follows them.

When nursing a patient who has had radium implanted, the nurse should employ distance and speed in her own protection. This means that whenever a nurse must go to such a patient to carry out a nursing procedure, she should carry it out as quickly as possible, so that she is near the patient for the shortest possible time. Nursing care of the patient should be shared equally amongst all the ward staff so that no one person is continually exposed to the source. The patient will need to have very careful explanation, about the reasons for this before the treatment starts, or he may get extremely depressed about the apparent lack of caring for him on the part of the staff.

When the radium is removed, special long handled forceps are used in its removal. Speed should be employed, and it is rapidly placed into a shielded container. On removal, the number of radium applicators must be carefully checked to ensure that no radium is missing. If such a loss has occurred the hospital procedure for dealing with such a loss must be followed.

In the case of the therapeutic use of radioactive isotopes, the precautions required will vary according to the type of radiation it emits, its half-life, and its rate of excretion from the body. Some of the following precautions may be necessary:

(1) Special care should be taken with excreta from the patient.

(2) Contaminated linen, as when the patient is incontinent, should be handled with special gloves, and kept separately for special laundering.

(3) Any suspected contamination should be reported to the appropriate authority immediately.

(4) It is especially important that a nurse who is nursing such a patient knows the precise instructions given about the nursing of the patient, the precautions to be taken and carries them out meticulously.

Any member of staff who works normally, in a radiotherapy department, X-ray department or on a ward where radium or therapeutic doses of radioactive isotopes are used with any frequency, wears an X-ray film badge during working hours. This blackens on exposure to ionizing radiation, the degree of exposure being indicated by the degree of blackening. This X-ray film badge is developed at set intervals and a record of the indicated dose received by each member of staff is kept. (For further details of safety precautions in hospital, refer to *The Safe Use of Ionizing Radiations*, London: Her Majesty's Stationery Office.)

Radiotherapy

The term 'deep X-ray treatment' implies the use of penetrating X-rays produced by the bombardment of a target by electrons travelling at high speed. The source of the energy required for this is high-voltage electricity, of the order of 180 000 to 2×10^6 V. This form of treatment is frequently used in cases of malignant growth and many such patients are treated by this method, often in conjunction with surgery.

Many require a large dose spread over a period of several weeks in order that a lethal dose can be delivered at the site of the growth without producing either generalized ill-effects or localized damage to the skin and surrounding tissues.

However carefully the scheme of treatment is devised the tissues surrounding the growth are likely to suffer at least some temporary ill-effects and this is especially true of the skin. Therefore great care is required during and for some weeks after the treatment. The skin of the areas treated must not be subjected to any chemical or physical irritants, therefore washing with soap and water, anti-septic lotions, hot or cold applications and the use of adhesive strappings must be avoided. The skin is less affected by the radiation from 'supervoltage' and cobalt units, but in every case the instructions issued by the Radiotherapy Department should be strictly followed. If a male patient is receiving treatment to the face or neck, shaving is usually forbidden for a time and the friction of a closely fitting stiff collar should be avoided. Mucous membrane reacts to radiation in much the same way as skin and some temporary damage to mucus-secreting cells will occur. If the mouth is included in the treatment area there will be a diminution in the secretion of both saliva and mucus. The patient may be very disinclined to eat on account of the discomfort and pain caused by a dry mouth and must be helped and encouraged as much as possible. Frequent non-irritating fluids to drink and frequent mouth washes will help. If the mouth is painful, lozenges containing a local anaesthetic—e.g. benzocaine—may be ordered, or aspirin gargles may give relief.

If an ulcerating malignant growth is being treated, the discharge is likely to be both offensive and profuse, and therefore frequent changes of dressings are necessary.

The patient's blood count is taken daily or at frequent intervals. A falling white cell count may be treated by drugs which increase the production of white cells, e.g. Prednisolone. In some cases radiation treatment may be suspended.

General effects of radiation are not usually marked when divided dosage is used spread over a period of weeks, but were fairly common in the early days of X-ray treatment when a single large dose was used. However, some patients may complain of loss of appetite, nausea, inability to sleep and general depression.

Radium Therapy

Radium is a naturally occurring element which spontaneously emits radiations of short wavelength. Radium is chiefly used in the form of its salt, radium sulphate, and in the form of the emanation or gas (radon) which is given off from it. The salt is placed in needles or sometimes in larger containers and the emanation is collected in radon 'seeds'.

Methods of Application

Surface application. The needles or applicators are embedded in a suitable mould made of Columba paste or Stent's dental composition, or may be attached to sorbo rubber or other suitable material which can be accurately applied to the desired area.

Interstitial irradiation. Needles or radon seeds are inserted into the tissues.

Cavitary irradiation. Applicators are placed inside natural cavities of the body—e.g. the vagina, cervical canal and the body of the uterus.

Rules and Precautions to be Observed in the Handling of Radium

Radium needles or containers, including radon seeds, should never be touched by hand but must always be manipulated with long-handled forceps the handles of which are covered with rubber.

When radium is removed from the safe and carried to and from the theatre a lead-lined box with a long carrying handle should be used for its transport.

The threading of needles and the preparation of applicators must be carried out on a special table provided with a lead screen. Proximity to the radium must be for as short a time as possible.

The time at which the radium treatment is begun and the time at which it is due to be terminated must be carefully noted. The success of the treatment and the safety of the patient depend on careful calculation of the dosage to be employed. The time during which the radium is in contact with the tissues is one factor in these calculations.

Careful checking of the radium is essential. The amount of radium, the number and size of the needles used are entered on a record card; unused containers are checked and returned to the radium safe.

Radioactive Isotopes

Radioactive iodine. This is often used in the treatment of carcinoma of the thyroid gland and thyrotoxicosis. In the latter condition most authorities consider that therapeutic doses of radioactive iodine should not be given to patients under 40 years of age. The radioactive iodine is given by mouth and absorbed into the blood stream from the alimentary tract. From the blood it is deposited in the thyroid gland and there acts as a source of localized radiation.

Radioactive phosphorus. This substance has been found to be effective in the treatment of polycythaemia, a condition in which the blood contains an excessive number of red cells. The phosphorus may be given by mouth or by intravenous injection.

Radioactive cobalt. This has a long 'life' compared with most other radioactive isotopes. It is now being used in place of radium or as an alternative to deep X-ray in a 'bomb' or beam unit in the treatment of malignant disease.

Radioactive gold. This isotope is used locally in the peritoneal or pleural cavities in cases of malignant disease where secondary deposits cause large peritoneal or pleural effusions necessitating frequent aspiration.

Precautions

When patients are receiving doses of radioactive iodine some of the material will be excreted in the urine. Nursing staff dealing with bedpans and urinals should wear protective clothing and rubber gloves. Should there be any suspicion of contamination of the hands or any skin area a thorough washing with soap and water must be immediately carried out. The radioactive urine must not be emptied directly into the sewerage system. The radio-activity, however, rapidly decays (the exact period of time which must elapse before the isotope is inactive varies with the different elements), and after storage for the appropriate length of time the urine can be discarded.

27

Bandaging, splints and traction

BANDAGES

Although a number of methods can be used to secure surgical dressings, there are still occasions when a properly applied bandage is the best way of retaining a dressing in position. Bandages are also used to fix splints, to apply pressure in order to stop bleeding and to give support and prevent swelling, as in the treatment of a sprained ankle.

Types of Bandages

Roller: 4 to 8 yd long, 1 to 6 in. wide. The parts of the bandage are known as the initial end, the drum and the tail.

Triangular: 1 yd² of material cut diagonally makes two bandages.

Many-tailed: tails 4 in. wide, the length varies from 42 to 72 in., width of the back 6 to 8 in. These measurements are for chest and abdominal bandages.

Jaw or four-tailed: 1 yd long, 4 in. wide, before cutting into tails.

Tubular gauze: for limb and head bandages.

Elastic net: can be used to secure dressings in all parts of the body. It is available in many different sizes.

Materials used for Bandages

Open-wove cotton: light and inexpensive, but does not give much support, and the edges fray unless the selvedge edge type is used.

'Kling': open-mesh cotton conforming bandages are very comfortable, light and porous and are particularly suitable for securing dressings on difficult areas, such as the breast and axilla.

Calico: harsh and inelastic, but firm; useful for slings and for applying splints.

Crêpe: comfortable and gives good support, elastic and easy to apply, expensive but washable.

Rules for Applying Roller Bandages (Fig. 74)

Stand in front of the part to be bandaged.
Pad the axilla or groin when bandaging near these parts.
Start with an oblique turn.
Bandage from below upwards, and from within outwards.
Applying the bandage with firm even pressure throughout.
Cover two-thirds of the previous turn of the bandage leaving one-third uncovered.
The drum of the bandage must be held uppermost.
Reverse on the outside of the limb.
Finish with a spiral turn, turning in the end of the bandage and securing it with a safety-pin arranged with point uppermost or with a small strip of adhesive tape.

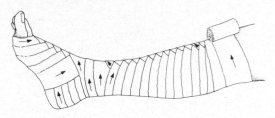

Fig. 74. Applying a roller bandage (figure-of-eight and reversed turn bandaging).

Points to Remember

The comfort of the patient is the first consideration except when arresting haemorrhage or correcting deformity.

Two skin surfaces should not be allowed to lie in contact under the bandage; if this point is not attended to, the skin is liable to become moist and sore.

The position of the part—place the limb in the position in which it can most easily be maintained by the patient without strain.

Neatness and economy of bandage should be considered, but the bandage must fulfil its purpose and must always completely cover the dressing.

Stump Bandaging

The stump is bandaged in order to prevent oedema, to encourage good venous return and tone up flabby tissue, to accustom the stump to being constantly covered, and to prevent an adductor roll of flesh in the groin. Crêpe or Rayolast bandage is used, 6 in. wide for above knee, or 4 in. wide for below knee stumps.

Start by placing the end of the bandage in the centre of the upper side of the stump at the level of the inguinal ligament. Then carry the bandage down and over the stump to the same position on the underside; ask the patient to hold the loops in position with his fingers as shown (Fig. 75). Continue to carry the bandage to

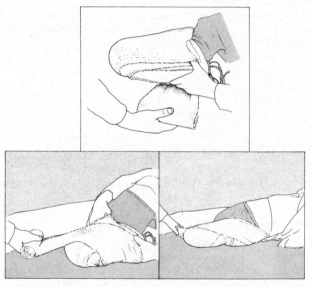

FIG. 75. Different stages in stump bandaging.

and fro over the stump, once covering the lateral side and once on the medial side. Fix the loops with a diagonal turn from the outside top to the inside bottom of the stump, and make a second diagonal turn in the opposite direction. Make straight turns round the stump making sure it passes high into the groin, pass it round the abdomen and cross on the iliac crest. Make sure the stump is not pulled into flexion. The bandage should not be uncomfortably tight but should exert slight tension on the stump.

Tubular Gauze Bandages

Tubular gauze bandages are a comfortable, neat and efficient method of retaining dressings in position. The gauze is made in various dimensions suitable for many purposes. For bandaging limbs wire cage applicators on which the gauze is stretched are used (Fig. 76). The applicator is passed over the part to be bandaged and then withdrawn leaving a layer of gauze covering the area. This procedure is repeated to give as many layers as are necessary covering the part.

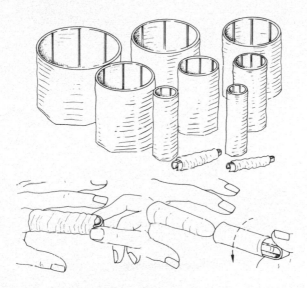

FIG. 76. Tubular gauze bandages. (top) tubular gauze applicators; (bottom left) tubular gauze gathered onto a finger size applicator and placed over the finger; (bottom right) applicator withdrawn and twisted at top of finger.

It is claimed that a great degree of control over the tension of the bandage is possible with this method and also that the bandage will retain its position better than the usual roller bandage. Many casualty departments find that tubular gauze is particularly useful for finger dressings and that the light, neat bandage is greatly appreciated by patients. Tubular gauze also makes a satisfactory and comfortable head bandage.

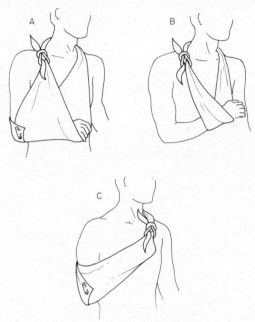

FIG. 77. Arm slings. (A) Large arm sling; (B) narrow arm sling; (C) St John sling.

Triangular Bandages

Triangular calico bandages are used as slings and as first aid bandages. They are also useful for holding dressings in position on areas where roller bandages would be difficult to apply or would be heavy and cumbrous.

Large arm sling (used to support the forearm). Stand in front of the patient. Spread the bandage over the chest, with one end going over the shoulder on the uninjured side, and the other hanging over the abdomen; the point should be beneath the elbow. Place the forearm slightly raised over the middle of the sling; bring the lower end up and tie on the injured shoulder to the other end with a reef knot. Tuck in the ends. Bring the point round to the front of the elbow, fold in neatly and pin (Fig. 77 A).

Narrow arm sling (used to support the wrist). Make a broad fold bandage by bringing the point to the base and folding in two, place one end over the shoulder on uninjured side. Place the wrist on the centre of the broad fold and bring the lower end up to the injured shoulder. Join ends with a reef knot (Fig. 77 B).

St John sling (used when the shoulder is injured and to give support to a fractured clavicle). Place the injured arm across the chest so that the fingers almost touch the opposite shoulder. Place one end of the bandage on the uninjured shoulder so that the point comes well beyond the elbow. Tuck the upper half of the base of the bandage well beneath the forearm and elbow. Carry the lower end across the back and tie the ends on the uninjured shoulder. Tuck the point in between the forearm and the sling. Carry the fold thus made around the outside of the arm and pin firmly to the bandage going up the back (Fig. 77 C).

SPLINTS

Splints are used to immobilize an injured limb, as in the treatment of fractures, or to prevent movement which might interfere with treatment (for example the use of a straight wooden splint to steady an arm or leg during intravenous therapy) and to prevent or to correct deformities. Examples of these two latter uses are splints used to prevent wrist drop or foot drop where muscles are weak or paralysed and splints used to correct talipes ('club foot') in infants.

The commonest form of splinting in general use is the plaster of Paris splint made for the individual patient. Other types of individual splints made of a variety of materials, such as plastics, resins, leather and metal, are mainly used in orthopaedic practice. Two that are frequently used for a number of purposes are the Thomas's splint (Fig. 78) used in conjunction with traction in the treatment

of muslin is unfolded at a time and loosely rolled as the plaster is rubbed into the mesh. It is convenient to run a red thread through the free end of the finished bandage so that the end may be easily found after the bandage has been soaked. Until sufficient experience has been gained in rolling plaster bandages some difficulty may be found in gauging the right amount of dry plaster to impregnate the muslin properly so that it is not, on the one hand, so full of plaster that the centre of the bandage remains dry when it is immersed in water and, on the other hand, so deficient in plaster as to be finally little more than a piece of wet muslin. Another common mistake is to roll the bandages so tightly that the water cannot soak completely through and a considerable portion of the bandage is wasted. A fine quality quick-setting plaster should be used. If it has not been stored in airtight tins it may be lumpy, and in this case should be sieved before use. The finished bandages should also be stored in airtight tins and may with advantage be dried out in a warm oven before being put away.

Application of a Plaster Splint

The nurse will often have to assist in the application of the splint, and in some circumstances may be entrusted with the carrying out of the entire procedure. Plaster bandages should be applied evenly but not tightly and no reverses should be made. The bandages should be folded to bring about a change in the direction of the turn. Plaster sets quickly and the moulding of the casting to the limb should be done during the application of the bandages. 'Moulding' means pressing the plaster into the natural hollow contours of the part to which it is applied so that it fits the part accurately and pressure on bony prominences is as far as possible avoided. Reinforcement of the splint may be carried out by strips of plaster bandage applied up and down the length of the limb and secured by further circular turns. Metal strips or pieces of Cramer's wire splinting are sometimes incorporated in a plaster splint. The finished splint should not be subjected to pressure, as for example by letting the heel of a leg plaster rest on the table, until it has set; this usually takes about 5 min. The limb should be supported on the flat of the hand in order to avoid making indentations in the plaster. Thorough drying of the plaster takes several hours, the time depending on the size and thickness of the plaster.

Plaster slabs are often used for limbs and have the advantages of being quick and simple to make, supplying a well-fitting splint which can be removed for any necessary treatment. The length is marked on a board or table and wet plaster bandages are folded lengthways up and down the marked area on the board until the requisite thickness is obtained. The slab of bandage is applied to the limb, moulded and then removed and trimmed. The splint is kept in place by a roller bandage.

Plaster shells may be used in the treatment of disease or injury of the spine. These are made by immersing long strips of muslin eight folds thick in thin plaster cream. The strips are applied and moulded on the patient's body usually directly on to the skin which may be previously oiled. One pound of dry plaster mixed with one pint of water makes a cream of the right consistency. The shell is removed for drying, trimmed and lined with wool or Gamgee tissue before use.

Following the application of a plaster the limb should be elevated and the bedclothes arranged over a cradle so as to allow free circulation of air to dry the plaster. The extremities should be inspected hourly for signs of interference with the circulation. If sufficient pressure is applied to a nail to blanch it the colour should return in a few seconds when the pressure is removed. If it remains white for any appreciable time this indicates inadequate circulation; blueness and coldness of the extremities are also danger signs. These signs should be reported at once as the plaster will probably have to be cut away or split and opened. After 48 hr, routine morning and evening inspection is in most cases sufficient. A sore may develop under the plaster and any complaint of pain at a definite point or a burning sensation should be reported at once, the area subjected to pressure soon becomes anaesthetic and the fact that the pain has disappeared does not mean that the danger of a pressure sore has passed. If a sore forms, the site may be indicated by the presence of a discharge on the surface of the plaster, the presence of a sore may also be detected by the unpleasant smell which develops when discharge is pent up under the splint. When a leg plaster is carried up to the groin special care is needed to prevent soiling. A piece of jaconet or plastic material may be required for protection of the plaster when the patient uses a bedpan. Rubber bedpans may be useful for the patient with a hip spica.

To Remove a Plaster

The plaster should be removed in a plaster room or a ward annexe otherwise infected loose particles are liable to be scattered and will add to the bacterial content of the air in the ward. The plaster should be moistened during the removal to reduce scattering of dry plaster.

A small light plaster can usually be removed by cutting through it with a knife. Great care must be taken to avoid cutting the patient's skin when removing an unpadded plaster, and in this case a pair of plaster scissors is to be preferred. Plaster shears or an electric saw will be required for cutting through a thick plaster.

After removal the plaster cast should be placed in a covered bin. The knives, scissors and shears should be boiled after use.

Plastic Splints

Light-weight splints made of plastics or resins are useful for infants and in cases where the splint is worn for a considerable time as, for example, in the treatment of a fracture of the scaphoid bone in the wrist.

THE APPLICATION OF TRACTION

Traction or extension is applied to a limb in order to exert a steady pull. This may be needed to prevent overriding of the fragments of a fracture or to prevent pain and contractures in the treatment of joint conditions, such as rheumatoid arthritis or tuberculous joints.

Traction may be carried out by the continuous pull of weights, or by fixed traction when the pull is maintained by fixation to the end of the splint. The traction may be applied to the skin of the limb, skin traction, or to the bone, skeletal traction. The latter is obtained by a pin or wire inserted through the bone below the fracture. In the case of a fracture of the lower limb skeletal traction is usually applied at one of three sites, the lower end of the femur just above the condyles, the tubercle of the tibia or the os calcis. For skin traction strips of adhesive material, such as Elastoplast extension strapping, are applied to the skin of the limb, or strips of gauze may be stuck to the skin with Sinclair's glue or Mastisol.

Preparation for Application of Traction

The bed (see also p. 90):
Fracture boards will be needed to prevent sagging of the mattress.
Blocks are often required for raising the foot of the bed.
A Balkan beam, Hoskin's overhead beam or some other type of frame with pulleys, will be needed unless a Braun's frame which forms a cradle and carries the pulleys is used.

The splint. If a Thomas's splint is used it must be the right size for the patient, the ring should fit comfortably in the groin resting against the ischial tuberosity at the back and the splint should be long enough to project about 6 to 8 in. beyond the sole of the foot. A flexion bar is usually attached to the splint to allow flexion of the knee joint.

Braun's frame is used in the Böhler method of treating fractures of the lower limb. High blocks are required for the foot of the bed and the splint needs to be firmly lashed to the foot of the bed.

Whichever type of splint is used, flannel slings will be needed to support the limb. The slings are double fold, the free ends being fastened to the outer bar of the splint by large 'bull-dog' spring clips. When the splint has been applied to the limb each sling is adjusted separately and secured. The upper and lower edges of each sling should overlap the slings above and below, if a gap is left the edges of the sling may press into the soft tissues of the limb.

Support for the foot in order to maintain it in a position of dorsiflexion may be applied in several ways, e.g. a foot support attached to the splint, or a cord and a weight attached to a wooden spreader fixed to the sole of a slipper worn on the foot of the fractured limb, the pull of the weight will be towards the head.

The slings should be sufficiently taut to support the limb in a position in which two-thirds of the limb is visible above the level of the metal side bars.

Skin Traction
Requirements

Adhesive strapping, 'orthopaedic' strapping, is the most suitable type as it will not stretch lengthways although it will stretch in width allowing it accurately to fit the limb.

A wooden spreader with a hole in the centre for the cord carrying the weight. The spreader separates the two lengths of strapping along the limb and prevents pressure on the prominences of the malleoli at the ankle. The strapping may enclose the spreader or may be fastened to it by webbing and buckles.

Extension cord and pulleys.

Padding for bony prominences such as the condyles of the tibia, head of the fibula and the malleoli. Folds of flannel, pieces of felt or wool may be used.

Crêpe, domette or woven edge cotton bandages, 3, $3\frac{1}{2}$ and 4 in. wide.

Safety-pins.

Tape measure.

Scissors.

Weights.

Requisites for shaving the limb should be provided, although some surgeons prefer to apply the strapping to the unshaved skin.

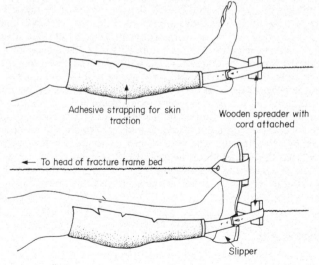

FIG. 80. Application of adhesive strapping for skin traction and method of applying slipper and cord for the prevention of 'foot-drop'.

Method of Applying the Adhesive Strapping to the Skin

The width of the strapping used is from 3 to 5 in., according to the size of the limb. It may be wider at the upper end and narrowed by being folded in at the distal end. The length of the two strips to be applied to the outer and inner aspects of the limb will be measured from the level on the limb indicated by the surgeon to about 3 in. below the sole of the foot. The last 8 in. are narrowed by cutting or turning in, and covered on the adhesive side with an 8-in. strip of plaster of the same width in order to provide a non-sticky surface in contact with the ankle. The edges of the long strips are snipped at intervals to allow the strapping to fit the limb without wrinkling (Fig. 80). An alternative method is to cut the strapping lengthways in three narrow strips as far as the lower 8 or 10 in., the three strips can be separated and, when applied to the skin, will lie more smoothly than one wide piece. The double thickness of strapping at the lower end is attached to the buckles

FIG. 81. Bryant's extension for fracture of the femur in infants and young children. Note that the buttocks are raised from the bed, so that the body weight provides counter-extension.

of the stirrup or spreader. If the spreader is to be enclosed in the strapping then two pieces are cut, one double the length of the single strips referred to above, and a shorter strip about 10 in. long. The spreader is placed in the centre of the long strip against the adhesive surface. The second strip is placed, also adhesive surface down, over the middle section of the long strip so that both strips are enclosing the spreader and a non-sticky surface is provided wherever the strapping may come in contact with the ankle. A hole is made in the strapping to correspond with the hole in the centre of the spreader. A crêpe or woven cotton bandage is applied over the strapping beginning at a point well above the prominence of the malleoli. A system of pulleys, cords and balancing weights is usually arranged to allow the patient to adjust his position. He is encouraged to exercise the muscles and joints by movement which can be carried out safely as the traction through the long axis of the fractured bone is constant.

Vertical Suspension with Skin Traction (Fig. 81)

This method is used in the treatment of fractures of the femur in young children under 6 years of age. Both the fractured and the sound limb are suspended vertically to a beam across the cot. The buttocks are lifted clear of the bed and the child's body acts as the counter-weight. In this position the child is easily attended to and the soiling of strappings or bandages is avoided.

Skeletal Traction

The insertion of the pin is carried out in the theatre. Steinmann's pin, which has a sharp point at one end and a nail head at the other, is hammered through the bone and the ends of the pin are held in a metal stirrup. Böhler's rotating stirrup is commonly used. The cord carrying the weight is attached by a hook to the ring of the stirrup. The sharpened end of the pin is covered with a metal cap or a cork. Denham's pin is similar to the Steinmann pin, but has a thread which grips the bone.

Kirschner's wire is inserted through the bone by means of a drill and the ends of the wire are held in a horseshoe metal stirrup. An S-shaped hook attached to the stirrup carries the weight cord. Kirschner's wire is not used as commonly as the Steinmann or

Denham pin because the fine wire tends to cut through the bone. The skin around the pin or wire is dressed with sterile gauze, and sealed with collodion or Mastisol.

Weight. The amount of weight used for traction will depend on the fracture, on the weight and muscular development of the patient and on the type of traction used. An average weight for skin traction is from 2 to 3 kg (4 to 7 lb.) and for skeletal traction from 4·5 to 9 kg (10 to 20 lb.). Maximum weight may be applied for the first few days, in order to overcome the powerful contraction of the muscles, and later reduced.

Following the application of traction the nurse should attend to the following points:

(1) The weight must exert continuous pull. At no time should the weight be lifted or allowed to rest on the bed.

(2) The cord must run freely over the pulley.

(3) The foot must be supported and kept warm.

(4) Where a Thomas's splint is used the limb and the splint must swing clear of the bed when the patient moves.

(5) When skin traction has been used the limb should be frequently inspected to make sure that the adhesive strapping has not slipped or wrinkled (in which case it is likely to cause a sore) or that it has not broken.

(6) Pressure areas, such as the medial and lateral malleoli and the head of the fibula, should be well protected by padding.

28

First aid and treatment in emergencies

FIRST-AID treatment is confined to the help which a non-medical person can give in cases of accident or emergency until a doctor arrives. In all cases of serious injury the immediate concern of the helper is to get a doctor to the patient or to get the patient to hospital as quickly as possible. In the meantime first aid must be directed at maintaining life, preventing unnecessary suffering and keeping the victim's conditioning from worsening.

The immediate threats to life which must be dealt with promptly are:

(1) Cessation of breathing, which will quickly be followed by death unless resuscitation is started without delay.

(2) Profuse bleeding, which must be arrested as quickly as possible. This fortunately, is not usually a difficult matter when dealing with external bleeding.

(3) Unconsciousness from any cause. An unconscious patient may lose his life unnecessarily if his airway is blocked by false teeth, or any foreign material, or by his own tongue, if he is left lying on his back.

RESUSCITATION

Cardiac Resuscitation

If the heart has stopped beating, tissues are no longer being supplied with oxygen. It is essential that the circulation be restored immediately. Cessation of the circulation to the brain is likely to lead to death of nerve cells within 2 min. Artificial respiration should be carried out simultaneously with cardiac massage. Ideally two individuals should work together, one inflating the lungs, and the other carrying out cardiac resuscitation.

In hospital, the times at which the heart stopped beating and massage was started must be noted, and the resuscitation team should be summoned so that defibrillation and mechanical respiration can be used as soon as possible.

Diagnosis of Cardiac Arrest

(1) Lack of carotid pulse.
(2) Fixed dilated pupils.
(3) Coma.

Method

The patient must be placed on a firm surface. If he is in bed, a fracture board must be in position, otherwise the floor should be used.

The operator places the ball of one hand over the lower half of the sternum. Having located this, he then puts his other hand on top of the first and gives sharp presses over the area, depressing the chest about 3 to 4 cm each time at a rate of about 1 per sec. The second operator gives a mouth to mouth, or mouth to nose, inflation, then waits while the first operator repeats the series of presses over the sternum. While waiting to repeat the inflation this operator checks the pulse in the external carotid artery in the neck. As soon as the pulse returns the cardiac resuscitation is stopped, but mouth to mouth inflations must be continued until the patient is breathing naturally. If only one operator is available he should give alternately five mouth to mouth inflations followed by ten cardiac compressions until normal breathing and circulation are restored.

Respiratory Resuscitation

Respiratory inspirations may cease although the heart continues to beat. In this case artificial respiration must be started at once.

Speed is essential if artificial respiration is to be effective. Whatever method is used, the patient must be placed in position as quickly as possible, tight clothing must be loosened round his neck and waist, and his throat must be cleared of fluid and debris by turning the head to one side and sweeping round the mouth with a finger.

Mouth to Mouth Method

The operator stands or kneels at the side of the victim, who must be lying on his back. The operator takes the patient's head in both hands, with one hand over the forehead and front of the head, presses the head back and extends the neck. The other hand is placed under the lower jaw pressing it forwards and upwards (Fig. 82). He then takes a deep breath, makes a seal with his lips around the patient's mouth and closes the nostrils, either by resting his cheek against the nose or by pinching the nostrils, and blows into the mouth, watching for the patient's chest to rise (Fig. 83).

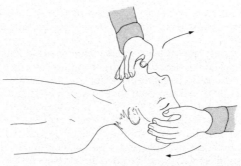

FIG. 82. Mouth to mouth resuscitation. The head is held in both hands and the casualty's jaw pushed upwards and forwards.

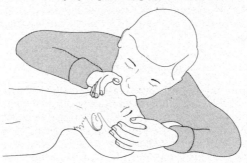

FIG. 83. Mouth to mouth resuscitation (infant or young child). Seal your lips round the mouth and nose and blow gently until you see the chest rise.

In the case of a child or small adult the operator's lips must seal the nose as well as the mouth. He then removes his mouth, takes another deep breath and repeats the inflation. This should be repeated six times as quickly as possible. If the patient has not started to breath spontaneously the procedure is continued at a rate of about ten inflations per min.

In hospital artificial respiration may be given by means of a two-way airway. This has one tube which is inserted into the patient's mouth and another through which the nurse can blow. An inflating bellows, e.g. Ambubag, Cardiff bellows, may be available and this can be used to inflate the lungs by squeezing the bag instead of breathing into the patient's mouth. It is still essential that an airtight seal is made by squeezing the patient's nostrils and the head must be fully retracted. A valve allows expiration when inflation ceases.

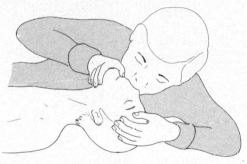

FIG. 84. Mouth to nose method. The lips are sealed on the casualty's face around the nose, and the thumb is placed on the lower lip to keep his mouth closed.

Mouth to Nose Method

This method is preferred by some authorities as providing a better seal (Fig. 84). It is also useful if the mouth cannot be opened, or if the casualty has no teeth when it may be difficult to obtain an effective seal. The procedure is the same as for mouth to mouth resuscitation except that the operator seals the patient's mouth with the thumb of the hand which holds up the chin; he then takes a deep breath, applies his mouth to the patient's face over the nose and blows into him.

Failure to inflate the lungs by either method usually means that the airway is obstructed at some point. Possibly the head is not fully extended and, therefore, the airway behind the tongue is not open. The first thing to do is to check this and adjust the position if necessary. The operator should then look in the patient's mouth, for there may be some obvious blockage due to vomit or fluid which can be removed. It may be necessary to turn the patient on his side and slap him smartly between the shoulder blades to dislodge foreign matter and empty out any fluid. A child may be held upside down and slapped between the shoulders.

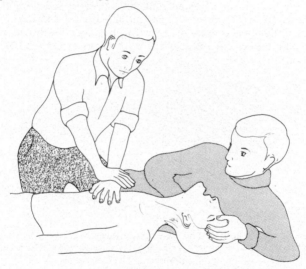

Fig. 85. External cardiac resuscitation and respiratory resuscitation being undertaken at the same time. Two first aiders working alternately.

Mechanical Respirators

If artificial aid is likely to be required over a long period, as in respiratory paralysis, some form of mechanical apparatus is used. The aim in all the various types of apparatus is to produce regular changes in pressure either on the lungs or inside the lungs in order that ventilation of the lungs may be maintained.

The three main types of apparatus are:

Negative–positive apparatus where negative pressure applied to the chest wall causes inspiration and expiration is produced by a slight degree of positive pressure

Positive pressure apparatus where pressure is applied to the chest and inspiration is brought about by elastic recoil when the pressure is released.

Positive pressure through the airway, either by means of a face mask, an endotracheal tube or through a tracheostomy tube.

SHOCK

Every seriously injured person will develop a degree of circulatory failure commonly known as 'shock'. The effect of this is slowing of the circulation and lowering of the blood pressure, leading to the condition of hypoxia, i.e. diminished oxygen supply to the tissue cells. Lack of oxygen leads to cerebral damage, cardiac, respiratory and renal failure. Blood loss is an important factor in producing a state of hypoxia and it should be remembered that the bleeding may not be obvious, as for example, bleeding into the tissues around a major fracture, such as a fractured femur.

There is no effective first-aid treatment for shock. Furthermore the signs of this condition, such as pale, cold skin and rapid pulse, may not be observable until a late stage, particularly in a healthy young adult. The first-aider should bear in mind that movement of an injured person increases shock and that any obvious urgent condition such as bleeding or a blocked airway must be looked for and treated.

The medical treatment is to increase the volume of the circulating blood as quickly as possible. The nurse should prepare for the intravenous administration of plasma or plasma substitutes and the collection of a sample of blood for grouping and cross matching. Morphine is likely to be needed and should be given intravenously, as it will not be well absorbed from the subcutaneous tissues or muscle.

Carbon Monoxide Poisoning

The patient should be removed from the atmosphere contaminated by the gas into the fresh air. If he has ceased to breathe, artificial respiration should be started.

The best treatment is inhalation of oxygen or a mixture of oxygen and carbon dioxide, and therefore removal to hospital should be as prompt as possible.

Electric Shock

If the victim is still in contact with the electrical circuit and the current cannot be cut off, efforts must be made to pull him away from the live wire.

It is necessary to insulate the hands in some way, otherwise the current will pass from the victim to the would-be rescuer. First of all it should be remembered that water is a good conductor of electricity, therefore, if the ground is damp the rescuer should stand on a piece of dry wood, or on a thick woollen coat or rug. The victim should be grasped by the clothing and the rescuer's hands be protected with some insulating dry substance, such as any rubber material, folds of dry newspaper or clothing. If the patient cannot readily be reached, as, for example, if the accident occurred on an electric railway, he might be dragged from the live rail with the aid of wooden walking sticks with crooked handles. Umbrellas are dangerous on account of the metal spokes; all metals are good conductors of electricity.

If these efforts are successful, the first treatment to apply is artificial respiration. The burns sustained by the patient will have to be treated later.

CONTROL OF BLEEDING

Bleeding from a wound will in most cases stop spontaneously by the formation of a clot and shrinking of the ends of the cut vessels. A small blood loss is not serious; indeed it acts as a cleansing agent washing the wound. However, if large vessels are severed the victim may lose a great quantity of blood in a very short time and, as already stated, this blood loss will increase the circulatory failure which is a feature of serious injuries.

Most authorities now agree that a tourniquet has no place in first-aid treatment. It is not easy to apply it effectively and by obstructing the venous but not the arterial blood flow, it may well increase the bleeding. If the tourniquet succeeds in arresting the flow of blood it is likely to be damaging to the tissues and may even lead to ischaemic paralysis of muscles or gangrene of a limb. It is also generally accepted that pressure over the various arterial 'pressure points', which has so long been a feature of first-aid teaching, is both difficult to achieve and time-wasting.

First aid in the treatment of profuse bleeding should aim at assisting the natural processes which enable the body to deal with blood loss.

Rest. The injured person should lie down with support and elevation of the wounded part. The blood flow to the area will then diminish and this will help closure of the ends of the cut vessels and the formation of a clot.

Pressure directly on the wound. This can be applied by holding a dressing firmly on the wound until such time as a bandage can be firmly applied. Pressure reduces the flow of blood and the dressing holds the shed blood and encourages clot formation.

In order to prevent infection of the wound a sterile first-aid dressing should be obtained if at all possible. If such is not available, then pressure may be applied with a large pad of any clean material to hand, such as a clean handkerchief or towel. If nothing at all is at hand and the bleeding is profuse from a large vessel, pressure can be exerted with the operator's bare hand.

In all cases where large quantities of blood have been lost it is essential to get the patient to a hospital where blood transfusion can be given.

In all cases too where the injury appears likely to have involved internal organs, or where internal bleeding is suspected, the patient must be taken to hospital without delay, but the first-aider should know what to do in certain special injuries and emergencies.

Bleeding from the Lungs

A crash injury or a stab wound in the chest is likely to injure the lungs and the patient, in addition to pain and difficulty in breathing, may cough up some blood. He will usually be most comfortable when propped up in a sitting or semi-sitting position. A puncture wound of the chest may be seen to suck air in every time the patient breathes. When air enters the chest cavity the lung on that side will collapse and, as the pressure increases, the action of the heart will be impeded and the opposite lung will be compressed. It is therefore necessary to prevent air entry as quickly as possible and this can be done by applying a large dressing and bandaging it very firmly round the chest.

Abdominal Wounds

In any injury which appears likely to have penetrated the abdominal cavity the patient must have immediate treatment in hospital. In the meantime no one must be allowed to give him anything whatever by the mouth.

Vomiting of blood is most often due to erosion of blood vessels in the stomach or duodenum by a peptic ulcer. The patient should be kept lying down while awaiting removal to hospital, and again nothing should be given by mouth. An estimate of the amount of blood vomited should be made and written down for the information of the doctor.

Ruptured Varicose Veins

Bleeding is profuse but easily arrested. The patient must lie down with the leg elevated. A firm dressing and bandage will usually control the bleeding at once. If, however, the first dressing becomes soaked and bleeding is obviously continuing, a second large pad or dressing should be applied over the first bandage and firmly secured.

Nose-Bleeding (Epistaxis)

Nose bleeding from a blow on the nose usually stops spontaneously in a short time. Nose bleeding with no apparent cause is likely to be more troublesome. The patient should lie down with the head and shoulders elevated. Then direct him to pinch the nostrils firmly together while breathing through his mouth. If this is not effective or if the bleeding recurs, a doctor should see the patient.

UNCONSCIOUSNESS

'The first-aider who is faced with a patient who has been found, or has become unconscious, is not called upon to make a diagnosis. He must, however, make an immediate assessment of what has happened' (*First Aid in the Factory*, Lord Taylor).

It may be obvious that the unconscious person has sustained a severe head injury or that he has been overcome by coal gas poisoning, or there may be evidence that he has swallowed poison. In many instances, however, there may be no obvious indication of the cause and valuable time may be wasted in trying to decide this before attending to the patient.

It may be necessary to move the patient from danger, for example if he is in a gas-filled room; otherwise he should not be moved.

No unconscious person should be allowed to lie on his back; in this position his tongue will fall back, obstructing the airway, and saliva will collect in the throat. Not infrequently an unconscious patient may vomit and if he is on his back the vomit will almost certainly block the air passages and also be inhaled into the lungs. The first step then is to turn the patient over on to his face or into the semi-prone position so that his tongue falls forward and saliva and vomit can run out of his mouth. The first-aider should then see that the mouth is clear of any obstruction and hold the chin forward, so preventing the tongue from falling towards the back of the mouth.

If the patient is still unconscious when transported to hospital he must be kept in the prone or semi-prone position while being moved.

The first-aider should never attempt to rouse the patient or to put any fluid, such as brandy or water, into his mouth.

In all cases of unconsciousness medical aid must be obtained as soon as possible. The only exceptions to this rule are the simple fainting attack when the person recovers almost immediately, or an epileptic fit occurring in a known epileptic subject.

FRACTURES AND JOINT INJURIES

Fractures

A fracture means a break in a bone. The two important classes of fracture are:

(1) A simple or closed fracture, where there is no communication between the site of the fracture and the external air.

(2) A compound or open fracture, where there is a wound which forms a communication between the site of the fracture and the external air and therefore danger of infection.

Signs and Symptoms of a Fracture

(1) Pain and tenderness over the site of the fracture.
(2) Inability to move the arm or leg in the case of fracture of a limb.
(3) Deformity: the limb is bent in a direction which would not be possible unless it were broken.
(4) Bruising and swelling.

The history of the accident is often helpful; the patient may say that he felt the bone snap. Quite frequently the diagnosis can only be definitely made by an X-ray examination, and in all doubtful cases the first-aider should treat the injury as a fracture.

General Principles of Treatment

(1) Avoid all unnecessary movement of the patient as this will cause pain and will increase the damage to the soft tissues around the fracture, or may convert a closed fracture into an open one.
(2) Immobilize the part by the use of a splint before moving the patient. A variety of improvised splints may be used, e.g. suitable flat pieces of wood, umbrellas, pillows bandaged around the limb or the patient's own uninjured limb or the trunk.
(3) Cover any wound with the cleanest dressing available.
(4) Arrange for suitable safe transport of the patient.

Fractures of the Lower Extremity

Femur. Fractures of the neck of the femur commonly occur in elderly persons whose bones are brittle. The usual history is of a fall followed by pain in the hip and inability to stand. Fractures of the shaft of the femur are the result of considerable violence, for example in road accidents, and there is frequently considerable bleeding into the tissues of the thigh.

The limb should be splinted by applying a long wooden splint from the sole of the foot to just below the axilla and securing it by bandages round the chest, hips, upper part of thigh, above and below the knee and round the ankle and foot. An assistant should apply traction by pulling steadily on the foot, keeping it at a right angle to the leg, while the splint is applied. Another method is to bandage the injured limb firmly to the sound limb, with bandages round the hips, thighs, above and below the knee and around the ankle and foot, keeping the foot at a right angle to the leg.

Fractures of the tibia. The tibia has very little muscle covering and a fracture is usually obvious. The leg may be splinted by wooden splints, one on the outer side of the limb and a second shorter splint on the inner side. Another form of splinting uses a pillow which is wrapped around the leg and foot and firmly bandaged.

Fractures of the Upper Extremity

Humerus. A simple method of splinting a fractured humerus is to bandage the injured arm to the chest, or to pin the sleeve of the jacket to the chest and to support the forearm in a sling.

Radius and ulna. Fractures near the wrist joint (Colles's fractures) are usually the result of a fall on the outstretched hand. Fractures of the shaft of these bones are commonly caused by direct violence. The forearm should be splinted from the elbow to the knuckles and a sling applied. Folded newspapers can be used to splint the forearm.

Clavicle (collar bone). A fracture of this bone is often caused by a fall on the outstretched hand. There is not much risk of displacement of the broken ends of the bone if the arm is immobilized. The first-aid treatment is to put a pad in the axilla, bandage the upper arm to the chest and support the forearm in a St John sling (Fig. 77 C).

Fracture of the Skull

The importance of these fractures is their liability to cause injury to the brain. Following a severe head injury the patient will be unconscious and may be bleeding from the ears and nose. There may be an escape of cerebrospinal fluid from the ear. First-aid treatment is that described for any unconscious patient. If clear fluid or blood is escaping from the ear a clean dressing may be applied. The patient must be taken to hospital as soon as possible.

Fracture of the Spine

If there is reason to suspect that a patient has a fractured spine, he should be kept lying still until sufficient help is at hand to lift him carefully on to a stretcher and convey him to hospital. It is important not to bend or twist the spinal column when moving the patient. The best position in which to transport him is lying on his back with small pillows or pads under the hollow of the neck, the small of the back and below the calves of the legs.

Fracture of the Pelvis

Fractures of the pelvis may injure the bladder, urethra or rectum. The patient should have a firm binder round the pelvis for support and should be lifted, without rolling, on to the stretcher.

Fracture of the Ribs

The special danger of a broken rib is that the ends of the bone may damage the lung. Following the injury the patient may complain of great pain on breathing and may cough up blood.

It is essential that medical aid should be sought early, as chest complications are apt to occur, especially in elderly patients.

The first-aid treatment consists of supporting the patient in the most comfortable position, usually sitting up.

Joint Injuries

Dislocations

A dislocation is a displacement of the joint surfaces of two or more bones and is accompanied by damage to the soft tissues around the joint.

Signs and Symptoms

(1) Deformity.
(2) Pain.
(3) Loss of movement.
(4) Swelling.

The shoulder joint is fairly readily dislocated; fingers, the elbow joint, knee joint and jaw may also be dislocated comparatively easily, but considerable violence is needed to dislocate the hip joint.

The first-aid treatment consists of supporting the part with a sling or bandages. A dislocation is most easily reduced immediately after the injury, therefore no time should be lost in obtaining medical aid.

Sprains

A sprain is an injury to the soft tissues of a joint involving the muscles and ligaments. The usual situations are the ankle, wrist and thumb.

Signs and Symptoms

(1) Pain.
(2) Swelling.
(3) Discoloration.

Treatment

The possibility of a dislocation or a fracture should be considered and the patient urged to get medical attention. In the meantime he should not use the limb and some support may be given by the application of a firm bandage. Elevation of the part and cold applications may help to prevent swelling.

BURNS AND SCALDS

A burn is an injury produced by dry heat, and a scald by moist heat. From the point of view of first aid the immediate results of the injury and the treatment are the same. Burns are likely to endanger life immediately as a result of loss of plasma from the burnt area and depletion of the volume of circulating blood. It should be understood that the patient's life is in danger from an extensive burn, even if it be entirely superficial; if one-quarter of the total skin surface is involved the injury is extremely serious.

Medical aid should be obtained as speedily as possible. Full treatment of the burnt area will be carried out only in hospital, but morphine may be required immediately for the relief of pain. The patient should be moved as little as possible and gentle handling is essential. A burnt patient may complain of thirst and small amounts of water may be given to relieve this. It is better to give small quantities frequently rather than to encourage the patient to drink large amounts as vomiting is not unusual.

The burnt area, if exposed, should be covered with the cleanest dressing to hand, if sterile dressings are not available clean towels or sheets may be used as substitutes. The surface which has been folded in, and therefore protected from dust should be placed

12

next to the burnt skin. Blankets and rugs should not be allowed to come in contact with an exposed burnt area as they are potential sources of heavy bacterial contamination. If the injured area is covered by clothing this is best left undisturbed.

The pain and severity of a small superficial burn may be reduced by immediate immersion of the affected part in cold water.

When the patient is admitted to hospital his immediate needs for fluid replacement are assessed. In all serious cases transfusion is started at once, usually with plasma or plasma substitutes. Blood may also be needed as, particularly in deep burns, there is considerable destruction of red blood cells.

Where burns are likely to be common accidental injuries, as for instance in certain industries, the use of a water-soluble cream containing penicillin or sulphonamide and 1 per cent cetrimide is one of the dressings recommended for use in first aid. Any first-aid dressing should be carried out with all the aseptic precautions that the circumstances permit. The dresser should wash her hands and dry them on a clean towel before handling any dressing material and an improvised mask, e.g. a clean pocket handkerchief, should be worn.

Scalds of the Throat and Mouth

Such accidents may occur in young children, who may suck the spout of a teapot or boiling kettle.

Medical aid should be obtained at once; swelling of the upper air passages may cause obstruction of the air way and tracheostomy may be necessary. The child should be put to bed and kept warm.

Chemical Burns

The chemical should be thoroughly washed off with warm water. If the nature of the substance is known, a neutralizing agent may be used, e.g. a corrosive acid such as nitric acid should be washed off with a solution of sodium bicarbonate or lime water. Strong lysol or carbolic acid splashed on the skin is best removed with surgical spirit or methylated spirit. Caustic soda burns may be treated with a weak acid such as vinegar.

Chemical burns of the eye. The eye should be opened (an assistant may be needed to do this) and then thoroughly wash out with clean

Examples of types of poisons, symptoms produced and appropriate first-aid treatment

Poison	Signs and symptoms	Treatment
1. *Corrosive poisons*, e.g. phenol or Lysol	Burns on lips and mouth. Intense pain from mouth to stomach. Vomiting. Marked shock. Thirst	Immediate treatment, dilute the poison by giving tapwater or milk if the patient can swallow. If the poison is a coal tar disinfectant, a stomach washout, using 1 per cent solution of magnesium sulphate (Epsom salts), should be prepared; 60 ml (2 fl. oz.) of liquid paraffin may be put down the tube after the washout
2. *Irritant poisons*, e.g. mercury preparations, arsenic	Pain in abdomen. Vomiting; the vomit may contain blood and mucus. Diarrhoea. Collapse	Give an emetic, prepare for stomach washout. Treat collapse by warmth and hot applications to abdomen. Following the emetic or washout a demulcent mixture of milk and egg may be given
3. *Poisons acting on the nervous system:*		
Hypnotic and narcotic poisons, e.g. morphine, barbiturates	Drowsiness, coma, slow respirations	If the poison has been swallowed, give an emetic. Prepare for stomach washout. Stimulate patient by giving strong coffee, inhalation of smelling salts or ammonia. Artificial respiration if necessary. The specific antidote to opium or morphine is nalorphine which combats respiratory failure. Drugs used to combat the effect of barbiturates include nikethamide, Methedrine and bemegride
Convulsant poisons, e.g. strychnine	Restlessness, delirium, convulsions	Emetic and stomach washout, if seen early. If patient is having convulsions, keep as quiet as possible. Drugs used to combat the convulsive poisons include anaesthetics such as thiopentone sodium and muscle relaxants, e.g. tubocurarine, Scoline

water for at least 15 min. The eye is then covered with a pad and bandage. Medical treatment is essential and urgent in order to prevent permanent damage.

POISONING

Poisoning by accident is a not uncommon emergency; children may swallow fluids or tablets left within their reach, adults may drink a supposed dose of medicine from an unlabelled bottle or may fail to read the label and swallow a dose of disinfectant or cleaning fluid. Deliberate taking of poison is usually with suicidal intent. Attempted suicide may be a way used by a disturbed individual to get help. Deliberate administration of a poison is of course done with the object of killing, or at least seriously harming, the victim.

The immediate course of action to be taken by the first-aider is to send urgently for medical aid and to try to find the nature of the poison so that an appropriate antidote can be obtained and to dilute the poison (if swallowed) as rapidly as possible. The nearest diluent to hand is usually water and the victim should drink four or five tumblerfuls of water at once. If it is readily available, milk is a good ciluent and demulcent fluid. Unless there is evidence of a corrosive poison (burning of the mouth and lips) the first-aider should try to induce vomiting. This may be effected by putting the fingers down the victim's throat or giving an emetic such as salt, two tablespoonfuls, or one teaspoonful of mustard, in a glass of warm water.

Examples of some common types of poisons, symptoms and treatment are given in the table on page 345.

29
Appendix

THERMOMETRIC SCALES

Centigrade Scale

$0°C$ = temperature of melting ice at sea level (freezing point of pure water).

$100°C$ = temperature of steam given off water boiling under atmospheric pressure at sea level (boiling point of pure water).

Table of Centigrade and Fahrenheit Equivalents

°C	°F	°C	°F
−30	−22·0	30	86·0
−25	−13·0	35	95·0
−20	−4·0	40	104·0
−15	5·0	45	113·0
−10	14·0	50	122·0
−5	23·0	60	140·0
0	32·0	70	158·0
1	33·8	80	176·0
2	35·6	90	194·0
3	37·4	100	212·0
4	39·2	101	213·8
5	41·0	102	215·6
10	50·0	103	217·4
15	59·0	104	219·2
20	68·0	105	221·0
25	77·0	106	222·8

To convert Centigrade to Fahrenheit:

$$°F = (°C \times \tfrac{9}{5}) + 32.$$

WEIGHTS AND MEASURES

Metric System

Measure of Mass (Weight)

1 microgram (μg) = $\frac{1}{1000}$ milligram or 0·001 mg.

1 milligram (mg) = $\frac{1}{1000}$ gram or 0·001 g.

1 gram (G or g) = weight of 1 millilitre (ml) of distilled water at 4°C. The accepted principle in prescription writing is G since g may be confused with gr (grain).

1 kilogram (kg) = 1000 gram.

Measure of Capacity (Volume)

1 millilitre (ml) = the volume of 1 gram of water at 4°C.

1 litre (l) = the volume of 1000 gram (1 kg) of water at 4°C.

Note: The cubic centimetre (cm^3) which is approximately equal to 1 millilitre should not be used as a measure of volume. The accepted abbreviation for millilitre is (ml).

Percentage Solution

The term 'per cent' is used to mean:
   (a) Per cent w/w = weight in weight.
   (b) Per cent v/v = volume in volume.
   (c) Per cent w/v = weight in volume.
One per cent solution w/v is equivalent to 1 gram in 100 ml.

To Dilute Stock Solutions of Lotions

Given stock solution = 1 : 20 solution.
Required: 200 ml of 1 : 80 solution.

Calculation:

$$\frac{1}{20} \div \frac{1}{80} = \frac{1}{20} \times \frac{80}{1} = 4$$

∴ 1 part stock solution required to 3 parts water to produce a solution 4 times weaker than original.

∴ $\frac{200}{4} = 50$, ∴ 50 ml of 1 : 20 solution + 150 ml water to give 200 ml of 1 : 80 solution.

Given stock solution = 40 per cent solution.
Required is 100 ml of 20 per cent solution.

Calculation:

$$\tfrac{40}{100} \div \tfrac{20}{100} = \tfrac{40}{100} \times \tfrac{100}{2} = 2$$

∴ 1 part stock solution required to 1 part water
∴ $\tfrac{100}{2} = 50$, ∴ 50 ml of 40 per cent solution and 50 ml water will give 100 ml of 20 per cent solution.

To Give Fractional Dose of Drug

Given solution of strength 60 mg per ml.
Required: 15 mg dose.
∴ $\tfrac{15}{60}$ ml required = $\tfrac{1}{4}$ ml of solution.

Young's Formula for calculating the proportion of the adult dose of a drug to be given to a child:

$$\frac{\text{Age of child}}{\text{Age of child} + 12} \times \text{Adult dose.}$$

Note: Young's formula is an approximation and should be used with reservation. Dosage is more often calculated according to body weight.

INSULIN DOSAGE

The standard strengths of insulin for injection are:
20 units per ml
40 units per ml
80 units per ml

For the injection of insulin a syringe of 1 ml capacity graduated in twenty divisions may be used and this is the type usually supplied to the patient who gives his own injections. If the insulin solution to be used is single strength, i.e. 20 units in each millilitre, then each division represents 1 unit, if it is double strength then each division is 2 units, and if it is quadruple strength each division is 4 units. Obviously the patient must be carefully instructed as to the exact amount to be drawn up into the syringe and this is particularly important if the dosage or the strength of the insulin is altered. For example, if the dose is 40 units and double strength insulin is used, then the patient must draw up 1 ml, 20 divisions; if, however, a change is made to quadruple strength and the dose remains at 40 units, then each division represents 4 units and the amount to be drawn is 0·5 ml, i.e. 10 divisions.

Syringes of 1- or 2-ml capacity are also used for the injection of insulin and these syringes may be graduated in 0·1 ml ($\frac{1}{10}$) or 0·2 ml ($\frac{1}{5}$) (Fig. 86).

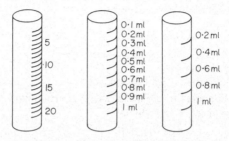

Fig. 86. Graduations on 'insulin' syringe and 1-ml syringe barrels.

Using a syringe in which each division on the barrel corresponds to 0·1 ml and with an insulin strength of 20 units per ml, each division represents 2 units of insulin. If the strength of insulin is 40 units per ml then each division represents 4 units of insulin, and with 80 units per ml each division represents 8 units of insulin.

Examples. (1) The strength of the insulin to be used is 40 units per ml and the dose ordered is 32 units.

The required dose will be $\frac{32}{40}$ ml = 0·8 ml, and since each division on the syringe represents 4 units, the amount to be drawn up will correspond with the eighth graduation on the barrel ($\frac{32}{4}$ = 8).

If each division on the syringe used represents 0·2 ml then, using insulin in the strength of 20 units per ml, each graduation equals 4 units of insulin. If the insulin strength is 40 units per ml each graduation equals 8 units, and with 80 units per ml each graduation equals 16 units of insulin.

(2) Using a syringe graduated in 0·2 ml and insulin in the strength of 80 units per ml, the dose ordered is 64 units.

The required dose will be $\frac{64}{80}$ ml = 0·8 ml, and since each division on the syringe represents 16 units the amount to be drawn up will correspond with the fourth graduation on the barrel ($\frac{64}{16}$ = 4).

Index

NURSING BOOKS

New Books

Hull & Isaacs
Do-it-Yourself Revision for Nurses: Books 1 & 2
Do It Yourself Revision is an entirely new concept which provides the student nurse with a systematic and interesting method of revision by which she can study a particular subject, answer questions selected from recent State Final Examinations, and mark her replies against model answers provided.

Book 1	144 pages	4 illus.	50p.	Books 3 & 4 ready June 1971
Book 2	144 pages	7 illus.	50p.	

Chisholm
An Insight into Health Visiting
Explains to the student nurse why she needs to learn about health visiting, what she will learn when seconded to the health visitor or district nurse, where she will see the health visitor at work and the difference between hospital and community nursing. *102 pages   60p.*

Miles
Baillière's Handbook of First Aid
The sixth edition of this famous Handbook has been extensively revised by STANLEY MILES. While the comprehensive practical first aid instruction of the original authors, which has given the Handbook its reputation as a complete and authoritative work, has been retained, there has been considerable rewriting of the text to include the technical advances in cardiac and respiratory resuscitation and the treatment of shock and burns which have taken place recently.
6th edn.   352 pages   180 illus.   £1.00

Mountjoy & Wythe
Nursing Care of the Unconscious Patient
This new book has been written to help nurses and others responsible for the care of patients whose level of consciousness is abnormal, for whatever reason and wherever the patient is being nursed.
104 pages   11 illus.   90p.

Meering & Stacey
Nursery Nursing *(A Handbook of Child Care)*
A complete textbook covering the syllabuses for the National Nursery Examination Board and the Examination in Nursery Nursing of the Royal Society of Health. In this new edition the age range covered has been extended to 7 years old.
5th edn.   approx. 400 pages   75 illus.   £2.50

BAILLIÈRE TINDALL   7 & 8 Henrietta Street
London WC2E 8QE

Reference Books

Baillière's
Nurses' Dictionary

By BARBARA F. CAPE, S.R.N., S.C.M., D.N.

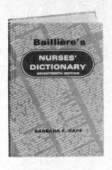

The latest edition of this ever-popular dictionary contains over 750 new definitions, and the 24 appendices are full of new information relating particularly to those subjects in which important developments are taking place.

17th Edition   *572 pages*   *8 plates*   *50p.*

Baillière's
Midwives' Dictionary

By VERA DA CRUZ, S.R.N., S.C.M., M.T.D.

This pocket dictionary, which has again been revised and brought up-to-date, is suitable both for midwives and for nurses taking their obstetric option. Obsolete terms have been omitted to provide space for new data, and the appendices have been heavily revised or rewritten.

5th Edition   *396 pages*   *140 illustrations*   *50p.*

Baillière's
Pocket Book
of Ward Information

By MARJORIE HOUGHTON, O.B.E., S.R.N., S.C.M., D.N., and ANN JEE, S.R.N., Part 1 C.M.B., R.N.T.

Fully revised and brought up-to-date, this book contains a multitude of useful information likely to be needed by nurses in their day to day work and of particular help to nurses in training.

12th Edition   *240 pages*   *6 illustrations*   *50p.*

BAILLIÈRE TINDALL

7 & 8 Henrietta Street
London WC2E 8QE

NURSES' AIDS SERIES

Standard Textbooks

WARD ADMINISTRATION & TEACHING
By Ellen L. Perry

"This is a book which has long been needed. Every trained nurse could learn something from it. While ward sisters put into practice the ideals and ideas outlined, we need have no fears for 'patient care' in our hospitals nor for the practical training of the nurse."   *Nursing Mirror*

304 pages   *11 illus.*   **£2.00**

SWIRE'S HANDBOOK OF PRACTICAL NURSING
Revised by Joan Burr

Changes in the syllabus of training have necessitated a major revision for this edition and Miss Burr has taken the opportunity to make many changes of approach to stress the human angle and to enable the nurse to appreciate her surroundings in the hospital and in the community. Care has been taken to cover the syllabus fully, and the use of simple language and illustrated examples ensure the maintained interest of the pupil.

6th Edition
308 pages   *57 illus.*   **£1.00**

MAYES' HANDBOOK OF MIDWIFERY
Revised by V. Da Cruz

"In this Seventh Edition, Miss da Cruz has incorporated the many new trends and advances made in recent years ... The text is set out with clear headings and good illustrations which make revision easy."   *Maternal and Child Care*

458 pages   *156 illus.*   *10 plates*   **£1.80**

BAILLIÈRE TINDALL   7 & 8 Henrietta Street
                                         London WC2E 8QE